BIG WOLF ON CAMPUS

COLLECTION ONE

AIDY AWARD
PIPER FOX

❀ Created with Vellum

COCKY JOCK WOLF

A BIG WOLF ON CAMPUS STORY

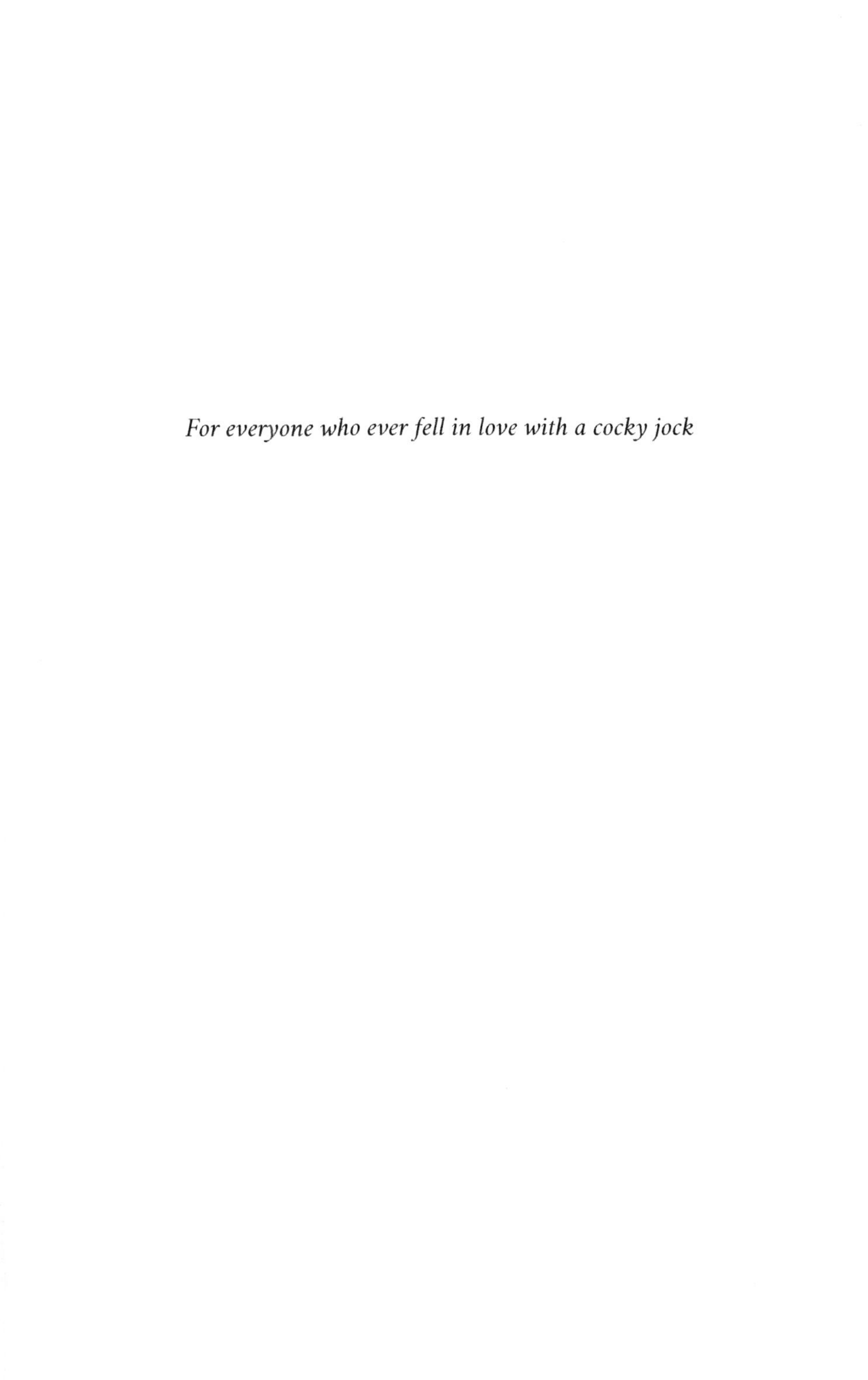

For everyone who ever fell in love with a cocky jock

I love how in scary movies the person yells out 'hello?'
As if the killer is going to be like 'Yeah, I'm in the kitchen. Want a sandwich?'

— SOMEONE HILARIOUS ON THE INTERNET

COCKY JOCK WOLF

Nerdy, chubby girls don't date quarterbacks... or werewolves.

Eli:

I just want one night off of being the all-star golden boy that the entire world, including my pack, expects great things from. Is it too much to ask to go watch my favorite horror movies and eat popcorn?

Apparently it is.

I just might get my chance if this cute AF nerdy book girl at the bar plays defense for me. As long as I don't let my wolf get a whiff of her ripe, delicious scent. The last thing I need to add onto my plate is a fated mate.

Charlize:

Go on a date or get fired - that's the ultimatum from my boss at the Moon Bean coffee shop. But I picked a real jerk and now I'm stuck at the bar with him.

I don't need anyone to save me, but a smart girl recognizes a good escape plan when she kisses one.

It's not like I'm going to fall for a jock with more notches on his belt than books on his shelf. But Eli is more than that and I'm developing some crazy feelings for him.

That is, until he turns into a werewolf straight out of a horror movie.

Cocky Jock Wolf is a fated mates New Adult paranormal romance with a nerdy, dirty, cute, and curvy girl and the captain of the football team (who is secretly a wolf shifter!)

ELI

One night. That's all I wanted. That's all I needed. Just one night under the new moon.

Not with a girl. That was easy. I'd racked up plenty of one-night stands. Came with the alpha wolf football star territory. I had a ball bunny knocking on my door most any evening, whether or not she knew I was a wolf shifter.

I was always down for some arm candy, or bed candy. The stream of cheerleaders, Bay State University Dire Wolves fans, and even a fresh out-of-school alum or two made me look like a sex god.

Lord knew my fucking life was all about what made me look good.

Good grades, great looks, stellar skills on and off the field. Being the best at everything got me what I wanted, prepared me to be the alpha of the Chincoteague pack someday.

Except tonight.

I just wanted one night off. Ten hours where I didn't

have to be the star, the jock, alpha heir to a pack, or the king of the campus.

Didn't look like that was going to happen. Because here I was at The Wolf's Den, everyone's favorite bar, celebrating the big win today with the entire offensive line. Again.

"Dude," Ty lifted his hand and gave me a stinging slap to the back, "when you threw that last pass, I couldn't even hear myself think over the fucking crowd going bonkers."

"School records are for pussies." Luka waved over the one and only female bartender.

"Whoo! Let's get our boy laid." Nik wrapped his arms around my shoulder. "You deserve a reward, man."

Kirill rubbed his hands together and scanned the room. "Game theory, guys. We hook Eli here up with the hottest chick and the rest of us get her friends."

Sigh. That wasn't even how game theory worked. But I would not be the nerd who corrected them. I let the guys scan the bar for chicks to pick up and ordered myself the Eli-Teagan-quarterback-special from the bar. Sparkling water, room temperature, with a twist. It was the season, and I was in training. No way I was fucking up my shot at going first round in the draft next year for a beer. I didn't need a scout seeing some TikTok video of me doing shots.

"Ew, get off me." The girl and her boyfriend standing next to me at the bar gave her guy a shove. He was clearly blitzed and didn't even notice when he bumped into me. My senses went on alert and my wolf rose up, seeking the danger.

Down, boy. It's just a bar, just a drunk guy, and just a girl who smells like ripe fucking peaches and moonlight.

"Come on," drunk guy swayed and grabbed the bar to

stay upright. "I just want to make out, maybe grab a tit. It's not like I'm going to fuck you, you're fat."

Oh, Goddess. Yeah, buddy, that's the way to get a girl to let you kiss her and feel her up. What a douche.

"This was a mistake. I wouldn't kiss you if you were one of my book boyfriends come to life. I'm leaving. Who cares if I get fired?" The girl grabbed her bag and her book off the bar and slid from the barstool.

This dickhead was crazy. The girl had curves for days. Curves for miles. Curves I could get lost in.

"You're not going anywhere. I bought you a fucking expensive froo-froo drink. You owe me." The asshat grabbed curvy book girl's arm.

Oh, hell no. I may have a string of one-night stands notched into my headboard, but no girl owed me or any other guy a kiss or sex or even a fucking smile. My wolf was feeling overly protective of this cute and curvy nerd, too. "I don't think my girlfriend has anything for you except the finger, asshole."

I grabbed the douche by his shirt and shoved him into my offensive line. They had my back on and off the field. Plus, three out of the four of them were also wolf shifters like me and could fuck this guy up if I wanted them to. Not that revealing ourselves as anything other than your average elite college athlete was allowed.

"Hey, Eli. Eli Teagan. Fuck. You're Eli Teagan. I didn't know she was your girlfriend. I'm sorry, dude." In an instant, three six-foot five two-hundred and fifty plus pound grouchy-ass wolf shifter football players had this guy surrounded, leaving me to check on the girl.

I pivoted and nearly forgot how to talk, looking at how god-damned pretty she was. "Are you all right?"

She stared open-mouthed at the huddle, flicked her gaze up to mine, and then back again. She hugged her book and her bag to her chest, shook her head, and backed away. The bar was extra crowded because of the win, and she was going to have a hard time getting out of there through the throng of people.

I slapped one of my guys on the shoulder. "I'm gonna take this one for the team. See you guys later."

When I turned back to book girl, the daggers in her eyes were aimed straight at my heart. She held up a finger. "A. I don't need you to save me, and B. you're going to take one for the team? Really?"

Shit. "I didn't mean it like that."

Time to turn on the charm. I put on my best you-know-you-love me smile and flicked my gaze down to her lips and back up again. Chicks got all swoony for that move. I let just the tiniest edge of my wolf out, too. That made all the girls go wild. There was always something extra sexy about being chased by a predator.

When I leaned in to whisper in her ear, she was mesmerized and didn't move a muscle. I couldn't help a glance down at the pretty skin beneath the collar of her shirt. Exactly where a mate mark would go. "Look, just pretend for two minutes that we're together. We'll walk out that door like we can't keep our hands off of each other. I promise we can part ways in the parking lot. You'll get away from the douchehole and I'll get the night off I've been hoping for. You in?"

I'm sure to the rest of the bar it looked like I was whispering sweet nothings into her ear, charming my way into her pants. Not a single guy would cockblock me and I could finally get the hell out of here without anyone knowing where I was going, what I was doing, or breathing down my neck.

She glanced at the mass of people she was going to have to push through, and her shoulders sagged. "Fine."

Rock on. I put my arm around book girl's waist, and it took the damn will of a saint not to grab her plump ass. "Excuse me, people coming through."

The wall of people shifted and cleared a path for us. Book girl stared up at me like I was a freak of nature. Weird. That was not what I expected. All I could do was grin like a loon back at her. She wrinkled up her nose at me and damn if I didn't want to kiss that look right off her face. What the fuck was wrong with me that I needed her to like me right here, right now?

Book girl stepped out of my hold on her waist, and I had to bring out the moves to keep up. I slid my hand into the small of her back and guided her through the crowd. The second we were out the door, she slapped my hand away.

I was so wrapped up in this girl that I hadn't noticed the guys had followed up and brought the asshole with them. One of them actually picked the guy up and tossed him into the grass between the street and the parking lot. He got up and wavered slightly, pointing to me and book girl.

Shit. He was about to call me out on the lie that she was my girlfriend. I could see it in his face, smell it in his scent. So, I did the only thing I could think of to save face. I kissed her.

CHARLIZE

He kissed me. He flipping kissed me.

I'd really like to say that I slapped him silly. But I didn't. I. Kissed. Him. Back.

What the hell is wrong with me? Ugh.

For being super smart, I'm super dumb. First off, I should have known better than to go to The Wolves' Den on a Saturday night after a football game. That's normally the nights we close the coffee shop up early and I spend a nice quiet night in reading whatever newest release we've gotten in for merch sales that week.

Tonight's was a new sports romance from one of my fave authors. I wouldn't have even considered entering the devil's den of iniquities next door if Selena, the coffee shop owner, hadn't threatened my livelihood.

Now here I was making out with the Dire Wolves' star quarterback. I might choose books over balls, but I knew who Eli Teagan was. Everyone knew him. At least the name, anyway. I don't think I'd ever seen him in real life. Just those enormous banners that hang from the athletic center.

He was actually a lot better looking in person, which was hard to do. I think half the girls enrolled at Bay State University probably masturbated to that particular image of our school's number one most eligible bachelor.

Not saying I had. I was more the Matthew Macfadyen as Darcy or Michael Fassbender as Rochester kind of girl. Romantic heroes did it for me, not jocks who didn't know better than to have sex in their socks.

Not that I knew or anything. The only jocks I'd ever slept with were the ones in romance novels when I fell asleep reading in bed.

My sense and my sensibility had clearly gone on a long walk through the moors, because I didn't even have the sense to break the kiss first. He was the one who pulled my tongue out of his mouth. When I blinked, we both kind of had that dazed what-the-hell-just-happened look. He rubbed his thumb over my lips and his voice was hot and husky. "Come on, let's get out of here."

"Okay." Was that really my voice, all breathy and whispery?

Geez. It was. Okay? Oh-kay? No. I was definitely not okay. I was not going home with a guy who had more notches on his headboard than books on his bookshelf. So why did I let him take my hand and drag me down the sidewalk that went between the bar and the coffee shop?

Maybe because Selena was right, and I was afraid of real life boys. Book boyfriends didn't break up with you and shatter your heart. Book boyfriends didn't tell you to lose weight, dress sexier, and hide your smarts. I never wanted to hear anything like that ever again. I had curves, liked to wear jeans and sweatshirts, and was here on an academic scholarship.

The thing was, I didn't give any guys a chance to be as good as a book boyfriend, because I never went out with any of them. But I did complain about them all being horrible jerks. Most of them probably were. But what if this one, this guy I had all the preconceived ideas about, wasn't a jerk?

I followed him down the sidewalk and into the alley behind the shops, hoping that I wasn't making a huge mistake.

As soon as we cleared the building, he pulled me to the side where no one would see and put his back against the wall. He took a long deep breath, closed his eyes, and lifted his face to the overcast sky. It was almost like he'd been trapped back there and could breathe now.

"Hey, are you okay?"

Eli blinked a few times and turned his head from side to side, stretching. "Yeah. Thanks for going along with that. I thought we were busted for sure. So, where you headed off to now? I'd offer you a ride, but I came with the guys."

Screech. That was my brain putting the brakes on every single one fantasy that had been running through my head. Once again, I was the smart girl who was also really dumb. I actually thought we were going to get out of there together. I thought he was going to take me back to his place and...

Dumb.

"I'm just gonna go home." That had been what I wanted to do tonight, anyway.

"Cool. You want me to walk you?" He looked at his watch.

"No. I live just across from campus. My car is right here.

I don't like to walk home at night after I close the shop. Don't worry, I'll be fine." Geez, I sounded like an idiot.

He gave me the eye. You know, the one that says he can tell I'm being weird. "You sure?"

"Yeah. I'm sure." I waved him off. The sooner he left me alone, the sooner I could go die of embarrassment. "Go do whatever it is you wanted to do."

"Thanks. You're the best. The next time you need a fake boyfriend at the bar, let me know." He gave me a salute and jogged down the ally in the opposite direction of the bar. I sort of thought he'd go back in. Spread his exploits of making out with me in the ally.

Not like I was brag worthy for a guy like him. He probably had a cheerleader, or the captain of the cheer squad, waiting for him and that's what he was in such a hurry to go do.

I got into my car and started it up with every intention of going home. Really, I did. But I was too keyed up. This was a weird night and a cup of tea and a book just would not do it for me right now.

There had been that flyer for the all-night old-school horror movie festival at the coffee shop. I was totally that kind of nerd girl. Yeah, I liked romance and horror. The best horror movies had a little romance in them, anyway. Like that one old Michael Jackson Thriller video, where he turns into a werewolf and then a zombie on his date.

The old one-screen theater off campus was only a few blocks. It would be easy enough to take in the next show and gorge myself on popcorn and Dots.

I pulled into the parking lot and hurried up to the ticket booth. The 1954 classic *Creature from the Black Lagoon* was starting in six minutes. Perfect. The only other classic monster movie I loved better was the 1941 *Wolf Man*. The guy ahead of me got his ticket and turned to go into the theater.

"Book girl? What are you doing here?" Eli looked around like I was the paparazzi, and he was waiting for the rest of the cameras and screaming fans to pop out of the bushes and start tearing his clothes off. "Did you follow me?"

This guy was a wreck. Kind of cute that he thought of me as book girl and not make out in front of the bar girl. I'd give him one brownie point for that. But he was losing it right away for not learning my name. "It's Charley, short for Charlize, not book girl, and no. I came to see the movie. Monsters who fall in love with human women are my jam. You too?"

I pointed up to the board listing the show and times.

"Oh. Yeah, uh, me too." He looked down at the ground and kicked at an invisible pebble. And he blushed. Like actual, adorable, embarrassed, blushing.

You could have knocked me over with a feather. Hot jock guys like Eli Teagan had the ego of a tyrannosaurus rex. I doubted his vascular system even knew how to make him blush from lack of experience. It hit me right in the old noggin. He wasn't here with a bunch of his jock friends. In fact, he'd done everything he could to get away from them to come here.

Aww. He was an old-school horror nerd and didn't want any of his friends to know.

That seemed ridiculous to me. People were allowed to like more than one thing. But maybe not in his world. Jocks ate, drank, breathed, and lived sports, as far as I knew. Probably especially during their big season. To get to where he was, he probably lived football twenty-four seven since he was a kid. Didn't leave much time for geeking out over black and white horror movies or anything else.

I'd been miffed at him when he left me behind the bar, but now I kind of felt for him. It has to suck to not be allowed to be yourself. I straight up knew I was kind of weird, totally a dork, a geek about a lot of things, and I fangirled out all the time, especially about my favorite authors' new books, especially the paranormal romance ones. I was okay with who I was most of the time.

Other people weren't. Society wanted me to be taller, thinner, tanner, to eat more salad, and be interested exclusively in the reality TV shows like *The Bachelor* instead of Hitchcock's *The Birds*. I dealt with that by not being around society.

Didn't seem like Eli had that choice.

"That's cool. Looks like there are a lot of good ones on tonight for their festival. Gonna stay for a few?"

He looked up from the ground all dorky shy-like. "Yeah. I bought the all-night ticket. We missed *Nosferatu,* but *Invasion of the Body Snatchers* is on later."

He skipped right over *Wolf Man*. I lifted my hands in the air like claws and prepared to howl up at the sky. "Hey, don't forget my werewolf fantasy come to life. Ahroooo!"

Eli choke-laughed and joined me in my wolf-style cry. He did a spot-on imitation. Almost sounded real. After he was all smiles. He really did have a killer grin. "Come on, lemme buy you some popcorn."

He also insisted on buying my ticket, even when I told him not to. I wagged my finger and shook my head at him, but when he wasn't looking, I secretly smiled. He didn't need to know I liked he insisted on paying, like this was a date or something. I was gonna get my feminist card revoked for goodness' sake.

We took way too long arguing the virtues of Dots versus M&Ms in popcorn and the theater was already dark when we got in there. Eli held onto my elbow to lead me all the way to the back of the theater like he could freaking see in the dark. "Wait, let's sit in the middle of the middle. Everyone knows those are the best seats for the acoustics."

"Yeah, but the back is darker, better visuals."

I wouldn't win this battle. It's not like I hadn't seen this movie a hundred times and knew most of the dialogue line for line. To the back we went. The second we sat down, Eli manspread, like he was the king of the theater. Legs wide and arms over the back of the seats. One arm over the back of my seat.

If he pulled the yawn and try the cop-a-feel move, I was going to... probably let him. In fact, if he didn't do the move by the end of the opening credits, I might just do it to him.

ELI

Yeah, I know the best seats in the theater are smack dab in the middle. We were sitting in the back in the dark so I could hide the rocket about to explode in my pants.

Charley smelled so damn good, not just like the ripe peaches from before, but also old books, and licorice. Even if I stuck popcorn up my nose, I was never going to forget her scent. Man had it been a huge mistake to put my arm around her, because now I had to use my other hand to balance the bucket of popcorn on my lap. Every time she reached for a handful, my dick screamed that she should be reaching for me.

My wolf was going so crazy inside, wanting to kiss her and lick her and bite her and... claim her.

I was not ready to claim a mate. I had the pressure of a career in sports while not revealing my true self, the future of our pack, and Professor Rojo's literature in translation mid-term coming up. None of those gave me time to even consider a mate.

Besides, she was a human and while it was no longer forbidden to mate with them, it still felt hella taboo. Which of course, made her all the more delicious. Sure, most of us grew up dating the humans in the towns we lived in, but we couldn't ever reveal who we were to them.

Why was I dying to let her see the real me?

Just because she was the hottest thing since Hot Pockets, and was funny and into old horror movies, and did I mention how hot she was? She didn't even seem to notice either my hard on or how much I was drooling over her and all those curves. I was going to have wet dreams about that ass. She was so far from the typical girl I dated or even took home for a fling, I didn't know what to do with myself.

She didn't seem the type to be impressed by game stats or whatever. She was sweet and... bookish, and she kissed like a fucking siren. I hadn't been this nervous around a girl since I lost my virginity and even then, it wasn't like I had to work for it.

"Dot?" She held up the box of sticky sweet candies. I hated Dots, almost as much as Good n Plenties. Yuck.

"Sure." I took one and stuck in my mouth. Ugh. Cherry or some shit. It was like chewing cough syrup.

"Ah." She sounded disappointed. "You got my favorite flavor. There are never enough red dots."

Yes. I almost fist pumped the air. This was my in. "I'm happy to share."

I leaned in slow to make sure she was down for this, and with the dot waiting between my front teeth, pressed my open mouth to hers. Her tongue snuck out and took the Dot, licking along my bottom lip. I tangled my tongue with hers and the candy. That was it for me. Charley Cherry was my new favorite flavor.

I snaked my hands into her hair and went all in, teeth clacking, tongues dueling, deep, deep kisses. I explored her mouth to the fullest. My tongue counted every one of her teeth and found her tonsils. The movie and the theater and the popcorn were all gone. It was just me and this fucking hot girl making out in the dark.

Goddess above, she was driving me crazier than any other girl ever had. My wolf certainly hadn't ever perked up and made its wishes known before. I'd like to do a way more with her in the dark. Or better yet, with the lights on so I could stare my fill of her amazing tits and her full ass. God, that ass. I grabbed a hold of her hip and pulled her closer.

"Ow." She laughed. The damn armrest was in the way and in this old-school theater, it wasn't going anywhere. I could rip it right off using just a tenth of my wolf's strength, but just like on the field, I kept that part of me reined in.

A quick glance at the screen told me we'd been making out for a good half of the movie. I'd happily spend the whole movie with my hands down pants and my lips locked to hers. But she'd mentioned she really liked this one, and I didn't want to be the asshole who made her miss it because I was horny as fuck.

Instead of sticking my tongue down her throat some more, I held up the box of candy and offered her another one. She smiled and picked out another red one, tempting me.

I tried to watch the movie, honestly. But this could have been my first viewing of *The Shining* in the theater, and I still wouldn't be able to pay attention. I didn't care if Jack was a dull boy. I wanted Charley to be mine.

She was rapt with the movie, so instead of trying to kiss her again, I pushed her hair back and started nibbling on her ear. That was the worst and best idea I've ever had. I could practically taste the skin at her throat begging me to bite and mark her.

"Mmm. Wow, that... that feels amazing. Do that again." She moved her head to the side, giving me more access to her delicious skin.

I was dumb, so, so incredibly stupid. I'd been looking forward to this all-night horror fest and an evening off of all the pressures of being the star quarterback, straight-A student, alpha heir to the pack for a month. I could get laid anytime.

Except that's not what it felt like with Charley. I'd just fucking met the girl and I was half in love with her already. She was more than a quick lay. I didn't know why, but she was. She was the kind of girl I'd give up Hitchcock for. She was also the only girl I'd ever been with who wouldn't want me to.

I wanted her. Not just in my bed tonight, either. "Char, I've got *Wolf Man* on my computer."

Charley froze. She stiffened right up and pulled away from me. Yep. I was officially a dumb ass. I should have just been happy to hang out and watch the movie, make out a little and not push her to come home with me. I knew I had a reputation as a ladies' man. She probably thought she was just going to be another notch in my belt.

For the first time ever, that bothered the hell out of me.

Charley glanced over at me, back at the screen for a long

time, and then back to me again. "You want me... to go home with you?"

Go big or go home. Alone.

"Yeah. We don't have to do anything you don't want to. We really can just watch the movie, just without these between us." I knocked on the old wooden arm rest.

"Shhh!" Some guy sitting in the middle of the theater turned and glared at us.

Charley stuck her tongue out at him. So fucking cute. She tilted her head to the side a little bit and looked up at me through her lashes, all cute and shy like. "What if I did go home with you?"

Oh, fuck yeah.

"We can do whatever you want." I was about to make a huge fool out of myself. "'Cuz, I like you, Char. I definitely want to take you home and I'd really love to take you to bed, but I also enjoy hanging out with you. I meant what I said. We can just go watch nerdy horror movies at my house. No expectations on my part for anything more."

Those pretty lashes fluttered again. "What if I wanted to do more?"

"Then we'll do more. Like this." I brushed my lips over her throat. My fangs dropped, and I dragged them so gently across the beat of her heart, bee-bopping in her neck, then down across her collarbone. Despite the push of my wolf to mark her and make her mine, not to mention the armrest poking into my intestines I leaned over and slipped my hand along her ribs and underneath her shirt, caressing the small of her back just above where her skin met her panties. "And this."

"Would you two please get a room or shut the hell up?"

We both ducked down, and Charley snickered. "I can't believe I'm going to say this, but my vote is let's get a room."

CHARLIZE

Eli and I snuck out of the theater so as not to raise the ire of the guy whose movie we'd probably already ruined. Once outside, we practically ran to my car.

"Where too?"

"Over by Greek Row. I share a house with a couple of other guys from the team. But don't worry. They'll either be out or in their rooms at this time of night."

Can't say I relished a walk of shame in the morning past the football team, but we couldn't go back to my place. I also shared a house, but it was only two bedrooms and four girls, so we shared the bedroom. But you know what? Fuck society. I wasn't doing a walk of shame in the morning. I wasn't even sure I was going to sleep with Eli. Even if I did, I wasn't going to be ashamed of it.

He was sweet and nice, and totally unlike what I expected the star quarterback to be like. He'd been a gen a knight in shining Under Armour. I hadn't been looking for that in a guy. In fact, I'd always wanted the opposite. I'm a strong independent woman, dammit. I don't need a man to rescue me, and most guys take a look at my plus-size curves and don't have any desire to.

Except for Eli.

I also thought we'd tear each other's clothes off the second we got into his room. I was a little bit nervous about that. No t-shirt to hide my muffin top, no jeans to smooth out the cellulite on my thighs. Turned out I didn't have to worry.

Eli showed me to his room, and then stood in the doorway while I looked around. He held his hands at his side like he didn't know what to do with them. I was pretty sure he did. There was that whole wolf in the sheets reputation he had. No way Eli Teagan was nervous to have me in his room.

"Sorry, it's kind of a mess. I didn't expect to have anyone over tonight." He grabbed a pile of books off his nightstand and shoved them into a desk drawer.

Weird. He didn't pick up the dirty socks, or the wadded-up papers next to the desk. He cleaned away his books. But he didn't get them all, and I was dying to know what a guy like him reads. "Here, let me help."

I pretended to straighten the remaining books, but I was definitely checking out the titles. H. P. Lovecraft, Robert Louis Stevenson, Mary Shelley, Shirley Jackson. All the horror classics the movies were made from. Then I spied his Kindle.

"Oh, no. You don't have to." He tried to snag the little e-reader from my hands, but I spun and flopped down onto his bed with it. One flick of the screen and it opened up to what looked like the last page of a book. I read aloud, "If you enjoyed Jakob and Ciara's story, there's a bonus epilogue."

I knew this book. I looked up at Eli, who was turning fifty shades of red. "You're reading a dragon shifter and curvy girl romance?"

Eli snatched the Kindle out of my hand. "It's action adventure with dragons and hot sex scenes. What's not to like?"

"You don't have to defend romances to me. It's my favorite genre. I've read that exact book, and the ten more in the series after it. Have you read her wolf books too?"

Eli's face did some weird contortions, and he mentally processed everything I'd just said. His face settled into a humored smirk, which I very much wanted to kiss right off of him. He sat on the bed next to me. "Uh, duh. Chronologically, the wolf series goes before the dragons."

"Yeah, but she published them while she was still in the middle of writing the dragons. Did you know--"

Eli put a finger to my lips. "Uh, uh, uh. No spoilers."

"Come on. I've got your spoiler, right here." I yanked Eli down onto the bed with me. It was a hundred percent fun being so brazen with him. Mostly because he seemed to like it as much as I did.

He was a big, powerful guy and didn't have to move a muscle if he didn't want to. So, it was extra delicious when he did come down onto the bed with me. We were both fully clothed, but his body over mine, pressing me into the soft blankets, had my girly bit on high alert. Like Defcon five... and a half. "Is this a spoiler alert? I want you to kiss me again."

"Nope, not at all. That spoils nothing, because I want to kiss you again." Eli brushed his lips across mine, not in a kiss, but a tease. "But I told you, we don't have to do anything except watch a movie together."

He rolled off the bed and grabbed a MacBook from his desk. "*Wolf Man,* the 1941 version, of course, or my personal, albeit controversial comedy horror favorite, *An American Werewolf in London*?"

Was I seriously going to have to talk this guy into getting naked with me? I both liked him more for it and wondered if there was something wrong with him... or me. "What? Of course, it's the campy John Landis flick for the win."

I sat up and propped myself up against his pillows. And we watched a movie. And we didn't have sex. He didn't even feel me up. Sigh.

Maybe he was having second thoughts now that he actually had me home and quite literally in his bed. There was one way to find out. Just as David was transforming into a freaky wolf creature, I stuck my hands down his pants.

Eli hissed as I stroked his erection. Also... that answered that question. He was hard as a rock star, hung like one too. He wanted me. Or he had a thing for Nurse Alex Price.

He grabbed my arm. "Char, if you keep that up, we won't be having half as much fun as we could tonight."

I gave him a little squeeze, and his eyes crossed. "I'm just getting the fun started is all."

In a blink, Eli had the laptop closed and on the floor, his body on top of mine, and my arms up and over my head. He kissed that spot along my collar bone he'd discovered at the theater again and I shivered. He chuckled because he knew I liked it. "Are you sure? We don't--"

The guy was about to give me a complex. I appreciated he was being a good guy and making me not feel pressured, but come on. I couldn't be a whole lot more ready and willing. "If you say we don't have to do anything I don't want to again, I'm going to, to--"

I didn't get to decide what torture I was going to inflict on him because Eli kissed me so deep and long and thoroughly, I forgot all about being worried or mad or anxious. He kept my wrists held in one of his big hands and used the other to slowly push my shirt up.

God. Did he really have to start his exploration of my body with my belly?

Yes. Yes, he did. Eli leaned down and swirled his tongue around my belly button and dipped in. I'd be worried about belly button lint, except he distracted me by kissing, licking, and nibbling his way up my stomach to where my shirt still covered my breasts. "Babe, you can say stop whenever you want, even if you think I don't want to."

"Don't stop." My voice was all sexy and breathy.

He let go of my arms and whipped my shirt right up and over my head. Thank goodness it was laundry day, and I had my one cute bra on because it was the only one left.

"Green polka dots are cute and all, but I've been dying to taste your nipples since our first kiss." He didn't do some kind of bad boy magic and whip my bra off. He pulled the cups down and licked one nipple until I was writhing underneath him.

"Fuck, I could get lost in your tits." He kissed his way across and gave the same treatment to the other breast.

Whatever reputation this guy had, it was well earned. I hadn't even taken my pants off yet and my panties were soaked. "Eli, take your shirt off. I want to touch you too."

"Hmm. It's my turn right now to get you as hot for me as

I am for you. Once my clothes come off, I want you wet and ready for me."

Any more ready and I was going to come just from his kisses. "I'm wet. I'm ready."

"Not even close." He finally let go of my wrists and my hands went straight for my pants or his pants, or both at the same time.

Eli pushed my fumbling fingers away and undid the button and pulled down the zipper of my jeans. He grabbed the waistband and started working them down my hips. He hadn't balked at my belly or the stretch marks on my boobs. I guess I wasn't going to freak out that he was about to see my hips and ass in all their plus-size glory.

I lifted my butt, and Eli pulled my jeans down. Before they got to my knees, he gave me a sideways look. "Are you wearing Slytherin panties?"

"Of course, they match the bra, and that's my house. Why, what are you? You're totally a Gryffindor. I can't tell."

"Something like that." He pulled my jeans off and tossed them to the floor, then he ran his fingers along the bottom edge of my undies, getting closer and closer to the center. "Fuck, you're fucking beautiful."

Aww. Not the most romantic turn of phrase, but coming from him with this sort of awe and wonder in his eyes, I'd take it over anything Jane Austen or any other romance writer ever wrote.

He kissed my belly again, lower this time, just above the waistband of my underpants. That sent tingles and butterflies and butterflies with the tingles all through my stomach and down between my legs. Eli grabbed the edge of the fabric between his teeth and pulled them down. I almost giggled until he shredded them with his teeth and licked his way between my legs.

Oh. Oh God. Was he going to...? God bless every chick who had ever been with this man before me and had taught him what women wanted. I wasn't super experienced, but this was college and I'd done my fair share of dorm room hopping and having mediocre sex in the middle of the night. Not once had a guy offered to go down on me.

I wasn't about to admit that either. Not that I could because within a couple of minutes, Eli had me seeing stars. Like actual, literal sparkles flying through my vision as he gave me the best freaking orgasm of my life. His tongue and lips and fingers eeked every last pounding, pulsing, name-screaming ounce of life out of me.

I was still breathing hard when he finally quit and crawled up my body. "You're the absolute most delicious thing I've ever eaten."

Just to prove it. He kissed me and I got the first taste of my own flavor mixed with the salty taste of him. I would never be able to eat popcorn or Dots again without getting wet.

ELI

Having Charley in my bed was better than throwing a game winning pass, better than when Mina goes for Dracula over Harker, better than hot fucking apple pie à la mode from the Sleepy Folk's pie shop in Rogue. I never wanted to leave, and I didn't want her to either.

Her face was flushed, and her eyes were all dreamy. She pushed her hands into my hair and scraped them across my scalp, kissing me back just as deeply. She whispered against my lips, "Do you have condoms?"

Boxes full. God Bless a sexy, confident woman in bed. I wanted her so bad I could hardly see straight and here she was the one taking this to the next level.

I didn't need protection, since wolf-shifters didn't get human diseases and we couldn't pass them on either. Hooray for shifter immunity. Unless this was a full moon and we were mated, she couldn't get pregnant either. But it wasn't like I went around telling all the ladies that and I'd never want them to feel unsafe in my bed. So, I kept a steady supply in the house. "Yeah. But we don't—"

"Don't try to talk me out of it. I want to feel you inside of me. I want you to feel as good as I do right now. I want you."

My heart exploded. Like right there in my chest. It went kaboom and melted into a puddle of goo. Plenty of girls had said they wanted me. Charley was the first one I believed wanted me for me. The me she knew about, anyway.

Fuck. Should I tell her now who and what I really was?

I was never fucking letting her go. She was mine. I knew it down to my soul. But for the first time in my life, I was worried about being a notch on someone else's belt. It had been ground into me from birth, never to reveal my true self. Wolves mate with other wolves. Not humans.

Only a handful of the highest-ranking wolves had claimed humans as their true mates. How the hell did they go about telling them. That wasn't something I could consider right now. I'd figure it out later. Right now, I was about to send my girl to the moon with more orgasms than she could count.

I rolled off the bed, shucked my clothes, and grabbed the box of condoms out of the desk drawer where I'd shoved the books. I hadn't wanted anyone to know I was reading for pleasure because that wasn't what the cool kids did. Charley didn't care. Actually, she cared and liked the same stuff I did. Stuff I hid from everyone else in my life because it didn't help me get a scholarship, lead a pack, get into the NFL, or get good grades.

For the first time in as long as I could remember, I wanted to talk to someone about what I liked and wanted to hear what she thought. I was already looking forward to a lot of long nights between her legs and then talking about what was between the pages of the books we were reading.

Look at me. Thinking about a long-term relationship. From one-night stands to night one with my true mate.

I slid a condom on and crawled back into bed. My cock was aching for her, had been all night. But this was more than a fuck. I liked more than her body and that was a way bigger turn on than I ever expected.

I spread Charley's knees and notched the head of my cock at her entrance. "I want this to feel good for you, babe. So, tell me what you like and what you don't. I'm gonna learn your body better than anything else in my four years of college."

She wiggled her hips and pushed the tip of me inside of her hot, waiting pussy. "Is it weird of me to say you're hung like a romance novel hero?"

"I've read romances. That's a damn compliment and an ego boost." I slowly pushed into her and good Goddess, she felt amazing.

She bit her lip, and I struggled to hold myself still so she could adjust. She wasn't wrong about my size. I'd spent enough time in locker rooms to know I had the goods.

"More, Eli." She panted the words. "I want more of you."

"You're so fucking tight. I don't want to hurt you." My wolf was pushing against me, driving me to flip her over, fuck her hard and fast with her ass in the air and her face in the pillows. For the first time in my life, I felt the alpha in me rise up, wanting and needing her submission.

"You aren't, I promise. Please, move. I'm going to go crazy." She wrapped her arms around my shoulders and dug her nails into my back.

Fuck. She was so hot and slick and sliding in and out of her pussy was like heaven. It wouldn't take me long to get close to coming, but there was no way I was going to come until she did. "Slide your hand between us. Feel me pushing into you and rub your clit. I need to feel your pussy squeezing me."

She did exactly what I told her to, and it took only a few flicks of her fingers and a couple of my thrusts and her back was arching up off the bed. "Oh God, Eli. Yes, yes."

The look on her face alone could have gotten me off. I pounded into her, taking us both over the edge. "Charley, fuck, you feel so good. God, yes. Fuck. I fucking love you."

My brain went haywire and the knot at the base of my cock enlarged. I shoved myself into her so deep I could feel her entire cunt coming around me. Never had I felt anything like this. My orgasm hit like a fucking thunderbolt, smashing into a freight train, crashing into a mountain. My vision tunneled and my heart pounded against my chest. Or was that my wolf?

The beast inside was pushing me to mark her, claim her, and make her mine.

I dropped my head to her shoulder and used my last bit of strength to keep myself from sinking my fangs into her, marking as mine. It took all I had not to collapse on top of her.

I could hardly breathe. I couldn't move.

No, like I legitimately couldn't move. The wolf's knot had gone full-on beast mode mating, and we were stuck together until my animal nature was satisfied she was mine.

I just told a girl I'd met a few hours ago that I loved her.

And I fucking meant it.

That was crazy, and I was a serious asshole. What the hell was she going to think of me now? Shit. She hadn't said anything back. It's not like I expected her to say she loved me back. I slowly raised my head to see what her reaction was, praying it wasn't revulsion. That she hadn't freaked the fuck out when she realized my cock was no ordinary human one and I'd just busted right out of the god-damned condom.

"Char? I...." Her eyes were closed, her breathing soft and even. She was asleep. "Charley?"

Well, hell. I'd fucked her into a coma. There was a dick-head part of me that was patting myself on the back for that. There was another part that was hoping and praying she hadn't heard me. I wasn't waking her up to find out, either.

I carefully held myself over her, so as not to squish her with my bulk, and had a long talk with my wolf. Which was weird since the wolf was me. I was the wolf. There was no real separation between the two parts of myself and I'd never felt more like I had a split personality than just now.

Look, wolf. She's not ready. If I reveal myself to her now, she's going to think I'm a monster and freak the fuck out. I don't want to scare her or hurt her. She knows nothing about the supernatural. If I'm going to talk her into being my mate, I need to ease her into this world.

The knot pulsed, pleasure rolling through me like a freaking orgasm aftershock. Oh, yeah. The wolf wasn't ready to let her go without a fight.

Char sighed so adorably that I quit fighting and pulled a blanket over us. I had no fucking idea what was going to happen in the morning, in the light of day. I'd never cared before. Girls came and went from my bed, from my life.

I wanted this one to stay. But she didn't know what I was.

My wolf didn't care.

How in the hell was I going to tell her? The beast pushed against me, and my skin and bones tingled with the magic of the shift.

No. Nuh-uh. Absolutely not. I was not having her wake up with a monster breathing and slobbering in her face. It took long, deep breaths to halt the shift, and I got another near orgasm pulsing in my cock for it. The knot swelled even larger, and Charlie's eyelashes fluttered.

Fuck.

Even without taking my animal being right in her face, she'd still realize there was something going on with me. My fangs were out, my eyes glowed with the magic inside of me, and with as much pleasure as was throbbing through my cock, I was on the verge of fucking her again.

Because I'm an asshole. Shit. I will not be that guy. Now the problem is not just how to tell Charlie, it's how to appease my beast to give me the time to figure everything out. Not only is everyone else in my life pressuring me, my wolf is, too.

I can escape my family, I can hide from the team for a night, but I can never escape the wolf. It won't back down until I do something to make Charlie mine.

Goddess, help me.

ELI

I pressed my lips to her throat, exactly where I would mark her. No matter how much my wolf pushed me, I would not mark her without her consent. She knew nothing about my world or what marking, claiming, or mating meant.

I couldn't help it and scraped my fangs across her skin. She shivered, and I wrapped her arms around my neck, pulling me closer.

"Ooh, again? You're an animal." She pushed her hips against mine and groaned.

This, I could do. I rocked my hips, knowing I couldn't pull out, but I had other skills. Within a minute, I had her eyes rolling back in her head and her cunt fluttering around my cock once again. Before I knew it, my balls tightened, and I came hard right along with her.

Then she did something I totally didn't expect. She growled and bit my neck.

She bit me. She fucking marked... me. I could feel the

magic tingling from her to me, across my skin and deep into my soul.

Like nothing else could, that satisfied my beast.

I wasn't sure how to feel about it. She wasn't a shifter. I would have been able to scent that on her. Charlie was a full-blooded American human woman. What the fuck was going on?

When she released me from her bite, she kissed my neck and then ran her thumb over it. "Oops. I gave you a hickey. Couldn't help myself."

"Next time, I'll give you one." She had no idea how much I meant that. I pulled out of her body and rolled over, wrapping her in my arms, tucking her head onto my shoulder. She was asleep in a few minutes again and I was in wonder of her ability to pass the fuck out.

I laid there, holding her tight in my arms, overthinking everything, letting all the pressures of the world pile on, and on, and on until the sun hit me smack in the face. Morning already. Ugh.

Charley was still and softly snoring. She had the cutest sexy bed hair, and I'd bet money my pillows were going to smell like her. I might never do laundry again.

I was gonna pull a pussy ass move and sneak out of here before she woke up. Put the ball in her court. I'd leave her a note and if she wanted to see me again, she could. If not.

I always had football and the whole damn world's high expectations to fulfill.

I dressed quietly and put her clothes on the desk chair. All except her adorable Slytherin undies. Those went into my pocket. With a quick scrawl on a sheet of notebook paper, I had my note.

Char,

You were sweeter than anything last night.

If I didn't have to get to practice, I'd happily spend all day in bed with you watching every version of Stephen King's It.

As always, no pressure. But if you want to see where this is going, swing by the field house any time today and we can talk.

Or do more.

--E

I wanted to make sure she saw it. Aha. I pulled one of the precious sleeves of mini donuts from my secret stash, that no respecting quarterback would have, and propped the note up against them. Then I made my way out of there as fast and as quiet as I could.

I caught a break because the other guys were already gone, off to the gym by this time. Coach liked us to do a light workout the days after a game, and the earlier we got it done, the earlier we were free. Except for me and few other key players. We got to watch film reels and pick over every god-damned mistake we made.

I hit the gym first and got the side-eye from my roommates. Shit. They surrounded me like a pack challenging an alpha.

They'd definitely seen Charley's car still parked in front of the house this morning. We'd all agreed at the beginning of the school year that no girls stayed overnight. I'd pissed plenty of cheerleaders off by taking them home in the middle of the night.

I put in my earbuds and started the twenty-minute warm up routine on the treadmill, to hold them off. That didn't work even a smidgen.

Ty, my well-meaning teammate number one, said, "Tell us she was too drunk to drive, so you took her home and she's coming back to get her car later."

I shook my head and upped the speed to give them the hint I wasn't in the mood to talk. "We weren't drinking."

"So, she's back at the house?" Luka, well-meaning roommate number two, asked.

"Probably." Fuck, this was uncomfortable. I was not used to being the one who broke the rules. We didn't bring non-shifter girls home. I knew that. We all knew better. We didn't even room with non-shifter teammates.

"Human chicks are a distraction you can't afford, man." Luka shook his head at me like I was a disappointment. "Fuck 'em and blow off some steam, sure. But don't be thinking you're finding a mate or some shit."

"I know, I know." They were right. My parents were counting on me playing a little pro sports before I came home to take over the pack with some money in my pockets. It was all about prestige and positioning, with so many powerful packs on the East Coast.

But none of these assholes understood what happened between me and Charley last night. I didn't fucking care if this blew my career.

My whole life was about everyone else's expectations for me. I wanted one god-damned thing for myself. I'd gotten a taste of life without all the pressure of my peers and teachers and coaches and family. Gotten a taste of Charley.

"You're going to taint your pack's pure lineage for the fat, nerdy girl? Dude, you didn't already tell her you 're a wolf shifter, did you?"

And just then she walked into the gym. Shit, if she'd been

a shifter herself, she probably would have heard everything we said. I glared at the bunch of them with my best shut-the-fuck-up face.

Kirill slugged me in the arm hard and pointed at Charley. "She must give some pretty damn good head, because there is no way you could fit your big old dick between those thunder thighs."

The other guys made the appropriate oohs and ahhs that went with the burn. All I could feel was the heat of a thousand suns on my face. Char had heard every fucking word, and the look on her face was breaking my heart.

She was hurt and scared. Of me and my asshole teammates.

I balled up my fists and literally shook with the rage. One more word from any of these assholes and I was going to shift right here in the campus gym and rip all their throats out.

Charley turned on her heel and ran out of the gym. I'd go after her as soon as I got myself under control. The best way to do that was to let out this pent-up rage on Kirill's face.

I knew better than to break my hand on his face. I used enough of my wolf's agility to jump over the treadmill's handrail and spun on the balls of my feet, switching direction faster than he could even blink to crack him across the jaw with my elbow.

He dropped to the floor like Tyson in the tenth at the Tokyo Dome. The rest of the group backed away as they should. I didn't even wait around, just took off after Charley. Either that girl was secretly a track star, or she had a penchant for hiding. The quad was wide open, and she was nowhere to be seen.

I jogged toward the student center, trying to find that sweet scent of hers in the air. I could track her if I caught even a hint of her scent. Maybe she went to hide in the library. I'd lose her in there since she already smelled of books. Shit.

Maybe she went back to my house? That was the opposite direction, but I could still catch her. We only lived a ten-minute walk from campus. I could get there in two if I sprinted the whole way, which I did. Her car was gone.

Fuck.

Fucking fuckety fuckballs. I didn't even have her phone number, email, snapchat. Nothing. I didn't even know her last name.

CHARLIZE

I should have known better. I did know better. But my hormones got the best of me. That had to be it. Because I was smart and didn't date or sleep with asshole jocks. Or dumbasses who thought they were actual dire wolves.

I'm so sure. *"You didn't already tell her you're a wolf shifter, did you?"*

Give me a break.

I never should have let anyone in the whole wide world know about my love of horror movies. Especially not some cocky jock. I saw him freeze up, and that gave me get the chance to get the hell out of the gym and the awkward morning after.

But what if... no. But... maybe? Did I believe in supernatural beings? A little bit. I was honest enough with myself that some of my love of the horror genre was that layer of what if. He had growled at me during sex.

Oh. My. God. What was wrong with me? Werewolves were not real.

Probably.

I hid behind the door like the big fat coward I was. I didn't want to hear any excuses about why he thought it was okay for his friends to make fun of my hobbies and especially not diss me and my body. Asshats.

Eli took off running toward the quad, sniffing the air like a drug dog. I waited until he was out of sight and beat feet to my car.

What I needed now was to escape into a good romance novel and forget about my non-existent love life. Except, crap. I'd left my book at Eli's house. I thought he might like the sports romance I'd just picked up. Dumb.

Fine. I steered my car instead to the coffee shop. The second I walked into The Moon Bean, I breathed a sigh of relief. Nothing like the smell of coffee and books to heal a broken heart. I was definitely not taking home a paranormal romance tonight.

"Uh-oh. I know that look. The date didn't go well?" Selena, the owner, came around the corner with a pile of books as high as her head. She'd said she wanted to expand the bookshop side of the business, but geez.

I grabbed a stack off the top, so they didn't all go tumbling to the ground. I'd a hundred percent forgotten about the date from hell. That felt like a thousand years ago and not last night. "Yeah. No. That guy was the worst."

"Hmm... yeah. I knew he wasn't the right one. But at least you got out there and now I don't have to fire you." She set her books down on the counter and started sorting them by author to put to the three new shelves we'd just gotten in.

A. How did she know that guy wasn't the right one and why didn't she tell me? And B. I'd thought for a hot minute that Eli was my guy. Should I tell Selena about him? No, definitely not. "You weren't really going to fire me, were you?"

"Hmm. It would be tempting." She tapped her finger on her temple. "I hate to see a girl like you be miserable, so I would have to let you go just so I didn't have to look at you moping around our brand new romance section every day."

A girl like me? What was that supposed to mean? But to be fair, I had made plans to mope around today. A new section of the store dedicated to shatter-my-heart-and-make-me-cry romance novels sounded like just the right place to do that. Sigh.

"That guy didn't break your heart or something, did he? I should have told you, but it wasn't the time. I will march right over to that bar and—" Selena brandished a book with a hot shirtless Viking holding a sword on the cover.

"No, no. It's not him that broke my heart." What was I thinking? That Eli was actually like a book boyfriend, all perfect and loving?

I fucking love you.

He'd said those words to me. I'd been too much of a chicken to say them back. Good thing. He clearly didn't mean it. Heat of the moment, I guess. Whatever. I didn't need Eli Teagan in my life.

Selena narrowed her eyes at me and sniffed. "Spill it."

I came straight here and without a shower. Did I smell like hot, schmexy sex? Crap. I backed away. "No. Everything is fine. I am perfectly happy getting a degree in literature with an emphasis on nineteenth century British authors, working at the coffee shop, stocking books, and avoiding boys for the rest of my life. I chose the wrong guy to give my heart to, so..."

I'd get a plant, and maybe a parrot. I'd teach the bird to say funny things like "I vant to suck your blood." and "Red-Rum, RedRum."

I could have long conversations with the ficus that would be just as intelligent as with any football player. Except Eli was smarter and funnier than a ficus. He'd get the horror movie reference I taught my parrot to say. If he even liked horror movies, that is.

Selena smacked the book down on the counter with a smack. "You're fired."

"What?" My face and hands went all cold and numb, then heated right back up as I got mad. "Because some guy who was clearly too hot for me treated me like dog poo?"

"No. Because I thought you were smarter than that. You're loud and proud and confident and never let anyone treat you like... poo, did you say?"

What? Like... is that what Selena, this badass take-no-shit woman, who pushed the rest of us to go after what we wanted, thought I was confident?

"You know who you are and what you like, and you've let no one else tell you otherwise. Not even fate." The tingle of the door opening and a new customer walking in sounded, but we both ignored it. Selena shook her head and rolled her eyes at me. "Why is it different with boys? What in the world makes you think you'd ever choose to open up to the wrong guy?"

Whatever. A love of horror movies and being good in bed does not a wonderful boyfriend make. He wasn't even my boyfriend, for goodness sake. He was a stupid one-night stand, and I was locker talk. That's not fate.

"I'm not the wrong guy. I swear to you Charley."

I spun toward the door and there was Eli, shirtless like he'd been at the gym, sweaty, and with an unnatural glow in his eyes. Were those fangs popping out from under his top lip?

Selena clapped her hands. "Ooh, I knew it. I just knew it."

I frowned at her. "Knew what?"

"And it's not even the full moon yet. Damn, I'm good. This is so going on WolfSpace later." Selena legit just walked away from me and Eli, talking to herself and ignoring me and my questions all together.

"Charley, I'm not sure what all you heard back there—" Eli stepped closer and reached out.

Nope. I turned sideways. "I heard everything, and I do not enjoy being made fun of."

"Shit. Everything?"

I folded my arms and gave him the stink-eye channeling my inner loud, proud, and confident woman Selena said I had inside. "Everything."

He swallowed hard. "Okay. Uh... let me explain."

"Explain how big of dicks your so-called friends are?" I was down for having him do some groveling.

"Yeah," he groused and cupped his neck, right where I'd given him a hickey. "That and... the uh, other thing."

"Like I believe that you're a wol—" Wait a second. "What's wrong with your neck, Eli?"

I pushed his hand to the side and where there should be a reddish bruise from my over-exuberance last night, there was a swirl of black and gray, like ink. I ran my fingers gently over his skin, in awe of what I was seeing. The marks were forming shapes, as if a magic spell worked on his skin. A wolf inside of a crescent moon appeared.

A wolf with glowing purple eyes.

"Eli?"

"Touch me like that again, Charley." His voice had gone down a full octave, and he was breathing a hell of a lot faster than a second ago.

Eli's irises were glowing with that exact same purple light, but his pupils were so huge I could see my reflection. I brushed my fingers over what now looked like a live moving tattoo. "I'm still mad at you, but what's going on? Is this some kind of prank you all pull on poor, unsuspecting one-night stands to get rid of us?"

Eli grabbed my hand and kissed the inside of my wrist. "You're not a one-night stand. At least, I don't want you to be. What the guys said about being wolf shifters, they weren't kidding."

"You're not getting out of this by distracting me with your horror cosplay fantasies or by turning me on with your well-placed kisses. Do we need to call an ambulance? Maybe an exorcist?"

"No, babe. Listen. I'm being serious, and —"

The bell above the door jingled again, and I pushed Eli toward the bookshelves. If he was having some kind of weird health problem and-or mental health attack, that was no one else's business.

"Hey, you, Eli Teagan. I've got a bone to pick with you, man." The douchepotato from last night stumbled into the coffee shop. He was three sheets to the wind, and it was barely afternoon. He was a real winner, winner, chicken dinner. That's what I get for going out on a date with the first guy who even vaguely flirts with me. I sure know how to pick 'em.

Eli stepped around me and pushed me behind him. "You don't want to do this, man."

The way he emphasized the word man was weird. Did these two know each other or was this just a dick measuring contest? Either way, I did not like being in the middle of it. "I think you could use a cup of coffee, my guy. It's on the house."

Bad date dude, whose name I couldn't remember for the life of me, snapped and snarled at me. "Stay out of this, you traitorous whore."

Uh, why were his eyes glowing like a wild animal caught in the headlights? Something was seriously wackadoo here. I needed to find Selena and call the police. Or maybe animal control. Or even Sam and Dean Winchester.

I glanced up at Eli to see if he'd caught that too or if I was hallucinating. And that didn't make me feel any better because his eyes were glowing too, but with an almost neon purple. When the hell had his freshly shaved face gone beyond five o'clock shadow? Holy shit, those were a canine style fang poking out from his upper lip.

Eli was a real life wolf man.

Cue the dreadful horror movie music where the heroine makes a dumb mistake and dies.

ELI

"Watch it, asshole." I stalked toward the guy who Charley had been harassed by last night. Fuck, was it seriously only last night? My gut told me I'd known her for a lifetime.

A lifetime together is what we'd get if I had my way. Just as soon as I took care of this douchecanoe and begged for Charley's forgiveness, on my hands and knees, if I had to.

The bad date dude was about to hulk out and in front of a human who knew nothing of the supernatural aspects of the world. That was not only dumb, it was arrogant. Which meant he was a god-damned one-blood. Assholes who thought shifters were superior and that humans should be subservient to us.

My father had dealt with them during the worst of the pack wars. He'd warned me they were dangerous. Dangerous because they were stupid and didn't think for themselves. Blindly followed the dogma of the worst of the Volkovs.

This was my school, and I didn't want anyone of his ilk

tainting our safe haven for higher education. Charley was my girl. Pieces of shit like him didn't belong anywhere near someone as special as her. It made me sick to think he'd ever touched her.

I kept my voice low, hoping Charley wouldn't hear, or if she did wouldn't understand. I'd explain about shifters and our society as soon as I could, but surprising her with it wasn't just dumb, it was against the code we wolves all followed. Punishable by death. "If you're challenging me for my mate, this is not the time nor the place."

"Why the fuck would you want to claim a human for a mate? Is the whole Chincoteague pack pussy whipped by these weakling human women?" Bad date dude sucked on his front teeth and shot a glance at Charley. "Or do you just want to fuck her? I'm happy to share her with you."

Okay, you want to play that game, fucker. I growled so deep and low that the alpha in me was ready to bust out and tear this beta to shreds for stepping out of line. Penalties be damned. "She is mine."

"Excuse me? I belong to no man... or beast." Charley snapped at us both. That's my girl. At least she didn't come out and get between us. Instead, she called for backup. Because she was a smart cookie, and I was being dumber than a box of rocks. "Selena, I think you need to come out here."

"I'm right here, *umnyashka*. I had to go close the shades and lock the door. Can't have any ball bunnies or campus security interfering with a challenge." Selena, who had definitely not been there a minute ago, popped out from behind one bookshelf and thankfully hauled Charley back a few feet. "We're in for a show. It's very exciting having two young strapping wolves fight over you. Ah, how I miss the good old days. Oh, stand back, I think that beta is in for an ass-whooping by your handsome alpha heir."

Yeah, he was. If Selena Troika, matriarch of the most powerful pack in the world and mother to the Wolf Tzar, was down for a challenge happening right here, right now, on her turf, I was going full fangs ahead. Beta one-blood boy needed to learn a lesson on how to treat women, human or wolf. Except that meant shifting, and Charley wasn't ready for that yet. Shit. Okay, so no shifting then.

"What? You mean wolves like raw, raw, go get 'em Bay State Dire Wolves, right?" Uh-oh. Char sounded a little hysterical and I couldn't do a damn thing to comfort her right now.

No, I had to make sure she was safe and protected from the likes of this guy. I narrowed my eyes at my opponent and snarled. Fucker needed to back off. He knew better. Or maybe not, because he hunched down and started circling like he was looking for a spot to attack.

"This is the best part. Now watch and keep an open mind." I couldn't take the chance to even take my eyes off this beta, but I could smell the popcorn and distinct giddiness. Like we were about to put on a show.

The scent of excitement wasn't coming from Charley, though. "Open mind? About boys fighting over me?"

"Just remember, the Goddess wouldn't have chosen you as a fated mate if she didn't think you couldn't handle it," Selena said like it was no big deal. Oh, that's right. To her, it wasn't. She was the head of the family that started the revolution. Before her sons, no one mated humans.

She broke all the rules, and I'd never broken a single one.

Maybe that needed to change.

Beta boy lunged for me, and I easily spun around him. He faltered on his feet, and I wondered what in the hell kind of training his pack gave him before sending him off to college. Not anything that involved agility. Probably didn't even hunt for himself.

His back was to the ladies now and from this position I could monitor them and d-bag at the same time. I gave Charley a wink and Selena a nod of thanks-for-the-solidarity.

"If you're gonna pick a weakling girl over your own kind, oh mighty golden boy, then you've made the wrong fucking choice." Beta boy's wolf shone in his eyes and was too close to the surface.

I should thank Selena, because I didn't care if the Volkovs themselves came and tried to tell me what to do. For the first time in my whole damn life, I was making a choice for myself. Not for my family, not for my pack, but for me. And my choice was Charley.

Assuming I didn't scare the shit out of her in the next ten seconds. I let my wolf push up and out. I'd chosen Charley as my mate, but ultimately it was up to her, and she couldn't make an informed decision if she didn't know who and what I was.

Beta boy may be forcing me into this, but that was a good thing. No time like protecting one's mate to expose the secrets entrusted to us all.

"What in the world is going on here? Have you all lost or minds or is this some kind of fraternity prank?" Charley's voice was nearing nuclear meltdown. I stared directly into her eyes and pushed my thoughts of love and lust toward her, hoping she'd get the message and not freak out.

My stomach went all tingly, and then my skin followed suit. Right in front of the first woman I cared anything about, I stripped naked, prepared to show her my true form, let her see the real me. The wolf, the alpha, her one true mate.

Selena took a bite of popcorn, and Charley's eyes went wide. "What in the actual hell? Is this actually a dick-measuring contest? I'd only been joking about that before."

Beta boy did the same and we both let the wolves take over. I dropped to all fours and let the bones break and reform, my fur burst through my skin, and my wolf senses take over. All without taking my eyes off Charley.

Her mouth dropped open, but Selena shoved a few kernels of popcorn in, forcing Char to chew. "Open mind, dear, not open mouth."

I wanted to trot over and push my nose into her hand, let her touch me, and maybe even stroke behind my ears. I would have if Beta boy hadn't decided to try his luck against me. He lunged and Char yelped. That almost distracted me, but both my wolf and the athlete in me knew how to turn off distractions in the heat of battle. If ever I needed my head in the game, this was it.

Before Beta boy got anywhere near my mate, I leaped into the air and tackled him to the ground, grabbing his throat in my teeth. Charley gasped, and I prayed to the Goddess of the Moon that I hadn't blown it with her. Please, oh please, oh please, let her be a tough cookie. I was pretty sure she was, but we hadn't known each other long enough to put any pressure on our fresh, shiny, lust-induced relationship.

I had to trust that I'd made the right choice just now, letting her see my wolf. The wolf was cocksure and confident, so I would be, too.

Beta boy struggled, and I gave him another shake. Since he wasn't in my pack and I wasn't yet a full alpha, we couldn't communicate in wolf form, but I growled in a way he should know meant I wanted him to show me his throat and submit to my dominance.

"Get him, Eli." Charley shouted and my heart sang. "Show him we don't take any shit from assholes like him."

That did not sound like a woman afraid of me. I fell all the rest of the way in love with her at that very moment. No one and no wolf would stand between me and my chance at a true mate.

I should have known better than to get that cocky.

Instead of submitting, Beta boy twisted and rolled, swiping his claws across my face. Blood spurted into my eyes, and I couldn't see. It was the advantage this dickbag needed. He slammed into my side, slamming me against the bookshelves and knocking the air out of me.

My wolf would heal my injuries, but nothing could heal my heart when I heard Beta boy's growl and Charley's scream.

CHARLIZE

It took me all of about three minutes after seeing Eli turn into the most amazing and gorgeous wolf for my brain to stop whirling around like a tornado straight out of Oz. Good thing I had to Good Witch of the South, or, err, of the coffee shop to help me.

Selena was not only not freaking out about two college boys turning in to wolves in the middle of our coffee shop, she'd made popcorn and was cheering Eli on. That is until Bad Date Dude started to win.

I got so mad that such an asshole might hurt the man I loved, even if he was a wolf, I screamed at him.

"Screaming won't help Eli, dear." Selena smirked at me, or maybe she smiled? "What else you got?"

"What else do you expect from me. I don't have fangs and claws." What was I supposed to do? Throw a book at them?

"You've got more power than you give yourself credit for. All women do, we just don't flaunt it like the men. Because we don't have to. Well, until we need to. Then look out." She waggled an eyebrow at me like I was in on some kind of secret with her.

I wasn't. Unless you counted the fact that werewolves existed. "What's my power?"

"What do you think it is?"

"This isn't a therapy session. That dickbag of a bad dog is going to hurt Eli. I need to save him." I didn't give Selena a chance to say anything else cryptic because said dickbag dog was creeping closer to all three of us.

Okay, what was I good at that could be my secret superpower? I was great at reading. Which wasn't useful here, but had exposed me to lots of fresh ideas and worlds. Maybe that's why I wasn't freaked the fuck out that Eli was a wolf. I was gonna go with that theory.

I was good at watching horror movies. Uh, yeah. That was sort of happening right in front of my eyes. Right. I'd seen about a million heroines who were too dumb to live run away from the monsters only to end up getting chased down and eaten. And not in the fun way.

I refuse to be the TDTL girl. What did the girls who lived do?

Aha. They embraced the weird and made friends... or became lovers of the monsters.

Check and mate.

Although, I was not making friends with Bad Date Dude.

I was missing one more piece of the puzzle. Selena cleared her throat and jerked her head at the rapidly approaching bad guy wolf. "Ahem... maybe try some of that loud and proud confidence?"

If Selena believed I had it in me, maybe it was true. I was

fantastic good at being loud and using my words. I should have done so when Eli's dumbass friends were being dumb asses. Eli could have used his words and told me who and what he really was. I never liked the part in the movies where the monster was silenced.

In my best unfreaked out, embracing the weird, and loud and proud way I could muster, I turned on the werewolf stalking toward me and smacked his nose. "Bad dog. Bad, naughty dog. Don't be a dick."

Bad Date Dude whined and stuck his tail between his legs. Huh. Okay, good. Guess he just needed a good telling off. I had plenty more where that came from.

The bell above the door of the coffee shop rang and in walked Eli's teammates from the gym. Uh-oh. I whispered out the side of my mouth, "I thought you locked the doors."

She whispered back, "I did. But I also called for backup. Your mate is an alpha, and he needed his pack. We're better with our friends and family around us. Why do you think I wanted you to find yours?"

Her eyes glowed a sparkling blue for just a minute, and then she tossed another piece of popcorn into the air and caught it between her teeth. Her very fanglike teeth.

A. Was everyone around here a wolf except for me? Were all these guys wolf shifters too? B. Ahh, Selena set me up. Crafty fox, I mean wolf.

Bad Date Wolf turned into a gray streak and bolted out the door, dashing between the legs of the football team. I had a feeling they could have stopped him if they wanted to. But all eyes were on me and Eli.

Shit. Eli.

I dropped to the floor and set his head in my lap, stroking his ears.

"Lucky bastard. I wish I had a girl who'd do that to do me."

With some creaking and cracking, Eli shifted back into his human form. He had three long scratches from his forehead to his cheek, but they were healing even as I looked at them. "Are you okay?"

I got up, and Eli followed me. Selena threw him his pants, and I'd need to remember to ask him about why he'd stripped down before shifting. "No more shifting today, kids. I've got a business to run."

The lot of them echoed some version of "yes, ma'am," and shuffled their feet until she shooed them toward the coffee counter. Selena re-opened the doors, and it didn't take long before more students filed in. There was an entire line outside.

"Yeah. Thanks to you, sweetness." He put his hand over mine and held it to his cheek. "Are you okay? You're not freaking out?"

"I did for a minute. But I think having a supernatural boyfriend and not freaking out is my superpower. Either that or it's not minding that you were naked in the middle of the coffee shop." I shrugged, and Eli laughed.

"I wanted to tell you, but it's complicated." He sat up and gave me a long, lingering kiss. Until the guys started hooting and hollering.

The asshole who had called me fat was standing right in front of the rest of his buddies. He deserved a good telling off. I'd smack his nose too, but it looked like he'd already hurt himself. Good. "Look here, dickface. I don't know what issues you have in your life that you feel you need to lash out at other people for not fitting into your little preconceived ideals, but I hope you get help with that."

The other guys around laughed and pointed at us like kindergarteners. Lord, save me from dumb jocks. Not that they were all dumb, but these didn't seem to have an original brain cell between them.

"The rest of you might take a good long look at yourselves in the mirror, too. You don't have to be empty-headed robots with no emotions who blindly follow the leader because he's got a big dick." Yes, I meant Eli. If more of them acted like him, I'd probably like them all better.

There were more snickers, but a lot fewer than before. Maybe I was getting through to them. Except they weren't looking at me. Oh... Eli's eyes glowed, his fangs had dropped, and he was snarling at the bunch of them.

I smacked him on the arm. "You could have said something, you know. You could have defended me."

"Doesn't look like you need me to. You put these douchebags in their places just fine. It's one of the things I love about you. You're not like the dumb bunny Barbies I used to go out with."

"Hey," a girl standing in line for coffee shouted. "I'm graduating with honors in theoretical physics and start at NASA in the spring, you bag of dicks."

Eli didn't even glance at the girl who did indeed look like engineer Barbie. He only had eyes for me. He was sexy and staring at my mouth, and did I mention I was suddenly very hot?

"I like that you know who you are and don't put on a facade for the world. Not like I do. Every move I make from the classes I choose to the friends I have is to make sure everyone thinks I'm the golden boy. But I'm not and I'm tired of fucking trying to be." His words were for me, but everyone here could hear him.

He thought I liked who I was. Selena had said the same. I mean, I tried, but I had a mask I showed to the world too. I wasn't hiding a supernatural secret like he was, but there were parts of me I didn't show to the world either. Everyone had that part of themselves they kept secret and safe.

I guess that's why I had fallen for Eli in the first place. We'd both let those walls down and shown each other our real selves, even before I knew he was more than your average bear... boy... whatever. "Eli, don't put me on some pedestal. I've got my own issues. We all do."

I dropped my voice to a whisper. "I understand the parts you have to keep secret, but I don't get why you think you have to hide your actual personality from everyone. You're a cool guy, and I don't just mean because you're the captain of the football team. You're smart and funny and I thought you were a nice guy until you got around these schmoes."

He glanced over at said schmoes and back at me. "Then help me be that guy, Charley."

Sweet. But no can do. "Don't put that on me. You gotta come clean on who you are and what you like all on your own."

Eli sighed and looked over at the other players again. Their opinions really mattered. I hoped not as much as mine. "Fine."

He stretched his neck from side to side and swung his

arms like he was warming up for a game. Then held his arms up to the air like he was declaring his faith. "I like classic horror movies."

"Dude. Who doesn't?" someone shouted from the peanut gallery.

Eli did that face people make when they are both shocked, pleased, and thinking - what the hell?

"Keep going," I prompted him and took a step closer.

His wolf flashed in his eyes again, but he nodded, acknowledging what I was really asking. "I also like nerdy girls with curves that blow my mind."

"Once again, dude. Who doesn't, besides this douchecanoe?" One guy shoved the fat phobic douchecanoe.

I stepped even closer.

Eli blinked a few times, and he licked his lips. I saw the tips of his fangs. He couldn't hide them from me anymore. I didn't want him to.

He hadn't expected his friends to be okay with what he was saying, and it was so cute to see how genuine acceptance hit him in the feels.

"And?"

He lowered his arms and held out a hand to me. "I like this nerdy girl right here, and I'd really like to ask her to be my girlfriend."

"Dude."

Eli turned and pointed at the guys. "Don't even say it."

I took that last step between us and put my arms around him. "I like this big mysterious guy right here, and I'd really like to be his girlfriend."

Even standing all the way up on my tippy toes, I still had to pull Eli's head down to give him the kiss we both needed.

"Get a room, you two."

Eli smiled against my lips. "I hear there's a werewolf marathon on tonight. Wanna come over?"

"Ahroooo."

"I'll take that as a yes."

ELI

Wasn't I just the luckiest fucker that ever lived?

This was Thanksgiving weekend, and I had to be back on Saturday to play in the Dire Wolves' game this weekend. That meant only one full day at home with the fam. That wasn't nearly enough time to eat a turkey and introduce my girlfriend, my mate, to my pack.

We were doing it anyway. The drive down to Chincoteague wasn't that long, and I didn't want to wait any longer. Tonight was a full moon, and it had just about killed me not to claim Charley on the last two moons. But I wanted to do this right, in front of my pack, so everyone knew she belonged to me and me to her.

"No, no, no." She wagged her finger at me. But I put her hand back on the wheel before she could get too riled up. "Nobody said anything about having sex in public. Eli Teagan, that is not my kink."

Char had taken to supernatural life like she'd been born to it, even though she wasn't one herself. She was going to make a fantastic matriarch someday. But I had waited to tell her exactly what the mating ritual involved until we were well on our way to my pack's home turf. I guessed on the road, a half hour away, was as close as it got. "Sweetness, it will be fine, I promise. It's not like anyone will watch us. Everyone else there will be getting it on with their mates."

She raised her eyebrow at me in the way that I learned meant I was in trouble. I loved getting her riled up. She was so damn deliciously adorable when she was mad. "So this is an orgy?"

"No. It's a sacred ceremony that has been a tradition for wolf shifters for centuries." Although, I'd kind of always thought of it as the wolf orgy. Not that I'd ever taken part, just watched once I came of age. It felt different this time since she and I would be the ones mating.

I thought I'd be nervous like human grooms always were on TV and movies. Those guys were dumb. I could hardly wait.

The GPS dinged for the turn down the long secluded one-lane road that led to my house, the pack house for the Chincoteague wolves. Char took the right and grinned at me. "You're making that up. You just want to have kinky sex. You could just say that. I've read plenty of erotic romance novels, you know."

Oh, I knew. There was an entire stack of them on my bedside table. Pornhub had nothing on erotic romance authors. "If you want, I can tie you up and blindfold you. The other wolves in my pack might think you're weird, but you're my kind of weird."

"Eli." She groaned and rolled her eyes at me.

She also squirmed in her seat. I easily scented her

arousal, and I'd use it to my full advantage if I had to. "I'll lay you down in a soft bed of leaves and tie your hands up over your head so your pretty tits are pushed forward. Your pink little nipples will be hard in the cool night air and just waiting for me to suck on them."

"This isn't working," she sing-songed.

Oh, yes, it was.

"And just when you're ready to beg me to fuck you, I'm going to spread your legs wide and eat that delicious pussy of yours until you're just on the verge of coming in my mouth."

"Uh huh." Her voice was nothing but a whisper now, and I knew I had her. She was rapt, and I was harder than rocks. We might have to make a pit stop before we got to the house.

"But I won't let you. Not until you say that you're mine for everyone to hear." She'd said it a hundred times before. My wolf demanded it from her and she gave it what it wanted because then I could give her lots of orgasms. But tonight was special, because my entire pack would know that I'd found my fated mate.

The first of the Chincoteagues to bring home a human mate.

She stuck out her tongue at me. "Meanie."

"You love it."

Charley blushed, mostly because we both knew it drove her crazy with desire when I kept her on the edge of an orgasm. The waiting made it even more explosive when I made her come after a lot of teasing, wanting, and needing.

There was one part of what would happen tonight at the mating ritual I'd left out. Tonight, I would mark her just as she'd marked me. A bite to the soft spot between her throat and shoulder that called to me like a siren's song. I'd been so close to marking her every time we were together, but I held myself back. Just like Charley, I knew it would be even better for the anticipation. The mark would make her night more than just another fuck...in front of my pack.

We pulled into my parents' driveway a few minutes later and I gave her a quick, hard kiss. "Come on, my mom's dying to meet you."

"What if your dad doesn't approve of me?" My dad had been wary of me bringing home a human, but one call from Selena Troika and he'd changed his tune.

"They're going to love you. Just like I do. You'll see." I dragged her out of the car and my mom was already at the front door waving us in.

My dad came trotting around the corner in his wolf form. I shook my head and called him out via our mind speak link. Dad. If you think you can intimidate my mate, think again. Remember, she's the one who smacked a one-blood on the nose and called him a bad dog.

I think that story, even more than the call from Selena, had changed my dad's mind about Charley. He liked anyone who stood up to one-bloods.

I know, my boy. But she's never met an alpha before. She might as well get the full feel of it right away, since she's going to be the matriarch of the pack someday.

Warmth spread across my chest. He had already accepted my mate if he was thinking of her future with the pack. I hadn't been sure he really would until now.

Charley took my hand and looked over at my dad's wolf. "Oh, is this your dog? Isn't he a handsome boy?"

Oh, Goddess.

She held out her hand like she was going to pet my dad and I almost died. Then she slapped her thigh and laughed hard. "I'm just kidding, Mr. Teagan. I figured out right away, you had to be the alpha Eli looks up to so much. Nice to meet you, I'm Charlize."

My mom joined us and put an arm around Charley. "I like her Eli. You picked a good one. Anyone who can give your father shit is a keeper in my book. Now come in the house, turkey is almost ready."

Charley and my mom headed to the kitchen and my dad shifted, threw on some pants my mom always kept by the door, and steered me toward his den. The sports channel was already on and we spent the next half hour talking about the teams and who we thought were going to the bowl games. But he seemed a little distracted, kept looking toward the kitchen. Maybe he was as eager for turkey and stuffing as I was. Mom didn't allow snacking on Thanksgiving, so we'd be nice and hungry for dinner.

On a commercial break, my dad muted the TV with the remote. "Eli, you know you don't have to play ball if you don't want to."

I just about spit out my drink. "I thought you wanted me to play pro for a few years before I come home."

He nodded slowly, but frowned at the same time. "Sure, that'd be great, but only if that's what you want, kid. You're a talented young man and you'll be a great alpha someday."

I didn't know what to say. Scouts were all over me and teams had come courting. I was just about ready to sign with an agent. Something had held me back from pulling that trigger, though. My dad had given me something to think about. I'd have to talk it out with Char. She always helped me figure what to do in a way no one else could.

He slapped me on the back in that way he had that always let me know he understood. "You two ready for the mating ritual tonight?"

I did not want to have a sex talk with my dad. Yuck. "Mostly. She's learned a lot from the other wolftresses at school, and Selena Troika's been like a mentor, but I'm not sure anyone is ready for their first time."

"No, I suppose not. I definitely wasn't ready for you mom and her wiley ways." He glanced toward the kitchen and his wolf rose up in the glow in his eyes. When they mated, wolves didn't necessarily get to choose their own mates. It was all political, but they fell in love. Disgustingly always thinking they were sneaky going off to screw around.

"Ew, dad. I do not want to hear about you and mom..." I made a barfing nose.

"Ah, but the way she glowed for me in the moonlight. It was like there was no one else in that sacred circle but her and me. You'll see, kid. You'll see."

I'd heard about this glowing for your mate thing, but my dad had never mentioned it before. Supposedly, it was something that happened for fated mates, but Charley and I had been too busy fucking like bunnies during the last two full moons to bother going outside in the moonlight. I wasn't sure I believed in such a fairy tale, but I also hadn't really believed in fated mates before I met her either. So anything was possible.

"Boys, dinner." My mom called us, but Charley stood at the door smelling like pumpkin pie and lust. I couldn't wait to eat her up.

We followed my parents to the backyard where we always set up the big wooden table so any pack members who wanted could join us for dinner. There were usually a few.

Not today, no. This wasn't a few. The entire damn pack was outside. When Charley and I walked out together, they clapped and cheered like we'd just won a game or something. They patted us on the back and shook my hand, and the wolftresses gave Charley kisses on the cheek.

I didn't know what to say, but Charley laughed. "Uh, I guess your family likes me."

"Yeah. I think so." We sat near the head of the table by my parents, and it took a minute for the rest of the pack to get settled at the tables that stretched halfway through the yard. When everyone was finally seated, my dad nodded at me.

I just stared at him until Charley elbowed me in the ribs. "He wants you to say grace."

Gulp. My dad always did that. He was the alpha. I grabbed Charley's hand under the table and bowed my head. "Today we give thanks to the Goddess of the moon, who blessed us with the ability to let our true natures roam free and gave us the gift of..."

I'd heard this prayer a thousand times, heard the ancient stories of a goddess who loved her people so much she came down from the stars and gave us the ability to shift into wolf form, be the hunters, warriors, protectors, and family we were meant to be. Never before today had I paid attention to the words.

I cleared my throat and squeezed Charley's hand. "Gave us the gift of her love. Join me today, my fellow pack, my family, my friends, in lifting our voices to her. For tonight we feast."

That's where the traditional prayer ended, but I added one more part because it's what was in my heart. "And tonight we find love. May you all be blessed with a true fated mate."

Every member of the pack lifted their faces to the sky and howled, a chorus of voices joining mine. Charley kissed me on the neck, right over the mark she'd given me on our first night together. Then she lifted her voice, but not in an average howl. No, she used her words and quietly howled into my ear, "I love you, too."

EPILOGUE

Standing in the forest, in nothing but a flimsy, sheer scrap of material, with a bunch of werewolves, was straight out of a horror movie.

I love horror movies.

I wasn't as freaked out about this mating ritual as I thought I would be. His dad said some words, they all shifted and howled at the moon, and then most went off to do their business. I knew they were around, but it didn't matter. They'd given us the modicum of privacy I'd hoped for.

Once Eli and I were here in his pack's sacred circle, I forgot about anyone else. With the moon shining down on him, I could swear he was glowing, especially for me.

He took my hands in his and gave me the gentlest of kisses. "You look so beautiful. I hardly know how I got so lucky to have you for my mate."

Aww. While I loved his gentle kisses, I loved our passionate, can't-wait-to-tear-your-clothes-off ones even more. I grabbed Eli around the shoulders and pulled his head down to mine, and did my best to kiss the bejeezus out of him. Luckily for us both, there weren't a lot of clothes to tear off.

Eli was already naked, and I was liking the fact that wolf shifters burst out of their clothes when they took on their beast forms. That meant they were naked a lot. I wasn't sad about seeing my boyfriend, my lover, my love in his sexy glory at any time.

We dropped to the ground, and he tore the light bit of material right off me. "Char, I know I promised to tease you and do all kinds of naughty things to you tonight, but goddess, I need to be inside of you. I swear I'll do all those other things later."

"Funny, I was about to say the same thing to you." I reached out and stroked his cock, partly because I loved seeing his eyes roll back in his head when I touched him, and mostly because I couldn't wait any longer either. "This entire day has been one big tease. I've been ready for you since breakfast."

Eli grinned and growled, which was one of my favorite wolfy things he did. "I know. I could smell your arousal all day. Why do you think I had a napkin in my lap throughout dinner? It's not like I have great table manners."

That was true. Eli and his teammates didn't just eat, they massacred meals. "Why Eli Teagan, are you saying you've been this hard for me all day? You must have blue balls by now."

"You have no idea, my love." He grabbed my butt and gave it a squeeze. "On your hands and knees. I need to see this lush ass when I'm taking you tonight."

While I didn't always like the size of my butt, Eli was slightly obsessed with it. I got onto all fours and waggled it at him just because I knew it drove him wild. He was over me in a second, and I heard his harsh breathing. I loved it when he let go and lost a bit of his control.

"Say you're mine, Charlize. Say it." The words were snarled, and that made my heart go ka-thump.

Normally, I did exactly what he wanted because we both enjoyed this part of our sexy times. But tonight, I wanted more. "You're mine, you say it first."

That did it. That let Eli's beast out exactly like I wanted. When he let himself be free like this, I knew I had the real Eli, the one I loved so hard that I never wanted to let go. Every day, average Eli was sweet, and kind and I loved that side of him too, but I knew he had to try to be that way. This was his true nature.

He fisted my hair and pushed me closer to the ground, but with his other arm, he grabbed my hip, holding me up so my ass was angled just right. He teased me with the tip of his cock, notching it just inside my entrance. "Tell me you're mine."

"You say it first," I repeated.

With one long, hard stroke, he pushed himself fully inside of me, filling me up so good it took my breath away. We fit together so perfectly that I groaned. "More, Eli. Tell me you're mine, make me yours."

"Fuck, Char." He thrust in earnest, fast and hard, like he couldn't control himself. In this position, he hit all the best spots inside of me and it didn't take long before my body was pulsing and pounding, so close to orgasm. Eli was close too, and he leaned over me, chanting in my ear, "Mine, you're mine."

He tipped my head to the side and scraped his teeth

across the tender skin between my neck and shoulder, in that sensitive spot along my collarbone. Zips and zings of pleasure zoomed through me when he did that. Tonight, it wasn't enough. I wanted more. I wanted everything from him.

"Give me all of you, Eli. I need the real you, I love you, and only you."

He paused for a moment, growled and then fucked me even faster and harder. "I am yours, Charlize, only yours, and you are mine."

He nipped at my earlobe and then pressed his mouth against that spot again. In another hard thrust, he bit down, sinking his fangs into me just as I opened my mouth to tell him what he wanted to hear. An orgasm like no other ripped through me and I screamed out the words. "I'm yours, Eli."

His cock pulsed inside of me as he came, and I felt the wolf's knot enlarge and lock us together. We collapsed onto the ground and Eli rolled so I was wrapped up in his arms instead of squished into the leaves and dirt underneath his enormous body.

We were both breathing hard, drifting in the glow of our bodies joined. With every breath he took, he whispered out that he was mine, over and over. Every time he said it, more warmth and tingles spread from the place he'd bitten me to run all up and down my skin.

I never wanted to leave his arms. "I love you, Eli, man or beast. I love you. You're mine and I'm yours, forever."

Those were the words his wolf needed to hear, and the knot faded, releasing us from its hold. My body gave one more little after quake of a shivering little orgasm and Eli chuckled. "You like the wolf's knot, don't you?"

"You know I do." I snuggled into him.

He kissed the spot where he'd bitten me and sent more tingles through me. "I hope you also like the new wolf's mark you have."

"Is that what you did? It felt amazing. I feel different now." It was as if a new hotter blood ran through my veins. I was down for being hotter for Eli.

"Different how?"

"Like my senses are heightened or something." I blinked to clear my vision. Then I sneezed. "Like there's more of me and more of you, and just more of everything."

Eli gave me a squeeze. "I'll always take more of you."

"Wait, umm, like for real, something is happening. My skin is all tingly and I don't think it's just because your made me come so hard I nearly exploded. What's happening?"

One minute I was in Eli's arms, feeling the afterglow of our lovemaking and mating, and the next I was wagging my tail.

My. Tail?

Eli?

Ack. His name did not come out of my mouth. It was like I was talking with my mind.

Eli smiled down at me and patted my head. "You're the prettiest wolftress I've ever seen." Then he scratched behind my ears, and I nearly fell over with pleasure. Oops, yep, I actually fell over.

Wolftress? Are you saying I'm a wolf right now? I said into Eli's head and tried to get up. Wolf legs were not like human legs. I was going to have to learn how to walk all over again.

Eli shifted into his wolf form and licked me right across the face, err, uh, snout. *Yep. You are. I'd heard some humans the Troikas mated got special powers, but I didn't know if it was true.*

You knew this was going to happen, and you didn't tell me? My tail started wagging again, so it was hard to hide that this was the coolest thing that ever happened to me.

Come on, let's go for a brief run and let you stretch your new form. Hopefully, you'll be able to shift back just as easily. Eli gave my side a shove with his nose and helped me back up to my feet.

Wait. Do we have to have sex for me to shift?

Eli trotted away, gave a howl to the moon, and winked at me. Guess we'll have to find out.

Need more Big Wolf on Campus?

Grab the next book in the series now, Bad Boy Wolf

Want more Eli and Charley? We've got a fun bonus chapter for you! Join Aidy's Curvy Connection to get it now!

BAD BOY WOLF

For everyone who ever fell in love with a bad boy, who was really just a burnt cinnamon roll.
Dark and crunchy on the outside, but ooey gooey and sweet on the inside.

Forget about prince charming! Give me the guy with tattoos and a bad boy attitude.

— SOMEONE HILARIOUS ON THE INTERNET

HUNTER

I closed the book and sighed, holding the paperback to my chest. "God, I love a good happy ever after."

Yes, I did read the last page of the book first. I had to be sure I'd get the warm and fuzzies from the ending. Later, in the safety of my room, I'd flip through and read the naughty bits. Only then did I start at the beginning and read the whole story.

"Even better when it's got all the sexy times." Charlize slid the book out of my tightly clutched grasp and put it back on the shelf. "I don't see how you can read the endings of every book in the shop and skip the sex bits. That's half the fun of romance novels."

Heat rose up my throat and cheeks like I'd been drinking a glass of red wine, and I stared up at the ceiling hoping Charlie wouldn't notice. I only blushed like this when I lied or had to get up in front of a class, or talk to people, especially guys. Okay, I blushed all the time and I hated it.

"Oh my God, you do read the sexy bits. Hunter, your

followers would die if they found that out." Charlize laughed and pulled a bunch of other books off the shelf from the erotic romance section. She thrust them into my arms.

Like I didn't know that. My blog, Insta and TikTok, the Hunter of Hearts was dedicated to reading romance novels, but my whole platform was built on skipping the naughty bits. No smutty books allowed. Even if I coveted them and stalked other influencers pages for their recommendations. "Urrgh. I know. But so would my grandmother, my father, his new wife, and my older sister."

I sipped my mochaccino and flipped through the stack of new releases Charlie had chosen for me and handed them all back. I'd already read every single one of them, some two or three times. But on my super-secret sneaky Amazon account that loaded to my Kindle where no one could see what I was reading. "It's too late now. I can't come out of the romance reading closet and be like 'Hey, everyone, I like to read super dirty books to get my jollies. Sorry for making you think I was a good girl."

My favorite coffee shop across from campus, the Moon Bean, recently expanded their business and added a bookshop that stocked everyone's favorite genre literature. I spent more time and money here than anyone reasonably should. But, come on. Two of my favorite guilty pleasures under one roof? What more could a lonely, horny girl with a goody-two-shoes reputation to protect ask for?

Selena, the owner, grabbed a copy of Maya Rodale's *Dangerous Books for Girls: The Bad Reputation of Romance Novels Explained* and handed it to me. "Hey, no literary snobbism allowed here. You can read whatever you want, whenever you want, for whatever reason you want. Just as long as you read."

"Tell that to my grandmother. She's already made it perfectly clear that majoring in contemporary literature is her worst nightmare. Unless of course it's just a stepping stone for law school or I get on at a Big Five publisher as an acquiring editor, which she is sure to make happen." I tucked the book into my stack of purchases for the day even though I already owned a copy. I'd give it away on my next TikTok live event. The booktok community went crazy for giveaways.

"Hunter, you need to relax, you're stressing me out and I can't write when you're freaking out." Rosemary, the resident creative writing major, who didn't want anyone to know she was writing a romance novel, shouted from her spot in the corner of the coffee shop. She was the only girl I knew who drank more coffee than me. I liked her and couldn't wait to read her book. It was sure to have all the naughty bits I craved in it.

Selena smiled and patted me on the back. "Don't listen to her, she won't even admit what she's writing about to the person who needs to know."

"Ooh, who needs to know?" Perfect opportunity to change the subject.

"Good try." She gave me a smirk. But you should listen to me. You need to relax."

The way she said relax, with the ah-sound all drawn out and with an eyebrow waggle indicated she meant more than getting a massage or taking a bubble bath. And there went the heat rising up my cheeks again.

Charlize blinked and held up a finger. "Isn't that what Rosemary just said?"

"Shoo. Go stock the new horror books we just got in. Your handsy quarterback boyfriend is reading me out of house and home." Selena made the go-away motion to Charlize and then propped herself against the shelf next to me.

"What you need is to go on a date and get some of this nervous energy out of your system." She wagged her finger up and down pointing from my toes to my head and back again.

"A date?" Yeah, that was my voice that sounded like Minnie Mouse. I cleared my throat. "I don't see how that's going to relax me even a little."

"Hmm." Selena examined me like I was some kind of book display that needed re-arranging. "No, you're right. Just any old date won't do for you. You're too wound up about the whole thing. What you need are some good old-fashioned dating lessons."

How did she know I knew less than nothing about dating and boys? Not nothing, I knew what book boyfriends were like. I was also smart enough to know that real life guys were nothing like romance heroes. "You're going to teach me how to find a boyfriend?"

"Oh-ho-ho. No. The best person for that job is a big flirt with charm to spare, so he can lend a little to you." She tapped her finger on her lips. Selena was this super gorgeous, mature, curvy woman who was more charming than anyone I knew and flirted with ninety percent of the professors and other older men who came into the shop. If not her, then who?

Wait. Did she say he? Ack. No. I clammed up like a

bonfire at the Cape if a cute guy even looked at me. Which they rarely did. College guys did not make passes at girls in glasses with big... well, you know. Let's just say, I was no Victoria's Secret model. I knew it. Guys knew it. End of story.

"I've got it. Pack up your bags, we're going next door." Selena shoved the books I wasn't going to buy into a bag and handed it to me.

"To The Wolves' Den? I don't think anyone there would to want to give me dating and flirting lessons." That place was notorious for hook-ups. Especially with the Dire Wolves players. The football team was too sexy for their shirts and not looking to find the love of their lives. Except maybe Charlie's boyfriend, Eli.

Those two were in mega love.

"Ah, you're wrong there. I know just the bad boy whose flirter is a well-oiled machine." Selena didn't wait for me to make my purchases or anything. She shoved my backpack onto my shoulder and led me by the arm out the door of the Moon Bean and down the sidewalk.

"No, Selena, please. I don't think this is a good idea. It's fine. I'm fine." Not only were my cheeks heating up, so was my throat and chest. Then there was ka-thumping in my chest like my heart was in an Edgar Allan Poe story. I might be fine putting myself on camera for my followers, but that was because I could use filters, and ring lights, and just the right angles to look good. In real life, I'd be practically bare.

Better to stick to book boyfriends. Or, uh battery operated ones. Or both at the same time.

Selena wrapped her arm around my shoulder and gave me a friendly squeeze. She treated all of regulars who hung out at her shop like an adopted family of sorts. I certainly felt more affection and care from her than my own grandmother or any of my string of stepmothers. "I'm doing this for your own good. Get your butt in that bar and learn to loosen up around the fellas, or you're fired."

"What? Wait. I don't work for you." My father insisted it was improper for me to work while studying. There would be plenty of time for that after I graduated. The only work I did was on my website and socials, and I'd been forbidden to monetize any of that, so it's not like it paid in anything but fans and books. I didn't need the money anyway.

"You're right, but you do use The Moon Bean to write your blog and get the latest and greatest romance novels. So, unless you go in there and get your flirt on, I'm banning you from the shop."

I gasped. "You can't do that."

Could I work on my hobby at home? Yes. Did I love being around other people who lived the book nerd life like me? Also yes, and having my own place off campus was boring and lonely. I'd go crazy if I didn't get to hang out at the Moon Bean.

"Of course I can. Now get in there." She yanked open the door to The Wolves' Den and shoved me inside the bar.

The stench of beer and bodies hit me first. I wasn't used to spending time in college dive bars, even though I was in college. This place was for rowdy beer-drinkers and risky shot-takers. That was so not me. I was more of a champagne bubbles tickle my nose kind of girl.

The second thing that hit me was the chest and six-pack abs of the guy I walked smack into while gawking at my surroundings and feeling out of place.

"Whoa, hey there. Walk much, sweetheart?" He grabbed me by the arms and kept me from falling right on my butt.

Once I got my balance, I looked up into the sexiest eyes I'd ever seen. They sparkled and everything, just like in the romance novels. Then he winked. Oh my God, he winked at me and my lady parts went haywire.

I blame them for what came out of my mouth next. Because never in my life had I ever said something so insane to anyone, ever.

"Will you teach me how to flirt?"

TY

I can't tell you how many hot girls come into The Wolves' Den to get their drink on and flirt with me. One of two things turns them on. Either the fact that I'm the bad boy defensive tackle with more quarterback sacks than any other Dire Wolf in history, or it's the motorcycle and my well-worn leather jacket that turns them on. It's like they can smell my wrong-side-of-the-tracks life and want to roll around in it. Half the time there's at least one sitting on my bike waiting for me when I get off work at three in the morning.

Coach hated that I did shifts at the Wolves' Den, but I'd never shaken the nocturnal life I'd grown up with in the backwoods of the Appalachians, hunting for my dinner, or avoiding the law. Tips helped pay for the stuff my athletic scholarship didn't, and flirting got me the big tips, and laid.

The sweet innocent eyes blinking up at me were not my type. Nope. Sure, she was practically made of money, I could tell that by the clothes and fancy leather backpack. One wink and I'd get a good hundred and twenty percent tip out of her. Didn't matter. She was the kind of girl I stayed far, far away from. The kind who wanted more.

My wolf disagreed. The beast inside of me ached for her. Mentally, I was already licking her up and down to see if she tasted like the ripe peaches of the natural scent of her soft skin.

Fuck.

I'd be lying if I said I never took any of the ladies up on their not-so-subtle offers to go for a ride on both me and my motorcycle. But I always went home alone.

I worked my ass off tending bar to keep a few dollars in my pocket, playing ball, and working toward my degree. It's not like I could ask my old man for anything but trouble.

It helped that I made damn generous tips from the ladies. It was the wink that did it. One little twitch of my eyelid got their panties wet and made me fifty bucks on a tequila shot order.

Not once in all that time had a single lady ever asked me to teach her how to flirt. Her adorable doe-eyed innocence got to me faster than the slutty come-ons I was used to. And that meant I needed to stay far, far away from this little bunny. I didn't have time for a relationship. Hell, I didn't even have time for a one-night stand.

"There's plenty of guys in here for you to practice your flirting with, chickadee. I've got to get to work." I let her go and kind of wished I hadn't. Shit. No use thinking more than a minute about her lush curves a guy could get lost in. "Come on up to the bar if you want a drink."

I high tailed it back behind the long wooden bar and found something to do that wasn't looking to see if the curvy chick took me up on my invitation. There were always glasses to be washed and cocktail fixings to be stocked. It was still early yet and only the late dinner crowd was hanging around. The place would get rocking in another couple of hours.

I served a couple of tables and did as much stocking of the fridges as I could before the evening rush. The next time I looked up from my work, I found chickadee sitting on a barstool right in front of the taps, a prime location for orders, with her laptop set on the bar, tapping away. Great.

I clanked the glasses I was washing nice and loud. "This isn't exactly the best place to do your homework, babe."

"Oh, uh. It's not homework. I'm making notes." She didn't even look up from the screen.

"Well, I suggest the library for that." Which meant, get a move on.

She turned fifty shades of pink and hunched down. It took her a full minute to come back with a response and I got the feeling most of that time was working up the nerve to say more than one sentence to me.

"Not unless you're going there. I'm noting how you flirted with those girls and how you keep calling me pet names." She bit her lip, and I couldn't look away. "Think that will work in reverse? Like what if I called you Shnookums or big boy or sport, does that get you in the mood?"

In the mood? This girl didn't have a clue and it was absolutely friggin' adorable. I wasn't going to be the one to teach her the ways of the force though. She didn't need my rough and tumble past smearing her life through the mud.

The football team may have taken me in like a pack never had, but I knew better than to think I'd ever be more than a lone wolf.

That life had given me the skills I needed to survive outside of this special bubble of four years of school. That included knowing how to keep myself out of trouble's way. If I could flirt my way into a woman's bed, I could flirt my way out of one too.

"Look, doll." I sidled right up to the bar and leaned across so my lips were close enough to whisper in her ear. "This isn't the place for a sweet little virgin like you. There's a cute coffee shop that sells books now next door. I'm sure they have a nice girl's guide to dating on the shelf you could buy. Better yet, get yourself a dirty romance novel, take it home, crawl under the covers, and get yourself off, because I'm not the one who is going to do that for you."

Her throat and face lit up with such a hot blush I could practically feel the heat from her skin. The scent of sweet peach rose up along with it and I knew to my soul, that was her arousal calling to me. If the suggestion of masturbating was enough to light her up like that, I could imagine what would happen if I did in fact become the one to get her off like she clearly needed. She'd probably spontaneously combust in my bed.

What a way to go.

I leaned back and watched her squirm. Her eyes darted all over the place looking to see if anyone else had heard my vaguely naughty words. "I never said I was a virgin."

I could scent emotions just as well as her need. Her innocence was like baby powder and but her fluster at my assumption was like a delicious, aged scotch. Dark and swirling. I'd been a hundred percent right on her sexual status. "Nope, but you are. I can smell your sticky sweetness from a mile away."

"You can... smell my virginity?" She sniffed her chest, and I couldn't stifle the chuckle.

I lifted her chin with a finger and waited until I had her full attention. Jesus, those eyes had me rethinking my stance on not fucking around with good girls. One last try to get her out of here. "Yes. I can smell it and so can every horny dickwad who walks in here. Unless you're looking for a whole lot more than you can handle, it's time for you to skedaddle."

She might not know this university was brimming with shifters, but I did and the thought of any of them even fucking touching her had my wolf pushing to get out and pee a circle around her.

Her eyes went as wide as the moon and her gaze went from nervous to a shit-eating grin that gave her crinkles along her nose. "Did you just say skedaddle? You're amazing at this flirting thing. Like you had me all on edge and then put me at ease again with your silliness. I'm learning so much. I gotta write this down really quick."

Silly? No one on the face of the planet had ever thought I was silly much less said so to my face. I thought sure that would have her running scared. She might be cute as hell, but she had the confidence of a ladybug.

Well, fuck. She wasn't getting the message and I needed this job too much to be outright rude to her. Fine. If she wasn't going anywhere, I was going to use her to my advantage. That was a lesson I'd learned young. Kids of loners had to.

Every barkeep knew ladies' night was to bring the men who'd buy the drinks in. My curvylicious virgin chickadee was going to be my lady that drew the men in because they would be panting after her. Right to my end of the bar and my tip jar all night long.

If I could control my wolf enough not to scare away any man who looked at her.

"What's your name, pumpkin?" Huh. I did keep calling her pet names.

"Hunter. Hunter Dean."

Of course it was. Hunter of my heart.

Goddess above, where the hell had that thought come from? No more of that kind of thinking.

"I'm Ty. You want to learn to flirt, Huntley, I'll teach you, but I'm going to need a couple of things in return." Like her number. No. No. No. Do not go there. This was business, and I needed money for books for spring semester.

"Oh. Okay." She straightened up, but her cheeks went pink again. I was dying to see where else she her skin flushed, like between her legs. "What do I have to do?"

I jumped up onto the bar, swung my legs over and dropped to her side. "First you have to put your computer away. That's a wall you're hiding yourself behind."

With a click, I shut her laptop and shoved it toward her bag. She sighed and then slipped it out of sight. "Fine. What's the other thing?"

"You're going to flirt your curvy little ass off tonight and get every other guy to walk in here to buy a drink, from me, for you."

"I am? I don't want to get drunk." She frowned. "I don't even like beer."

No, she wouldn't. She was more of a white wine spritzer kind of girl. "I got you, boo. I'll be watering down your drinks and giving you plenty of direction. You're not going home with any of the schmucks who hit on you, either."

"I'm not?" She tilted her head to the side in the cutest way. "Isn't that kind of the point?"

"You're not going home with anyone but me. Got it?" Dammit. I hadn't meant to say that. What was wrong with me? She and I were not compatible. The only way the two of us ended up together was if she was going through a rebellious phase and wanted to bring home a bad boy to daddy to make him lose his shit.

It's not like fate had declared her the one and only woman for me.

I certainly wasn't going to mark her, claim her, and make her my mate.

"Oh." Her lips made the sexiest oh and her eyes went all dark and sparkly.

I could easily be that bad boy for her. I could be her protector, her alpha, her mate.

Fu-uck me.

Time to get my head, and not my cock, back in the game. Precious Hunter with her two-thousand-dollar laptop, her pearls, and her rich girl sweater set were nothing but a tool to me. One that was going to make me lots of money. I needed to remember that. "Now, lose the pearls, let down your hair out of that school-girl ponytail, and let's unbutton the top of your sweater."

If I was a real douche, I'd undo those buttons and look her up and down till I was rock hard. I was having a hard enough time as it was keeping my eyes off her chest. "We need to get you the look. That is half of flirting."

She unfastened just the very top button and bit her lip.

"Then I'm doomed. Guys don't look at me that way. I was hoping the flirting would make up for, you know..."

Hunter rolled her eyes at herself and shrugged her shoulders, then she waved at her side and ass.

Was she serious? The junk in her trunk was what had me with a semi in my pants since she'd smacked into me at the front door. She was every guy's wet dream and then some. She had curves on curves and any guy would be like a giddy teenager to get to run his hands up and down that soft place where her waist dipped and her hips--

I licked my lips. "I know just the thing to get you looking all sexed up."

Puffy lips, that flush to her cheeks, a little out of breath, that would drive the men wild for her. She had me on edge and I was going over.

A group of my teammates walked in, rowdy as can be, and I did the dumbest thing I possibly could have. I staked my claim and kissed the daylights out of Hunter right there for everyone in the bar to see.

HUNTER

Ty. Kissed. Me.

Me.

I did not see that coming from a million billion miles away. It's not like I hadn't already fantasized about what it would be like to kiss him. But I certainly didn't expect he ever would take me in his arms and kiss my freaking bobby socks off. If I hadn't wrapped my arms around his neck, driven entirely by instinct, I probably would have fallen right off my barstool.

If this was a flirting lesson, I liked it. I wanted a whole lot more lessons. But not just with anyone, and I wasn't planning on using this new skill Ty was in the middle of teaching me with anyone else.

There was something special about this guy, this one guy, that had me head over heels for him. And it wasn't simply that he was the first guy who'd ever kissed me. It wasn't even because our tongues were currently doing the cha-cha.

I liked him. A lot. Too much. He was easy to talk to when no one else ever had been. He didn't look at me like a weirdo or with disgust because I wasn't a size two, or even a size twelve. But it was more than that. We had a connection.

Didn't we? Was this all in my head?

What was I doing? Ack.

I pressed my hands on his chest and gave him the tiniest of pushes to break the kiss. He was big and strong enough that if he didn't want to move, he wouldn't. With a groan he pulled his mouth from the best minute of my life. I didn't want it to be over, and neither did Ty. He brushed his lips over mine, feathery soft, and then nipped at my bottom lip.

That's when I heard the cheering coming from the bar and the chants, from what was surely the entire football team, that we should get a room. This time the blush didn't just light up my face, my entire body went supernova. I hid my face in Ty's shirt more embarrassed than I'd ever been in my life.

This is why I didn't put myself out there in front of the world. I whispered and only not loud enough that I meant him to hear. "Why did you do that? Everyone is..."

I hated that the entire crowd was looking at us, judging. They were probably all wondering what a hot guy like this was doing kissing a chubby nerdy bookworm like me. I was wondering the same thing.

"Shh. Don't mind them even a little bit. They're a bunch of dickwads and none of them matter at all. This, right here, is between you and me." Ty grabbed my chin and angled my face to look at him.

I kept my eyes down. The easy rapport I'd had with him early was gone with all my confidence. "I thought you were just going to teach me how to flirt."

Ty growled, like a freaking sexy beast. "You don't need a

damn lesson from me, and one taste of you has me feeling possessive. If you don't want this to go any further, if you've got plans to get your flirt on with every guy in here, say so now. Otherwise, we're going for a ride."

I swallowed hard. My skin and chest and fingers and hair jittered like I'd had too much caffeine or some kind of upper. Ty was my drug, and I was afraid to get high.

"What do you want, Hunter. It's your choice. I won't move another muscle without your consent."

The overthinking and worrying already revved in my brain. What did I want?

Everything.

To feel like I belonged with someone.

A connection.

Ty.

I wanted Ty to be mine.

Which I was about to blow if I kept being the scaredy cat who waited to see how everyone else reacted for my own self-worth. For once I was telling those mean girl voices in my head to shut the hell up. Selena said I needed to relax. She wasn't wrong. If I was ever going to be like the heroines in the books I loved to read, this was my best chance.

I bit my lip to keep my fear of what might happen, what other people might think of me inside. I was tired of being what everyone else wanted. Exhausted by the worry of what the people around me thought.

Was I insane for even considering taking it? Yes. Was I going to anyway? Also, yes.

All because of one kiss? Again... yes.

Ty kissing me and asking me if I wanted to do something more was my personal call to action. Just like the girls in the book. This was my one shot to break away, to have something for myself, for my very own. A giggle of excitement with a touch of fear bubbled up. I was going to do it. I was going to go crazy with this bad boy. "Where would we ride to?"

Okay, so the crazy version of me was still a work in progress. Ty might not want to give me flirting lessons, but if I was super lucky, he was about to give me a lesson in letting loose. I cleared my throat and tried again. "Yes, I do want to go on a ride with you. I don't care where you take me as long as we go a little crazy."

He grinned at me like he'd won the lottery, then glanced over at the guy behind the bar. "Hey, boss. I'm gonna need the night off."

Ty didn't wait for the reply, which was just a bunch of grumbling anyway. He grabbed my hand and my backpack and led me through the group of football players and toward the front door. One of them started clapping and my breath stuttered. Ignore him, ignore him, ignore him.

"Dude, I gotta get me one of those curvy girls. Yowzah."

Was that yowzah about me? I peeked at the guy who'd said it and he waggled his eyebrows all suggestively at me. Maybe I should have gone out and done this meeting guys at a bar thing a long time ago. Who knew?

But if I had, I might not have met Ty and that would have been a tragedy.

We pushed out the back door of the bar and into the parking lot lit with one too many lights to be romantic. I was all gaga eyes imagining Ty on his motorcycle anyway.

"You ready to go on a wild ride with me, Huntley?" He held out a helmet to me.

I took it, but I was surprised. "I thought bad boys who rode motorcycles were all about taking risks."

Ty laughed and grabbed a second helmet that looked well-worn and popped it on his head. "I may be a bad boy from the wrong side of the mountain, but I'm not stupid. I grew up around bikes and saw my fair share of bashed in heads. My old man would pitch a fit if he knew I even owned a helmet much less had one for my girl, but I'd rather use my brain to graduate from school than see it smeared on the highway."

His girl? I'm sure he didn't mean it that way. A hundred other women had probably worn this thing when he'd taken them for a ride. That sounded way dirty in my head.

"We'll have to get you a jacket of your own, but for now, you can wear mine." He brushed a kiss on my shoulder and then slipped his black leather jacket around me.

God, it smelled like him. Like fresh air, leather, and something I didn't know how to name, it was simply...sexy man smell. His attention on me, his scent on me, and his kiss still lingering on my lips had my whole body going into overload. I was either ready to fly to the moon or melt into a puddle of goo at his feet.

Was this what love felt like?

No, I was being silly. This was simply a crush on a guy who was being nice to me. Extra sexy nice.

"Come on, let's go be a little crazy." Ty helped me onto his motorcycle, and I had to hold the hem of my flowy summer weight skirt to keep it from riding up my thighs.

Ty eyed the newly bared skin and gave me a cheeky grin. Then he climbed in front of me. "Hold on tight."

He started up the bike and its deep rumble hit me right

in the uh...right places. Holy crow. Was this why girls liked to ride on the back of motorcycles? I had a hot guy between my legs and a huge machine vibrating my whole body. I was already having more fun tonight than I think I'd ever had in my entire life.

We roared out of the parking lot, and I squeezed my arms tight around Ty's waist. Speeding through traffic, whizzing in and out of cars took my breath away. I wanted to be that girl in the movies who throws her arms up over her head and lets the wind whip through her hair while the hot guy on the motorcycle drives them off into the sunset.

Why was I even still thinking about it? I was that girl now. I straightened up a little bit and pulled my arms back, still gripping Ty's shirt. On the count of three.

One.

Two.

Before I got to three, Ty gunned it like he knew exactly what I needed. I held on tight for another second more so I wouldn't be thrown off the back, and then I threw my hands up and howled up at the night sky. Blood and excitement rushed through my ears in a roar, and I felt free. For the first time ever, I was doing something no nice girl with a disapproving grandmother, and a haughty father would ever allow, and I loved it.

I couldn't hear Ty laugh, but I felt his back move like he was. Somehow, I knew he wasn't laughing at me, but with me, feeling the joy coursing through me. It was as if his free spirit had spilled over into me, and I was returning it threefold to him. We were connected, we were one.

Ty steered the bike toward the edge of town and out to the hills where our school's giant wolf head symbol of our mascot was laid out in great big white rocks for the entire world to see our school spirit. This quiet road was also known as our town's lovers' lane.

An hour ago, that would have freaked me out. Honestly, with any other guy, I'd be having a panic attack. Instead, I was having a case of the giggles.

We pulled into a scenic overlook that showed off the night lights of our cute college town and then the dark shimmer of the ocean off in the distance. Ty took his helmet off and hung it over one of the handlebars. I did the same but handed it to him to take care of. I snuggled up against his back and enjoyed the moment. No thinking about what I was supposed to be doing, simply happy to be in the here and now.

"Have fun? Crazy enough for you?" His voice had this contented tone that I envied.

"Absolutely." He was the best time I'd ever had. Sure, sure. One motorcycle ride wasn't all that crazy, but it was miles beyond anything I'd ever done.

"Good, let's have some more fun, because now I really am going to drive you as crazy as you're making me." Ty twisted on the seat and grabbed me around the waist, pulling me onto his lap.

"Oh. Be careful. I don't want to squish your junk." He'd said he liked my curves, which I was still a little flabbergasted about, but even so, I knew how heavy I was.

"My junk is doing just fine." He wiggled his hips around and whoo boy, yes, he was happy to see me. "Look, we don't have to do anything you don't want to. I need you to know that."

But I wanted to do everything with him. "You're sweet.

There's a whole lot I'd like to do with you. I've been missing out on the fun long enough."

"I'm not sweet, Hunter. Before we go any further, you should know that. I'm so far from a nice guy, you're bound to get dirty, and I don't mean in the fun way. Although, I'd sure as fuck like to get down and dirty with you."

"I've never been more ready in my life to get dirty." I proved it by sliding his jacket off, then pulling my dress up and throwing it over my shoulder. My usual blush didn't creep up my cheeks this time because I had nothing to be embarrassed or ashamed of. Not with Ty.

TY

Holy fuck. I was in so much trouble with this girl. She was offering herself up to me like a virgin feast and I wanted to eat up every bite of her. She should not be giving her virginity to a low life like me. To a good girl like her, her first time meant something and if it was with me, that memory would be tainted forever. She was the girl who waited until marriage, and let some one-percenter give her babies, if not orgasms.

The thought of her letting anyone else between her plump thighs made my teeth ache. Wondering if some jag-off human, even worse, a husband, knew how to make her come just pissed me the hell off. The need to mark her, claim her, and make her my mate was overwhelming me.

I was about to be a real selfish asshole, because I wanted prim and proper, nice girl Hunter all for myself. That alone didn't make me the asshole, the fact that I was going to ruin her for anyone else forever did. But I couldn't help it. In the span of a couple of hours, she'd become mine.

Her virginity was mine, her body was mine, her kisses

and her orgasms were mine. I didn't have much to give in return, but my heart was hers. If she'd have it.

I'd figure out how to ease her into the supernatural aspect of my life. It's not like I had a pack to introduce her to. In fact, if I was careful, she might never need to know the real me.

Except I wanted her to. The way she glowed in the moonlight out here in the wide open had me wanting to howl my thanks to the Goddess of the Moon for bringing her to me. Tonight, I would do nothing more than make her feel worshipped and satisfied. Then tomorrow I'd talk to Eli, quarterback and team captain, who happened to have a human girlfriend.

I wasn't good at asking for help from anyone, but my teammates were the closest to a pack I'd ever had, and they'd do right by me and my girl.

Yeah. My. Girl.

Hunter was mine.

"Then let's get dirty." I shoved my hands into her hair and crashed my mouth down onto hers. Our first kiss had surprised her, she was ready for this one. Her tongue danced with mine, and she let out the sweetest little whimpers. Having her thighs and arms wrapped around me while I rode through the cool night air had been a turn-on and a half. With her on my lap, pressing her hot little cunt against my cock through our clothes was testing me like a teenager.

The brazen way she'd lifted her dress over her head had me near to becoming a slathering beast. The only thing between us were her panties and my zipper. My dick was pressing so hard against the metal teeth, I'd have marks in my skin for a month. I'd rather have her teeth marks on my cock any time.

Hunter broke our kiss and reached for my jean's button. I did love a confident woman. She wasn't that a few hours ago. I felt like the biggest baddest alpha for making her feel she could be confident with me. I put my hand over hers to stop her from getting my cock out. Which made my cock and my wolf unhappy with me.

"Huntley, wait. Your first time should be somewhere nice, like a bed of roses or some shit. Not on the handlebars of my bike." If I had more than twenty bucks in my bank account, I'd take her to a swanky hotel or something. But as it was, this was happening at either her place or mine.

She smacked my hand away. "No. This is perfect. I don't need some fairytale. I want you. I want to be with you, right here, right now."

God, I hoped she didn't live to regret this. If ever my life growing up in the Fangs and Fur MC was good for anything, this was it. I lived my life on motorcycles and one thing I knew how to do was have sex on one.

"Then take your panties off and give them to me." I was never giving them back either.

"Uh." She got that deer in the headlights look went all pink again. "What if I take them off but you don't get to see them?"

For a second, I thought I'd pushed her too far and this night was over. But I figured out the real problem as she held her hands over her luscious cunt and squirmed. She was wearing granny panties and thought I hadn't noticed yet. "No way, doll. They're mine now and if you don't take them off, I'm going to rip them off. Either way I'm keeping them and using them to jack off with when we aren't together."

Her mouth made that adorable oh I was coming to love. I was going to love it even more when it was wrapped around my dick. I slid her off my bike and set her to standing on the ground next to me. She didn't move to do what I told her to do. I crossed my arms and narrowed my eyes at her. "Don't make me wait, because if I have to take those panties off you myself, you're going to be laid across my lap with your bare ass in the air getting a spanking for being a brat."

She scrambled to get them off and I'd have to remember the spanking threat. It would work until I actually spanked her for the first time, and she found out she liked it.

I let her fumble with trying to get her panties off and over her shoes and took my time undoing my fly. I slid my jeans down just far enough to let my cock out. Jesus, I don't think I'd ever been this fucking hard before.

"You're not wearing underwear?" She gaped at my cock, and I gave it a stroke just for her. "Of course you aren't. That's so, so, sexy."

"Nope. Now give me your panties." I held out my hand and waited for her to hand over some kind of floral print cotton with a wide waist band. She dropped a pure white scrap of lace in my hand. Holy mother of God. She'd been wearing nothing but lace under that skirt this whole damn time, and they were wet.

I wrapped them around my cock and gave a couple of hard fast strokes. Fuck, that felt good. But nothing like what being inside Hunter's wet pussy would be. I was leaking cum just thinking about it. I wiped the pearl at my tip with her scrap of lace and shoved them in my pocket. I grabbed the condom in my wallet, which I kept around for human girls who wanted to feel safe and held it up for her to see.

"Honey, I'm clean as a whistle, and for reasons I'll explain later, I'm not going to get you pregnant, but if you want me to wear this, I will."

Nine times out of ten I busted out of the condom anyway, but unless we were fucking under full moon, my seed wouldn't take root.

"I'd rather be safe. I know that's not how I'm supposed to act when we're doing the whole let be crazy thing, but, yes, please."

That's what I thought. She might be having fun stepping out of her comfort zone, but at heart, she was a safety girl. "I'd wear a whole damn hefty bag if it would make you more comfortable."

Hunter stared at my hand gliding over my cock putting the condom on and I swear I grew bigger and harder just for her. "Wow. Um... wow. I know I don't know anything about man bits, but are you sure that's going to fit?"

She didn't mean the condom. "I promise, not only is it going to fit, it's going to feel so good filling you up. Come back over here and climb on my lap. Wrap your legs around me."

I would steady us with my feet on the ground. This position would allow her to control how we started. But it wouldn't be long before I had her bent over the handlebars fucking her from behind.

My wolf pushed so close to the surface with the thought of fucking her like an animal that I almost lost control and shifted right here in front of her. Down boy. She's not ready for all of that. I had to be gentle with her. Tonight.

"I won't fall off?" She laughed at her own question, and I found myself smiling too. Sex had never been fun before. Hot and sweaty and needy, but not fun.

"I promise. I won't let you fall." I planted my feet on the ground, using the bike for something to lean against. She'd be doing most of the work and those thick thighs of hers weren't going to hold out long, which was fine by me. I was already fantasizing about holding her hips tight while I pounded into her. Because I was an asshole.

That wasn't going to change. Except for this one brief moment where I took her virginity.

Hunter stepped onto the running boards, and I pulled her to me. Before she could straddle my cock, I cupped her cunt in the palm of my hand. She was soaking wet. "Have you ever had anything inside this tight cunt?"

She sucked in a shuttered breath. "I... I have a vibrator."

Christ. That was something I'd like to see, her getting herself off. I slid my fingers in between her hot, needy pussy lips and found her clit. I circled it a few times and watched her closely to see what she liked. Her eyes fluttered shut and I carefully slid a finger inside of her. "No man before me, right?"

"No," she whimpered.

Certainly no other wolf.

Good. I didn't want her pussy to know any other but me. I slipped another finger in and carefully fucked her, opening her up, getting her ready. "Put your hands on my shoulders and wrap one leg around my waist. I'm going to put just the tip in, you must do the rest. You decide how much of me you can take and how fast. Okay?"

"Me? I thought you would--" She rode my fingers, getting

wetter by the second and her breathing was ratcheting up. She was already getting close and that's just how I wanted her.

I didn't want to just take her virginity, I wanted her to give it to me. "No, doll. You're in charge."

She swallowed and nodded. "Okay, yeah. I'm in charge."

So fucking hot. I pulled my hand from underneath her skirt and gave my fingers a lick to show her what was coming later. She tasted salty and sweet, and I was going to spend an hour eating her out. Later. I smeared the rest of her juices over my cock, lubing myself up for her.

Hunter took a deep breath, put her arms on my shoulders and swung one of her legs up and around my hip. it took me less than a second to find her hot entrance. This was going to be pure fucking torture.

The best kind.

HUNTER

Little girls dream of white weddings and handsome grooms. Big girls dream of white satin sheets, rose petals on the bed, and candlelight for their first time. Girls like me, the ones who somehow never found the right guy in high school to lose their virginity to, start dreaming of frat houses or the back seats of some dude's car.

Anything to get rid of the dreaded V-card. I never imagined I'd lose mine under the stars on the seat of a motorcycle. I wouldn't have it any other way.

Just the head of Ty's cock pushing at my entrance felt huge. My body seemed to know what to do better than I did because I would have happily stood there with his brilliant, almost glowing blue eyes staring into my eyes for a lifetime. Such a silly fantasy. A lifetime, with Ty.

I tentatively pushed my hips forward and oh, God, his cock stretched me almost to the point of pain, but also giving me incredible pleasure. So much so that I got brave and pushed forward until he was as far in as he could go. "Oh, God, Ty this feels amazing."

He shoved his hands into my hair and pulled me in for an intense kiss. He moved his hips, rocking them so he moved in and out of me only a fraction of an inch, but it felt incredible.

"Fuck, doll. I know this was supposed to be for you, but you've got me so wound up I don't know where your pleasure ends and mine begins. Tell me what you need, because I'm so fucking close I can taste it, and there's no way I'm coming before you do, and I get to feel your tight cunt milking me."

My inner muscles literally clenched when he said that. I panted out my words. "Keep talking like that and I'll be right there with you."

"While I'd love to talk dirty to you all night, I don't think that's going to push you over the edge. Wrap that other leg around me and hold on." He kissed me again and stood up holding me under my butt.

If he hadn't been inside of me, I would have protested that he should not be trying to pick me up and carry me around like a fairy princess. We didn't go far anyway. In the next second he had us swapped in position, with me sitting on the leather seat and his cock pushed deeper into me with the new position.

"Grab onto that bar on the back of the bike, and hold on tight, doll. I'm about to rock your world."

I reached over my head and found the bars where motorcycle saddlebags were latched and grabbed on. Then I closed my eyes and let the night and the sex take me away.

"Hunter. Look at me when I fuck you. I want every part of you to know it's me you gave your virginity to, it's me making you come, it's my name you're going to cry out."

Ty didn't move until I looked up at him. "That's right, doll. You and your body are mine now."

"Yours." I think I had been since the second I ran into him at the front door of the bar.

He pulled back his hips and I groaned at the loss of him inside of me. That didn't last long. In another breath he pushed in even deeper than before and set up a rhythm that had me gasping for air. This was like no vibrator I'd ever used, and I was throwing mine out as soon as I got home. Assuming Ty came home with me.

"Oh God, Ty. This feels incredible. Yes. God. Yes." Man alive, I had been missing out.

"You're so fucking tight, it's incredible. I can hardly wait to see how tight your ass is." His words were a husky growl that sent tingles along every nerve ending I had.

He was so dirty, and I loved it. Deep down inside, where I'd never let anyone see, I was a dirty girl, and he was my perfect match. Seeing and knowing that was a hotter aphrodisiac than any food or drug in the world.

"Now, I want to see you come apart for me." Ty reached between our bodies and without missing a beat, found my clit with his thumb and pressed on it like a little pleasure button. He'd definitely found my orgasm switch. I gripped those metal bars with all I had and cried out his name as the orgasm crashed into me.

Ty didn't stop fucking me for a second. He thrust faster and harder and flicked his thumb over my clit drawing this orgasm out until another one hit me like a freaking earthquake. My back arched up off the seat, and every muscle in my body clenched. I couldn't breathe, I couldn't scream his name. The full body orgasm had me in its grips and seeing stars.

"Fuck, Hunter. That's it, doll. God, yes. Fuck, fuck." He bent down over me, burying his face in my neck. He scraped his teeth across my skin and nipped like he was going to bite me. Holy moly, that tiny bit of pain sent me into an instant orgasm, this one much more intense, making my entire body lock. I couldn't breathe, couldn't think, only clasp his body tight to mine.

Ty growled deep and low and finally lost his rhythm. His hips jerked as he came just as hard as I had, thrusting even deeper into me, stretching me, making us fit together so I didn't know where I ended, and he began.

Neither of us moved for a long time, and I for one, loved being in this one true moment, joined as one. If I wasn't lying on the back of a motorcycle, I could fall asleep in this blissful place between Earth and Nirvana.

Ty was the first to move. He licked over the place he'd nipped me and then kissed that exact spot. Then he worked his way up my neck and jaw to my lips and kissed me with so much passion and yet so tenderly I thought it would make me cry.

"I think you killed me, love. You are pure fucking heaven. I've never felt anything like that in my life." He gathered me up in his arms and we just held each other for a while.

"Come on, let's find your dress and I'll take you home and fuck you properly in a bed this time."

"You want to do this again? This wasn't like a one-time wham bam thank you ma'am kind of thing?" I didn't want it to be, but I also didn't want to assume he'd fallen for me like I had for him.

Surely there were books on the subject of how to make a guy fall in love. I needed to check them all out so that I could do everything right and get him to feel the way I did.

Ty didn't say anything, but he did frown at me like he was mad or something. My dress was on the front tire, and he snagged it. He didn't simply hand it to me though, he helped me put it on and then pulled my hair out of the collar, playing with it for a long quiet eternity.

"Is everything okay? Did I say or do something wrong? Oh crap. You're trying to figure out a way to say you want to go back to my place and fool around some more but that you don't want more than that, aren't you?" Even if he did brush me off, I knew exactly what I wanted now, and I was going to do everything in my power to make him fall in love with me.

He grabbed my jaw and kissed me hard. When he pulled away, he didn't let my face go. "No, Hunter I'm not. You're the one who is going to have to tell me you don't want anything more from me, not the other way around. I have fallen so fast and hard for you I can hardly see straight. But I need you to tell me to fuck off, because I'm not good for you."

I grabbed his wrist and yanked his hand off my face so I could say what I wanted to say and make it very clear. "Are you insane? You're the best thing that's ever happened to me."

"No, I'm not. I come from trash, and I know a rich girl when I see one, Huntley. If my old man gets even a whiff of your money, he'll make both of our lives hell to get his hands on it." For all the insisting that I look him in the eye, he was having a tough time doing the same right now.

"Are you going to try and steal my money?" I already knew the answer, I just wanted him to hear himself say it.

"Never," he snarled.

"Then I don't give a hoot about your dad."

"That's because you don't know who he is. My old man is the president of the Fangs and Fur motorcycle club. He'd sell his own kid if he thought he could make a buck."

Why did I have the horrible feeling that wasn't a hyperbole example? I'm not normally privy to the criminal underworld, but I was crazy about those true crime novels, and I'd read one about the F and F Club. He wasn't wrong when he said they were scary. They were the worst kind of criminals. They didn't care who they hurt and there were even rumors that they either sacrificed animals or did some kind of ritual where they pretended to be wolves. They were wanted by the FBI and PETA.

At least Ty's skeletons were out in the open. Mine were worse because they were hidden. "Your dad is honest about who and what he is. Mine has probably hurt just as many people, or more, but he lies to himself and the rest of the world by saying it's just business. I guess I learned to lie from him. If you're no good for me, then I'm not any better for you."

"What have you ever lied about?" He rubbed his thumb across my lips like he couldn't believe anything but rainbows and sparkles ever crossed my lips.

"Pretty much my whole life is a lie." Something I was just realizing for the first time tonight. "Except for how I feel about you."

Ty shook his head. I wasn't getting through to him. "There's a lot you don't know about me and I'm not sure how much to tell you, so you don't go running away screaming."

Screaming with orgasm maybe. "We don't have to know everything about each other tonight."

"Besides who and what I am, I don't have any money. If not for my athletic scholarship, I wouldn't even be in college. I can't take you on fancy dates, or buy you presents. You don't want a man in your life who is barely scraping by. "

"Ty. This is the first date I've ever been on in my life, and it was pretty damn great. It was the best free date ever. All I want is to be with you. The rest we can figure out as we go." I wasn't doing a particularly good job of talking him into being with me. What else could I do?

Ty was a man of action, he'd more than proven that tonight. I'd also learned tonight about how being very intense and serious, then breaking that tension with something funny could get someone's attention and open their hearts. So, I took action. I grabbed his keys and hid them in my fist. This was a dumb idea, but it's all I could come up with on short notice. "But to do that, we have to actually make a go of it. I really, really want to do that. With you. Are you in?"

I dangled the keys in front of his face and then I dropped them straight into my bra. "If you are, you'll take back your keys, with your tongue."

Ty looked deep into my eyes, studying me for far too long, and then slowly the edges of his mouth turned up and he laughed. "You need to work on your pickup lines, doll. I'm in. I am all in for you. I will do everything in my power to make sure you never regret being with me and to make you happy."

My little heart could explode with all the love between us. Love I never thought I'd find with anyone. I wasn't sad that it had taken this long though, because Ty was worth the wait.

"You forgot to answer with your tongue."

Ty shook his head and laughed at me. Then he found his keys. But it took him a while and several orgasms before he did.

TY

After I made her come about a dozen more times and my sweet mate was well satisfied, I took her home. I shared a place with some of the other guys on the team and that was no place for a nice girl like her. At least it was better than the stinking one room apartment above the bar my pops and his MC crew extorted.

I rolled the thoughts of Hunter being mine around and around in my head. She was my mate. After my cock went supernova, and the wolf's knot expanded inside of her, locking us together, I knew. I knew without a doubt she was my fated mate.

Fairy tale or not, she was mine just as I belonged to her. Now to figure out how to bring her into my world of shifters, demons, and magic. There was a reason marking and claiming a human as a mate was taboo. They didn't always respond well to seeing someone turn into a beast. That's what sent our kind into hiding in the first place.

Not that I thought Hunter would go all demon slayer on

me, but she'd clearly led a pretty damn sheltered life. I didn't know how she'd react to seeing me shift into a wolf.

Even now that the new Wolf Tzar had declared we could mate anyone we wanted, it still felt wrong to even be thinking about telling her. Which made having Hunter in my arms and on my cock all the more delicious.

I may not agree with the way my pops lead his lone wolf life, but I was a rebel born and bred.

I finished typing up the paper for my Russian Literature in Translation class and submitted it online. The very early morning hours were the time I had to get my classwork done.

When your old man thinks education is for chumps, it's hard to talk him into helping pay for school. Even harder when he's a lone wolf who doesn't want anything to do with pack politics. I learned how to ride a bike from him, but I got my love of books from my mama, God rest her soul.

If I didn't want to show up with a permanent tent in my pants at the early bird workout with the starter squad before my seven-a.m. class, I needed to go jack off to thoughts of the pretty moans and whimpers Hunter made when my face was between her thighs.

I hit the shower, then raced over to the student athletic center a few minutes late. But that second orgasm imagining Hunter's mouth wrapped around my dick instead of my hand was so worth it.

"Tyoma Orion, get your ass on the field. You're fucking late." Coach had that parental way of using our full names when we were in trouble. Wasn't the first time he'd yelled at me, wouldn't be the last. But he knew I worked my ass off.

Anyone one else tried to talk to me like that and I scare the shit out of them with a partial shift. But I respected coach.

I used a burst of my supernatural speed to catch up to Eli. Using our extra-human abilities was frowned upon when we were playing against teams that didn't have shifters in the ranks. But most of the starters on the team this year were one kind of a beast or another. While I wasn't used to relying on anyone, knowing we shared this secret from the world gave me the guts to talk to someone about what the hell was happening between me and Hunter.

I hated talking about feelings and shit, but I didn't know that much about wolf lore. Most of my knowledge was gained after I moved in with the other shifters on the team. They were all raised in packs and just assumed I did as well.

I had yet to fess up to any of them about my real past. I wouldn't if I could help it. So, it was best to just make this out to be locker talk. "Teags, you look like shit, man. Keeping your girl satisfied wearing you out, man."

Eli gave me a shit-eating grin. We all knew he was getting his dick wet way more than the rest of us ever since he'd marked Charlize. "That's none of your fucking business, is it, Orion."

Unfortunately for me, football players loved a good ribbing and the second Luka and Kirill heard me poking at Eli's sex life, they joined in. Kirill took every opportunity he could to make sure we all knew every detail of his sordid affairs. "It's our business when Charlie keeps the rest of us from getting any fucking sleep because she's screaming your name during peak napping hours."

Most of us slept for at least a few hours in the middle of

the day since we were awake at night. Especially around full moons.

"Better than us having to hear you slapping your own cock around wishing you were getting some." Luka gave us all the wanking hand motion.

Kirill raised his voice an octave doing a piss poor imitation of a girl's voice. "Oh, Luka, there's a fire in my pants, won't you come and put it out for me?"

"You only wish you were a firefighter, dickmunch. We get all the pussy cats."

Swear to God, these two could go on all day like this. Thank fuck for Eli's achiever drive insisting on being serious about practice. "Shut up, assholes. If we want to win our own fucking Homecoming game this weekend, you need to get quit thinking about your dicks and concentrate on playing ball."

"Got it, Cap. Concentrate on our balls." Kirill saluted with one hand, grabbed his crotch with the other and then took off in a sprint to finish his laps. If he didn't do everything first or win at everything, he was one cranky son of a bitch.

I waited until he was out of earshot and our little group were back on pace before clearing my throat to say anything. "Teagan, you marked Charlie, right?"

Eli's chest puffed up like a proud fucking peacock. "Fuck yeah, I did. Don't want any of you jerk-offs even sniffing around my girl. Not that she wouldn't cut your heart out with a spoon if she needed to."

"And your pack was okay with that?"

Luka and Eli, both gave me a weird look. This was definitely not my regular kind of locker talk. The wolf flashed in

Eli's eyes, and he took a good long whiff of me. I may have showered for a good thirty minutes, but there was no hiding the scent of sex from another wolf. That was nothing new on me, but Eli wasn't the captain of the team for nothing. He was a natural alpha and would inherit his pack someday.

Anyone paying attention would be able to scent ever bit of my new feelings for Hunter. Eli was paying attention now. "Yeah. They were. You thinking yours won't?"

This conversation was not going where I wanted it to. No way was I getting into that my pops would rather use humans for their money than anything else to do with them. He thought wolf shifters were the superior race and that we should rule over everyone weaker. Which is exactly what he did with his MC. Pack or not, they followed his orders and liked it.

"Uh, not so much. I'm thinking I shouldn't have anything more to do with her." Even thinking about pushing sweet Hunter away gave me a fucking stitch in the side of my ribs.

Eli slowed to a cool-down walk and turned so we walked across the fifty-yard line. "But you can't stay away from her, can you? She's your moon and stars and you'd die for her, wouldn't you?"

How the fuck was he in my head? He adjusted his pants and I realized he wasn't talking about me, but himself and Charlize. Duh. He'd already marked her. He planned on claiming at mating her too.

I cleared my throat and looked around to make sure no non-shifters were within earshot. "I came this fucking close to marking her last night. My wolf almost completely took over. I don't know what the fuck to do. This is way unfamiliar territory for me."

Luka kept pace with us and was listening in awfully intently for a guy who got about as much action as I did. We were both love 'em and leave 'em kind of guys. Leave them well satisfied, but I never had more than one night with any of the chicks I fucked.

All I wanted was one more night, then one more, and one more, for eternity with Hunter. I didn't understand what exactly was different with her. I just knew all the way down to my soul that it was.

"You want my advice, man? Or is this just talking to figure your shit out?"

Except for maybe coach, I didn't really have anyone else to talk to about this and no way I was going to figure it out on my own. "I'll take any advice you got."

"Okay, but just know that you're going to think this is insane." Eli shrugged and picked up a ball. He indicated for Luka to go out for the pass and threw it long before he said anything to me. "You need to go talk to Selena at the Moon Bean. I'd tell you what she told me and Charlize, but I doubt you'd believe me. Take your girl with you."

"The wolftress who run the coffee shop?" I had no doubt Hunter already frequented the place and probably knew the owner. "What is she like some sort of matchmaker that helps humans find wolf mates?"

Har har. Wouldn't that be hilarious.

"Trust me. She explained everything to Char. Well, not everything. I did practically have an alpha challenge right in front of them. But Selena helped Char not to freak out about it."

Huh. Guess I was skipping my afternoon nap, so this place better have good strong coffee. Except, I heard something rumbling nearby that gave me a shot of adrenaline that spiked my awareness well beyond what any caffeine could do.

Motorcycles. Older shitty ones, like my pops and his crew rode. At least six of them. And they were headed this way. Fuck a fucking fucker.

Before I could even go warn coach, my old man rode right onto the practice field and parked in the end zone. Coach blew his whistle and called everyone in. Most jogged over to him. I stood my ground.

What are you doing here? I used the mental connection I had with my father so no one else needed to be privy to this conversation.

He laughed and pulled his cigarettes out of his vest pocket. "Look at you, being a team fucking player."

My wolf rose up and pushed against me, wanting to shift and ready for a fight. My pops rarely even came out of the mountains, much less all the way to the shore, and never to my school. He was here for a reason, and it couldn't be good.

This is no place for you. If you want something from me, it will have to be after practice. I clenched and unclenched my fists to control the angry energy fixing to burst out of me.

My father's eyes shifted to their supernatural ruddy red color. Even he knew better than to shift in front of a bunch of humans, but he loved to push that edge. "I can wait until your done playing your little games. But I don't know if your girlfriend would like that much."

The beast inside of me rose up instantly to protect my mate. My fangs dropped, my claws extended, and my bones were ready to crack and reshape so I could become the murderous beast inside. A hand on my shoulder and the voice of an alpha, even if he wasn't mine, stopped me.

"Don't let him bait you, Orion. Stay cool and we'll work together to make sure your girl is safe, and this lone wolf doesn't cause any more trouble." Coach stood at my side, along with Eli, Luka, Kirill, and the rest of the shifters on the team.

I took several hissed breaths to keep my wolf contained, but it was a close fucking thing. How in the hell was I going to admit to all of them that this piece of shit lone wolf was my father? A shiver went through me at the look he was giving me and my teammates. This wasn't going to end well.

"This ain't none of your business, coach." He said coach like a slur. "This is between me and my kid."

Well, fuck. Guess my secret was out now. Time to man up. "You haven't been a father to me in a long time. Don't think you can come riding in here now and think I'm going to do shit for you."

My good old pops didn't even flinch. We both knew he had a whole crew around the corner that would fuck us all up in a less than fair fight if he merely whistled for them. "Oh, I think you will do whatever I want."

"Not likely."

He pulled the half-smoked cigarette from his mouth and flicked it on the ground, still lit. "I'm proud of you son."

I only had a single four-letter word as a response to that. "What?"

My father had given me praise a single day in my life. Nothing I ever did was what he wanted. Because he'd never really been able to control me. Never. What he couldn't control, he hated. Proud wasn't even in his vocabulary. "You picked out a mighty fine girl. Couldn't do much better."

A chill like the arctic itself was blowing on the back of my neck froze every cell in my body. He'd mentioned my girl earlier, but I assumed it was his standard shit-talking. The greedy look in his eyes now told me now that he not only knew about Hunter, he had plans for her.

I was going to fucking kill him.

HUNTER

"You are cut off, Hunter. I am officially declaring anymore caffeine off limits for you." Charlie stood behind the counter being incredibly mean to me. "And nothing with sugar in it either."

I couldn't even be mad at her. I was on cloud nine, and ten, and even eleven. "Come on, Char. I promise I haven't even had one cup of coffee today, and I was up extremely late last night. I almost slept through my classes this morning."

"Yeah, right. A. You haven't missed a class, ever. And B. If you haven't had any coffee than you need to lay off the crack." She gave me the evil eye but poured me a cafe au lait anyway.

Selena came up to the counter from the back of house with a load of her famous rhubarb danishes for the bakery case. "She's going to be riding high for a while if I had to guess. She had a date with fate last night."

"Ooh. I love that phrase. Can I use it for my book?" Rosemary came up to the counter for a refill too.

Selena looked her dead in the eye and said, "No. I've got other plans for you." Then she handed us both a danish and walked back into the kitchen. But then she did something weird. She yelled through the doorway, "Don't eat those. I have it on good authority that you're gonna need them in a minute."

"Uh, need them for what?" I said to Charlize.

She shrugged and picked out one for herself. "I don't know, but I have learned that around Selena, it's best to just do what she says."

A rumble like thunder only louder and at street-level sounded from outside. Within a few seconds it was so loud I had to cover my ears. Selena came back out and I did a double take at her. Her eyes were...glowing. "Rosemary, can you please run over to the English Department and give this to Professor Rojo for me? Quickly."

The scary tone in Selena's voice, calm but also urgent as all get out, plus her eyes had Rosemary flipping her laptop shut and hurrying to get that note. Selena had her go out the back of the coffee shop instead of the front door. And we all saw why.

Out on the street, or rather the sidewalk in front of the shop, were four big and burly men on motorcycles with leather jackets. They dismounted and came pushing in the front door. The little bell overhead jingled and gave me the heeby jeebies. I never thought a sound like that could ever be so ominous.

The tall, thin guy who looked more like a vampire from Forks than a gang member looked right at me and grinned. Out of nowhere, my heart went haywire beating faster and for the first time since Ty and busted by V-card, I felt myself blushing.

"Hello, welcome to the Moon Bean." Selena greeted the scary dudes while at the same time putting herself between us and them.

"Out of the way, wolftress. We don't have no business with you." The biggest guy who looked like he could snap each of us in half with his pinkies folded his arms and glared at us.

"Funny that you came into my place of business then." Selena was a badass and I was about to pee my pants. Wait. Did they just call her a wolftress? Was that insult?

"Don't mess with us, lady." Creepo vamp dude glared at Selena, and she recoiled from him. "Just give us the girl and we'll be on our way without fucking up your little fun times with the humans."

I whispered to Char out of the side of my mouth. "Am I hallucinating, or did he just refer to us as humans?"

Char grabbed my hand and closed her eyes, then nodded. "Eli and his, umm, friends, will be here in a minute. I'm gonna tell you what Selena told me. Keep an open mind and don't freak out."

"I'm already freaking out." I was used to greedy corporate types who would sell your retirement out from under you to make a few bucks, not hardened criminals and the evil version of Edward Cullen.

I'd always been team Jacob anyway.

Wait, how did she know Eli was on his way, and by friends did she mean Ty? Because I would love to be wrapped up in his arms right about now. Was I being a princess wanting to be rescued by my bad boy prince? Yes.

Did I care that I was setting feminism back fifty years for even thinking that sentence? Nope.

I'm coming Hunter.

Whoa. What in the hell was that? Ty's voice, but like, inside my head. I looked around like maybe he was nearby, but there was only us women and the motorcycle thugs.

Sweetheart, I know this is beyond weird, but I need you to trust me just like you did last night. I won't let anyone hurt you. Okay?

Okay? No. None of this was okay. Apparently, the threat of having a motorcycle club staring at me like I was a juicy piece of fruit was more than my brain could handle, because I was definitely hearing voices. Or just one voice.

Tell me you're not hurt, and no one has taken you, Hunter.

Maybe this wasn't the time to talk to my new imaginary friend in my head, but what else could I do? "I'm fine, thanks. How are you?"

Good girl. I'm almost there. Don't freak out when you see me. I've got a plan. You with me?

"I guess so." If you're not with them, join them.

I glanced at Charlize and Selena, but neither of them seemed bothered that I was presumably talking to no one. Char might even be talking to her own imaginary friend because her lips were moving, and she was staring off into space.

Creepy stared at me and I felt another wave of whatever hit me before, this one making my skin tingle. That dude was trying to do some crazy hypnosis or something on me. Maybe it was working and that's why I was hearing Ty's voice in my head.

I didn't know what to believe.

Selena picked up the tray of rhubarb danishes and

grabbed the biggest one. Now was not the time for snacks. Maybe she was just trying to placate the scary men until help arrived. She winked over at me and Charlie and in the next breath, she flung the pastry at the silent burly guy to the side, and the rhubarb goo on top smacked him right in the nose.

He grabbed his face and dropped to his knees, screaming out in pain as his fricking face melted off like that scene in Indiana Jones and the Lost Nazi's movie.

Both Char and I controlled our own screams, mostly, and when Selena gave us a look, we grabbed danishes and brandished them like shields in front of us. Which is the strangest thing I'd ever done in my life. It was all I could do to keep from tossing my cookies watching some Hell's Angel dude dissolve in front of me.

"Imaginary boyfriend, now would be a fun time to show up in real life." I whispered the words under my breath so no one would either hear Ty's plan or think I was insane. Especially the Vampire Lestat over there.

Selena snarled at the big guy who'd been making demands. The guy had barely flinched as his compatriot's skin merrily melted away. There were black scales where his skull should be, and those cookies were coming closer to being hurled.

"That'll teach you to bring a demon dragon wyrm to a wolf's domain." Professor Rojo strolled in like this was any other day at the coffee shop. I didn't understand how he got here so fast. Rosemary only left to get him like twenty-seven seconds ago.

He gave Selena a nod, me and Char an eyebrow of irritation, and proceeded to spit on the guy melting on the floor.

And when I say spit, I mean he spit lava. The dude screeched like a weird, creepy, screeching bird sound and poof, he was nothing more than a disgusting oil stain on the tile.

Here came those cookies. I covered my mouth and turned away. But what I saw behind me was even worse.

A man who looked like an older version of Ty but who drank and smoked too much pushed his way into the coffee shop with my real-life boyfriend in a headlock. But Ty didn't look like his usual self. His eyes were glowing, and he had freaking fangs. He was snarling and growling like a wild beast trying to get away from what I had to assume was his father.

I was ready to fling my rhubarb pastry at his dad, but Ty gave me the smallest shake of his head. He was afraid for me. I could see it in his face.

"Well, well, well." The burly blond man looked me up and down and sucked his teeth. "She's ever purdier in person than in her Tiky Tokies. You done picked a good mark, son. We ain't just gonna milk her and her family dry. With them pretty blue eyes and that shiny blonde hair, she'll bring in a decent price to the highest bidder. I know just the pack who'd like to have her."

Ty struggled but couldn't get out of the hold. "You're not fucking touching her."

Okay, I don't know what was going on, but threatening me and trying to choke out the best thing that ever happened to me. No. Just no. Big mistake. Huge. If last night with Ty had taught me anything it was to quit being so damn scared of life all the time. I never did anything even the slightest bit risky until I asked him to teach me how to flirt.

If I'd gotten so much more than I ever expected from that one tiny chance at putting myself out there, then surely, I'd reap all the rewards if I took a real risk. Plus, imaginary Ty had said he had a plan. Now was the perfect time to enact it. I hefted the danish, grabbed Charlie's and tossed them both at Ty's dad's face. "Look out, Ty."

The danishes hit their mark dead on. One stuck to his face and the other smacked him right in the chest. Except... he didn't start melting or screaming or letting Ty go.

Instead, his face morphed, and he grew a snout, whiskers, ears, fur, and fangs. What in the hell was in these danishes? I'm glad I didn't try to eat one. "That was a mistake, girly. I'm no demon dragon wyrm."

He shoved Ty to the floor and swiped the goo off his face. That was his second mistake, because it gave team Moon Bean time to react. And when I say react, I mean everyone but me and Charlize turned into a freaking wolf. Except Professor Rojo who sprouted big red wings and the head of a freaking dragon.

There were tatters of clothes everywhere, including a Dire Wolves practice jersey where Ty used to be. Instead of my sexy bad boy boyfriend, a beautiful, but angry, honey blonde wolf with glowing amber eyes stood in his place.

I closed my eyes and took a long breath. "I'm not freaking out, I'm not freaking out. I. Am. Not. Freaking. Out."

When I popped my eyes back open, the scene out of a supernatural horror movie was still there, and I was totally fucking freaking out. This is what I got for going outside of my comfort zone and thinking I could have a boyfriend and super-hot sex. This was a tale as old as time, where the good girl is corrupted by the temptations of the flesh and the moment she gives in, she'd punished by the beasts of hell and a horrible death.

I'd been living in a stupid dream instead of reality thinking I could have the romance novel book boyfriend. Unless, of course, this was a paranormal romance.

The wolf that was Ty leaped across the back of one of the bad motorcycle riding guys who'd turned into wolves and slammed into the other blonde wolf. He sent his father careening into the counter and a whole pile of mugs fell on top of him.

Ty turned to me with his tongue lolling out and a sparkle in his eye like he was having a jolly old time. *There was just one thing wrong with the scared and mean girl voice inside your head, love. It's wrong.*

The feelings I'd been so used to for years did not like that. Every bit of negative self-talk I'd ever thought about myself reared its ugly head, like a dragon who spewed fire on my poor sensitive soul. Oops. Maybe not like a dragon. Professor Rojo might not like me thinking like that.

All my insecurities and the horrible things the world had taught me to think about myself were more like that demon dragon wyrm thing and if I was going to survive the rest of my life, much less this afternoon, I needed to kill all those thoughts and feelings and turn them into an oily stain on the floor too.

"You're right." I didn't feel debased or depraved. I'd spent my whole life thinking I wasn't special. Being with Ty had me feeling more like my real authentic self than I ever had in my entire life. The fearful, faux persona I'd created to please my family and society was the corrupt one. "I'm not going to listen to them anymore."

I had no idea what this weirdo crazy life I'd just stepped into where my boyfriend was a werewolf who fought off creepy monsters in a motorcycle gang, but it was better than the first world hell I'd been living in. "I have no idea how to do anything helpful besides social media posts that go viral, but let's kick some bad guy butt."

I whipped out my phone and started filming because I may not have supernatural skills on my side, but I did have cancel culture to back me up. Three million followers across all my socials could make these guys wish they'd never messed with us.

You know what doesn't make for a good video? Seeing your werewolf boyfriend get attacked by three other huge wolves and have his guts spilled all over the coffee shop.

That's exactly what I captured on my phone as it happened right in front of my eyes.

TY

Fucking bastards. It's not like I didn't know my pops and his crew fought dirty. In fact, I'd prepared for it and had some dirty moves up my own sleeve, err, fur. But trying to slice my belly open in front of humans? That was a low blow.

"Ty, noooooo!" Hunter screamed and ran toward me, skidding across the floor on her knees at the last second.

Dammit. She was putting herself literally into the thick of a dog fight. I didn't expect her to be so brave, even though I should have. She was the fucking bomb. But it meant I needed to go off the game plan.

I almost had my father and his cronies lulled into their false sense of security. Coach and Eli would be jumping in on my signal, but too soon and we wouldn't have the backup we needed to truly take the Fangs and Fur down. If someone had to die in that time, it wasn't going to me or Hunter.

Because I was young and worked out every damn day, I had fifty pounds of muscle on any of the other wolves here. It also meant my wolf's supernatural healing ability was faster and stronger than the rest of them. I could take risks, they couldn't.

But the nature of risks was that the risk-taker didn't always get what they wanted.

Hunter, get behind me. I could see that she was scared, but for me, not herself. Still, she was a smart cookie and did what I told her too.

"Ty," she whispered and touched my side. "You're bleeding so much. If you die, I'm going to be really mad at you."

I'm not going to die. My wolf will heal my injuries quickly. Don't you worry your smart and savvy brain with me.

No way the Wolf Tzar was here yet. The plan coach, Eli, and I had come up with on the fly to find Hunter and take down Fangs and Fur was barely in motion. I needed to hold out a bit longer.

Because I'd just lied to my sweet Hunter. I was hurt way worse than I was read to admit. I'd lost too much blood and my wolf was having a challenging time getting me patched up fast enough. I couldn't take another hit and I saw in my father's eyes, that he knew it as well as I did.

He wasn't my alpha, so when I'd shifted for the first time during puberty, he lost his ability to mindspeak with me. I hadn't heard any other voice in my head until Hunter. Now I fucking wished I did have a powerful alpha aside from the Wolf Tzar who was alpha over us all.

This was exactly why I wasn't ever going to be worthy of the mate fate had bestowed onto me. Fuck.

The blood loss was starting to take its toll on me, and my vision wavered, growing dark around the edges. I focused directly on my pops and growled putting up a front as long as I could. Thank the Goddess that years of playing football had taught me how to think on my feet and push through pain.

I prayed with all my heart and soul that I had an ounce of alpha blood in me. I could take my father down and end his motorcycle club's reign of destruction myself.

I took one step forward and bared my teeth at the cronies trying to advance on us and pushed the plan into the front of my thoughts, praying that I could get the gist of it to Hunter. If I failed her, I still needed her to be safe.

If I go down, tell Char to bring in the back up ASAP.

Charlize and Eli had the same kind of connection I did with Hunter. I had no doubt he would have let her in on our plan to make it seem like my father had captured me knowing he would lead us straight to where he'd taken Hunter.

Anyone else would think the scent coming off my beautiful Hunter was plain old fear, but I smelled the second it changed. She was still frightened, but there was a new determination. She didn't freak the fuck out, and she didn't say a single word. Her hands slipped into my fur and gripped it tight, like she wasn't ever going to let me go.

"Where you go, I go."

I'd wanted someone in my life ever since I could remember who was my ride or die. Now I had her, and I didn't know if I could keep her. Hunter's touch sent a rush of emotions through me. What little blood I had left, sang for her and my skin tingled. The feeling was either love, or death come for me.

Turned out it was the Grim Reaper. Because that's when I died.

The world around me went completely black and my lungs and heart stopped. Or maybe time did. I could still see the shadow of everyone around me, but they weren't moving, or rather they were, but so slow it was hardly detectable.

I lifted my arm to cover my eyes... wait, what the fuck? How the hell did I lift my arm if I was dead and how did I even have arms? I'd died in wolf form.

Well, kid. That's because you aren't dead. My honey bunny just stopped time for a sec so we could... wait, umm. Love of my life, what is it we're doing with this wolf again?

Who the fuck was talking? I blinked a few times, and I couldn't see a thing, just vague streams of rainbow light floating around in the air, as if someone was shining a flashlight through a prism. But that voice resonated in my head as strong as any alpha's. Whoever was talking was immensely powerful.

Kur, you're just being a fuddy duddy because this isn't one of your dragon sons. The words echoed as if from very far away. But then the most beautiful woman dressed all in white floated toward me as if she were an angel.

Are you the Goddess of the Moon? Is this what happened when a wolf shifter died? While belief in the Goddess was just a part of wolf life, I never really believed there was much more to it than myth and legend.

No, young man. She's... a little preoccupied at the moment. I am a friend of hers though. Normally we wouldn't interfere with one of her chosen ones, but you are mated to the daughter of a dragon, so I thought it was only fair.

Hunter's father is a dragon? Had she hidden her true self

from me? Maybe this was why she hadn't freaked out when a bunch of wolves shifted right in front of her.

Oh, her dragonblood is quite a few generations back, but it's there none the less. The woman waved her hands, and a warm wind blew across my skin. *Kur give him a little of your dragon's breath too. We need him hearty and hale to protect our girl.*

A puff of green smoke wafted out of nowhere, and I cringed. Dragon's breath was what I had the morning after drinking all night with the guys when we won our games. The moment the dragon's magic touched my skin, all the pain from my injuries evaporated.

Thank you. I didn't know what else to say. Not sure why they healed a dead guy.

The rainbow flickered and shimmered in front of me. *Now you can get back in there and use your alpha voice to tell that piece of trash who calls himself your father to fuck off.*

But I wasn't an alpha. These weird deities, or whatever they were, had me confused.

Oh, shit, sweetums, do you have the Moon's gift, or did I leave it at home? Was it in my other pants? Wait, maybe I left it in Siberia?

The woman in white held up her hand as if touching someone and smiled. *Stop teasing him.*

Teasing me? About what? If this was a weird riddle, I had to solve to get into the wolf afterlife, I was screwed.

The woman turned her smile on me. *You asked your Goddess for something and since you're already one of her chosen, I thought we'd just give it to you in her absence. I'm sure she won't mind too much.*

What had I prayed to the Goddess for? If bringing

Hunter into my life was her doing, she'd already given me more than I ever deserved. *You'll keep Hunter safe for me?*

Oh, you'll do that yourself. But do us a favor when you kick those douche bros that call themselves a motorcycle gang in the ass. Make sure to rip the head off that incubus. He shouldn't have brought a Galla demon into this realm and he needs to pay for that.

Incubus? Sex demons? *He and his sex allure aren't why Hunter and I--*

No, don't be a douchecanoe. She's your one true mate. And sexy times with your mate is like no other. Did I already give you my standard advice to my sons about giving their mates lots and lots of orgas--

Poof. The rainbow smacked me in the face and like I'd been tackled by a three-hundred-and-fifty-pound lineman, I smashed back into my wolf form with a power flowing through my veins so intense I could howl at the moon. So, I did.

The sound of my bay shook the glass on the windows and made everyone here either drop and cover their ears or whine with the sheer magnitude of the sound. That was no ordinary howl. That was the sound of an alpha declaring dominance.

The only person who wasn't affected by my howl was Hunter. She stood tall and proud beside me like a warrior princess. She whispered out of the side of her mouth at me. "I thought you were dead."

I thought you were sweet and shy.

My father and his cronies, including what I now recognized as in incubus advanced on us. It didn't matter if the

Wolf Tzar wasn't here to take these assholes down and out of my life. That was my job now.

Sweetheart, I'm going to fuck these guys up. You in?

Hunter gave me a quick nod while not breaking eye contact with the incubus. He didn't have her bound in his allure, of that, I was sure. She had a mad on for him though. Good. I was thoroughly enjoying her warrior woman side. I'd love to see her fuck him up.

Hunter's voice rang in my head. *Dire wolves for life.*

The howl I'd let loose was the signal for the rest of the football team, the supernatural players anyway, to move in. Within ten seconds the other wolves busted into the coffeeshop. The MC guys didn't stand a chance. They fought for only the blink of an eye before they were surrounded and trapped by a bunch of wolves, a couple of bears, a jaguar, and a thunderbird. Professor Rojo even got in on the action and snagged the incubus with his big old dragony talons.

Hunter crossed over to the incubus and smashed a danish of all things into his face. "Take that, you asshole. I may not know much about what in the hell is going on here today, but I know when someone is manipulating me. Just so you know, you're flirting game needs work." She smiled at professor Rojo and then kneed the incubus straight in the ball sack.

The only one left was my dear old dad. He was wily and dodged everyone's efforts to attack. But Selena Troika in her wolf form had him backed into a corner.

He's mine, I said. Selena shouldn't have been able to hear me, but she did.

She slowly backed away, giving me room, and wink. *I knew you had it in you, kid. Give him hell.*

Only alphas could hear and talk to other wolves. Holy moon and stars in the sky. That was the gift from the woman in white and the rainbow had given me. I had prayed to the Goddess to be an alpha in my own right so I could defeat my father.

He lowered his head and growled, inching his way forward, trying to intimidate me. He looked so weak and ugly to me. How I was ever scared of him, I couldn't even fathom.

Stand down, you fool. Your fight with me is over. The sound of my voice boomed like never before, the alpha in me coming through.

My father cowered at my words as any lone wolf would before an alpha. *You're not my alpha, you can't command me. Don't forget you ain't nothing but a piece of poor white trash.*

This fight was over. He already knew he'd lost. I almost felt sorry for him in that moment, knowing that he was about to hit rock bottom. He'd never had much in the first place, and I was about to take it all away from him.

Because the one thing he valued the most was his control over others. He no longer controlled me.

The door to the coffee shop opened then and an imposing man strolled in like he wasn't bothered by a supernatural fight between wolf shifters wasn't going on in broad daylight. The air around us all went from charged and crisp to electric. Probably because he was no mere man. Not even a mere wolf. This was the almighty Wolf Tzar, Nikolai Troika.

My team members who were in wolf form tipped their

heads to the side in deference to the alpha of alphas. I didn't. Not because I didn't respect him, and I think he knew that.

The Wolf Tzar took one look at my father, then at me and raised one eyebrow as if very unimpressed. Hunter didn't like that. "Don't be giving my boyfriend the stink-eye, dude. You may be super-hot, but you're either team Dire Wolves or you can eat a danish."

The Wolf Tzar's other eyebrow went up and the corner of his mouth twitched like he was trying to quash a smile. "Don't worry, feisty young matriarch, I'm team wolves all the way."

Then he turned his gaze back on my father. "He may not be your alpha, but he is one, nonetheless. Are you declaring an alpha challenge?"

Didn't matter whether my father wanted to challenge me or not. He was already defeated. I answered for him. *He is not. This wolf is lone and will never have a pack of his own. He doesn't deserve one.*

My father, knowing he was truly the loser, shifted back into his human form and turned his back on us all, staring straight at the wall. I wanted to tell the Wolf Tzar to take my father away, but I didn't want to push my luck. Hunter pushed it for me. "I take it, you're the law around here. You should lock this asshat up."

My delicious mate did not yet understand that wolf justice meant that my father would be killed for his life of crime. But anymore, I cared little about him and his fate. He'd get what he deserved.

My fate with Hunter was all that mattered now.

If I was an alpha now and she was to be the matriarch of my pack, I needed to find us some territory and a sacred circle to make everything official. With the Wolf Tzar standing right in front of me, this was an opportunity that I couldn't pass up. I shifted and stood before him.

Hunter gasped, pulled off her cute little cardigan, and held it up in front of my junk. She whispered as if everyone else here hadn't noticed. "You're naked. Which is something I personally enjoy, but I'm not sure your sheriff guy appreciates."

The rest of my teammates shifted, and they were all naked too. Hunter took one look around and went pink from her head to her toes. I hoped that adorable innocence hadn't been lost with her new badass awakening. I wrapped my arms around her and tucked her into my chest. "I promise to teach you everything I know about wolf shifter society, but the first lesson is that we're naked a lot."

She giggled. "That is a plot twist I did not see coming. Which of course are the best kinds."

"Sir," I addressed the Wolf Tzar. "I'd like to have a proper mating ceremony with my mate and start our pack out the right way, but I have no sacred circle."

Not to mention not a lot of experience knowing how to be the leader of a pack or how to be a good alpha. I only knew I wanted to be the best I could for Hunter.

The Wolf Tzar nodded, thinking. "I hear there is some territory in the Appalachians that has been without a good pack for some time. It's yours. But after you graduate. Until then, I invite you to any of the Troika lands, Serenity Bay, the Bay of the Sea Wolves, or even the sacred circle in Rogue for the upcoming full moon."

My soul felt a thousand times fuller at his offer, and

knowing that I could, would make Hunter truly mine, and belong to her in the true wolf way.

Now to explain the mating ritual to her, where we'd have sex in front of all the other members of the Troika wolf pack as witnesses to our union. I was looking forward to that full-body blush.

HUNTER

CHAPTER 9 - HUNTER

The second Ty explained the ins and outs of the wolf mating ritual, I knew right then and there that we were waiting on that. Did I want to be his mate? Abso-fucking-lutely. Really, I already felt like we were connected in that deep way he said mates felt. I didn't need a ritual to know he was my one and only.

"I really want our sexy times to be just about you and me, for now." I really did understand how important this new role of alpha was to him, and I was there to support him one hundred percent. "While I'm not ready to do the whole mating in front of a pack of wolves thing, I am pretty excited for you to teach me all about your world of the weird and unusual."

Ty waggled his eyebrows at me. "Oh, you're ready to get kinky, are you?"

Maybe. "Don't you think we'd better try out some of the regular stuff first? Like a bed for instance?"

We did not, in fact, try a bed that night or the next day, or the next. Who knew there were so many other places to get down and dirty? Even my plethora of naughty romance novels did not prepare me for love in an elevator.

I barely had time for my blog or my socials anymore, so I was really looking forward to the week off for Thanksgiving. Let me tell you, actual romance was way better than the kind I'd been reading about.

Selena invited us to a very weird Thanksgiving dinner at a strip club one of her sons owned in Rogue. My father and grandmother were...ahem... very displeased I wasn't coming home for the holiday. They'd expect to see me for Christmas. I'd go, but I was bringing along a surprise bad boy wolf boyfriend. That and the necklace and note I'd found in my room one day telling me I was a descendant of a freaking Gold Dragon. They wouldn't be able to avoid telling me about our family heritage any longer.

Strippers were nothing like what I thought. They were really cool. I was already planning on going to Helena's pole dancing workout class in the morning. She was the manager of the club and curvy like me. Between her and the other girls, they made it very clear that big girls could be sexy and pole dance too.

The other women and their mates were all nice and welcoming, but I gave Ty's hand a squeeze and did the whole mindspeak thing. I loved that we had this intimate connection between us that allowed me to see and feel his thoughts and emotions and vice versa. Plus, it was great for surreptitious sexy time meetups. *Any chance we can sneak out of here without making the Wolf Tzar mad?*

I also sent Ty a mental image of me riding something that wasn't a pole or a motorcycle. He snorted his mashed potatoes out his nose. He covered his face with a napkin and gave me a smirk. But he cleaned himself up and stood, pulling me up with him. "Tzar, Tsarina, Selena, thank you all so much for the dinner. I'd like to show Hunter the sacred circle if I might?"

The Wolf Tzar looked at his wife, uh mate, and she gave him a soft smile. Now I could tell most of the time when someone else was mind speaking. The Tsarina winked at me, and I liked knowing she was on my side. The Tzar waved Ty off. "No need for formalities, kid. Go, have your fun, but keep your senses open. Troika territory is never completely safe from one-bloods who want attention."

It wasn't long before we found ourselves making out under the full moon in the Reserve in Rogue. The protected forested area was beautiful, but it was also freezing cold. Ty led me to an area where the trees opened up, but the canopy of branches swirled overhead forming an almost chapel-like peace and quiet in the middle of the woods. The streams of light of the moon poured down and as we stepped into the center, Ty's skin sparkled and glowed.

He stared down at me, and I could see his wolf in his eyes. "Hunter of my heart, you're glowing."

"You are too. Is this some kind of wolf shifter magic?" I couldn't look away and I was no longer cold. The heat inside of me grew along with my need for him.

"I don't know. I thought maybe it was you doing a spell on me." His voice was barely above a whisper, and I could hear the love he had for me in every awe-filled word. "I've never wanted you so badly before. I want to say I'll make love to you, but I don't think I can be soft and gentle right now."

Oh, gawd. I loved when he lost a little of his control and let the bad boy come out to play. I also knew how to push his alpha wolf's buttons. "You'll have to catch me first."

I took off running, full well knowing that he could catch me before I even took a step if he wanted to. He loved the chase and I got at least ten yards before he tackled me, rolling so he took the brunt of the fall, and I was wrapped in his arms.

Right away he rolled us over, so he was on top of me and pushed his knees between mine, spreading my legs open. He sniffed the air and the wolf in his eyes glowed with a deep amber. "Mmm, you do want me, don't you, my naughty girl? Just how long have you been squeezing your legs together so I wouldn't scent that on you?"

Like I would ever hide how much I was eternally turned on by him. Still, it was fun to tease him. "Hours. Hours and hours. I was starting to think I'd have to go hide in the bathroom and take care of it myself."

"Never gonna happen. Besides, if you'd even tried, we would have had our first round of bathroom stall sex."

God, I loved how dirty he was. "Too late now. What are you gonna do about it?"

"This," he growled and rolled me over, flipping my long skirt up over my back and ripping my panties. There went another pair. Good thing I had a stake in Rihanna's lingerie company to keep myself stocked in new undergarments.

I could hear Ty unbuckle his nice pants he'd gotten especially for this dinner, and then unzip them. To be fair, we'd been through quite a bit of his clothing too. I'd taken to gifting him new t-shirts and jeans for every silly little anniversary we had. He gave me sex toys. I got the better end of that deal.

He laid himself over me and his cock pressed against the flesh of my butt. "Do you feel how hard I am for you, Huntley? I had to think about statistics and imagine losing every football game for the rest of the year to keep myself from having a fucking tent in my pants all evening."

Aww. He hated to lose. "Why? Because we were in a strip club?"

"Yes."

Okay, he knew I was teasing him, so his answer was not what I expected. "Oh."

"Because I was imagining you up on that pole, teasing me with your tits and your soft cunt, barely covered with the sexy lingerie you insist on wearing all the time just to drive me insane." He spread my legs wide with his knees again and reached one hand between us to cup my pussy. "I've been hungry for you all day."

In one quick move, he sat back and pulled my hips up, so I was on my knees with my ass in the air. "Fuck, yes."

Before I even knew what he was planning, he gave me a little bite on the behind and then licked his way down to between my legs. We'd done plenty of oral before this, but never from behind. How was he even going to... Oh. Oh my god.

He pushed his tongue into my channel and swirled around and around making sounds like a man dying of thirst and enjoying a long cool drink after days in the desert.

I clenched the muscles in my inner thighs and groaned. He hadn't even touched my clit yet, and it felt so good. My legs were already shaking, and we'd barely started.

He pulled away and I heard him smack his lips. "You're fucking delicious when you're about to come. But don't even think about it yet. I want to be inside of you when you explode."

"Then you'd better hurry up and fuck me, because one touch of my clit and I'm ready to go over the edge." If my hands weren't preoccupied keeping me from face-planting into the leaves and dirt, I'd do it myself.

"Not yet." He dipped back down and grabbed one of my lower lips into his mouth and tugged with his teeth. Then he did the other one. He knew exactly how much the tiny edge of pain turned me on. I wasn't into real pain, and Ty knew exactly how much to give to get me really going.

"Ty, oh please. You're so mean to me." All my begging got me was a chuckle and more teasing with his teeth and tongue. He knew I couldn't come without him playing with my clit, but whew boy, this was the closest I'd ever been to exploding from teasing alone.

There was something different about being with Ty tonight. Maybe it was this place, maybe it was the full moon. Maybe it was that I was so completely ready to give myself to him body and soul. "Ty, I need you, now. No more teasing, please. I need to feel your inside of me."

I wanted nothing more than our joining, to become one, to make him my one true mate.

He didn't even hesitate. We both liked to have fun with teasing and sexy times, but he was always so incredibly careful with me, showing me what I didn't understand or hadn't yet experienced, always listening to what I wanted and what I didn't.

When they say consent was sexy, they were talking about the way Ty was with me.

"I'll give you everything you've ever needed and more, love. Everything." He pushed his body over mine again, lowering us both to the ground and coming over me like a giant blanket with a rocket in its pocket. I rested my cheek on my arms and waited with pleasure at how he would treat me next.

With his face right next to mine, he nibbled his way from my ear, licking that sensitive spot on my neck and then scraping his teeth from there down to my collar bone. Sparks of light burst in my vision, and I shivered. "Do that again."

He did, but this time with more pressure from his teeth. I let out a long groan and the muscles in my chest clenched as if my heart needed help being contained in my chest. "Please, Ty, more. I don't know what you're doing to me that you haven't before, but I need more of it."

He kissed the spot right above my collarbone. "This is where I'll mark you. It will hurt, because I'm going to sink my wolf's fangs into your skin, sharing the magic the Goddess has given to all wolf-shifters with you. But with the pain will come such intense pleasure, you won't be able to contain your body's reaction."

"I'm going to come from your marking bite?" We'd talked about the mark, but he hadn't mentioned orgasms.

"You are, and I want to be fucking you hard when you do." Ty scraped his teeth over the spot again and my nipples went hard just like they did right before I orgasmed.

I wiggled my butt, to entice him to get this party started. Much more of this anticipation and I was going to be a puddle of goo in the grass. Ty took the hint, or he finally figured out I was going to die if he didn't get me off soon and pushed just the tip of his cock inside of me.

I held my breath and pushed back against him. He loved it when I took charge of this part of our joining. I got to decide how fast, how hard, how far, and how deep to go. This time I wanted all of him as quickly as I could get him.

"Fuck, Huntley, fuck. You feel so good. Your cunt is already pulsing and fluttering around me."

Like I didn't know. I was about to pass out from how amazing it felt to finally get our bodies together again. "You have to take over now, I don't have any leverage like this."

"I know, sweetheart, and I'm sorry. My wolf is demanding your submission and I thought this way would be the easiest."

Geez. Why was that so frickin' hot? "I'm yours, Ty. Take me so your wolf knows it too."

He growled and I got exactly what I'd hoped for. His wolf's knot swelled at the base of his cock, pushing at my entrance, just like it did every time we had sex. A simple touch of that knot sent Ty into the most extreme pleasure, but he rarely let me near it. Something about getting stuck together that I didn't quite understand.

He slid out, taking away the lovely pressure the knot had against my entrance. But with a hard fast thrust, he shoved back in, and then did it again and again. "You're mine, Hunter. Mine."

The words were barely more than a grunt, but he said them inside my head at the same time. "Yes, I'm yours."

And he was mine.

When I said those words, he let out a short howl and pulled my knees up again but placed one hand on the middle of my back, keeping my chest and face down. Ty pounded into me hard, saying either my name or that I was his with each thrust. It all felt so right and perfect. We were both breathing fast and hard, and I was so close to coming, but couldn't quite go over that edge.

With each thrust and each word, I could hear he was almost more beast than man. His body may be that of a college sports star, but his wolf had control of his mind. "Ty, mark me. Claim me. Make me your mate."

I don't know where those words came from. It was almost as if they'd been placed into my mind, especially for me to say to him in this exact moment.

He howled, longer and louder this time, and grabbed my hair, pulling me up so our bodies were flush. He scraped his teeth across the spot he'd promised to mark and reached a hand between my legs, finally, finally sliding his fingers over my clit. He growled in a way that if anyone else heard, they'd think he was deadly dangerous. "Say that again, mate."

"Mark me." The words were a soft prayer on my lips. He answered them with a pinch and pull on my clit.

I gasped and said, "Claim me."

Ty pushed his cock deeper inside, the knot urging my pussy to open for it, and his groan matched my own. He tugged on my clit again, stroking the little bundle of nerves until I could barely see straight.

I swallowed and forced the air out of my lungs to get the final words out. "Mate me."

With a final dark growl, Ty pushed my head to the side

with his own and bit down into the skin at my neck, piercing my body with his teeth. He fucked me with long, deep thrusts, and flicked his fingers across my clit.

I lost all control and let my body take us both into the pure nirvana of pleasure, erupting into the most intense orgasm, I'd ever experienced. Not only did I see stars, I saw rainbows and wisps of white magic all around us.

As I cried out his name to the moon above, Ty thrust into me one last time, forcing the wolf's knot fully inside of me, filling me so completely. He ripped his teeth from me and bayed up at the moon, calling my name into my mind. He came inside of me, filling my pussy with his seed, and for the first time ever, I hoped my womb too.

He'd said he could only get me with child under a full moon, and I wondered if this night was even more special than either of us expected it to be.

We stayed locked together like that, for a long time. I rested my head back on his chest, and he licked the wound he'd given me with his marking bite. Neither of us said a word and just stared up at the symbol of his Goddess. I thanked her for bringing him to me.

EPILOGUE

HUNTER

In the very early morning light as Ty softly snored in the bed we shared at the adorable Rogue bed and breakfast place we'd checked into on Thanksgiving, I snuck out from under the covers and over to my desk. I pulled my laptop from my bag as quietly as I could and booted it up. I didn't want to be out of Ty's arms long. Besides, I had a morning blow job to try out on him. But there were a couple of things I wanted to take care of first.

We couldn't stay in bed all day. We had get back to campus so he could play in the big game tonight. And I needed some serious girl-talk with Char about marks and mating rituals. Someone really needed to write a girls guide to dating the paranormal. Maybe we could get Rosemary a wolf boyfriend and she could write it for us.

Nah. She was into one of the other guys on the team. I

didn't know who all was a shifter yet because there were like a hundred guys who played for the Dire Wolves and it's not like I could go around asking each of them if they were a wolf, a bear, a scary ass bird, or a wild panther. Besides, we all knew Rosemary had it bad for her best friend who I doubted was a shifter. He was also a volunteer firefighter and I doubt wolves went around rescuing kitties from trees.

I sent off a quick email to the Dean foundation to recommend a student at Bay State University for the education grant we had available every year to students who went to my school. My father was stingy enough that he refused to advertise the grant and only those aware ever applied for it. Those in the know were his cronies and their kids didn't need the money.

But I knew just the guy who would love to finish out his next three semesters without worrying about where the money for books and a roof over his head came from so, he could play more football and do a whole lot less flirting. He'd borne the brunt of obligations long enough and I wanted to ease that burden just a little bit if I could.

The second message was a little more near and dear to my heart. It took me a few minutes to decide what to say, but once I figured it out, the words flowed.

Dear readers and faithful followers of the Hunter of Hearts,

I've fallen in love.

Not with a book boyfriend this time. I'm head over heels for my very own bad boy and I must tell you something important.

He's great in bed.

I thought by pretending that sex didn't matter, that if I told that to the whole world, not only with this blog and my social media accounts, but with my everyday actions, it wouldn't hurt as much when I had to admit, I was a twenty-one-year-old virgin.

I thought it wouldn't hurt as much to think that I would never fall in love if I pretended that love was only in books.

I was wrong. In so many ways.

I've lied to all of you and to myself for far too long and I won't do that anymore. I'm doing my best to be my most authentic self from here on out and it's going to take me some time and effort to discover exactly who that is. But with the help of a really great guy, I'm on my way.

This will be my last post and I'll end it by saying just this one thing - I read the naughty bits and so should you if that's what makes you happy.

Wishing you lots of love like I have found and many orgasms.

Yours,

Hunter

PS - I'm also trying out a new genre I think you'll all love too. Paranormal romance is my new jam and let me just say... wolf-shifters are my favorite.

I posted to my blog with a recommendation of a couple of paranormal romances for my more open-minded readers to try.

Yeah. That felt good. I'd make a TikTok that would probably break the internet later today. Maybe I'd even get Ty to wave hello. Hopefully, he wouldn't care that I mentioned wolf shifters. That wasn't outing his world. Plenty of people already liked paranormal romance anyway. I can't believe I waited this long to read it myself.

I closed the lid of the laptop but remembered one more email I needed to send.

Dear Selena,

I might not be in the store as much seeing as I've found my very own bad boy. Except this one is real and not just a book boyfriend.

Thanks for firing me even though I don't work for you.

Yours,

Hunter

P.S. - Tell Rosemary to get her nose out of her laptop and let her fireman football player know how she really feels. I promise her, love (and orgasms) is worth the risk.

--H

I was surprised that I got an email right back.

Dearest Hunter,

A. I told you so.

B. Has anyone told you yet about WolfSpace? I think you'd probably blow up on there with a dirty book blog. Just saying.

C. You leave Rosemary to me. I'm already plotting ways to get her fired. Up. Fired up.

--Selena

Ooh. Was WolfSpace like Facebook for the wolf shifter community? I was so in for that. Rosemary was in for it. In all the best ways. If I could, I'd bring every girl on campus into the Moon Bean to get a little matchmaking from Selena. Because if they could all be as happy as Ty and I were, the whole dang world would be a better place.

I closed the laptop and crawled back into bed with Ty. Honestly, I'd much rather spend my time loving on him than any social media. I'd spent most of my life wishing I knew what love was, and now I'd found it. I'd never, ever give up my romance novels. They gave me the comfort and now that I didn't have to feel ashamed about what I read, I was going to read even more.

No reason I couldn't have the best of my book boyfriends and then go see if Ty wanted to re-enact all the hottest parts. For the rest of our lives.

Which of course, I mean the happy ever afters.

NEED MORE Big Wolf on Campus?

Grab the next book in the series now, Heart Throb Wolf

WANT MORE TY AND HUNTER? We've got a fun bonus chapter for you! Join Aidy's Curvy Connection to get it now!

HEART THROB WOLF

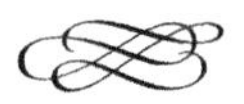

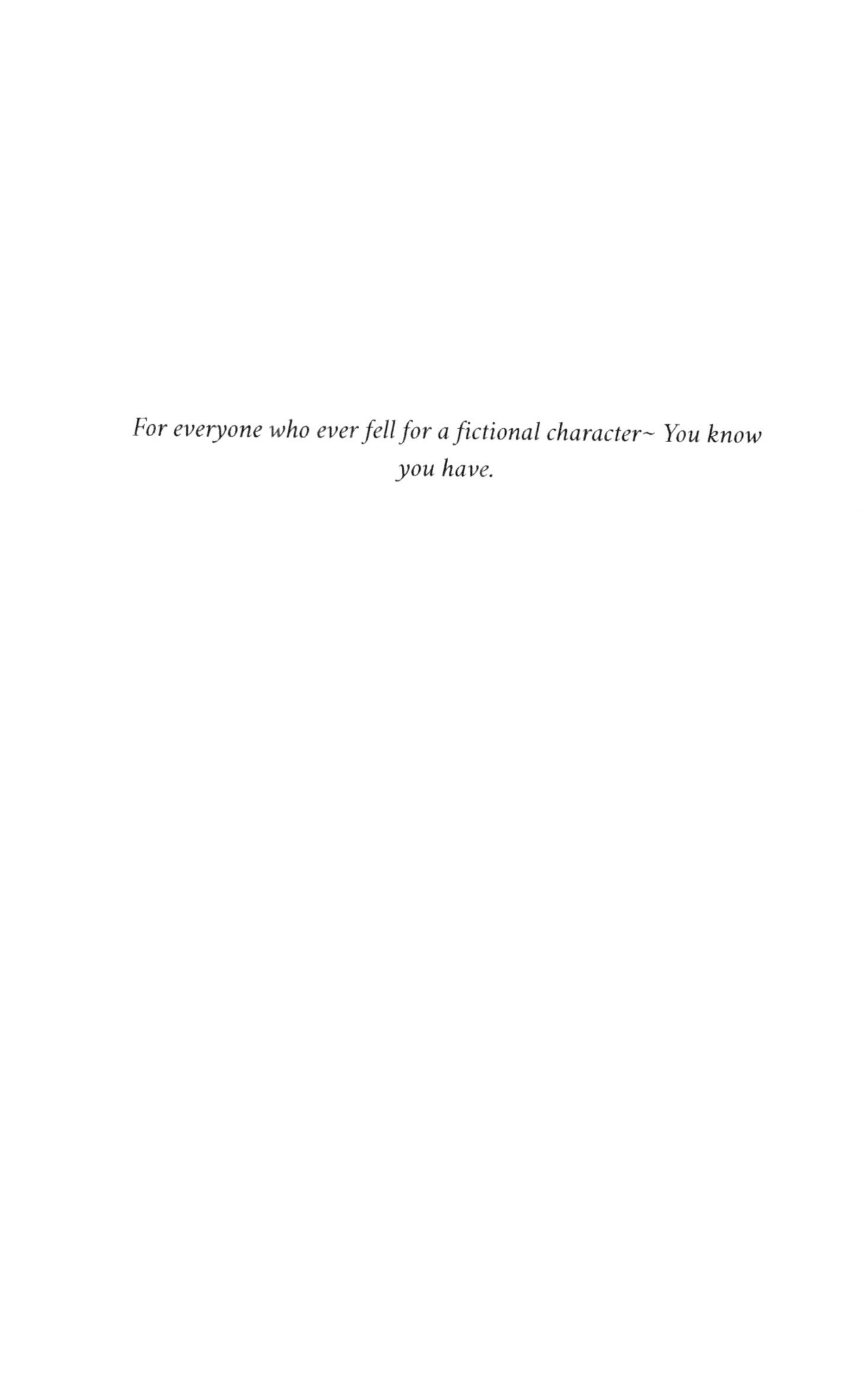

For everyone who ever fell for a fictional character~ You know you have.

In the end, we all become stories.

— MARGARET ATWOOD

ROSIE

Oh no. No, no, no. They couldn't make me do it.

No way was I having a big book launch party at the Moon Bean.

"If you don't have your launch party here, your fired." Selena slapped one of the one hundred paperback copies of my book she'd ordered down on the counter, making my cappuccino jump in its saucer.

"Once again, I don't work here." We'd already had this conversation once when I didn't want to hit the publish button. I'd never intended to let anyone else read my werewolf firefighter romance novel, much less put it out into the world for someone to stumble upon. Someone like Nik.

Selena had won that round too, and not only had it ended up costing me a few hundred dollars to hire a good editor and to buy a book cover featuring a hot AF fireman holding a hose suggestively and sporting a wolf tattoo on his chest...I put my dirtiest fantasies about my best friend into eBook and print for all the world to read.

God, what had I been thinking?

I'd hoped liked hell no one would read it. Except my friend, and fellow romance addict/bookworm Hunter had Tiktokked about it. She'd shut down her book blog, but her TikTok had blown up after she'd admitted to reading and loving the naughty bits in romance novels. Now all she had to do was sneeze about a book and people, a lot of people, bought it.

"Don't you?" Selena waved my book around, and I tried to grab it from her before anyone saw it. She was too fast for me and tossed it to Charlize in a horrible game of keep-away. "How many words of this book were written right over there in my cafe?"

Uh-oh. Here we go again. And of course, Selena was right. She owned the Moon Bean, which was my favorite coffee shop, book store, and writing spot all wrapped into one. I practically lived here. "All of them."

Charlize, who also worked here, was a horrible friend because she started reading the book right there in front of me, to complete my feelings of mortification. She didn't even look up when she said, "Dude, you're not going to win. Also...what page do the sexy bits start on?"

"That's right." Selena crossed her arms and gave me the eyebrow of doom. "And since your shiny, new fans are clamoring for you to write the next book, where do you suppose you'll write that?"

Great. I was crap when I tried to write at home. Netflix was the frenemy of all procrastinators like me. I could go try to find another coffee shop, but this one was right across from campus. Besides, it felt like a second home, but one filled with books and coffee. "Umm, same table?"

"Not if you don't have your launch party here." Selena

grinned like the Cheshire Cat she was. "Besides, it's too late, I already put it on the shop's website. Be here Saturday night to sign books, You'll get the profits from the sales split with me fifty-fifty."

"Book launch party, did you say?" A pretty girl perusing the romance books on display raised an eyebrow and looked between me and Selena.

"Yes. For Rosemary Roman. Her debut book, *The Fireman's Growl,* comes out this week and the Moon Bean is hosting her exclusive launch party. You can preorder your copy at the register."

"I think I will." The girl turned and walked straight over to the counter where Charley handed her a flyer and rung her up.

Damn it. She knew she had me. My scholarship covered my tuition, but didn't give me extra money for books. I'd cut my hours waitressing at the Wolves Den bar and grill next door down to just two nights a week to give me more time to write. I needed that two-hundred or so bucks the sales of the paperback would get me for next semester, because the royalties from the eBooks wouldn't hit my account until after school started.

"Fine. You win. I'll be here, you monster." Selena had no idea what she was doing to me.

What if Nik found out?

I'd just have to make sure he didn't come. If I was really lucky, he'd have practice or even better a game, or a fire to go put out. I would totally consider becoming an arsonist just to keep him away from the Moon Bean.

My phone rang and of course, it was Nik. "Hey, what's up?"

"Hey, babe. I need a favor."

He always called me that. It didn't mean anything. We were just friends. Had been ever since senior year of high school when I'd first moved to Rogue, and Nik had signed up for English tutoring with me. He'd been embarrassed at first, but once I figured out he was dyslexic and told him he wasn't stupid, we'd been best buds ever since. I was just one of the guys to him.

Except he didn't call any of the guys, babe.

I shook my head at myself, at how I got butterflies every time he said it.

"What do you need?" I didn't even squeak or sound out of breath.

"Dire Wolves have a bye this weekend." I could practically hear the eyebrow waggle in his voice. He was planning something.

Crapballs. If he didn't have a game on Saturday, he and his team buddies might accidentally end up at the coffee shop. They always hung out at the Wolves Den bar and grill next door , and more often than not, he'd come over and try to get me to go drinking with them instead of sticking my nose in my computer.

"I got myself and the boys at the firehouse a side gig on Saturday. I'm bringing' a couple guys from the team along too. Wanna come with? Be our talent manager or our body-guard for the night, so the ladies keep their hands off the goods?"

Yes.

Not yes I could go, yes he wouldn't be able to come to the launch party. "Can't, sorry. I've got a... uh...a book thing I have to go to. You know, for school."

Oh God. I sounded so weird.

The line was silent for a second. "Why do you sound weird about it?"

Sigh. Busted. There was only one solution to this. "I'm not weird, you're weird."

Thank goodness we were best friends and I could say stuff like that to him, and he wouldn't even blink twice.

"Fine, but you're going to miss out. Some lady hired us to be at a party, in our fire gear, but with no shirts on."

Umm. Maybe I was changing my mind about not going with? "Uh-huh."

I definitely squeaked that time.

"She swore it's not like a stripper thing, she just wants us to hold some product she has for sale. I hope it's sex toys. She's even sending a limo to come get us, so we arrive in style at her party. Isn't that nuts? But you know how we get pawed at those kind of things."

Whoever this lady was, she wasn't nuts, she was smart. Nik and his crew at the firehouse were hot, seriously hot. I'd buy anything they were holding. "Sorry I can't be the cock-blocker for you. Wait, what do you call it when it's in reverse? No, forget I asked that, I don't want to know. Be sure to take lots of selfies and send them to me. I'm sure I'll be bored out of my mind at the book thing."

"You're still coming to the house on Sunday for the game though, right?" He didn't sound worried even a little.

Because of course I was. Nik knew how to make exactly two dishes, spaghetti—heavy on the meatballs—and steaks. He needed me to provide the game day goodies that weren't simply meat on a stick. That meant brownies. Yum. "My chocolatey, gooeyness and I will be there. You're sure you don't mind that I invited Charley and Hunter to our game day ritual?"

"Babe," I could practically see the shrug of his ridiculously huge shoulders as he chastised me with the pet name. Tortured me with it too. "Of course not. The more the merrier, especially when the more is my teammates' girlfriends. I already asked Eli and Ty if they wanted to come along too."

While I was looking forward to brownies, barbecue, and vegging in front of the TV on Sunday, I was going to be pile of nerves until then.

Saturday turned out to be the longest day of my life. Selena forbid me from coming into the Moon Bean until the start of the party. I was too antsy and decided to spend the hour beforehand at the bar next door at the Wolves' Den.

"Hunter warned me you were coming over. Here's your margarita, light on the tequila. She said she'd kill me if I let you get drunk before your big night." Ty slid a fancy margarita glass in front of me and shot me a smile.

I smiled, grateful Hunter had called ahead to her boyfriend to have this ready. He only tended bar on the nights the football team didn't have a game, since he was one of their star players. I inhaled the slushie green drink and pressed my palms to my temples to stave off the brain freeze. "I won't kill you either if you keep me supplied with those and enough chips with guac to calm my nerves."

"Oh, so you are the guest of honor tonight, huh?" That same girl who'd been at the coffeeshop the day before held up her ticket to tonight's party. She'd emphasized the word 'are' like she'd questioned that she heard right yesterday.

"I guess I am." Eek.

"So, do you write about your real life in your books?" Why did this girl sound more like a lit snob than a fan of romance?

Must just be my nerves. No way I was answering that truthfully. Like I was going to admit out loud that I'd written a book about me and my BFF falling in love. "Oh, uh, no such thing as werewolves, right? So I guess that's a no."

I snort-laughed and buried my face in my bowl of chips. until the alarm on my phone went off right at six, and I just about dropped it trying to turn the ringer off. Okay. Keep calm and carry on.

There probably weren't even going to be very many people there. Who even went to a book launch for an unknown romance author, anyway?

I downed the rest of my second marg, got another brain freeze and spent the walk from the bar to the bookshop rubbing my tongue across the roof of my mouth, trying to warm my head back up. Which is ninety-percent of why I didn't notice the four kazillion people in the book store, until I pushed in through the front door.

The whole room started clapping, and I forgot how to breathe. Were all these people seriously here for me?

Selena came over and wrapped her arm around my shoulder, "This way, Miss Author. You're signing table awaits."

Selena steered us through the crowd, and I caught a glimpse of our destination. My usual table in the cafe had been replaced by a long, rectangle table with an enormous stack of my books to one side, a sparkling tablecloth with a stylized version of my pen name on it, and a whole line of people waiting for an autograph. The pile of books I expected, the sparkly table cloth was a nice touch. The winding line of people, I did not, and made me regret not ordering a third margarita.

The introvert in me reared up in revolt, but I beat her back down with an image of what I thought an famous author should look like. I squeezed my eyes shut and whispered to myself, "I can do this."

Selena squeezed my hand and gently tugged me to the table. "Of course you can do this Rosie, don't be foolish. Besides I got you an assistant to help you along. Now, let us launch this book."

And I totally could have, totally would have. Until I saw him. My mouth fell open wide enough that flies could set up camp and roast marshmallows. I'd shut it, but the muscles in my face had gone numb. Or maybe they'd just gone dumb.

The completely unexpected, never-even-crossed-my-mind backdrop for the book launch came in the form of a very hot, totally ripped, and mostly naked fireman with a wolf tattoo on his chest holding my books in his hands like he was holding the .

Nik.

My best friend.

Right out of my dirtiest fantasies I'd put in the book. Brought to life right out of those pages and standing before me.

Holy crap.

NIK

When the limo this rich lady who hired us to model products for the night pulled up in front of the Moon Bean coffee shop, I was damn sure it stopped short, and we were going to the Wolves' Den next door. Maybe for some kind of new alcohol launch or something. I'd seen sexy girls in short, skin-tight dresses with beer logos slapped across their chests give out t-shirts and shots, or whatever to boost sales and brand recognition. Any first-year marketing student knew that. Plus the Den was the stomping ground of every player on the Dire Wolves squad.

My athletic scholarship paid for school now, but I had contingency plan on top of contingency plan for after graduation. That's why I was double-majoring in Fire Science Technology and Business. I had no grand ideas of playing professional ball after school, and my pack needed someone to keep the Reserve open space where we roamed free in our wolf forms safe from fires.

Gear for football and books for a big course load were

expensive. That's why I'd so readily agreed to be a piece of fiery hot man-meat tonight. My savings account never seemed to get more than a few hundred dollar in it. Couldn't pay for books, balls, or babes that way.

But Selena Troika, the mother of our alpha and former matriarch of my pack, came out herself to usher us into the bookshop side of the Moon Bean. It was packed too. Mostly with women who were all going gaga over some book with a shirtless firefighter on the cover.

I glanced at windows that were covered in six-foot tall posters of the cover. Jesus, it could have been me on that book.

"Hey man, you know who this Rosemary Roman chick is? Is she like famous or something?" One of the other guys from the firehouse that I'd corralled into this gig tonight picked up a book from the display and looked it over.

"I don't know. Her name sounds kind of familiar though. She must be somebody to draw a crowd like this." Besides the fact that Selena was paying us a thousand bucks to stand around with...I guess books, in our hands.

"Nik? Good, you're here." Selena Troika was a force to be reckoned with. While no one would say it, we all knew she'd been involved in the revolution against the Volkovs. I didn't really understand what she was doing here running a little coffee shop and bookstore at the university.

But my mama always said trust your matriarch no matter what, so that's what I was doing.

I raised my hand. "Present."

She looked me up and down and with every inch, her smile got wider. "Yes, this is exactly what I was hoping for.

You'll be stationed at the signing table. Charlize will show the rest of you to your places."

Charley was my best friend Eli's girl. I waved at her, feeling kind of stupid standing there all oiled up and shirtless. But she was doing a damn good job of pretending she didn't know me. Shit.

Had I done something to piss her off? While Eli wasn't my alpha, he was the future alpha of the Chincoteague pack, and my parents would be really upset if I did something to harm the relationship with another local pack. Especially one with so many wolftresses they could arrange a marriage for me with.

I'd have to ask Eli, or better yet, Rosie if she knew what that was all about tomorrow at the barbecue.

Selena grabbed me by the suspenders and dragged me into the cafe portion of the bookstore where a long table and stacks of books was all set up. "You stand right here and look like you came right out of those pages, okay?"

"Yes, ma'am. Will we get to meet this author?" Maybe I'd grab a copy of the book for Rosie. She loved to read. I was surprised she wasn't here anyway. She spent pretty much most of her time sitting in the coffeeshop with her nose in her laptop. I guessed since the coffee shop was closed for the event, she'd made those other plans.

Maybe I shouldn't get her the book though. I wouldn't want her to think I was trying to tell her something by giving her a romance novel with a firefighter on the cover. How embarrassing would that be? She was my friend, totally just one of the guys. Sort of. None of the guys had a great rack or a luscious ass. Not that I was noticing. Nope. Not me. Hadn't been noticing since high school.

"Hmm. She'll be here soon. Maybe peruse the pages of her book while you wait." She handed me one of the books and waggled her eyebrows all suggestive-like. What was she up to?

I flipped the book over to read the description on the back and see if there was a photo. No picture. But how totally weird that it was about a fireman who was a werewolf. I flipped the book over and saw that the model had a wolf tattoo that was eerily similar to mine on his chest, and a blue glow to his eyes.

Was Selena trying to tell me that a human had discovered our secret and it was somehow my fault? Charley was in on our secret since she was mating Eli. Was that why she was mad at me? What the hell?

I didn't get a chance to read what the book was actually about because the whole room started clapping and Selena escorted someone through the crowd toward the table.

That someone was Rosie.

What the actual fuck? She'd said she had some book thing...oh. Oh. Holy shit. Rosie was Rosemary Roman. Holy shit.

Holy.

Shit.

Rosie wrote this romance novel.

About a firefighter... who was also a wolf shifter.

Did she know? I'd always been so damn careful around her, even if I'd wanted to tell her a million times.

For a hot second I thought she'd been weird about her other plans because she didn't want me to know she'd set this whole thing up. But then I looked at her, standing there with her mouth hanging open.

"Nik?" She looked like an adorable deer in the headlights. She definitely had no idea I would be here.

Besides that wasn't my Rosie. She was a wide-open book. She didn't keep secrets from me.

Except she hadn't told me she was an author.

I didn't know why that fucking bothered me so much. I needed to get over that right now, this was her big moment, and I'd be there for her no matter what. Just like she'd always been for me.

"Hey Rosie oops, I mean Rosemary Roman, author extraordinaire." I sounded like a Neanderthal who didn't know a novel from my ass. "I had no idea you wrote a book."

I held up the one in my hand and pointed to her name on the cover. "Grandma Roman would be proud."

The scared look on her face drained away and she smiled shyly, pulling her lips between her teeth to hide it like she always did. "Yeah? I hope so. That's why I picked it. You don't think it sounds dumb for a pen name?"

"Naw. It's perfect." We'd spent plenty of hours at her gran's kitchen table, them both trying to teach me how to read after I'd been told for years that I was just dumb. "If you'd have picked anything else, I'd be mad."

Selena pulled out the chair behind the table and waved Rosie over. "Ready, Miss Roman? Your fans await."

Rosie made a can-you-believe-this face, then plopped down behind the table and was immediately swamped with people who wanted her to sign their copy of her book. We didn't get to talk much for the next couple of hours. I watched as she smiled at each and every person who came up to her to get her autograph. She chatted with them all and listened to their funny bookworm stories, making each person feel special, seen.

She was born for this.

That was fucking hot.

Whoa. Where had that come from? I hadn't thought about her that way in years... okay days... fine at least ninety minutes. Rosie was so much more than a hot chick. She was my friend, and I'd never jeopardize that friendship to get my dick wet.

I'd learned to ignore my wolf when Rosie was around. Which wasn't always easy since she had the kind of curves that made me hard and always smelled like ripe peaches.

Not even my wolf could talk me into dicking around with her. Sure, I'd had my fair share of fantasies about her when we'd first met, and my wolf went all crazy trying to claim her. I tamped those ideas down real fast once she made it clear she was here to tutor me and nothing more. But she had done more. She'd believed in me when no one else had.

Now it was my turn to support her.

I handed book after book over to the people in line, took all of the comments about my fireman's pole, or hose and returned them with a smile. When they asked if I would growl for them I actually did it, and had at least a dozen phone number shoved into my pocket.

A girl with a real resting bitch face cut in line so she was next. The women she cut in front of deferred to her. Prey instinct. The cutter was a wolftress. There had been several other wolftresses, she-bears, and a few female felines here tonight too. There were plenty at Bay State U, but I didn't recognize this woman, even though she was around our age.

She glanced at me, then at Rosie, then the cover, and back to me. "So is this story about you?"

I politely deferred with a shrug. Rosie had paused to take a drink and almost spit out her water. "Oh, geez. Sorry. Who do you want me to make this out to?"

"Erika. No wait, just your signature is good." Rosie signed and the wolftress took the book and sauntered away like we were beneath her.

What a bitch.

When there was just one copy left, I swiped it and hid it behind my back. "Sorry, ladies. It appears we're all out."

That statement was meant with boos and jeers and ahhs. Selena waved the rest of the people in line toward the cash register, promising them all vouchers which they could return for signed books as soon as the next shipment arrived.

That left me and Rosie alone together for the first time all night. She was absolutely fucking glowing, and I was sweating.

"Wow. I'm exhausted, my cheeks hurt from smiling, and I think I might have carpal tunnel." She dropped her pen and shook out her hand.

"I hope you've got it in you to sign one more." I showed her the secreted book and flipped it open to the front page. "Sign it, 'To my sexy firefighter inspiration, Nik.'"

I thought she'd laugh, but she grabbed the book from me and picked up the pen, stuck her head down and signed the book. She didn't even look up when she said, "You don't have to buy the book. Really. I should give this copy to—"

"No way. This one is for sure mine." I snagged it from her

even though she kept a tight grip on it and stuck it down the back of my pants.

"Nik. Really. Don't read that. It's just, umm...you know, it's for girls." Cute, adorkable Rosie was turning fifty shades of pink in the face, and I wanted to lick my way up one side of her flushed throat and down the other.

Shit. Down boy.

"No way, babe. This is a major accomplishment. Of course I'm going to read it."

The other guys came over to join me, each with a book of their own in their hands. Kirill, the Dire Wolves football team calendar model, had actual lipstick marks all over his chest. He'd begged me to come along even though he wasn't even the least bit interested in firefighting. Dude loved getting man-handled at stuff like this.

"Don't be trash talking romance novels and saying they're just for girls. Where do you think I learned my highly attuned ladies-man skills. My mom had hundreds of these at home. I like the ones with dragons and wolves and stuff in them the best, so you know, you can't go wrong with a fire-fighter wolf-shifter hero." He winked at Rosie as he snapped the suspenders on his borrowed pants.

Kirill was officially uninvited to tomorrow's game day barbecue.

"Oh my God. Selena gave you each a book? Kill me now." Rosie laid her forehead on the table.

Selena sauntered over. I'm sure she felt like the cock of the walk for having such a packed store tonight. "Don't you boys worry about Rosie. All authors think their books are horrible. Here's your pay. The limo is waiting outside to take you all home or wherever you want to go. Now shoo. I'm closing up shop in a few minutes."

I really wanted to stay and talk to Rosie about her book, but it seemed like she wanted to avoid the subject. I'd see her tomorrow. Maybe I'd even stay up late and read some of it. I wasn't a fast reader, but I was sure I could get through a few chapters. "See ya later, Roses. Congrats again on the book."

She didn't even pick up her head, just waved half-heartedly. She was probably super tired.

We had the limo drop us back at the station so we could change out of our gear, and the other guys wanted to hit the bars. "Next time, fellas. I've got ribs to marinate for tomorrow."

"Is that a euphemism for read the sexy bits in this romance novel and jerk-off?" Kirill slapped me on the shoulder with his copy.

"Don't be an asshole." I grabbed the book from him. He didn't deserve it. "This is Rosie's work and you will respect it and her, or I will kick your fucking ass."

"Whoa. Okay. Sorry. It's not like she's your girl or something." Kirill snatched the book back from me, and took off running up the stairs.

She might not be my girl, but maybe she should be. I was all mixed up over this book I hadn't even read yet. "See you guys tomorrow afternoon. Bring beer. Don't bring Kirill."

It only took me a few minutes to take care of the prep for having the guys and Rosie over tomorrow so I settled in on the couch with *The Fireman's Growl.*

I read it straight through. Nothing like finding out exactly how your best friend feels about you by reading a hot as fuck sex scene in a book.

And her depictions of life as a wolf-shifter were eerily accurate.

Had I said holy shit earlier? Because I meant it now. I glanced at my phone. Two forty-three in the morning.

Fuck it. I was going over to Rosie's.

ROSIE

By all rights I should have been exhausted after the signing and talking to all of those people, but I couldn't sleep. I might never sleep again. It was almost three o'clock in the morning, and I was pacing back and forth in my living room, surrounded by cold mugs of tea I kept making and then forgetting.

I never should have let Nik walk out of the Moon Bean with my book.

I really wanted to blame it all on Selena, but I was the one who wrote a romance novel about my best friend and then handed a signed a copy to him. My sexy firefighter inspiration. He had no idea.

This could go only one of two ways. Either he'd freak the fuck out and never talk to me again, because I was a weird, creepy, obsessed girl who'd written a dirty book about him or... Probably it was just that one outcome.

No way would hot, gorgeous, funny, kind, delicious Nik read my book and decide he'd always been in love with me too. I mean, have you seen him? He's like a thousand times hotter than the guy on the cover of my book and I'm, well, chubby is an understatement. I've never even had a boyfriend, much less one that wanted to do all the dirty things to me I'd written in my book.

The whole thing was a fantasy. One that I should have freaking kept in my dreams. Now the entire world, including Nik, his firehouse buddies, and probably the majority of the football team, knew I was in love with my best friend.

Maybe no one wouldn't notice since I'd also turned him into a werewolf? Yeah, right. Making the story paranormal didn't hide a thing. Not to mention Nik's sexy wolf tattoo.

I might not be able to sleep now, but I could rest when I was dead. Because I was definitely going to die of embarrassment the second I saw Nik. Fine. I would just have to avoid him. For the rest of my life.

Except I didn't want to. He was my best friend in the whole world. I loved hanging out with him. And what if he did pick door number two? The scenario where he liked me back?

Stupid to get my hopes up. If nothing had happened in the last four years between us, nothing ever would.

"Rosie?" A loud, fast knock sounded at my door. "Rosie open up."

My stomach dropped right down to the floor and rolled away. My heart jumped rope in my throat. What was he doing here? It was three in the morning. "Nik?"

"Rosie, open this door right now, before I kick it down." Did he just growl?

I was so freaked out, I couldn't figure out if he was mad or excited or freaking out too.

"Umm, don't do that, I'll lose my deposit. Probably you should just come back tomorrow. Or better yet, I'll see you at the barbecue." I pressed my hand to the door and willed him to go away.

"I don't want to have this conversation through a door where the entire neighborhood can hear, but I will." He was already loud enough that the people next door were likely going to complain.

"Okay." I prided myself on having a brilliant vocabulary. Not today. Every word drained out of my brain when the panic came flooding in.

"Okay, what?" He jiggled the handle. "Okay, you're going to open the door?"

"No." I squeaked that at a pitch so high only dogs could hear the answer.

"Fine." His voice got quieter and closer like he was leaning his head against the door. "I read the book, babe."

Fuck. I was now down to one syllable swear words. Wait, I don't think I said that one out loud.

"You named the firefighter Mick and the girl Thyme."

I thought I was being all clever. Nik and Mick, Rosemary and Thyme. It was a stupid name. "It's an interesting name."

"They're best friends who fall in love." He stayed silent after that.

I knew deep in my heart if I didn't say something right here, right now, it was over. He'd walk away feeling confused and betrayed. A thousand snarky replies stuttered through my mind, every single one of them designed to push him away, keep my heart safe from the rejection he was about to slap down on me.

That wasn't fair to him or me. If ever I was going to take a risk on love, this was it.

I yanked my long sleep t-shirt down as far as it would go, and unlocked and opened the door. It looked like he'd run here. Nik's hair was sticking up like he'd been running his hands through it, and his eyes had that gorgeous blue glow that flashed whenever he was riled up about something.

I peeked at his face to see if he was mad, or irritated, or upset. For the first time since we'd met, I couldn't read him. He wasn't giving me a single clue to how he felt about my book...about me. I bent my head, closed my eyes and took a deep breath. Then I slowly raised my face, swallowed hard and whispered, "I know, Nik. I wrote the book."

"Is it about me, Rosie? About you and me?"

I'd never lie to Nik. I couldn't. He was my best friend. There was no going back now.

"Yes."

He stepped through the doorway, grabbed my face with the book still in his hand, and kissed me.

Nik.

Kissed.

Me.

I melted into him, lost all sense of time and space. There was only me and Nik, our lips, our tongues, and our hunger for each other.

I wanted to say it was the best, most sensual kiss in my entire life, but I had nothing to compare it to. I'd never been kissed. Ever. I guess that makes it the best still. I hoped I wasn't doing it really badly.

What if I was like slobbering on him too much. Gah. I broke my mouth from his, but then couldn't help taking just a little bit more and brushed my lips back and forth over his once, twice, three times.

"Rosie, my sweet Rose. Why didn't you ever say something?" He pushed his fingers into my hair and gave the strands a stiff little tug.

God, that sent tingles all along my scalp and I forgot what the question was for a second while I wondered if real-life Nik was as kinky as the wolf-shifter fireman Mick in my book. But that could wait. He had asked a question I couldn't leave unanswered.

"I didn't mean for you to find out this way."

"You mean you didn't mean for me to find out at all, don't you?" He lowered his face to the crook of my neck and scraped his teeth across an insanely sensitive spot on my skin. "Don't deny it. I know you too well."

"Busted?" I whimpered the single word. It was all I could get out. Was this the part where he gets mad? I'd prefer we went back to the kissing part instead.

"You're worried that I won't feel the same." He growled those words into my ear, then lifted his face and looked so deep into my eyes he could probably see my whole soul.

Nik was the only one I would ever let see all of me. Emotionally, anyway. I nodded, or maybe I thought about nodding, because I don't think my head moved.

"I thought so. I'm going to show you exactly how I feel about you, babe." Nik shoved the book into my hands and then picked me up like a freaking princess, kicked my front door shut with one foot, and carried me down the hall toward my room.

"Oh God, put me down. You'll hurt yourself. I'm too heavy." I dropped the book and wrapped my arms around his neck, scared to death we were both going to end up on our asses.

"I will never drop you, Roses. You're mine." His words were filled with such sincerity that I knew he was talking about more than this single moment.

Nik went straight into my room, set me on the bed, and gave my shoulder a push. I fell back into the pillows, and he crawled over me like a panther. "You say stop and I will, but don't say it because you're scared of what I think about who and what you are. I want to be here, and I want to be with you. Got it?"

"Uh-huh. But umm, I've never—" He and I knew everything about each other, but there were some things a girl just didn't talk about with her guy friends—even if he was the guy I shared everything else in the world. A girl just didn't blather on to the guy she was in love with for the last four years that she was a virgin.

Except right now that little fact felt like the giant virgin elephant in the room.

"Shh. I know." He kissed one of my temples. "Did you think I don't know? We're best friends. We tell each other everything. We always have."

He kissed the other temple and then my jaw, and then my neck. I wanted his lips everywhere. I wanted my lips everywhere on him. He had me pinned down to the bed, which was—ahem—straight out of one of my fantasies, but I couldn't move to touch him. Mostly just my head. I tentatively pressed my lips to the spot right behind his ear that starred in more than one scene in my book.

He groaned and my panties got a whole lot damper. "But you haven't told me about any of your girlfriends."

"That's because I haven't had any." He said it so matter-of-factly that I almost missed the meaning. That and because he was swirling his tongue around the shell of my ear.

"What? I don't..." I was about to say that I didn't believe him. I hadn't ever seen him with a girl. He'd never talked about anyone with me. "You're... uh... in your sexual prime. You're the star of the football team, and you're a hot, sexy firefighter. You must have the ladies lined up at your door. I just assumed we didn't talk about that part of your life."

Nik rolled to his side and let out a long huff of breath.

For a moment, I thought I'd blown it. I shouldn't have questioned him.

"Babe, I'm horny as fuck all the damn time. I jack-off like twenty-four seven." He took my hand and placed it right on the fly of his jeans.

Holy crap on a cracker. That was no banana in his pocket, that was the whole damn banana tree.

"Feel how hard I am for you. Every inch of this is for you. I came twice while reading your book, and you know I was imagining you and me in those sex scenes. They were very... descriptive. But there hasn't been anyone since you moved to Rogue. Not since high school, not since I met you."

"What? What do you mean since you met me?" My head was spinning in so many circles with so many what-ifs.

"I could tell you, but you know I'm not good with words. Let me show you how I feel." He sat up and whipped off his shirt and I drank in every single one of those six-pack abs.

He reached for the edge of my t-shirt and gently lifted it about an inch and a half before I stopped staring at his perfectly honed body and realized he was about to see mine.

"Nik, stop. I... couldn't we just leave my clothes on? And

we could turn off all the lights. You don't want to see my jiggly bits. Talk about a turn off."

"Rosie, Rosie, Rosie." He took both my wrists in one of his and shoved them up over my head. His eyes went from the stomach I was trying to hide, up to my chest where he lingered and licked his lips, up to my mouth. He flashed me a look filled with dirty promises and then kissed me so long and hard that I might have forgotten my name.

He broke that kiss by nipping at my lip. "Later we're going to have a long talk about the way you put yourself down. Right now, we're both getting naked, because I do want to see every single part of your body. I'm going to worship you from the tips of your toes to these fingers way up here, and when I'm done, I'm going to start all over again."

I wanted that, oh how I wanted it. But I was having a really hard time believing he was into lumps and bumps where muscle tone and flat bellies were supposed to be.

"I recognize that look, Roses. It's the one that means you're feeling self conscious. Whose body do you think I was imagining when I was reading your book? Whose body do you think I stroked myself to? The last thing I want you to do is hide from me in the dark with your clothes on."

This time when he yanked my shirt up, I let him. I had some serious body issues to get over, but I couldn't think of a better way to start than by letting someone I cared about show me exactly how much he loved my curves.

NIK

Fucking hell. Rosie had the greatest tits on the whole fucking planet. I was going to get lost in them for a hundred years, kissing and licking and fucking them. I'll admit having watched a little porn in my time, and it all starred women with big tits, and hips, and thighs. Just like Rosie's. I couldn't wait to come all over them. Make sure my scent was all over her and let every other shifter know she was mine.

That was for later. This first time for us together was going to be something special.

I'd let the animal out on our next go around. My wolf was howling inside about claiming her right here and now. But I still didn't know for sure if she understood what I truly was. I wasn't marking her until she was ready for that commitment.

She was the one for me, forever. But it was her right to make her own choice about whether she wanted to become a part of my world permanently. I shouldn't even make love to her until we talked about it. But I couldn't wait any longer. I had to have her.

Especially if I might lose her later.

My wolf wanted me to flip her over and take her from behind. I'd bet my favorite hose that Rosie had a wild side and would enjoy that as much as I would. She sure wrote like she did. But this first time, she needed gentle, loving, and reassuring from me.

It took way longer than I anticipated to get her naked because of her insecurities about her body. It would take time for me to convince her that she was desirable. Society was the one that was fucked up. But the wonderful world of wolves loved a girl with meat on her bones.

"God, you're so incredibly gorgeous." I knew exactly how she was going to react to that. She never could take a compliment, much less one about how pretty she was. I'd given up on telling her because she usually reacted so badly. That was my mistake. I'd tell her everyday for the rest of my life.

The rest of our lives.

Yeah. I was thinking long term. My own parents made my future very clear. Mate with a nice wolftress from a neighboring pack, and do my duty to them and our pack. Even if the Wolf Tzar said we could now mate whoever we wanted instead of only other wolf-shifters, I still didn't exactly believe in the whole fated mates thing.

Until I read Rosie's book.

Because I wasn't just in love with her. She was my one true mate. I just hadn't let myself believe it before.

I could blame it on my parents, but if I was real honest with myself, I hadn't wanted to screw up the best thing that ever happened to me. Being in her life was more important than anything else. Now that I knew she was in love with me too, it was as if the fire-hydrant had been opened up full and everything was gushing out.

"You don't have to say that." She looked away, hiding her face halfway into the pillow.

I grabbed her jaw and pulled her head back so she had to look at me. "I should have been telling you that all along. I know you don't believe it, but I think you're the most beautiful woman in the world. I'm going to keep telling you until you believe it too, even if it takes years."

She gave me a shy smile that melted my heart because she didn't hide it like she usually did. "Years?"

"Yeah. I'm thinking like the next fifty. Or a hundred." I winked at her and began my quest to show her how I felt about her and her body. I started with a quick hot kiss, pumping my tongue in and out of her mouth until she was groaning and panting for breath. "That was just to show you what I'm going to do to your pretty pussy next. Now you hold onto the headboard until I tell you what to do next."

My wolf needed to dominate her, wanted to see her submit to me. I was running on pure instinct now, and maybe a little inspiration from the sex scenes in her book.

I didn't give her a chance to protest. I pressed her knees open and my mouth watered with the sight of her panties glistening. Her sweet pussy was already wet for me. My cock fucking twitched wanting to get inside of her, and my wolf howled inside, ready to stake my claim on her body. Images of the wolf's knot buried deep inside of her popped into my head.

Not yet. First I was going to make sure she was nice and

relaxed and ready. I tugged her panties to the side with my teeth and gave her one long lick, getting my first taste of her. I almost came right then and there. Being between her thighs was beyond heaven. This was why Rosie always smelled like peaches to me—it was the scent of her emotions when she was aroused.

She was hot, for me. Right here, right now and that was a bigger turn on than anything else.

"Whoa. Oh God, Nik. Do that again."

That's my girl. "Put your fingers in my hair, let me know what you like as I do it."

I remembered the scene in her book where she described the fireman wolf going down on Thyme and everything he did that drove her crazy. I swirled my tongue around her clit and slowly sunk one finger inside of her. She was so damn wet, and so tight. Rosie moaned my name and her fingers dug into my scalp. That was all the signal I needed to know she was getting off on this.

The thing was, I was getting off on this too. My dick was so damn hard I could feel the blood pulsing through it. My wolf was closer to the surface than ever.

I had every intention of getting Rosie off before I fucked her, but once I got my cock into her tight pussy, I wasn't going to last more than a few strokes. This first time, I needed her to be as close to coming as possible so we could come together.

I don't know why that was so damn important to me, but it was. I wanted the first time I made love to my sweet Rosie to be special. This was the moment when we'd look back and remember how connected we were. Because then perhaps she wouldn't freak out on me when I revealed my wolf to her.

I continued to lap at her clit and slid a second finger in to her hot, wet pussy, pumping my fingers in time with my licks. Rosie's ass came up off the mattress and her inner muscles clenched down on me. She was close and we'd only barely gotten going. She was just as worked up about being together as I was.

I gave her one long last lick, sucking her clit into my mouth and flicking my tongue over the tight little nub until her legs shook and the pitch of her moans grew higher and higher. I released her from my mouth and pulled my fingers from her body. Then, I swiped them up and over her clit, giving her one more jolt of pleasure before I pulled away entirely.

"Please, Nik, don't stop. Please." She'd squeezed her eyes tight and fisted her hands into the sheets the same way they'd been gripping my hair.

"Don't worry, babe. I'm not going anywhere. I want you to taste yourself on me." I licked her bottom lip and rubbed my jaw, wet with her juices across it.

She opened her eyes and her tongue darted out, licking up her own essence. So fucking hot. Her eyes went dark and sparkled with need. She would make a beautiful wolftress.

I had no way of knowing if she would become a shifter when I claimed her, but my alpha's mate had, and she'd been a human before they met. The blue glow of the Troika pack would be the prettiest thing I'd ever seen shining in her eyes.

"Good girl. I wanted you to see me do this." I licked the two fingers that had been inside of her up one side and down the other. "You're fucking delicious."

Rosie gasped and sucked in the rest of her breath, in and out slowly with pretty, rounded lips that I was going to fuck soon. I wanted to take her every which way two people could fuck each other. My need to mark her body as mine and only mine grew stronger by the second.

It would kill me not to mark her tonight. But I wouldn't do that to her until she could say yes to being my true mate.

"But why did you stop? I was so close." Her whimper was so sexy and I loved it.

"Give me your hand." I unwrapped her fingers from where they were twisted in the sheet and slid them between her thighs. "Keep yourself hot and wet for me while I get undressed too. But don't come. I want to be inside of you when you do. That orgasm is mine."

Her eyes went wide and she licked her lips. "Like this?"

Rosie's fingers stroked into her plump pussy lips and her fingers were coated instantly. She swirled the wetness of her clit and God damn, if I didn't get inside of her in the next two seconds, I was going to be coming on her belly. "Yes. Exactly like that. That's is the hottest fucking thing I've ever seen. I am definitely making you finger yourself for me all the time."

I turned and sloughed my jeans off and onto the floor, and ripped my t-shirt over my head. That's when I noticed the dildo and the packet of condoms on the floor next to her bed. Fuck. Had she been masturbating before I got here? Was she thinking about me when she did?

I grabbed the package and the dildo from the floor and held them up. Rosie said, "I touched myself after I wrote every one of the sex scenes in our book. That's how I made myself come thinking about doing all those things I wrote with you."

Holy Goddess. I had to grip the base of my cock hard so I didn't come all over her right now. "Fuck yeah, you did. Don't stop doing it now. I want those fingers right there while I fuck you. I want you coming so hard with my cock inside of you that you can't see straight."

She didn't know that we didn't need these condoms. Wolf shifters didn't get diseases like humans, and we certainly couldn't pass them on. And unless it was full moon and we wanted a baby, she couldn't get pregnant either. But I wanted my Rosie to feel safe with me. I ripped open one of the packets and rolled the condom on.

It split halfway up my cock. Rosie glanced down at the mess in my hand and she blinked. "Holy crap, Nik. That's, I mean, you're... holy crap. That's not going to even fit. God, you're so big."

I smiled like a loon as I very carefully tried again to put a condom on. It was too fucking small and it would probably break while I fucked her, but she didn't need to know that. I crawled back onto the bed and pushed my way between her thighs again. "It's going to fit just fine. I'll go as slow as I can, you just keep fingering your clit."

She swallowed hard but nodded. Her eyes fluttered shut and I took the opportunity to kiss her again. Her hand was going crazy between us, and she had to be close. "Open your eyes, Roses. I want to see your expression when I put my cock inside of you."

Her breathing shuddered but she did look back up at me. Her fingers slowed and I gripped my cock in my hand. Just like I guessed, the damn thing split. I kissed her and chucked the broken condom aside hoping she didn't notice. I didn't want her to think I was an ass, but I needed to get inside of her and satisfy us both really fucking soon.

I broke the kiss and slid my cock through her juices, getting it nice and wet before I pressed just the tip inside of her tight entrance. "That's it, good girl. Get yourself closer, babe. I'm not going to last long inside of you. I want you on the verge of coming."

"I'm there. I swear, much more and I'm not going to be able to keep from coming." That soft whimper I was coming to love was in her voice again.

"Good girl." I pushed in deeper and her pussy gripped me tighter than my own fist when I'd been jerking off earlier. This was so beyond anything I'd ever felt in my entire life. I was barely halfway in and had to grit my teeth from pushing all the way to the root with one long thrust.

"More, Nik. I need more. Please."

Thank fuck. Inch by agonizing inch, I sunk into her body until she cried out. "Fuck, Rosie. I'm sorry if I hurt you."

"No, no." She shook her head, but her fingers had stilled. "I, I just feel so full. Give me a second."

It was going to kill me to hold still. I already had sweat beading along my spine from the effort not to just take her fast and hard like my wolf wanted me to. I would take every second of torture for her, to make sure she was ready.

She took several long breaths and then her fingers moved between us again. "I'm ready. Fuck me, Nik."

Holy hell. This girl was everything I'd ever wanted and more. So much more. I moved my hips just enough that we both got a little of the friction we needed. She wasn't ready for me to really pump in and out of her body. Even that small movement sent fireworks off in my cock. I moved another inch and thrust back in, then again, and again.

Rosie moved her hips in time with mine and her fingers between her legs faster than that. "God. This feels so incredible perfect."

I couldn't hold back any longer, and I thrust deep and pulled out, pushing us both into a fast and hard rhythm. She closed her eyes and arched her back. Her throat was right there for me to bite, to mark, to make my claim on her.

I would if I didn't do something to stop myself. "Look at me, Rosie. Look at me when you come.

Her eyes shot open again, and I swear to god she was glowing from the inside out. I reached between us and stroked over her clit to drive her closer to the edge. Her pussy fluttered around me and she screamed out, "I love you, Nik."

Her body clenched hard as the orgasm took her body and I thrust as fast and as hard as I could into her. I felt the base of my cock swelling, the wolf's knot grew and if I pushed into her, the wolf wouldn't be satisfied until I marked her too.

I couldn't do that to her. The wolf part of me needed to make Rosie my mate, right here, right now. My parents expected me to mate with a wolftress. They'd never accept my sweet Rose as my mate.

I pulled out, kissed her, and came harder and longer than I'd ever come before all over her pussy, thighs, and belly. The knot throbbed and ached and I grabbed it, stroking my fingers around it. My whole cock was so sensitive the slightest touch almost hurt.

I bet it wouldn't have if I'd been inside of her. But the

knot would have locked us together, and I knew from somewhere instinctually deep that we'd be stuck that way, my cock inside of her, until I marked her, claimed her, and made her my mate.

The knot slowly receded and once again I could breathe. A different ache crept into my chest.

I loved her, but I couldn't have her. Not permanently.

Wolves mated wolves, or at least they still did in my family. We had to get as much loving in now before my parents found out and broke us apart forever.

ROSIE

Nik and I made love twice more. Once at dawn and then again around noon when we woke up from the nap after our last bout, where we'd tried doggy-style and he told me all the dirty-naughty things he wanted to do to my ass and with my dildo.

I couldn't help but notice that he pulled out each time and came on me, instead of in me. I don't know why that felt so... wrong.

He apologized about the broken condom after our first round. I got that they were the wrong size and he'd tried to use them. I was have to going to invest in extra, extra, super-duper, quadruple XL size for him.

He even asked me if I was concerned, and if I wanted him to run out and get some better ones. He was a good guy and since we'd both been virgins—which still had me flabbergasted—I wasn't worried about diseases. We'd been a little too anxious to get going again and didn't talk about pregnancy though.

Honestly, that wasn't likely either. I had a long line of

women in my family who battled infertility and PCOS. I was a miracle baby. My mom had made that very clear. She believed that was to blame for my eternal chubbiness.

Even after we decided we didn't need the condoms, Nik still pulled out when he came. I guess I couldn't blame him for not wanting to have babies. But the mean voices in my head said it had nothing to do with the fact that we were still in school, too young, and not married. Every insecurity I had was screaming that he didn't want to be tied to a fat girl the rest of his life.

Fat girls were fine for fucking, but not for marrying. The whole world made that very clear to me. It hurt to think that Nik believed it.

Sigh. I was being ridiculous. He loved me.

Although, when I said I loved him, he hadn't said it back. Still, I knew we had a deeper connection, and maybe he just needed to come to terms with our new relationship before he could say it.

Grr. I was all up in my head, over-analyzing every little thing, picking myself and this brand new beautiful thing to pieces instead of enjoying what I had. I vowed to try harder not to do that and snuggled deeper into his arms.

We didn't wake up on Sunday morning until his phone started buzzing non-stop from his pants pocket, where they still lay on the floor. He groaned, rolled over, kissed me, and then fumbled around trying to find the damn thing on the floor.

"'Lo?"

He listened for a second and then sat bolt upright on the bed. "Fuck man, sorry. We'll be there in a few minutes."

"Oh no. The barbecue." I swiped my hand down my face.

We'd both forgotten about Nik's game day party at his house. "I can't go smelling like sex. Give me a few minutes to take a shower."

"I love the way you smell like sex and me. But I'll agree to a shower... if we do it together." He made sexy eyes at me and yanked me out of bed and into the tiny bathroom off my room.

We did not take only a few minutes. It took a full ten just to figure out we weren't going to be able to have shower sex in my little stall. Instead I dropped to my knees and gave him my first ever blow job. He insisted on coming on my chest which I didn't even think I'd find sexy at all, but watching him actually coming was incredible, and I couldn't wait to do it again.

After that we washed up, but that took another ten minutes because Nik insisted on making sure my pussy was incredibly well scrubbed.

He pulled his clothes on from the floor and I grabbed a dress and a cardigan from my closet.

"Don't wear any panties. I want to know you're naked under there all day." Nik lifted the skirt of my dress and smacked my bottom. A day ago, I'd have been mortified if anyone touched my butt, or saw it, or even thought about it.

It was just so big, it was like round, and like out there. I mean... gross, look.

Except Nik didn't think it was gross. I still didn't love my jiggly bits. But if Nik did, that went a long way to me thinking that maybe, just maybe someday I might not think my body was so bad.

The panties stayed in my top drawer, which felt so incredibly naughty, and I loved it. We drove over to his place along with a bag of stuff from my kitchen so I could make the brownies at his house. I'd meant to make them this morning. But instead I made love.

When we got there, everyone was scattered in and outside. Waiting. The guys from the firehouse had broken in through his back door and already had the grill started, and his football teammates were passing around beers and sodas. We opened the door and received a round of applause when everyone spotted us.

"Nice of the host to show up, asshole," one of the firefighters said.

"Yeah, sorry. I had a fire to put out." He kissed me on the top of the head and gave me a squeeze.

Oh. Okay, I guess we were going to be right out in the open with our shiny new relationship. That made me feel almost instantly better. He wasn't hiding the fact that we were together. I'd been a little worried.

We were subjected to a round of oohs and awws, and one "I fucking knew it," from Kirill.

Before we could get ribbed any more, Charley and Hunter and a woman I'd never met dragged me off to the kitchen for girl talk.

"Girl," Hunter clapped and squealed, "This couldn't have worked out any better, right? Oh, sorry. This is my cousin Eva. She just gotten a job at the library. Don't worry, I told her all about your wolfy firefighter book and your, uh, wolfy football-playing firefighter."

Hunter leaned in and whispered, "But she doesn't know the boy's, umm, secret. So ixnay on the olfway talk."

What? Eva must not be into paranormal romance like

Hunter and I were. I laughed and shook her hand. "Welcome to my crazy life, Eva."

"It's awfully romantic what you did, writing a whole romance novel just to tell the man you liked how you feel." She smiled at me and got a wistful look on her face.

"That's not exactly what I'd planned, but I guess it worked out that way." I glanced through the window to the back yard where Nik was definitely getting grilled by the guys.

"Yeah. Thanks to us and Selena," Charley said.

"Wait, what?" I played back all the events of the past couple of weeks and especially the last few days in my head. "You set this up so Nik would find out about my book? Is that why you guys sent me running off to the English department that one day?"

Charley and Hunter exchanged a weird look, but then Charley nodded and grinned. "Uh, yeah. Selena's been working on you for months. As soon as Hunter read that one sex scene over your shoulder and figured out who you were writing about, she told Selena. And that set this whole thing in motion. She's going to be so happy to hear you guys hooked up."

Eva frowned at us. "Who is this Selena? She sounds like a meddling—"

"Don't say it." Hunter held up her hand, stopping Eva's protest. She's the reason Charley and I found our guys too. Just beware if she ever tries to fire you—you're about to meet or get together with the man of your dreams."

"She can't fire me, I don't work for her." Eva sounded so adorably uppity, like it was beyond possibility that anyone could meddle in her affairs.

All three of us laughed and exchanged knowing looks.

Nik walked into the kitchen and grabbed me around the waist. "Ladies, would you please excuse us. We have some brownies to make."

Hunter winked at me and grabbed the other two, dragging them back outside.

"Is that code for something, you dirty wolf?" I giggled. I was decidedly not a giggler before last night. I guess happiness can do that do a girl.

Nik set me on the counter and placed himself between my legs. "Yes it is. Well, no. I really do want to make brownies with you. I love your brownies, and it's not game day without them. That's what I wanted to talk to you about. Not brownies, I mean—fuck. I'm fucking this up."

Aww. I hadn't seen Nik get flustered about asking me about anything since our very first tutoring session all those years ago. "You can ask me to make whatever you want. But it's hard for me to make anything while I'm sitting on your kitchen counter."

"Yes, but it makes it easy for me to do this." Nik ducked down, put my knees over his shoulder and his head beneath my dress.

I would have protested, but I forgot how to talk the second his tongue slid across my clit. Anything I was going to say turned into moans. I had to put my own hands over my mouth to keep from crying out when he pushed those naughty fingers into me.

"Oh, hey." Someone's voice floated into the kitchen and back out again. "I hope you're not planning on making anything on that counter. Food and safety violations galore going on there."

I didn't recognize the voice, but that could be due to the fact I was coming so hard I couldn't think straight. Nik popped back up, clearly pleased with himself from the self-satisfied grin on his face and kissed me, snaking his tongue in and out of my mouth just like he had down below.

"I couldn't stop thinking about how you weren't wearing any panties." He helped me back down off the counter and good thing too because I was a bit wobbly on my feet after that killer orgasm.

"I may never wear them around you ever again." Although, maybe when our friends were around.

"That's probably best. Hey, babe?"

"Yeah?" If he was going to ask me anything that required a real answer, I needed to find my mushy, gushy, sex-addled brain and pop it back into my head. I could hardly think at the moment.

"This is gonna sound weird, but how did you come up with the idea of shifters? For your book?"

Okay, that came out of nowhere. "Umm, it was Selena's idea actually. She piled me up with a bunch of other paranormal romance books, and said I should consider making my hero a werewolf."

"Selena?" He said her name like I was on crack.

"Yeah, why? Is it too weird? It's not like it's bestiality or anything."

"It's not weird. Well, I mean," Nik glanced out the window, and Eli gave him a thumbs up from over by the grill. What in the world was going on?

He rubbed the back of his neck, and I got this ache in my chest. Something bad was about to happen. Nik didn't act like this around me. But up until yesterday our relationship had been completely different.

He huffed like he was psyching himself up for a tough play or to run into a fire or something, he started again. "It's just that I—"

"Fire!" One of his firefighter buddies stood up and sniffed the air. Then pointed toward the front of the house. "Three, maybe four blocks away."

Nik narrowed his eyes and sniffed the air too. Must be a firefighter thing. "Shit, babe. We gotta go check that out. Keep the girls and the football team entertained for me for a few minutes, will ya?"

"Yeah, sure. Go do what you gotta do. Be safe."

I watched as Nik and the other firefighters bolted out the front of the house, and we all heard a car screech away. Charley, Hunter, and their boyfriends were still out back at the grill. Time to do my hostess duties. The brownies still weren't made, so I grabbed a bag of pretzels and a container of chocolate hummus I'd brought over last week that none of the guys would even touch, and took it out to the yard.

"I'm sure they'll be back in no time." I laid the food out on the table and turned to find Charley and Hunter staring at me, or rather staring at my neck.

They looked at each other, then to their boyfriends, and shook their heads. Hunter took my hand and pulled me away to sit with her next to the unlit fire pit. She glanced over at Eva, who was occupied talking to Eli, and then patted my hand. "So, did he tell you?"

Uh. "Tell me what?"

NIK

My wolf was torn in two—the pure animal wanted to run, run back to Rosie to mark her and make her mine.. But the part of me that was a pack member, pushed so hard against my skin that I could barely stop from shifting as the tires squealed and car skidded to a halt. Because it wasn't some random fire.

It was the fucking Moon Bean.

I jumped out of the car and didn't even think about what I was doing, going purely on instinct and training. Smoke billowed out the door as people fled the building, but I had the opposite game plan.

We had to get everyone out of the Moon Bean to safety. There wasn't anything I could do to stop the flames until the fire trucks arrived, but I sure as hell could make sure Selena wasn't in there.

Smoke stung my eyes and the power was out, but my wolf vision could see in much dimmer light. I scented the fear on the people left in the building. My crew was on point and we flashed some hand signs to each other indicating a search pattern.

The smoke was thicker as we made our way to the coffee bar. A barista crouched behind the counter with a tiny hand-held fire extinguisher in her hand.

"Oh my god, help! I don't know what happened, one minute I was making an oat-milk flat white, and the next minute the fire alarm went off and the whole place filled with smoke."

"Hey," I knelt down beside her and squeezed her arm gently, and carefully took the unused extinguisher from her hands. "You're gonna be okay. Give me your apron."

She scrambled out of her apron and I held it under the faucet, then crouched down to her level again. The scent of her fear burned my nostrils even more than the smoke. I didn't recognize her, but then again, I only ever really came to the Moon Bean for one thing, Rosie.

I pushed the soaked apron back into her hands. "Hey, what's your name?"

"M-M-Madison."

"Okay, Madison, you're doing great. Here's what you are going to do. See my buddy behind me? He's an off-duty fire-fighter. He's going to get you out of here. Hold this over your mouth and breathe through it, so the smoke doesn't make you cough. Can you do that for me?"

She wrapped the apron around her face. "L-like this?"

"That's great. You got it, Madison. Now I'm going to check the rest of the coffee shop and make sure no one else is stuck in here. I'll see you outside." I looked over my shoulder and watched my buddy disappear with poor Madison. Two of us left. We pushed on, past the cafe side to the bookstore section, where the smoke was the thickest.

"Selena," I shouted, catching her scent. "Selena Troika, it's Nikita Grimm."

Before she could reply, I spotted her huddled next to a shelf on the floor. "Nik you are here, thank the Goddess."

I fell to my knees beside her as she looked up at me with Troika blue glowing eyes, her own wolf close to the surface. She was a little scuffed with soot and maybe even a bit singed around the edges, but no damage her wolf couldn't heal quickly. "Can you stand?"

"Of course I can, don't be ridiculous." She batted my hand away and gave a curt nod over to where Rosie's table signing table was still set up. "But I'm not sure about the young wolftress hiding over there. I've been trying to coax her to leave, she is the last one here. I smell no blood, but perhaps she is injured."

"Maybe she is just scared, fire will do that to some." Even wolf-shifters. We may be tough and heal faster and easier than humans, but we aren't immortal.

Selena frowned and shook her head. "That one is not the scared type, *moy dorogoy*."

The gleam of amber wolftress eyes flashed through the sooty air. No, definitely not the scared type. More the scary type. The girl hiding was none other than Resting Bitch Face from the signing.

"Is there anyone else left in the coffeeshop, Selena?" I couldn't only rely on my senses, not in this much smoke.

"Madison was it, but I saw your friends help her out."

I looped my arm beneath Selena's and guided her over to

my final firefighting compatriot along with the extinguisher. "Go now, I'll get her out, whether she wants me to or not."

Time to rescue Bitch Face. I crawled closer and could see her watching me through the smokey air. The hair on the back of my neck stood up, my wolf warning me of danger.

I crouched down and held out my hands, palms up, like you would approach a stray dog. Did her lips curl into a smile of sorts, or was it a trick of the smoke playing over her features? "Hey. I'm Nik."

"Yes, Nikita. I know you."

"That's right. We met at the signing." Not that I'd given her my full name. Weird. Something to worry about later when we weren't in the middle of a fire trap. The books in this section could go up in flames at any moment. Heat was building behind me, and a bead of sweat rolled down my back. I needed to get this girl out of here. Fast.

"Are you injured?"

"I don't believe so, no." She sputtered out a mewling little cough.

Super fake. Ugh. What in the world was going on here?

"Okay, what's your name?" If she was scared, I hoped using her name would keep her calm like it had with Madison.

"Erika."

Now I was getting somewhere. "Good, Erika, we're going to get you out of her, okay?"

She tipped her head to the side, studying me. "Okay."

Great. I'd earned at least some of her trust. "I need you to stand up, but stay crouched down low like me. Okay?"

She reached out for me, but as if she had no strength. I had the distinct feeling she was feigning helplessness.

I stretched my open hands to her and lifted my eyebrows in a practiced encouraging gesture. Behind me, the bookcase collapsed, sending cinders and sparks dancing around my feet. Erika screamed loud enough to make me jump. No more screwing around. I grabbed both of her hands, pulling her up and out from under the table.

"You saved me," she huffed out in a whoosh, before falling limp in my arms. Her head plopped down on my shoulder and her lips slid over my neck. It sent a shiver like cold needles down my spine. I shook her just a little, and she did a bobble-head routine, but her eyes stayed closed.

So, I did what I had to do. I picked her up and slung her over my shoulder in the classic fireman carry. I had no patience for games, not in a fire. It sure as shit felt like Erika Bitch Face the wolftress was toying with me. None of that mattered now. All I wanted to see was fresh air, clear sky, and Rosie.

I ran through the coffeeshop, dodging an over-turned chair and tables in the coffee shop. A second later I was through the front door and free. I jogged towards my crew and Selena, and Erika let out a groan that grew louder the closer we got to my friends.

She squirmed and wriggled against me. "Niki, put me down."

"You got it." I dropped my hands to my sides and let her slide down, but her knees buckled like a boneless little rag doll. I caught her by the hips, before she tumbled to the ground, and Erika leaned in. That girl leaned in for all it was worth. She wrapped her arms around my neck, and pulled herself close until every inch of her touched every inch of me. Her head fell back and her eyes glowed up at me.

"You saved me, Niki," she breathed the word outs slowly and seductively, and followed them up with a slitty-eyed, half-opened smile. "I was so scared, and then you appeared like an answer to all of my prayers to the Goddess. Strong, fearless, and so powerful. It is like fate has tied us together. You are so—"

She kept staring up at me and talking, but her words were drowned out by the deafening honk and screeching siren of a fire truck as it stormed down the street. Before it came to a stop, the geared-up fire team went to work, pulling hoses, and getting briefed by my boys.

I itched to be over there, telling them what I saw, and lending a hand, but Erika was still attached to my neck. I reached up and tried to peel her away, but she hung tight like she didn't want to ever let go.

"Niki, don't you feel it? We are made for each other, destined for one another. I am promised to you, and you to me."

"I'm not promised to anyone. If you'll excuse me, I have a barbecue to get back to." I would miss out on all the fire fun, but I needed to extricate myself from her immediately.

"Oh, but Niki... it is true. We are meant to be together. We are such powerful beings, and I could never mate with a lesser wolf. My parents spoke to yours. It is all settled. Together you and I will bring our packs closer together and make them great again. I cannot wait for the next full moon, for our mating ritual."

It's all settled? Mating ritual? With her?

She closed her eyes, and pulled my head down, reaching up for a kiss.

A kiss that I would never give. There was no way. My

parents had talked about me mating a wolftress because they didn't believe in fated mates. They had always been anxious for me to make a good match. It was half the reason I came to Bay State University where there were other shifters in school.

They couldn't have...they wouldn't have... arranged a mating for me, would they? It had been pretty common practice until Max, the Troika alpha, and Galyna, a human woman, had started a revolution declaring that we didn't have to mate other wolves. But I still thought I'd get to choose my own mate. How could they make a mating deal without even mentioning it to me?

I took a long step backward. "I need a minute here. I've got to call my parents."

"Of course. You will want to tell them how we met so unexpectedly. This has all come together so magically, like kismet."

The phone rang, and rang. "Please pick up. Please, please, please—"

"Hey sport." My dad laughed into my ear, like he was the funniest guy on the planet while I was ready to puke.

"Hey dad. I need to ask you about... mating—"

"You met Erika? That's great. We meant to introduce you to her and her parents after the game next weekend. She's amazing, isn't she? Such a pretty girl, and so smart. Both of you are so ambitious."

I tried to interrupt, to stop this flood of enthusiasm from him. "Dad, I don't know how to—"

"No need to thank me, Nik. We are so thrilled to have helped bring about such a prestigious match. Erika's family is part of the former Crescent pack."

Uh, nobody called them that anymore. Once the Wolf Tzar and his mate defeated their alpha and took over, they became Serenity Bay. The Crescent's old alpha was a one-blood. I got that same cold needles shooting down my spine feeling as before.

"I'm sure I don't have to tell you, but they are a powerful pack. A union of a good Grimm pack son with a Crescent daughter will bring our pack back into the position we deserve."

What the fuck was going on? My parents had pledged their fealty to Galyna Troika, when she killed the horrible Grimm alpha in an alpha challenge a few years ago. With Galyna being mated to Max Troika, our two packs were basically one. Few of us made the distinction between the two, except when it came to last names. So why was my dad talking about Grimms and Crescents now?

"Uh, yeah. Right. Okay, gotta run dad. See you next week." I hit end before he could go on gushing about Erika or their plans for us and closed my eyes. They stung with smoke and disappointment.

Erika's fingers snake through mine, and didn't even try to shake her loose. What the hell was I going to do?

When I opened my eyes, Selena was staring at me from her place beside the firefighters. The fire chief was talking to her about the damage, said it started in the romance section. That was right beside where Rosie sat with her laptop every day, writing her book about me. About us.

The fire chief pitched his voice low, but my wolf's enhanced hearing caught every word. "Off the record, Selena, at least until the fire investigator arrives and makes it official, I'd say you are looking at arson."

Selena shifted her gaze back to me, then did one of those thousand yard stares. "Someone did this intentionally, then?"

"I'm afraid so, ma'am. But the good news is that the damage to the building is minimal. Mostly smoke. You should be able to open again in no time."

Selena allowed herself to be led away on the chief's arm but not before giving me another pointed look. Or was she looking at Erika.

"Niki?" Erika pressed herself closer to me.

"Yeah?" My voice sounded dead. For the first time in my life, I wished I wasn't a wolf shifter.

"I feel so shaky, so exhausted and overwhelmed. I don't think I can drive. Will you take me home?"

"Hey, Nik," Kirill shouted from where he was leaning against the car I came in with the guys. They were all exchanging fist bumps.

"Where the fuck did you come from Kirill?" I didn't have any patients for his antics today.

"I was just pulling up to your house when I saw you take off with your fire buddies. I smelled the smoke too, and thought you might need a hand." That was the least douchy thing Kirill had ever said. Maybe ever done, and I wanted to do was pick a fight with him, feel my fist connect with his solid jaw, have him hit me back until my outsides matched my wrecked insides.

"It's under control." I shrugged. It was the simmering coals of dread in my stomach that were burning out of control.

"Let's go eat some ribs then man, I'm fucking starving. Who's your new girlfriend, and does she have a hot sister for me?"

She wasn't my fucking girlfriend. But I did have a duty to her, my parents, and my pack. Dammit. Fuck. Fucking dammit.

From where she was stuck to my arm like a day old pizza stain, a throaty, quiet laugh rolled out of Erika, "Aren't you going to introduce me to your friend, Niki?"

I didn't know what the hell to do here and I needed time to figure it out. I wasn't going to be an asshat in the meantime. "Uh, Kirill, this is Erika. Erika, Kirill, he's plays for the Dire Wolves with me. He's a Bay pack sea wolf."

Kirill took her hand and kissed it like she was a princess. He was such a fucking cheesedick, but at least he was diverting a little of Erika's laser-focused attention away from me.

Erika chuckled softly, "Yes, I can see he's all wolf."

Was she fucking flirting with him?

"Niki, sweetheart, I don't want to take you away from your friends... don't worry about me. I'll be fine." She stumbled over the word fine and her lower lip trembled. She looked like she was going to cry. I couldn't keep up with her moods.

"No, I'll take you home. I'm sure you're exhausted." Wait, where was her home? If she was Crescent come Serenity Bay she likely lived up in Cape Cod. Yes, I could drive her home, shift and run back, and work off all this worry. That would give me time to figure out what to do.

"Dude." Kirill winked at her. "She's probably on adrenaline burnout. She shouldn't be alone. Probably just needs a triple margarita and some food."

More tinkling laughter floated from Erika's pouting face, and she squeezed my arm. "If it's not too much trouble, I would love to go to the barbecue with you. I don't really want to be alone. Not tonight."

Leave it to Kirill make a painfully horrific situation worse. She held up her keys and jingled them lightly.

The nausea from before roiled in my gut. She wanted me to take her to my house? Where Rosie waited for me?

Shit. It wasn't her fault I'd fallen in love while our parents arranged our futures. I took her keys and held her car door open as she floated down into the passenger seat. "I cannot thank you enough, Niki."

"Sure, uh, don't mention it." The engine turned over, and I died a little with each turn of the tires. My only consolation is that Eli would probably still be there. There's no way Charley would leave Rosie at the barbecue alone. I sent a little prayer up to the Goddess that he, being the future alpha of his pack, would know something, anything about getting out of an arranged mating.

ROSIE

Hunter, Charley and I were in the kitchen rooting through Nik's kitchen for more snacks. Football players were bottomless pits, and I wouldn't let them eat all the meat before Nik and his firefighter buddies came back. I caught them exchanging glances for what feels like the bajillionth time that day. "Really, really? We're back to knowing looks?"

"Settle down." Charley popped up off her stool and steered me over to the third stool at the kitchen island. "Now sit."

"And stay this time. Don't make me duct tape you in place. I love you, but it's not that kind of love, " Hunter threw her arm around my shoulders.

"Very funny. I'm beginning to question the love you two profess for me. Secrets don't make friends."

Charley opened her mouth like she was going to say something and Hunter slapped her hand over it. "No, Charley. You know it's not our story to tell. Nik would freak out if you try to talk for him."

"Oh my god, you are both totally impossible. You know that, don't you?" I scooted off the stool before either could stop me and headed over to the refrigerator. "If you refuse to divulge whatever this stupid secret is, then I'm making you both help me with another batch of brownies."

"I think three pans of them is more than even the football team can consume in one day." Charley pushed the eggs I'd set on the counter back towards me. "I seriously can't take another round of stress-baking, Rosie. Just sit your ass down and drink margaritas with us, like a normal human woman."

"If you love me like you said you do, you will start cracking those eggs." I pushed them right back.

"He's gonna be fine, Rosie. I promise." Hunter slipped the measuring spoons out of my hand.

"You're not going to let me bake, are you?" My answer was a group hug that made me feel equal parts shy and loved.

"Not a single batch. But I will happily make you a margarita while you tell us what's going on in your head," Charley answered.

I was worried about him being off at a fire, sure, but we all knew that's not why I was a fidgety mess right now. "Everything just happened so fast. I can hardly believe he read my book, that he loves me, that we slept together. And that I am finally able to tell him that I—"

The door flew open with a bang, and Nik's crew of fellow firefighters spilled into the crowded living room, filling the house full of male energy, high-fives, and celebratory whoops. My shoulders dropped about a foot as all the stress poured out of me in a huge, whooshing sigh.

They were back. Everything was okay.

Everyone in the backyard filed into the kitchen, and the small house filled with talk of my beloved Moon Bean, which was damaged, but going to be fine. I cringed when I heard them talk about hearing the fire chief's arson theory. Who would want to burn a bookstore? Nazis were all I could come up with.

Kirill sauntered in last and closed the door behind him.

I rushed forward, "Wait. Kirill, where's Nik?"

"Dude, he's fine. He's in another car, be here in a minute. Chill."

A moment later, the door opened half-way, and I knew it was Nik. I could feel him. My face split in two, I smiled so wide. It was all I could do to stop myself from running to him, jumping up to wrap myself around him, and slather his face with kisses. All of that was definitely happening when everyone went home.

Kirill turned and bellowed out, "Nik, my man. Dire Wolves forever, you fucking dick-swinging, chick-saving hero. Everybody give it up for Nik and Erika."

Hanging off of Nik's arm was a woman I didn't want to recognize, but did.

My mouth gaped open like I was trying to catch a herring like a trained seal at the zoo. The girl from the launch party who didn't want an inscription in her book, just my name. The girl who looked at me like you would look at dog poo stuck to your shoe. The hot girl with the tiny waist and big boobs, who looked like some Siberian ice princess lingerie model. That Erika?

"What is that bitch doing with her manicured talons digging into Nik?" Charley took the words right out of my mouth.

I want to shout at her, tell her to stop, but nothing comes out.

Nik floated his hands up then slowly dropped them, quieting everyone down, "Look, I didn't do anything today that any of these guys didn't do too."

He gestured around to his friends, and everyone claps. Everyone except for me, because my arms were frozen, along with my lungs, and my heart.

"I'm no hero, seriously. But if I ever hear who torched the Moon Bean, I will rip them to fucking shreds." His words brought another round of whoops and calls for retribution. I know it's not right, but it warmed my heart that everyone wants to defend Selena and the Moon Bean. It sort of thawed me out, and I stepped closer to Nik.

My emotions were running through me like an iceberg on speed, and I was shaky and off balance. All I knew was that I needed to talk to Nik, touch him, hold him. I pushed my way through the crowd, but I stopped cold when Erika start to talk.

"It is not true at all, he is one hundred percent a hero today. I was so scared, afraid for my life. Then Nik appears through the smoke and fire. He picked me up and carried me to safety. This man saved my life today. He is my hero."

I stood there watching dumbly as Erika stood up on her tiptoes, lifted one dainty foot up behind her, and wrapped her arms around Nik's neck. She pulled him down and planted a kiss right on his lips, a kiss that she drew out until I had to take a breath for them. The crowd erupted in back-slapping, cat-calling applause.

Oh no she did not. "Excuse me, pardon me, let me through." I rudely shouldered my way toward Nik. I tried pushing between two big Dire Wolf linesman, and got stuck. "Hey guys, you're squishing me."

"Rosie sandwich," one of the players joked and then handed me through and right into Erika.

She did that duck thing with her lips that women do when applying lipstick. I hated every inch of her. I tilted my head and gave her a wide, toothy smile. "Hiyeee. So glad Nik was able to save you from the fire. Can I get through, please? Thanks so much."

I moved, then Erika moved. I shifted to the side, and she shifted in front of me. Then she spun around and gave me her back. Oh, this hag was going down. I gave her a fierce poke to the shoulder, "Get out of my way. I need a minute with Nik. My boyfriend, Nik. Without you hanging all over him."

Erika spun slowly on one of her pointy-toed, high-heeled boots. She narrowed her eyes, and I would've sworn they glowed red. She grabbed my shoulder and pushed me back through the crowd, right back to where I'd started. No one was paying any attention to us, they were all so rapt by Nik retelling the story. "Oh, you're still here. How cute that you are concerned about Nik. But he is mine. We are engaged."

"You... you're what?" I stammered like an idiot. "He would never be with someone like you."

"Someone like me? Someone who gets what she wants?" Erika unfolded her arms and sniffed me, like I literally smelled. "How little you know him. We are the same, Nik and me. So be a good girl and run along. Go write another book. Who knows? Maybe you will get lucky, and someone else will pity fuck you. Just like Nik did. Go."

How did she— Her words and the fact that she knew Nik and were together last night, wasn't the real problem here. She growled, and opened her mouth in a feral-looking snarl. It wasn't just the sneer of a vicious, mean-girl. She had an honest to god mouth full of fangs, like I was stuck in one of Charley's horror films.

Erika's face transformed, her mouth stretched, elongated, and when she snapped out, "Run," it was through a fur covered snout. She raised her hands as if to push me or maybe grab me. But instead of her shiny gel manicure, her nails were sharp claws.

All the blood drained from my extremities and I almost threw up on her.

The Erika monster laughed, then stopped abruptly. She was just a bitch-faced mean girl once more. Until she flashed those awful fangs at me, a string of spit connecting one terrible tooth top tooth to the bottom. So I did what she told me. I ran.

"Rosie?" It was Nik. Nik who I had loved forever. Who I thought loved me back, until two minutes ago. His footsteps pounded in my ears, and my lungs were on fire. I burst out into the now empty backyard before he caught up to me.

"Rosie, stop. Please stop." He spun me around, catching me in his arms, pulled me against him, and kissed my head.

"Rosie... " he kissed in front of my ear.

"Rose... " he kissed down my neck.

"Roses... " he kissed that spot that shot heat through my body, and most desperately between my legs.

I closed my eyes and imagined being naked in his arms, saw his eyes staring into mine. "No. No. Don't ever call me that again."

"Rosie, please. I...I love you."

"You can't do that. Not now. I'm way to freaked out for you to try to make everything better by saying those words. I need you to be one hundred percent honest with me, because I deserve the truth."

He slowly took a deep breath. "Yes you do. You totally do."

"So what is going on? Are you engaged to that awful girl? Is she even a girl? Her face... she threatened me... came at me with claws and fangs."

Nik hung his head. He didn't even need to tell me, not really. It was all true. He was marrying a monster. What did that make me?

He rubbed his hand over the back of his neck. "Rosie... it's complicated."

"Well freaking un-complicate it for me."

"I wanted to tell you. I was going to last night. Not about Erika, but well, this is gonna sound so crazy, but just listen. Erika is a shifter, a wolftress. She's from a powerful pack, and our parents got together and decided we should align our packs... through mating... which is basically marriage."

Erika was a wolf shifter, a werewolf. Was he making fun of me? No. This was no joke. Did that mean...? I took a step back, and a rush of every hair on my skin rose and fell.

"You're one too, aren't you? A wolf shifter?" This couldn't be real. Werewolf boyfriends were only in books. Paranormal romance novels. Or horror stories.

He slowly nodded his head, but his eyes were locked on mine. He didn't move, and I didn't either. "Show me."

"Rosie, I can't. We aren't even supposed to tell humans, much less let you see us shift."

"I have known you for five years. We've done things together that I would never even consider doing with anyone else. I think if I want to see you as a freaking werewolf, you should show me. Right now."

Nik didn't say a word, but a flurry of emotions I didn't, couldn't understand, flashed in his eyes. He pulled his shirt over his head. He undressed with evident frustration, kicking off his shoes and getting stuck as he stripped off his pants.

Never would I have thought naked Nik would make me miserable. I had to remind myself that I did nothing to create the misery. It was all Nik. And Erika, horrid awful Erika.

He stood naked. And glorious, because he was Nik. He held out a hand, a slow, tentative invitation to join him, and every tiny fiber of my heart screamed yes... but I shook my head no.

He exhaled and threw a look over his shoulder at the house. Then he turned back to me, seemingly satisfied that no one was watching, and closed his eyes. He rolled his head and pulled his shoulders back. My eyes traced over those ridiculously defined shoulders, the etched ripped abs, and of course, his thick cock.

Then it happened.

His skin split and fur pushed up, and like with Erika, Nik's mouth stretched and his even teeth grew into pointed, flesh-tearing fangs. His eyes, so full of sorrow, flashed and he dropped to all fours. Bones cracked, warping, reforming, and I gagged thinking of the pain he must be going through. But before I could blink, the wolf stood before me.

He was terrifyingly huge, wild and predatory.

I knew full well I should be scared. But he was marvelous. Better even than the werewolf in my book.

He took a silent step towards me, and stopped. His humongous wolf head cocked to the side. I nodded, and he padded to me, pushed his snout into my hair.

"Nik, are you really in there somewhere?"

He circled me, brushing along my backside. His fur felt glorious against my skin, soft and warm. He rested his huge head on my shoulder and I clung to him and filled his fur with tears.

His voice popped into my head. *Don't cry. I love you so much, Roses. You are everything.*

He shifted again into the man I loved, held me, stroked my hair, rocked me until there were no tears left.

I clung for a few moments more and then stepped out of his arms, "This is a lot. I need some time to process."

If I didn't put some actual space between us, I would give in. He'd lied, by omission, both about Erika, and about who he truly was.

The back door slid open and I heard Erika's voice. "Nik? Come back inside, this party is so boring without you."

Someday I would write her into a book, and give her wolf pox. By then, they would be married, or mated, or whatever.

"Rose." Nik grabbed for my hand, and I pulled back. I should have known better than to think he could or would ever be with me. Nik was a fire-fighting, football hero, wolf, god. And I was the girl who lived her life by watching or writing love stories for other people.

I turned and walked away because I had to. I needed some unconditional love and a warm cup of tea to chase away my cold reality. I pulled my phone out and ordered up an Uber to Grandma Roman's. She made everything better, always had and always would.

A half hour later, my face screwed up as I walked through the cozy living room to my nan's kitchen. I heard voices. Ugh. I wanted Grandma Roman all to myself.

"You have to find out who set that fire and why," nan said.

"First I have take care of that mess they made of my beautiful books. Then I will make them pay."

Selena... what was she doing here? My sweet Grandma Roman was friends with her? Selena who was my biggest supporter but also sort of scared the poop out of me? I peeked my head around the corner, "Hey, do you have another cup of tea in that pot for your favorite granddaughter?"

Grandma Roman popped up out of her chair and wrapped me up in the warmest hug. I sagged in her arms, and then the tears just started flowing non-stop.

"Oh my sweet girl, come and sit and tell me what's wrong." She held me at arms length and inspected me. "Who or what has made you so sad?"

She fussed over me and slid a plate of lemon cake over. "Selena said your book is selling like crazy. This should be a time for celebration, not tears."

Grandma love is strong stuff, and just what I needed.

"If I may, I believe this is about a very handsome Dire Wolf firefighter by the name of Nik, is it not?"

I looked across the table at Selena. Her eyes sparkled over her tea cup, or more like glowed. Like Nik's. "You're one of them?"

Selena took a sip of her tea and nodded. "A wolf shifter, yes."

Grandma Roman's eyebrows raised, and she gave Selena the side-eye, but didn't freak out or laugh or anything.

"Don't look at me like that, Dotty. It is time for Rosie to hear it all. She has to choose whether she wants to grow into an interesting woman, or stay a girl who only writes things about other, pretend interesting women."

Nan went over to the cupboard and came back to the table with a bottle of whiskey. She poured a healthy slug into each of our cups. "Here's to interesting women."

NIK

My feet dug into the turf, and I was ready to run all-out. My knees bent, and I pushed off the ground with every muscle fiber in my legs. The leather made a satisfying slapping sound as the ball snapped into my hands. Another good catch. But then my body shut down, and I let go.

Not of the ball. I'm not an idiot. One foot landed and then the second. And I took one step back before stopping, then I just closed my eyes. Kirill did exactly what I wanted him to do. He hit me hard, knocked me off my feet and plowed me into the field.

Fuck, it hurt. My ribs screamed in protest, because this was the third time I just stood still and took the hit. I deserved the pain. Every single bit of it.

The coach blew his whistle so hard and long I was afraid his head might explode from the pressure, "What the holy hell are you doing out there? Do you think you're playing freeze tag, because the last time I checked, this was football.

You catch the ball and you run—catch and run, catch and run. Someone go help Nik screw his head on right."

I ran to the bench with the rest of the offensive line. I grabbed my water bottle and sucked on it just to avoid talking to anyone. Kirill shoulder checked me from behind, making me spew water all over the bench.

"Looking good out there, fuckwit. At least, you're making me look good out there. Keep it up. But seriously, dude, you gotta reserve a little energy for the field. Not that I can blame you. That Erika is beyond bang-able. So much more my speed than your last hookup."

Before I could stop myself, my wolf reared up and I lunged, fangs and all. I wanted to plant my fist into Kirill's stupid fucking mouth and tear out his shit-talking tongue. But Eli grabbed one arm, and Ty had the other.

"Down boy. Take a deep breath," Eli said. "If you knock him out, he might lose one of his two remaining brain cells, and we need him for game this weekend."

Kirill shrugged off Eli's insult. "Jesus, Nik. I'm just giving you shit, because you suck so bad today. Trying to snap you out of your head and into practice."

"What the fuck is going on? Talk." Ty finally let go of my arm, but followed up with a less than friendly shove. He meant more than just the game today. The lot of them wanted to know what was up with Erika and Rosie.

I hadn't told anyone that Rosie ran away from me. They all just thought she... well, I don't know what they thought because I didn't even tell anyone she left the party. But of course Charley and Hunter had noticed. I'm sure they gave Eli and Ty an earful.

If it were any other day, any other circumstance, I would

have just told them all to fuck off and I'd figure it out on my own. Dudes didn't talk about feelings. Although, we'd sure gotten an earful of them when Ty hooked up with Hunter. And come to think of it, Eli was all mushy gushy about Charley all the damn time. Maybe we did talk about our emotions with each other.

Huh.

Since I was frustrated and tired, not to mention completely destroyed by guilt, I wasn't thinking straight and could seriously use their help. Well, maybe not Kirill's, but he just sort of came with the package.

I plopped down on the bench and just let it all out. "On one hand, there's Rosie. She's lived deep in my heart, for years and being with her is everything."

She made me feel complete. Made my heart beat stronger.

"On the other hand, are my parents, my pack. Mating with Erika would create a powerful alliance between Grimm and Serenity."

I felt trapped. Stuck between expectation and desire.

"Why didn't you just say Rosie was your fated mate, you dumbass? " Kirill smacked me in the head. "I'll take Erika off your hands."

Kirill's jackassery, rubbed me the wrong way mostly because he was irritatingly right. Rosie absolutely was my fate mate.

I answered like a complete dickhead, "Yeah, well I don't even know if fated mates are even real. My parents had an arranged mating, and they have a great relationship. Wolves have clearly been doing just fine just mating and leaving fate out of it for freaking centuries."

"Nah. You don't believe that." Kirill glared at me like he was the one being offended, "Try again, asshole."

Eli nodded, although looking a little surprised that Kirill was so astute. "What he said."

"Listen, I appreciate what you're trying to do. But right now, I need to put my head down, wolf up and do what's expected of me. I have a duty to my parents and the Grimm pack." Even if that responsibility felt like hot rocks in my stomach and chest.

"Your duty?" Kirill threw his hands up in the air. "That's the stupidest thing to ever come out of your mouth. Mating isn't about duty. Especially when you have obviously found your one, true mate. Do you know what most wolves would give to have that. Fuck you, Nik."

We all sat there silent for a solid minute. Kirill wanted to find his own fated mate? What kind of an alternate universe was I in right now?

Eli patted the huffing, hulking-out Kirill on the back and then stared down at me. "I used to be just like you, Nik. I felt all the pressure in the world bearing down on my shoulders to be the perfect future pack leader. I thought I had to do what everyone expected me to do too, but it was all in my head."

Eli was the god-damned golden boy. I never would have thought he felt any kind of pressure.

"When fate brought me to Charley, I held on tight, because life without her would be like living in a world without color or flavor. Everything is better with her, literally everything in my life. My parents get that."

"I totally agree, man." Ty stepped up and clapped a big hand on my shoulder. "I'm an alpha now, with my own fated mate. I put everything on the line for her, even when I didn't think I deserved her. Hunter doesn't just make everything better. She makes me better."

They were right. But Eli was destined to lead his pack, and now Ty was starting his own. I wasn't an alpha and that mean trying to the make the best decision for everyone.

"Nik, if you don't just pull your head right out of your stupid fucking butt and chose your fated mate over some wolf pack socialite, then you're a total dumbass. That's it." Kirill actually kicked dirt at me, like we were five.

"You're right." I threw my hands up, "I know you're right. But to break off this engagement to Erika, I'm going to have to tell my parents that I am going to throw away an opportunity that they worked hard to put together."

They'll understand, man." Eli folded his arms and nodded all sage-like.

"Maybe, but then I'm going to have to go see Galyna. As in Galyna Troika, as in the alpha of Grimm pack who literally tore the head off another wolf to claim the pack. And then we'll have to go to Nikolai Troika. The fucking Wolf Tzar, because he's her pack alpha. You think either of them are going to be falling-down happy to hear that I want to sever a highly desirable alliance between Grimm and Serenity Bay?"

Eli and Ty both winced. At least I was getting some sympathy instead of a load of shit.

"I don't envy you. At all. But Niko Troika is a good Tzar, and he fought for his own fated mate. He'll want you to as well." Ty held out a hand, and when I took it, pulled me in for a half-hug-half-back pat.

"Go, get it done, numbnuts. Don't fuck up your one

chance at happiness." Kirill shoved me toward the locker room, and I let him.

Because once again, he was fucking right. Rosie was my chance at real happiness. Nothing else mattered, not even duty to my pack or my parents.

I didn't even change. I ran to my car and headed straight for Rogue. I spent the entire ride rehearsing my talking points in my head. These were words I didn't want to fumble. By the time I opened the door to my parent's house, I was a ball of stress all over again.

"Mom? Dad? I'm home."

My dad stuck his head out of his den. He took one sniff of me and his spine stiffened like he had been struck by lighting. "Nik. What are you doing here? We're not supposed to see you until this weekend, with the Crescents."

Uh-oh. This wasn't starting off great.

"Oh, honey. What a lovely surprise." My mom walked into the hallway from the kitchen, wiping her hands on a towel. She was probably making something big and juicy for dinner.

"Yeah, uh... well, hi. I'm sorry I interrupted your evening. But I need to talk with you." I shuffled my feet and only looked at my mom. I could already smell the irritation pouring off my dad.

See? I knew they weren't going to be happy.

"Come on into the kitchen. Dinner's almost ready and there's plenty for you too." My mom waved the two of us in and grabbed another place setting for me. We sat down, and before I could launch into the speech I prepared, my mother peered closely at me, then tilted her head. "Nikita, you don't have to marry her."

My jaw dropped. What the? How did she do that?

She grabbed my dad's hand, and he scowled but squeezed hers back. They'd clearly already been talking about me and my future with Erika. Or rather my non-future with her. Dad didn't look totally on board, but when my mom got going, there was no stopping her.

He stabbed a piece of the meat from the platter, and pointed at me with it. "No son, you don't. I heard your trepidation on the phone. I'm not stupid. Why didn't you say something then?"

I sat there just blinking at my parents for a second trying to keep up with these people who looked like my parents but reacted like aliens.

"Really, Nikita, you've never had a girlfriend, never talked about anyone. We waited forever to see if something would come of you and Rosie, but we finally just gave up on it. When Erika's parents approached us, we thought we were helping."

"Wait, wait." I held up both of my hands and closed my eyes, "Erika's parent's approached you about the match?"

"Yes. They're a strange lot, insist on calling themselves Crescents instead of Serenity." My dad finally put his meat on his plate and then shoved a piece in his mouth.

My mom continued for him. "But they're daughter seemed pretty, always smiling in the pictures they showed us of her. They're very anxious for her to be mated. If you two aren't right for each other, or if you've maybe met someone else, well, we just want you to be happy."

"I can't mate with Erika. I don't love her. I love Rosie."

My mom pumped her fist in the air, like she was

watching me score a touchdown. "Yes, I knew it. I am so happy to hear you say that. Does she feel the same?"

"I don't know." Goddess, I'd fucked everything up. "I though she did. We sort of connected, okay we really connected."

My dad scowled. "You should have told us you and Rosie had finally gotten around to getting in each other's pants. Have you marked her and claimed her too?"

"Dad!"

"Well, We would never have pushed this arranged mating on you, but it was such a good match. It would have been a powerful alliance."

My mom gave my dad a pinch, and he backtracked, "I just wanted you to quit fucking around if Rose didn't have the same feelings for you as you've had for her since the beginning."

Did everyone but me know the two of us had been in love for all these years? "You aren't upset that she's human?"

My dad made a face, but my mother waved a hand around, "That isn't even a consideration. All that matters is that you have found your one, true love. Your fated mate. I am so happy I can't stand it."

"But I don't see how I can back out of this arranged mating without creating some serious bad blood between our packs. Galyna is going to want to skin me alive."

My father sat up straight. "We'll go to Max and Galyna's and sit down with them tonight. The sooner this is sorted out, the better."

"We?"

"Yes. Your mother and I set this in motion. You will have

to speak your heart to Galyna, alone. But we stand with you, Nik, always."

Secretly their open support made me feel all warm inside. We went straight over and Galyna welcomed us graciously, but being a shrewd wolftress, she clearly sniffed out what was about to go down.

I took a deep breath. "I'm sorry to intrude on your evening, but I would appreciate speaking with you."

I followed her down a long hall, and she led me into a set of massive double-doors. We sat, her on one side of a big desk with pictures of their kids decorating the surface.

Galyna steepled her hands and leaned forward, elbow on the desk, solely focused on me. "What brings you to my home, Nik?"

"Ma'am, I have to talk with you about the arrangements my parents made on my behalf to mate with Erika, uh, Crescent."

Galyna raised on eyebrow in a way that let me know she'd caught the pass I'd thrown when I called Erika a Crescent versus a Serenity. "Then let's talk."

Here goes. "There's nothing between us, and it seems like the mating of a wolf to his mate should be everything. I prepared a speech in my head, and it was so much better than this... But what is comes down to is that I want to break off the arranged mating."

She was silent for what felt like forever.

"If it's alright with you, young man, I'd like my mate to join us."

Shit. Okay. I nodded and Galyna called Max in. Please, please, please. If anyone should understand wanting to be with a fated mate, it should be these two, right?

Galyna filled Max in quickly and he sat on the edge of the desk, then deferred to his mate. She tipped her head. They'd definitely done some communicating with their own wolfspeak in their heads in between.

Galyna started, "Breaking an engagement is a serious step. Erika and members of her pack might harbor some deep resentment if you do this. Can you tell us why you want to break it off?"

"I don't mean to cause so many problems, ma'am. It's just that I... well, I believe that I have found my true fated mate." If anyone should understand, it would be these two. But they weren't relenting.

Max and Galyna shared a look, and then he spoke up for the first time. "Does this wolftress have a name? Does she belong to any pack we know?"

I swallowed hard and looked between the two of them. "She's human."

Just like Galyna had been. Max showed zero surprise. No emotion whatsoever. No one was reacting the way I anticipated. "Does this human have a name?"

"Rosie. Rosemary March. She's Mrs. Roman's granddaughter."

Galyna smiled and some of the worry melted away. "And are you absolutely certain that Rosie is your fated mate?"

"When I am with her, everything feels right. It feels like my heart is beating outside of my body, and there isn't room in my brain for anyone except Rosie. We're meant to be together."

Galyna and Max looked at each other and my alpha shook her head. Shit.

Did I blow it? Fuck.

Fuck. Fuck.

Blood rushing through my ears whoosh, whoosh, whooshed and I thought for a minute I was going to black out.

But then Galyna stood and crossed over to me. "Relax kiddo. Sorry for the third degree, but I'm afraid you and your parents have gotten caught up in some pack politics and I had to be sure of where you stood. Of course you and Rosie should be together. We'll take care of the, uh, Crescents."

Muffled laughter and the sound of glass clinking echoed at opposite end of the hall. "Come on, Nik. They're waiting for us."

As if some wizard, god, or Goddess had snapped their fingers, the entire world became sharp, I could see, hear, and feel again. My heart beat a fast, steady rhythm in my chest and... oops, my cock went rock fucking hard.

Rosie was going to be mine. Shit. After I won her back. Right now she still hated me. But I would do it. I would woo her and wine and dine her, and show her exactly how much I loved her. I followed after Max and Galyna back to their kitchen, anxious to say our goodbyes and get back to campus.

I stopped in the doorway and took in the scene. Nikolai Troika, the fucking Wolf Tzar sat at the head of the table nearest me, with his mate Zara by his side. She gave me a bright smile and raised her wine glass to me. There was my mom and dad, who also had glasses of wine in their hands, and Selena, who was unexpectedly sitting at the other end of the table.

And then my mouth fell to the floor.

Because next to Selena was Rosie. My Rosie.

Rosie stood, her sweet lips curving up in a soft smile. I practically vaulted over the table to get to her. I had her in my arms and pressed a kiss to those sweet lips that was far too deep and far too long for present company. She kissed me back, and my wolf rippled through me with a suppressed howl.

My senses filled up with Rosie—the taste of her, the smell of her, the feel of her luscious curves. Nothing else existed, no one else mattered. Just Rosie.

Selena turned to Niko and said, "You see, it is just as I told you it would be. These two grow so brightly together that they outshine the sun. How do you not need sunglasses to look at them?"

ROSIE

"You're here." Nik stared into my eyes like I was the moon and the stars and the entire solar system. A gaze that threatened to ignite a four alarm fire in my lady bits if he didn't stop.

"Of course she is here, Nik. I thought it was best to have him around for the fall out regardless of which way you stood. Niko can get the arrangement part taken care of right here, right now." Galyna Troika, our local librarian, who it turned out was a human who mated a wolf and took over a whole pack, patted my shoulder.

Nik was back to staring at me, his intensity and naked want made my cheeks so hot that I thought the blush would be permanent. Not to mention that my panties were ridiculously wet. Everyone at the table was a wolf shifter. Could they tell? They could probably all smell me.

God how embarrassing.

Nikolai, the Tzar or King or whatever of all the wolves, broke me out of that spiral when spoke aloud, "It is official.

The arrangement is broken. I will speak with Erika's parents tomorrow. I think perhaps we have several items to discuss."

A smile split Nik's handsome face in two, and his eyes glowed like mad at me. I should've felt like an outsider, because something decidedly wolfy just went down. But I didn't feel left out, because I wasn't. Besides being at Gran's, this place I slipped a hand around Nik's neck and pulled him in for a kiss, sweet and tender.

"Come on. I have a place I'd like to show you." Nik pulled me from the house and we walked over to the Reserve, which of course I'd been to a hundred times before, but never after dark. That was against the law, and also creepy. No one went to the Reserve at night. But he led me down a path I hadn't even known existed.

"The Reserve is really special to the pack. This is where we can roam free in our wolf forms."

It was beautiful. The moon was waning but still full enough to light our path. When I looked up at him, he was lit up like a glowing lightning bug. Made my insides all squidgy. "So this place you're taking me is a wolf-shifters only place? You won't get in trouble for showing me?"

He laughed lightly and kissed the top of my head. "It is *the* wolf place. Just for us. No other shifters come here, and folklore keeps most humans from venturing very far beyond the picnic areas and walking paths. And no, I won't get in trouble. You're part of the family now."

"No other shifters? As in there are shifters who aren't wolves?" It squeaked out of me, and I was embarrassed by my reaction. Maybe I came from a long line of mouse shifters and just didn't know it yet.

"Yeah. Dragons, bears, you know."

I didn't, but I nodded as if it was all normal and not super duper paranormal.

"You aren't freaked out by all of this, Rosie? I should've told you."

I squeezed his hand tight. "It's a lot, but it isn't too much. I promise. I'm weirdly totally okay with most of this."

Nik shook his head. "Seriously? Isn't this when you round up the villagers and chase us all out of town with pitchforks?"

That made me laugh, in a comfortable Rosie and Nik sort of way. I looped my arm through his. "You know, I think I sort of knew all along. Going to high school in Rogue, well, there has always been kind of weird stuff going on. It escalated when I started at Bay State U. I mean, there is always strangeness going on around campus."

Nik stiffened. "Like what?"

"Like college football players who make plays the pros can't, and move faster than they should. Stupid fights at parties where guys are legitimately snarling at each other. Don't get me started on the weird motorcycle gang that rolled into town last month. They were totally freaky, feral looking. But then Selena sent me across campus before anything exciting happened. Then no one would tell me what happened, but poof, no more strung out leather wearing thugs to be found in town."

Nik stared at me with wide eyes. "You don't miss a thing. Those guys were bad news. It was Ty's dad. He was a lone wolf with a chip on his shoulder."

"Poor Ty. That must be rough."

"I was seriously worried about you. You were in real danger that day and I hated that I couldn't say a thing." He growled, and I'm not even sure he knew he was doing it. "I patrolled outside your house for weeks after all that went down, to make sure that they didn't come back, and that you were safe."

"I had no idea." I thought back. "Well... that's not entirely true. I maybe thought I saw a gigantic wolf... but I wrote it off to an over-active imagination, because I was in the middle of writing a werewolf romance book."

"Really? I thought I was being so stealthy and sly." Nik looked genuinely disappointed that I had caught him out.

I giggled at him. So freaking cute. "You definitely were. The stealthiest."

"And the slyest?"

"For sure."

Just then, we stepped into a hidden clearing, lit up by the moonlight. The trees formed a circle around the clearing and the moon shone overhead illuminating the leaves and trees and flowers as if this were a fantastical painting. "Wow, this is beautiful."

"It's our sacred circle," he pressed my hands together and warmed them between his. "It's where we hold the Troika and Grimm pack mating rituals."

"Like a fated-mate wedding? That's so magical." I immediately envisioned myself walking down an aisle in a flowing, flouncy sort of gauzy dress complete with boho flower crown. Nik would be waiting for me at the end, in a linen shirt, and—

"Uh, it's not exactly like a wedding... it's more like the wedding night."

Somehow I didn't think he meant a night wedding. "What does that mean, exactly?"

"Well, shifters like us don't have fancy weddings, because we are more, uh, nature-oriented. So, our rituals are more around acts of nature. The sort of acts that only a couple engages in." He looked up at the moon and back down at me, and his breathing had sped up and his eyes had gone glowy and dark. "Like when I say mating rituals, Rosie, I mean literally mating under the full moon with the pack bearing witness."

"Witness as in watching? As in having sex in front of the whole pack?" Were wolf shifters kinksters?

"Yeah. That's pretty much it. Except the full moon also gets all the other fated mates in the mood for their own mating rituals, so it isn't like they very many are stand there just staring. There are lots of couples, umm, mating."

Oh. My. God. I hadn't even wanted Nik to see me when we had sex, and now I was supposed to expose every bit of me to a bunch of strangers in some kind of wolf shifter orgy? I squeezed my eyes shut and did some deep breathing. "In through the nose, out through the mouth."

"Rose?"

I needed a sec to get my careening insecurities under control. That was the sort of negative thinking that kept me from revealing my love for Nik in the first place, kept me alone and lonely. The sort of thoughts that would keep me from ever having my own happily ever after.

"Look. I have a way to go toward learning to accept that my body isn't bad, just because the world around me tells me it is. You're the first person who has ever said that I was anything but... well, fat, ugly, unlovable."

"I get it, Roses. I really do. You're the first person who told me that I wasn't dumb, the first person to believe that I could actually graduate from high school and get into college. Doesn't mean I don't still get frustrated that my brain doesn't work the same way other people's brains do. I still feel stupid sometimes."

"But you're a good student. You're going to graduate from Bay State with two degrees. Clearly you are smarter than the average bear, uh, wolf."

"And you're the most beautiful woman I've ever known."

Yeah, but would he say that when I was old and fat? Then boom, it hit me so hard it made my heart do a back flip. He would, because he loved me... and deep in my heart, I knew the opinion of everyone else in the entire world didn't matter. Only Nik's. I'd like to say that my own opinion was the only one that mattered, but my thoughts were... broken, by society, by mean people on the internet, by media, by my own internalized fatphobia.

But when I was with Nik, I didn't feel broken. Even when we were pretending we were just friends, he never made me feel like I was anything but wonderful, anything but his best friend. He made me feel like I belonged. And I wanted to belong to him forever.

I was still working on the liking myself part, but this last week went a long way to me seeing that I'd been looking at life through a lens of fear and doubt and negative self-talk. I made a mental note to thank Selena for helping me take those anti-rose colored glasses off.

"I'm going to choose to believe you instead of the stupid people in the world. If you think I'm beautiful, then I am beautiful."

His eyes flicked from mine, down to my lips and back up. "Oh, I definitely think so."

"Okay, then that's settled. What do we do now? I'm not sure ready to have sex in front all of your pack. Is there like, a couple of steps that we could do before?"

"Yeah, it's something you only do with your mate. It's called marking, and it is the most powerfully sexy thing I can think of ever doing with you. I literally had to bite my tongue not to mark you the other night when we were together."

"Powerfully sexy sounds really good." I bit down on my lip to keep from laughing at my bold self.

Nik leaned in and kissed me, softly at first, but in seconds heat was blooming so full and fast. He lifted his head back just enough for me to be able to see his eyes. They were glowing the brightest blue. He slid his hands down over the small of my back, over my butt, to my thighs. And then he lifted me up.

"Ack, Nik, no." I called out, completely freaked out that he was even trying to pick me up. "I'll break you."

"Shut up, Rose, and wrap your legs around me." He started with the kissing again, tasting me, pressing his tongue against mine. No arguing if you can't talk. I pulled my feet up and wrapped them around his waist.

He walked us over to the center of the sacred circle without missing a step like I was made of rainbows and bird song, and pushed my back against the tree. God, I'd read about this in romance novels and never ever imagined I'd get to live anything this hot in my life.

I looked up at him, my arms still wrapped tight about his neck. And then I looked again. "Nik. Nik, look. You're glowing. We're glowing."

I reached toward the moon and danced my hand through

the air. My skin was luminous and beautiful. It was like we were phosphorescent.

His eyes went all soft and sexy, making me gooey and warm in so many ways, "I've pictured you like this, so many times. Fuck, you're gorgeous."

Nik dropped a slow volley of kisses from the corner of my lip to the spot just below my jawline, making my breath hitch. He took his time, kissing and nipping at my neck until there was nothing else in the world except for Nik's mouth on my body. He pressed his lips against my throat, and scraped his teeth across that spot that made me moan, "Right there, Rosemary. Right there. I will sink my teeth into you and mark you as mine. A mark that will last forever, tell everyone that you are off limits, that I claim you, forever, Rose. Forever."

"Yes, Nik do it. I want it. I want you to mark me, forever. Right now." Good thing I told him what I wanted then, because he ran his tongue over that spot, deliberately, taking such sweet, sweet time, I lost all ability to speak, to think, to move.

Nik rumbled a low, sexy growl, and sunk his teeth into the tender spot on my neck. I went from pleasantly floaty and wet to super hot tsunami. My pussy sent a shock wave through my body that made me cry out in pleasure and writhe against Nik like he was my personal stripper pole. He shifted against me, and I shamelessly rubbed my center over and over him, riding the best orgasm of my life out as Nik lapped at my neck like melted ice cream.

He chuckled all self-satisfied against my neck. "This helps your mark heal faster. I didn't know marking would drive my gorgeous, sexy fated-mate into a screaming orgasm."

"Nik. Nik. Nik." I threaded my fingers through his hair and tugged just a little to get his attention. His eyes met mine and it felt like home. "Make love to me, Nik."

"Anything you want, Roses, anything at all."

Warm fingers traced up my thigh, as I tugged at Nik's shirt. Just as his clever fingers found the edge of my panties, the sound of a branch snapping made Nik go motionless. He kissed my deliciously throbbing bite mark once more, then gently disentangled our bodies, and straightened my clothes with an excessively pleased, proud smile lighting up his face.

"It's Niko. He called us back to the house."

"I heard a twig break. How do you know who it is? I didn't hear a word."

"The twig was just to get our attention, he used wolf speak, you know like when I talked to you in wolf form?"

Alphas can use it to talk to their packs, and fated mates to each other.

As I watched Nik, I realized that his mouth wasn't moving. Nevertheless, I heard his voice, like a bell... in my brain. "Oh my god, I thought I imagined you talking in my head earlier. Like a stress induced hallucination. That is the coolest thing ever."

I thought those three little words meant only for him and watched his eyes to see if he caught my thoughts.

He did and it took us a few more minutes to extricate ourselves from each other and head back to the house. We pushed in through the back door to the Troika's and I blindly followed Nik back to the crowded-cozy kitchen table while I daydreamed about exactly what the two of us were going to do all night long.

The Wolf Tzar gave us a nod. "My apologies for interrupting your, uh discussion."

Nik took my hand in his and brought it to his lips. "I've marked my mate. I know that I am supposed to put pack before self, but Erika and her parents can go fu— uh, away. Rosie is mine."

"I applaud your conviction, Nikita. Your instincts about Erika were spot on. While you were walking through the Reserve, the fire chief called for Selena. Erika has been arrested."

"Arrested?" Nik and I both said at the same time.

"She set the fire on purpose." Selena spat the words out. "Her parents too are being detained by the Grimm county sheriff as we speak. Turns out they're one bloods who've been hiding under the Serenity Bay banner. Pieces of trash."

I leaned over to Nik and whispered, "What's a one-blood?"

"I'll explain later, but it's bad."

Selena's eyes glowed and her nails went all wolfy. She was pissed and nobody wanted to get on Selena Troika's bad side. "Apparently Erika read Rosemary's book, told her parents about it, and they all devised a plan to start a fire at the Moon Bean to draw you away from Rosie, Nik and hurt me."

Although the news about Bitchy McBitchface was great, the mark on my throat throbbed with unfulfilled desire. I caught Nik's eye across the room, and poured every bit concentrated mind power into one thought, and beamed it at him, "*Take me to bed before my lady parts burst into flames.*"

"*My hose is yours to command. Let's go start a fire.*" Nik lips curved up into a promise of a wolfish grin. "Mom, dad, alphas, thank you for everything. If you'll excuse us, we have some place to be."

I didn't even care that they all gave us knowing looks and chuckles as we fled the room. All I cared about was me and Nik, in a bed, or even the backseat of a car. We had years of lost time to make up for.

NIK

I didn't think the night could possibly deliver me any further surprises, but as I watched Rosie search through her handbag for the keys to her apartment, I realized that I was wrong. Because contrary to past experience, a woman scrambling to find something in a handbag was the hottest fucking sight I'd ever seen. Then again, it wasn't just any woman dumping an assortment of hair ties, old receipts, a kindle, her cell phone, and pens and paper on the ground. It was Rosie. My mate. My well-marked, fated mate.

Rosie looked up with flushed cheeks and a Cheshire cat smile. She jingled the keys in her raised hand. "Found them."

I reached out and put a hand on her luscious, curvy hips. "You need to get in that bedroom right this minute. You should know that if you refuse, I might suffer permanent damage, because I think all of the blood in my body is concentrated in the raging hard on I have for you. I legit might pass out."

"We can't have that. If we are being open here, I should

tell you, that if you don't take me to bed, the mark you left on my neck might cause the rest of me to combust and burn up into a pile of ash."

I pulled her against me and ran my tongue gently over my mark.

"Mmm, do that some more."

"You know, Rosie," I gave her another lick, "I get it now."

"Keep licking. What do you get?"

"Why I never wanted to have sex with any other girl."

"What are you talking about? And give me another lick."

"I mean, I was ridiculously, painfully, obnoxiously turned on all the time... but never for a some randy ball bunny, or a cheerleader, or any wolftress. Just you, Roses, only for you. My wolf has always known that you were my one true mate, and it just felt wrong to even think about having sex with someone who wasn't my mate... who wasn't you. It's only ever been you, Rose. Now and forever."

She pulled down on my collar, and softly glided her lips over mine, before she looked up at me with glassy eyes. "*Only you, Nik. Now and forever.*"

God, hearing her using wolfspeak in my head was so fucking hot. I picked her up with a growl and padded into her bedroom. "*I want to be inside you.*"

Rosie laughed and switched back to talking aloud, "As fun as it is to have you in my head, I want to hear you whisper it in my ear."

I lowered her down on the bed, and slid up beside her, my free hand finding the soft skin of her thigh beneath her skirt. I leaned in close, my breath stirring the strand of hair tucked behind her ear, "I want to be inside you, Roses. More than I have ever wanted anything in my life. Say you want that too. Goddess above, I want to hear you say it."

My fingers gently skimmed over her panties, already wet with her need, and I rubbed her clit through the thin layer of soft fabric. I wanted to make this moment, this night perfect, and satisfy my mate in every possible way. I continued to stroke her slowly, and kissed her neck, moving my fingers in time with my mouth, my tongue lapping over and over the mark I made.

"Tell me what you want."

"I want you. But wait, I got something."

Rosie rolled over, leaving me feeling cold and terrible, just to be without her warmth for a second. She rolled back by my side and pushed a flat cardboard package into my hands.

"G31, TheyFit condoms? Measure for Pleasure? Rose, what are these? It sounds like I could use them to invade a foreign country."

Rosie snorted. "Uh, the world's largest condoms."

"Really?"

"Really. I did a Google search, and these are it, Nik. I noticed that the last ones didn't do you justice. Now you can explore as much as you want without fear of making a little Nik junior."

I swept my arms around her, and rolled her over on top of me, the better to peel her clothes off her. Running my hands under her dress over her sides, I worked at the clasp on her bra. "You are an amazing researcher but, we can go without them altogether."

As soon as the words left my mouth, I knew I had fucked up—Rosie turned as rigid as granite under my hands.

"Nik, I'm not ready for a child. I know that diseases aren't an issue since we both just lost our v-cards together, but you do know that there are serious repercussions with unprotected sex, and relying on pulling out isn't a smart birth control tactic."

"I'm such an idiot. One of the benefits to being a wolf shifter is no human diseases, and I can't get you pregnant except under certain circumstances. I am all for fulfilling your every desire, including using the missile condoms if that's what you want."

Rosie shook her head. "Seriously? Wolf shifter sex is like... I mean, you can't... that means that I can just sit back and enjoy myself with zero stress?"

"Yeah, babe." I chuckled at her excitement. "That's exactly what it means."

"Then why did you pull out our first time? Every time we did it, you pulled out and came on me instead of," Rosie's voice quivered, "instead of in me?"

"Aw, Roses, I'm sorry. I just couldn't explain to you then," I took her hand, and gently kissed each of her finger tips, "I was so afraid that you would freak out and never want to see me again."

"Okay, so tell me now because I am freaking out, but I definitely want to see you again."

Just thinking about my wolf's knot and being inside of her had me on edge for her. Maybe that girls guide to dating shifters was a good idea. "The wolf part of me desperately wanted to mark you, claim you as my mate."

She grinned like a loon. "You wanted to mark me that night?"

"Rosie, I've wanted to mark you since we first met." I

couldn't resist scraping my teeth over the mark. It had fully bloomed into the tattoo like wolf and moon symbol of me on her soft skin. "When I fuck your sweet pussy, my cock gets a wolf's knot so that the animal is satisfied you're claimed too."

"What's a wolf's knot?"

She'd been thrown in the deep end of shifter life, I hope this wasn't the one thing that pushed her over the edge. "Okay so, just like in nature—"

"Ooooh. You and me baby aren't nothin' but mammals. Are we going to do it like they do on the Discovery Channel?"

Rosie cracked up, which made me crack up, which made any thoughts of worry about her drowning in the whole wolf thing float away.

"Okay, when wolf shifters are with their one true mate they want to claim, and not just anyone, we get this knot at the base of our cock when we come—"

"Oh." Her eyes went all wide and she glanced down between my legs. "It's seriously wolf-like."

"Yes, so if we were to do it, right now, and I came inside of you, the wolf's knot would keep us locked together, my cock in your sweet, sweet pussy, until the wolf was satisfied that you were claimed properly. I couldn't exactly come inside of you that first night, without explaining why my throbbing, aching cock was stuck fast in your body."

"Oh my god, really?" Rosie snaked an inquisitive have over my abs and circled my shaft with her fingers, making me almost come right there and then. She traced a light line down the backside of my hard-on,

"That makes me really happy Nik."

"Really?"

"Yeah. I'm really relieved. I was kind of focused on you pulling out, and I thought of so many reasons why you did it... and none of them were really good. I thought it was me."

"Oh no, Roses, I'm sorry. I probably should've just told you everything. I know it sounds stupid, but so much happened so fast, and it was amazing... a little overwhelming. We went from best friends to best lovers before I even knew what I was doing."

"No regrets?"

"Are you kidding me right now? No regrets, Rose. Okay maybe one. I regret that it took me this long to get you in bed."

She kissed my lips as her clever fingers stoked up and down my shaft. "I can't wait to feel you inside of me. I love the idea of being locked together."

I had Rosie out of her panties in less than a second, and rolled her over once more so I was on top. I stripped off my jeans before as she pulled my shirt over my head, and stretched out against her, going for as much naked skin on skin contact as I could manage. "Fuck, you feel so good, Rosie."

I teased her a little before, I place the tip of my cock at her opening, and slowly press myself inside, feeling her tight, warm walls stretch to accommodate me. She groaned and I took both her hands in one of mine and stretched her arms out above her head, making her arch her back. I loved the way her soft, lush body, molded to mine, making us one.

"More Nik, I want it all, I want all of you inside of me."

I gave her another inch, and another, and slipped my free hand between us. I was so fucking close to coming, but no way was that happening unless she was coming with me. I found her clit, as hard as my dick, and I move my fingers back and forth as I moved my cock in and out.

I pulled one of her hands between us, moving her fingers to take my place, "I want that more than I want anything, Rosie, but you feel too damn good. Show me how you liked to be touched so I can make you come with me."

She nodded her head and rocked her hips against me, moving our hands together through her slick folds, caressing both her clit and my cock. "Fu-uck."

I thrusted deep and hard into her, and held myself in that hot, soft, magical place until Rosie's cunt flutters with the beginning of her orgasm. "Tell me Rose. Tell me to fuck you until your mine."

Her tongue slid across her bottom lip and she sucked in a harsh breath. "Yes, yes. I need you. Fuck me."

That is all I needed to hear, that and her moan as I drove into her again and again until I wanted to explode, and I felt the wolf's knot swell and grow. She ran her fingers across my slick shaft with each thrust and grazed them gently around the knot at the base. It was pure nirvana to have her touch it, and I was afraid that I would come if she touched me for much longer.

I pulled out and grabbed her hips. My wolf was totally taking over and I needed to fuck her fast and hard now. I needed to claim her. Without a word, Rosie shifted onto her belly. She turned her head to face me as she lifted her hips into the air, and wiggled her adorably delicious looking ass back and forth, "Discover channel. Now. I need you to take me like this, right the fuck now."

My wolf nearly exploded, and I felt a rush and a tingle as my skin threatened to give way to the wolf.

I grabbed Rosie's hips and thrust into her so deep, I didn't know where I ended and she began. She groaned out my name and I was lost.

"You're mine, Rose. Mine."

I reached my hand around, and stroked her hot clit until her cunt clenched around my cock. My wolf took over and I pressed her down against the mattress and fucked her hard, and deep, and fast. Rose squirmed against me, backing that sweet ass into my dick, and cunt tighten around me until I could hardly move. I flicked my fingers across her clit once, twice, and when she whimpered my name, I thrust my wolf's knot fully inside her. Rosie flexed against me, and I squeezed my eyes closed as I saw stars.

"Say you're mine, Rose March." I spilled me seed into her body, my knot locked us together and we both shattered into a million pieces. "Say you're mine."

Rose gasped and tilting her hips higher, and I sunk my fingers into her hips, holding her tight. "Say you're mine."

"I'm yours, Nik. Only yours."

I lost all control and came again, erupting with the purest pleasure in the most intense orgasm I ever experienced. I was buried so deep into Rosie's pussy with each pulse of my seed into her, the wolf's knot went deeper, until I felt Rosie shudder and her second orgasm clenched me harder. I pulled her hips back, savoring the feel of her body squeezing my knot, riding out my orgasm and hers in a moment of shared, perfect pleasure.

We were locked together in bliss and I lowered myself on top of her, grazing my teeth over the mark on her throat, nipping at her neck making the little pussy flutters go on and on.

I wrapped her in my arms and shifted to my side, pulling her over with me, and spooning her tight and licking at the mark. "Are you okay, babe?"

"Oh, yes. It's like every little part of me is filled with you." She ground her ass against me, and I couldn't stop the growl from rumbling up inside.

"You're so fucking sexy, Roses. If you keep pressing up against me, we are going to be stuck together like this all night."

"And that's bad why?" She reached up and threaded her hands into my hair, pulling my lips down to her throat again. She loved me teasing her mark as much as I did. "You sent my body into a nuclear meltdown. The Chernobyl of orgasms."

"That's what I'm here for, Rosie. To make you glow like you are radioactive." To prove it to her, I kissed and licked that spot until I felt her tighten around me again, and her breathing grew shallow. I took one of her full, luscious tits in my hand and rolled her nipple between my fingers pinching her lightly. I scraped my teeth against her throat, and she moaned out my name.

I shifted and reached lower, cupping her sweet pussy, tracing my finger around her clit. She arched her back, pushing the knot even deeper. I bit her again, and lapped my tongue over the fresh marks.

My cock twitched with pleasure and the knot pulsed in time with Roses' movements as she ground against me. Still hard as a rock all over again, I thrust as much as I could. "Is this what you want, sweet Rose? Tell me what you want me to do."

She moved her head to the side, "Bite me, Nik. Claim me. Make me yours again and again."

I sunk my fangs into her, as the knot receded and I could once again I thrust deep, in and out. Her tight pussy grew even tighter, as she came again, clenching around cock over and over. I kept my mouth on her throat, scraping her soft skin with my teeth as I pounded her harder and faster. The orgasm ripped through me, and as I exploded, the knot grew again, locking us once more. "I'm yours, Rose. I love you. I am yours and you are mine, forever."

"I'm yours, Nik. Forever. I love you... so much."

Rosie stretched her arm around behind me and pulled me closer against her. She took my free hand in hers and hugged me to her tightly. My eyes closed and I drifted in and out of sleep, listening to her heart beating in time with my own.

Never in my life had I felt so relaxed, so at peace, so... loved. "I think I've always loved you Roses, from day one. I think I was afraid I would do something and fuck it up, and lose you forever. I just didn't want to believe that we could be anything more than friends. Until I read your book. I should have made a move on your back in high school."

"Aw, Nik. Honestly, if you had made a move on me in high school, I probably would have run away screaming. And ruined everything. I didn't really like myself much back then. I'm not sure I would have believed you."

"You believe me now?"

"Absolutely. I will admit that when I ran away from you the night of the barbecue, I spun up all sorts of scenarios, came up with a million reasons why you wouldn't choose me. But then I thought it through, and I knew you loved me. I love you so very much, and it would be absolutely dumb of me to deny your love."

"You're my very favorite smart-girl bookworm. What do you say I help you outline the sex scenes for your next book?"

"I think it will be a bestseller. A very dirty bestseller, if I'm lucky."

I kissed her mark. There would be no doubt in anyone's mind that Rosie was taken. "I'm the lucky one."

HOT SHOT WOLF

For all the ladies who love both a yummy football player butt and a growly wolf shifter.
We can have our football wolf and eat him too.

Love is game that two can play, and both win by losing their heart.

— EVA GABOR

ADDY

I wasn't going to make my tuition payment. Well, I could if I skipped my rent. And sold my soul to the devil. Also, if I didn't eat this week. Or next. Luckily, I could scarf day olds and chug coffee at the Moon Bean Bookshop and Café where I worked, which would fuel my brain for trying to figure out another way to get the money I needed.

"Addy, we're going out." My friend, Hunter, sauntered in and dropped onto the cushy couch favored by the bookstore patrons for curling up with a latte and a new book. Her boyfriend worked at the Wolf's Den, the bar next door, and she was always looking for company to hang out with while he worked.

Her life came easy. She barely studied and got great grades, her family was old money, and guys, girls, theys, and gays lusted after her for both her curves and her kindness. She was the girl you wanted to be or be with, so it was hard to hate her. I had no idea why in the world she'd decided to be friends with me. I was nothing very special.

Except tired. I was damn near exhausted.

"I'm working." And when I got off, I was taking a nap. I'd been up since four yesterday afternoon studying for my econ exam and then work. I hated pulling all-nighters, but Friday evening was my one night off, so I'd done it knowing later I had a date with my pillow and a vibrator.

"You work too much, so I'm kidnapping you, and we're going to the bar so you too can meet a real-life man. The kind that can take you to bed and make you forget all your worries." By the waggle of her eyebrows and the mind-in-the-gutter tone, Hunter was already planning all the ways her boyfriend could help her forget everything, including her name.

He could do it too. I'd heard them having sex before. I'd accidentally come across them getting down and dirty in the stacks at the library. Let's just say Ty was talented when it came to making Hunter forget how to say anything but, 'Oh, God.' and growling in a way that was scary sexy.

No, I wasn't jealous. Not even a little teeny tiny eensy weensy bit. Nope, not me. Never.

I'll admit, I was tempted to ask her to use her powers for good and set me up with one of her rich dudes who would happily give me one million dollars. Okay, I didn't need that much, but the difference between a million and school tuition wasn't much when you had nothing, including that long lost scholarship.

Of course, I'd never actually ask Hunter to do that. I could make it on my own and I certainly didn't need a man to save me.

"You have been working every night for weeks." She thrummed her nails on the table and stared me down. I could practically see her evil plans for me forming in her head. "A night out with some hot guys is exactly what you need."

"I don't have any—" Oops. I'd almost admitted I had zero experience with hot guys. Or guys in general. Who had time to date, or even hook-up when I had to work every damn day, and lots of nights? "—thing to wear."

"Ha. I knew you were going to say that, and I brought you an outfit." Hunter pulled out a bag from a plus-size lingerie shop and dangled it from her fingers.

"I'm not wearing lingerie to a bar." I'd never worn anything besides my functional, cheap, plain, white, cotton briefs. Bras in my size were never cute or pretty anyway. They held the girls in, and when I was lucky, had straps that didn't dig into my shoulders.

"It's not only lingerie. There's a sexy dress in here too." She pulled out a beautiful black dress that looked short enough that everyone would see my butt, or at least my underpants, if I wore it.

"It's not that I don't trust your taste in going-out clothes, but… kidding, I don't. You can pull off the short skirt and rock it. If I take two steps in that my butt will hang out beneath the material." I grabbed the bag from her anyway because the dress was stunning, and I couldn't afford anything like it in the next thirty years according to my school loans.

"You don't give your fine ass enough credit. There are lots of hot guys who are totally into junk in the trunk, and bellies, and hips, and thighs like ours." She waggled her eyebrows at me. "Like the guys we're meeting up with. They will be drooling over you in this."

I fingered the material. Ooh, it was silk. "Wait, we? And what guys?"

"Charlie is bringing Eli, which of course means, his ever-present teammates will be coming along. We're meeting them and a few of my sorority sisters at the Wolf's Den in a half hour when the coffee shop closes."

"No way." I had bags under the bags under my eyes and hadn't showered or slept in way too long. Plus, I would look ridiculous in that dress. Like a plus-size Barbie doll that someone else had dressed up.

Hunter pointed at me with a smiling smirk that I didn't like one bit. "You're coming. Get dressed."

I sank down behind the counter to hide from Hunter's I'm-not-taking-no-for-an-answer glare. "I can't."

Selena, my boss and the owner of the bookshop and café, strolled in and grinned at me. "Yes, you can, and you must."

"Selena," I whined. I knew what was coming and I didn't like it. Selena had a way of making people do what she wanted even when it had absolutely nothing to do with work. She was the master of invading all of our private lives. I'd seen her do it to Charlize, Rosie, and Hunter.

In fact, I'd gotten this second part-time job just a few weeks ago when Charlie had asked to cut back her hours to spend more time with Eli. They'd gotten really serious, really fast. I did not have room in my life for a relationship like that.

"Adeline." Selena folded her arms and stared me down with a twinkle of mischievousness I feared. "You have to go out. You're celebrating."

Crap. "Celebrating what?"

Selena looked at Hunter who shrugged and said, "Uh, the fact that it's the weekend?"

Selena shook her head. "Nope. The fact that Adeline didn't get fired today because she did as she was told and went to the Wolf's Den for a paid night off."

I couldn't go. Kirill Zaliv was a Dire Wolf player. Not that I kept tabs on him or anything. But the Bay was a sports crazy college, especially when it came to football, and it was hard not to know who the stars of the Bay State University Dire Wolves were. Especially if one of them was your older brother's ex-best friend who maybe knew I'd had a crush on him since puberty.

"I want to say I'm not going, but I don't have a choice, do I?"

"Sure, you do." Selena shrugged. "We always have choices. You can choose to go, or you can choose to get fired. I won't have any lonely hearts working in my establishment if I can help it. Bad for business, you know. I'm guessing you're going to find that someone special tonight."

"What? I don't think so." Did she know something? Like my unrequited crush on the one man who really didn't even know I existed and never had?

The bell that indicated someone entering the bookshop tinkled, and Selena walked in their direction laughing. At me. "I know so."

Hunter thrust the dress at me for a second time. "When she says she knows, she knows. It's like a weird superpower she has. So quit stalling and go get dressed already. There's some make up in that bag too. Use it."

Gah. There really was no getting out of this. I couldn't

resist against both Hunter and Selena, damn it. Those two were in cahoots and conspiring against me.

I took the bag to the little employee locker room and pulled everything out. It was too much, and I would have to find a way to thank Hunter. Well, we'd see how the night went before I went thanking anyone.

It's not like I knew Kirill was going to be at the Wolf's Den for sure. It was a Friday night. He probably had a date or a booty call. Except I also maybe knew that he hung around with Eli. I wasn't a stalker. Who said I was being stalkery when I just sort of, kind of paid attention to his schedule in all of my negligible amount of free time? A girl has to have a hobby, right?

No?

Just me?

Fine. Perhaps I had decided to go to Bay State U because Kirill was here and there was nothing like watching him score touchdowns. Not that I cared if the Dire Wolves football team won or lost. I couldn't care less about their record or any other team. That's not why I watched each and every televised game, even if I had to bribe one of my roommates for their ESPN password with lattes.

My older brother would absolutely die if he found out I didn't even have a clue about the rules of his favorite sport. But seriously, who cared about offsides or offense or off-anything-else when there were men like Kirill Zaliv in tight pants?

"Hello? Adeline? Come in, Addy." Hunter waved the dress in front of my face.

"Uh, right. I told you I was tired." I mean, I was, but that was not why I'd spaced out. Nope. I was thinking about football butts. One in particular.

"Good try. I know that look. You were thinking about someone you hope to see at the bar tonight. Selena was right. I can't believe you have a crush on someone and haven't told me yet. Is it one of the bartenders?"

I quickly changed out of my clothes and into the new ones. The barely there panties wouldn't be seen even if someone could see my butt hanging out, and the bra pushed my boobs up so they were practically in my face. But the dress... oh the dress. It slid on like it was made of fairy dust and hugged my curves, but also flowed over them so the material didn't cling where it wasn't supposed to.

"Ooh, yes. Now let me put some blush, bronzer, lippy, and mascara on and whoever you've been thinking about will be gaga for you." Hunter whipped out the make-up and was brushing it on my face before I could get away.

"Really, this isn't, you don't have to—" I didn't even get to finish before Hunter had me puckering my lips for the gloss.

"There, all done." She smiled and applied the lip gloss on herself too. "You look snackaliscious. I hope you're ready for some attention tonight."

I took a quick glance in the mirror over the sink and hot damn. I did look ready to party. Now I didn't know whether I wanted Kirill there so he could see me looking all grown up, or I'd be too... no... I was about to say too embarrassed. But Hunter's mini make-over gave me the confidence boost I hadn't even realized I needed.

In fact, maybe tonight was the night I met someone new, and could leave my childhood crush behind.

KIRILL

The music, the chatter of ball bunnies, and the coin drinks at the Wolf's Den were not what I had in mind for tonight.

I'd had been taking hits all day. Coach had decided to make it his mission to get the defensive line to sack my quarterback, and being the biggest, baddest center in the league, I couldn't let that happen. The Dire Wolves had a shot at the championship, and there was no way I'd let Eli get taken down.

What I needed now was a big meal, a long soak in a hot tub, and then to head to bed to jerk-off for some real relaxation. What I had was a cold drink and a long shot at getting laid.

"Come on, man. Take one for the team, buddy. Please, I'm begging you." How the hell a two-hundred and fifty-pound defensive lineman had perfected pleading puppy-dog eyes baffled me. But this fucker had the look and the tone down pat.

"That might work on the chicks, man, but I am not

taking out the girl with a good personality so the rest of you dickheads can get up close and personal with her hot friends."

The other guys shook their heads and laughed. Fuckers. Eli already knew he was off the hook because he had a sexy AF girlfriend who'd invited the girls to the bar in the first place.

I should have known better than to come out with the guys tonight. The ball bunnies will be warm and willing, they'd said. Nobody said anything about me getting stuck with babysitting duty.

"You haven't even seen her yet. She might be hot. Any chick will be glamorous standing next to your ugly mug," Eli said.

"You can all fuck off."

"I could, but they're on their way over." Eli turned on his million-dollar alpha of the pack smile and nodded toward the entrance to the bar.

Damn it. "You guys owe me."

Luka slapped me on the shoulder and bobbed his head, vying for the first look at the ladies. "Yeah, sure. I'll take the next one."

"The next three."

We were all a bunch of assholes who were going to hell. But we had a good time, and never let anything get very serious except for football. That was exactly how I liked my relationships with the ladies.

I was a junior and still trying to talk my pack alpha into allowing me to be drafted next year. Shifters weren't supposed to get into any spotlights that would expose us to the non-supernaturals. But I was in the prime of my college career, I'd made a name for myself in the league, and no one had a clue I was anything more than a talented, plain old human athlete.

I wasn't going to blow that by getting sucked into mating like Eli, Ty, and Nik had. I was very careful about who I revealed my wolf nature to. Ever since high school, when I thought my best friend could handle it. He couldn't. So now I stuck with being friends with other shifters, and absolutely was never falling for a human girl ever again.

But screwing around with them? Abso-fucking-lutely.

The giggles coming from halfway across the Wolf's Den had me rolling my eyes. I didn't even have to look to guess what they looked like. Bottle blondes, fake boobs, no butts, and the brains to match. I hadn't gotten tired of them in the last three years at the Bay, one more night wouldn't kill me.

Except I wasn't getting one of the ball bunnies. I had the responsibility of entertaining that one friend all groups of pretty co-eds had and felt obligated to bring out with them. The girl who was badly in need of a makeover and usually an attitude adjustment.

Whatever. I'd get all touchy feely with her, tell her how pretty her eyes were, and have her eating out of my hand before the other yahoos even got their girls' numbers. Then I'd take her home, dazzle her with my trophies and my prowess in the bedroom. She'd be talking about her one night with a Dire Wolf for years.

"Ladies," Hunter's feminine voice started the introductions, "meet Luka, defensive end, Jordan, kicker, DeShawn, cornerback, and—"

"Kirill?" The sweetest voice, like honey and eternal youth, washed over me.

I couldn't move fast enough, the world became a slow-mo instant replay. Getting off the stool and turning around to see the specter of love lost took a monumental effort.

I scanned the group in front of us. These were not your typical ball bunnies. From left to right there was curvy, sexy, Charlie, curvier, sexier Hunter, sex on a stick brunette girl, and a gaggle of less than curvy blondes. Those last ones were definitely ball bunnies.

Screech. My brain hit the brakes and then rewind. My wolf reared up and I had to take several fast breaths to contain my beast.

Sex on a stick. She fucking smelled like ripe peaches, and had curves in all the right places, a butt I could grab onto, and a great fucking rack. The smattering of freckles across her nose had me hard in an instant. Freckles I could distinguish from any other in the whole world, because I'd imagined kissing and licking every single one I could see, and a few that couldn't.

Her brother was the one thing that had stopped me from indulging in those fantasies.

"Adeline? What are you doing here?"

"Hi Kirill." Addy pursed her lips, hiding her smile, exactly like I remembered.

"Addy, you know one of the guys on the football team and you didn't share? You've been holding out on us," ball bunny blonde number two said.

She tried to sidle up to me, but I only had eyes, and arms, and time for one girl.

I called upon my highly refined blocking skills to use her momentum and moved blondie right into DeShawn's waiting arms. I quick stepped around the other girls until there was nothing between me and Adeline but air and memories.

I quickly made eye contact with my teammates sending my best mental telepathy to take a girl and distract them so I could talk to Addy.

Eli nodded and gave the guys a head jerk as his signal. Luka, Jordan, and DeShawn all made their moves and started talking to Addy's friends like the whole thing was a perfectly executed play. That left me with my girl all to myself.

"You don't really remember me, do you?" Addy leaned in and spoke directly into my ear to be heard over the music and mass of people at the bar.

Her breath smelled of cinnamon and lattes and sent shivers from the back of my neck straight to my cock. I needed to cool my libido. Addy was no ordinary chick. Not the kind I normally picked up at the bar, and definitely not the type I took home.

I'd been head over heels for her in high school. Just looking at her now, I was already half in love with her again. Her brother had made sure I understood she was off limits.

Whoa whoa whoa. Keep your cool, dumbass. I grinned and shout-whispered back, "You're not someone I would ever forget, babe."

Addy stayed nice and close, so she could hear over the crowd around us. God bless loud bars. It gave me the chance to watch her blush.

"I haven't seen you since graduation." And the fight with her brother. "Where you been?"

Addy shrugged. "I grew up. I guess we all did."

I didn't miss her quick perusal of me, flicking her eyes

from my shoulders on down. She lingered below my waist long enough to deepen the color on her cheeks.

I took the opportunity to focus on her lips, the ones that had starred in most of my wet dreams. I didn't need to look her up and down. I knew every single one of those curves. "You definitely grew up good. You're even prettier than you were in high school."

Her blush went darker and spread across her chest, just like I hoped it would.

She shook her head but smiled. "You always were a flatterer. I never believed a word that came out of your mouth."

"You should have." Especially the bit about choosing what she wanted out of life and not letting her asshole of a brother determine who she could and couldn't kiss.

The smile stayed on her lips, but a flicker of unhappiness flashed in her eyes. "I should have done a lot of things."

What was that supposed to mean? I had a million questions to ask her, including how she'd ended up at Bay State University and why she hadn't called the second she got here.

"But I'm not thinking about any of them tonight. I'm out to celebrate and have fun with my girls." She grabbed my bottle of water and downed it in a couple of gulps.

I could watch her swallow all day long and into the night. And here came my cock rising again. Down boy.

A pulse-pounding song blared out into the bar. Happy hour must be over. Loud music meant loud talking meant dry mouths meant more drinks. We should get out of here. Together. Good plan.

"What are you celebrating?" I needed to know if it was

important enough to hang around with her friends at the bar or if I could help her celebrate… all night.

She held a hand up to her ear. "What?"

"What. Are. You. Celebrating?"

"What?"

It wasn't that I didn't like being this close to her, but we couldn't have a conversation this way. If we couldn't talk, I couldn't talk her into my bed. Where I would show her every single move I had to keep her sated and satisfied. There was no denying it, I wanted to fuck her senseless.

I pushed a hand into her hair and pulled her to me. Getting her close enough to whisper into her ear was certainly no hardship. The softness of her skin, the vanilla scent of her shampoo, all brought back an infinity of memories heating me from the inside out.

Her eyes went all big and then darkened. Well, hell. If she thought I was coming in for a kiss already, maybe I should.

"Addy, let's go dance." Someone literally shouted and snatched her right out of my arms.

Fucking hell.

I stalked after them because Addy was mine.

The wolf part of me agreed.

Mine.

ADDY

I let myself be dragged away by Hunter and Charlize. I needed a minute to contain the explosion of emotions seeing Kirill again had started. A night out with the girls was like a shot of espresso, so much potential if you added the right mix ins, but on its own kind of boring and bitter. Kirill was the extra shot and the pumpkin spice sugar syrup that had a riot of yumminess spilling all over my emotions and reawakened needs.

Most of those needs had settled right between my legs.

A pounding beat and flashing lights were not conducive to deep thoughts or conversation. This night wasn't supposed to be about either one.

Hunter gripped my hand and gave it a tug. "Holy hotness, Addy. You and Kirill were looking like you wanted to eat each other up."

I'd had the biggest crush on him forever, and of course, I couldn't hide that. But was he looking at me that way too? "We went to high school together. Did you know he would be here tonight?"

Charlie and I had worked together at the Moonbean all semester, her in the bookshop and me in the café. And Hunter was one of my best friends, but that didn't mean the two of them wouldn't conspire against me along with Selena, to find out my secret crush and make something like this happen.

"Sure, I did, but I didn't know you were into him." Hunter dipped her chin and whispered, "He's kind of a dick to be honest. I'm a little surprised. Not who I would have picked for you. Luka is so cute and adorbs. I was already shipping you two in my head"

Kirill? A dick? Never to me. Like, I couldn't even imagine him being that way. He was all alpha, but like a cinnamon roll on the inside.

"So, are you going to hook up with him?" Charlie waggled her eyebrows.

"Don't be ridiculous. I'm sure he has half a dozen girlfriends." All of which were probably absolute sexpots, not inexperienced virgins. Or his former best friend's little sister.

"Don't underestimate your power over men." Hunter flashed her eyes up and down my body, pausing at my cleavage and raised an eyebrow.

Was I in the midst of a slightly stressful body image moment? Yes. Was I pushing through that and playing the fake it till you make it game? Again yes. "You made me wear this dress, and I'm not having this conversation with you. Let's just dance."

I felt too big for a place like this and more than slightly awkward dancing with so many people around, but I was going to do it anyway. Plus, bonus points if it distracted

Charlie and Hunter from asking any more questions about my lifelong crush making me blush from head to toe with nothing but a look, I would happily bump butts with a baker's dozen of strangers around me.

Or better yet bump and grind with a particular Dire Wolf. Nope, no. Not gonna go there. Kirill was just being friendly, just like he always was. Time to calm my crush down, get over it, and relax my overactive hormones.

"Ooph." My rear end knocked into someone. Oops. I moved a bit to the left and swayed my arms and hips in time to the music. I used to love to dance before I had to work and go to school, and there was always music in our house growing up. Screw self-consciousness. It was my night to have fun, or so the girls said. I could do whatever I wanted as long as it wasn't studying or making coffee for bookworms.

What I not so secretly wanted to do right now was catch-up with Kirill. Three years was a long time to hold onto a youthful crush. I had a better perspective on how silly I'd been to think I was in love at fifteen.

He was still a handsome devil, maybe even more so now. I'd always been a sucker for a tight football-player butt. It was most of the reason for going to the high-school football games in the first place.

I tried to squeeze past a couple who really needed to get off the dance floor and get a room. The guy had his front smashed to his girl's back and his hands wrapped around holding her tight. Did that even count as dancing?

"Where are you going?" Charlie shouted.

"I'm gonna go find Kirill. I'd love to catch-up on old times with him."

"I'm right here." His voice, laden with husky sexuality, came from right behind me.

I jumped and smashed some other dude's toes. "Sorry, sorry."

I smacked Kirill on the arm. "Don't sneak up on me like that."

Instead of replying or apologizing, he grabbed me around the waist and pulled me into his body. He formed a barrier between us and the rest of the writhing bodies on the dance floor. My heart went supersonic. Dirty dancing with Kirill? Only in my dirtiest of dreams.

He was warm, strong, and all kinds of off limits for me. But he felt so damn comfortable, and I relaxed. He swayed his body, bringing mine along for the ride. It wasn't the fast bump and grind of the people around us, but a slow back and forth, like a power ballad at prom.

And then we were there. His senior prom that I'd talked my way into attending even as a sophomore, as the ticket taker for the Rogue High School student council. His date was throwing up drunk in the bathroom and he'd pulled me onto the dance floor, our bodies swaying together to the beat of our own song.

I'd never wanted that night to end.

But it had.

He and my brother, Ryan, had some huge fight later that night and the next thing I knew, they weren't friends anymore. I didn't even see him again that whole summer, and then heard he'd gotten a scholarship to play for the Dire Wolves. Before I knew it, he and my brother had both left for colleges on opposite sides of the country.

The lights of the club flared in my eyes. This wasn't high

school, but I felt like the same girl who could have been sweet talked into his bed. I pushed at his arms and took a step back and faked a smile. "Don't get any ideas here, buddy. I'm not going back to your parents' beach house with you later."

"I've got my own apartment now, baby." His voice was smooth and practiced.

I laughed. "Don't baby me, Kirill Grimm. Save those moves for somebody you actually want to take home with you."

He leaned in, brushing his lips over my ears. "I don't want anyone but you."

So many emotions poured over me, some like warm melted chocolate, others stinging and painful like hot steam. I shouldn't feel hurt that he was joking around. He'd always flirted meaninglessly with me. He didn't mean it then and he didn't really now either.

Was that why everyone thought he was a dick? His harmless flirting might not feel harmless to some girls who actually thought he was interested. I knew better. I'd always be Ryan's little sister to him.

I probably wouldn't even see Kirill again after tonight. I hadn't most of the semester. We just ran in different circles. Him with his jock friends and me... well, in the work hard, study hard, no time for anything more than one night out a semester circle. So why not have some fun on my one night?

I still wasn't going home with him, but dancing because I never got to, a few drinks, and some reminiscing about old times wouldn't hurt. It might even be the fun I was supposed to have tonight.

I poked him in the chest. “Stop trying to sweet talk me and dance.”

“Yes, ma’am. You asked for it.” Kirill pulled me back to him, spun me around and grabbed my hips. It was so damn easy to follow his lead. He ground his pelvis against me and moved his body up and down my back to the beat of the music.

“You’re insane,” I shouted, but laughed and did my best to make him keep up with me. I might feel completely ridiculous, sure I looked like a flailing albatross dancing with a graceful, athletic swan, but I was having fun.

“Whoo hoo, you go on with your bad self, Addy.” Hunter winked at me and started up her own sexy dance. She and Charlie were doing their own brand of dirty dancing with their boyfriends. Hunter's other sorority sisters had attracted the attention of half the bar. Before the song was over, the five of us were in the middle of a group of guys all vying for a chance to dance.

One song transitioned into another with no sign of slowing down. After one more, I’d drag Kirill off the dance floor and see if we couldn’t find a quieter corner to grab a drink and talk.

“Hey there, wanna take a turn with me?” A tall guy in a Bay State U Basketball team shirt popped up in front of me.

“She’s with me, man,” Kirill said in a very snarly tone.

I wasn’t exactly with him, but I didn’t have any interest in dancing with Sir Dunksalot.

“Let the lady speak for herself.” Basketball dude grabbed my hand and tugged, trying to pull me away.

I tugged it right back. “Uh, no thanks.”

"Come on sweetheart, don't worry, I don't care how big your ass is. I'm a tits man anyway."

Before I even blinked, Kirill was between me and the other guy. The immediate crowd of people all stopped dancing and formed a circle around us.

"I said, she's with me. Back the fuck off, ball boy." Kirill rose up to his full six-foot six height and holy cannolis, the man had muscles on top of muscles. And were his eyes glowing?

None of that seemed to scare off his rival. "You football players think you're so hot, prancing around in your tight pants and sticking your hands between each other's legs. Yeah, that's right man, I know who you are. You can't come at me. You'll get kicked off your precious team. So, give up on your chubby chase and we won't have a problem."

Ugh. Casual fatphobia was so 1990s. What an ass. I stepped between him and Kirill and held up one finger ready to give him a piece of my mind. He didn't even spare me a glance.

"You gonna hide behind this fat cow, little football boy?"

Oh goody. Fatphobic and misogynistic. Great combo. My favorite. A million needles pricked in the back of my neck and worked their way through my body and into my eyes. I hadn't expected such a blatant dig, and it wasn't even to my face.

I'd learned from middle school on up that men like this didn't deserve my attention. I owed no one an explanation of my body or my life. But Kirill clearly hadn't ever seen this gross side of men and how they behaved around girls who looked like me. He was itching for a fight.

The best way I knew how to make it all stop was my

standard go to—remove myself from the situation and pretend it wasn't happening.

I ducked my head and pushed away from them all. Shouldering my way through the crowd was harder because people would not get out of the stupid way.

"Addy, wait."

No way. I pushed against the crazy bar-goers, using every ounce of adrenaline to flee. More scuffling and the sound of someone hitting someone else came from behind me.

I slipped out the front door. The fresh air felt so good on my hot skin. I stepped to the side and leaned against the wall. Some girls' night out this was.

The rest of my group burst out of the door a moment later. The girls were laughing and breathing hard like they'd run a sprint. The guys acted more like they'd been playing a game, not in a bar brawl.

All except Kirill. He looked worried. Or maybe that was the cut near his eye and the way the skin around it was red and purple and swelling.

Hunter came over and hugged me, then joined me on the wall. "Addy, ha ha ha. You were brilliant. The way you ducked and pushed that asshole with your butt, just when he went to make his move. Totally threw him off his game. Kirill knocked the crap out of him. Boom. He went out for the count."

What? "I didn't—"

Eli slapped Kirill on the shoulder and smiled over at me. "Seriously. You've got yourself quite the scheming little lady there. Wasn't sure we were getting out of there unscathed until your girl there saved our asses, with her ass none the less."

"But—" I shook my head and looked back and forth between everyone who were all sure I'd made a calculated move.

Eli's phone buzzed and he frowned at it. "As much fun as we're having standing around out here, campus security is headed our way, and I really don't want to get kicked off the team for brawling at a bar with those dumbass basketball players." He grabbed Charlie's hand. "Who wants to come back to my place and keep the party going?"

Kirill stepped forward, took my hand, and spoke up for the first time since they'd all come out after me. "You all go on. I think it's time Addy went home."

Yep. Still just Ryan's little sister to him. I trudged ahead and waved him off. Of course, overprotective older brother's friend had to chase after me. "Go have fun with your friends. I'm not really up for any more partying."

"I'm not either, but we don't have to go home if you don't want. What do you say we find a cup of coffee somewhere and we can just tell old stories and have a laugh?"

Sigh. "Fine. But if you even mention the words chubby or chaser, I'll sock you in the other eye."

He winced. But now, close up, his injuries didn't look half as bad as I thought they'd been. There was no cut at all, and hardly any swelling or redness.

"We better get some ice on that too."

He half shrugged. "I'm fine, it's nothing."

I should go home, just like he said, but that's not what came out of my mouth. "No, come on. There's ice and a first aid kit in the kitchen at the Moon Bean."

He took my hand and I let him. We walked around to the back entrance, and I was grateful for the darkness because it hid the way I was feeling ooey gooey and twitterpated walking hand in hand with him. We didn't say anything for a few minutes, walking slowly, stretching out the scant yards to our destination. "Did you really knock that guy out?"

"How could I not?" He shrugged and gave me one of those infamous flirty smirks. "I had to protect you. You're my girl."

That thing I said earlier about not needing a guy to save me? I didn't know it would make me feel so swoony inside when one did.

KIRILL

My heart was still working overtime like I'd just run a whole series of hundred-yard dashes or had been hunting along the beach in ninety-degree heat on a humid day. It would be hours before the rush of adrenaline faded. I welcomed the feeling in my wolf form or during games, but walking down the street, holding hands with the girl who'd been off limits for me until now was no place for me to be all amped up.

I couldn't help it. Nobody, not nobody insulted my girl.

Damn.

My. Girl.

She was mine.

Her older brother Ryan had made it perfectly clear she wouldn't ever be my girl. Even when I'd tried to tell him I was in love with her. Even when I'd revealed my true supernatural nature and told him she was my fated mate.

I wasn't supposed to do that. But he'd been my best friend for a long time, and I thought if there was any human I could trust, it would have been him. I was wrong.

Which made me think I'd been wrong about the whole one true mate thing too.

But Ryan wasn't here now, and little Adeline Austin was all grown up. Moon above was she ever grown up. The wolf inside of me snarled and howled to be let out. It growled at me to mark her, claim her, make her my mate here and now.

I wasn't going to risk having her freak out like Ryan did. Every instinct told me she wouldn't be like that. Just one touch of her, and I knew all over again that she was meant for me and me for her. My three and half year long shitty mood lifted. I'd been denying myself the one thing that made me feel whole. That would drive any wolf insane.

And that was why I couldn't risk exposing what I was to her yet. I was not losing her again.

I also wasn't letting this opportunity to woo her pass me by. So far, I wasn't doing such a great fucking job of it. The moment she'd been in trouble, she ran. She had no reason to trust me. I couldn't let her slip through my fingers again.

"Addy, I saw, I mean, you were..." my brain to mouth synapses weren't firing in the right order. I wanted to make sure she was really as all right as she said, but without stupidly insulting her even more. "Are you sure you're okay? I mean after what that dickmunch said back there?"

She sighed and I didn't like it. I wanted to take care of her, never let anyone or anything ever hurt her again. That included me.

"I'm fine. It's nothing I haven't heard before. I'm pretty good with who I am and what I look like most of the time. So, it doesn't really matter if some guy calls me fat or a cow. That's a him problem, not a me problem."

What? She acted as if people called her horrible names all the time. That wasn't right. "Addy, you're beautiful."

Shit, that didn't come out right. "I don't mean being fat equals being ugly. You've got curves that a man can hold on to. My dick has been hard more than half the night thinking about how I could grab hold of your hips and you'd fill my hands instead of poking into them."

She didn't say anything, and I was sure I'd completely blown all chances of not only getting in her bed but getting her to give me shot at winning her heart.

Shit.

Probably because I really was an ass and reduced her entire being to nothing more than a sexual object. Fuck. Why did I have such shit for brains when I was around her? My hormones and my beast were why. I had to make a better impression on her than this if I was going to win her heart.

"Uh, and you know, I'm a dick... who is clearly thinking with my cock. But I do know that you're more than your body. Sorry for not being any better than that shithole at the bar."

She didn't say anything but searched my eyes, back and forth, like she was looking into my very soul. I was being weighed and measured with no idea what she thought of me. She probably thought I sounded like I was making shit up to get on her good side.

I might do that to the ball bunnies, but not my Addy. I was a dick, but never to her.

She squeezed my hand and thank the fucking moon. She could have left me standing there with my dick in my hands. Instead, she guided us around to the back alley behind the bar and the row of shops. "You're a rare breed. Most guys don't think like you do. I almost didn't believe you, but you'd never lie to me."

"Never. But make no mistake, *rybwy,* most guys absolutely want a smart girl with curves. Nobody I know wants someone who can't carry on an intelligent conversation, or a little stick under them in bed. I'm pretty sure I'd break those girls into pieces if I even tried to hold them, much less talk to them aside from flirting."

She pursed her lips in that trying not to smile way. "Like I said, you're not the typical guy."

"You've been dating the wrong kind of guys then, and I can tell you, they're assholes." Even thinking about her with any other man had me wanting to mark her right the fuck now.

I hoped to get at least a smile out of her for that. Instead, I got another sigh. Damn. I'd just have to show her how amazing I thought she was.

We stopped behind the Moon Bean coffee shop, which I'd been avoiding as of late. Ever since I'd worked for Selena at those book signings, I felt like she had her eye on me. She was the former matriarch and mother to my alpha, and I didn't need her taking any extra notice of me.

Didn't look like anyone was home though. Maybe we could make out in the sheltered doorway here in the back where no one would bother us. I could definitely show her how hot she was then.

"You wanna get something to eat? I could definitely use a coffee and a donut as an end of the night pick me up." She searched through her little handbag and pulled out a set of keys. She popped them in the door lock. "Trust me, the coffee here is way better than any late-night diner. I promise."

"Oh, I could eat. I love to eat."

We went inside and she slipped behind the counter, wrapping an apron around her waist, and pushed her hair up in a bandana with little books, coffee cups, and cats on it. With her short dress, the apron, and her hair up, she had a very sixties housewife vibe. That wasn't normally my kink, but it might become one.

She'd be even sexier without any of it on. Nope. No. I would fucking sit on my hands to keep them to myself. She was not a sex object, no matter how much my cock wanted her to be. She was my mate, and she deserved a little fucking respect.

I would show her I was worthy of her. If she fell for me, maybe she wouldn't be sacred out of her mind when I revealed my inner beast to her.

"What do you want? I make a mean dolce de leche macchiato." Was this her version of coffee shop girl flirting?

Fucking adorable. She was just so damn easy to be with, and I'd missed being in the Austin family circle of trust. "I don't know what you just said, but I want it in my mouth right now."

There was a lot of Addy I wanted in my mouth. Her lips, her neck, her—

"Ahem." Addy made the universal sound for you're-busted-checking-out-my-chest and my-eyes-are-up-here.

"There's more tasty treats in here than the lattes, babe." Shit. Close your damn mouth, asshole.

"Such a sweet talker." Addy snorted.

Phew. I never could resist her smile, or her lips, and I'd

had lots of fantasies starring her tongue. Fu-uck. My one-track brain was being driven by my one-track wolf.

How in the hell had I ever let her get away? Dumbest ass move I'd ever made. She was more beautiful today than when we were in high school, but there was something different, more sensual than just her looks. She had a different kind of confidence than before.

She might have run away from the bullying words tonight, but it wasn't because she was some sad, frightened little bunny.

She shook her head and blew me off. Probably thought I was flattering her, not being sincere at all. This wasn't casual flirting for me. This time I wasn't giving up, and some dirty talk and flirting wasn't going to win me her trust or her heart. I swallowed, pushed my horny ass wolf down, and manned up.

"I shouldn't have walked away from you."

We both went still. I literally bit my tongue, floundering for her reaction to my admission. We'd never talked about the fight I had with her brother. I'd never told her how I felt about her. I stupidly went to her brother first, being a dumb teenager raised in a pack that had never valued women. Not until Kosta became our alpha and showed me what a real relationship with a mate could be.

Tension rippled across her shoulders as she processed what I'd just admitted. I couldn't tell her back then, and my balls had shriveled up in fear, so I didn't even truly say it now. But she knew. She had to.

Addy rolled the complications of our past off in a shrug. Fuck, she was going to deflect. "You had a new life at college to get to, a scholarship. It wasn't like you were my boyfriend or anything. You didn't need some kid with a crush tagging along behind you."

"I still should have told Ryan to fuck off." I had no idea how much she knew about my fight with him. He might have told me in no uncertain terms to stay the fuck away from her, but I did know that he kept the secret of the Bay pack to himself. Had he even told her why I disappeared on her? "Instead, I slunk away believing in the bro code instead of my feelings for you."

She busied herself with making a frothy cup of coffee, taking her time drizzling the top with some kind of sweet syrup. I literally sat on my hands to keep myself from yanking her across the counter and kissing the daylights out of her. I wanted her so badly. Not just physically either. I wanted her to see me, to know me, to accept me.

"We were all just kids, and we all needed to grow up. Including me. Life isn't some teenage rom com. It's hard, and exhausting." She slid the mug over to me, and finally looked up at me. Her eyes held so much sincerity, but also pain. Pain that was my fucking fault. "You two were best friends. Whatever he said to you that night was more important than what we might have had. Which wasn't anything if you remember. "

Time for me to man up and tell her how important she was to me. Now, and back then too. "Doesn't mean I wasn't in love you."

ADDY

I snort-laughed. I didn't mean to, it just popped out, like a tiny explosion of happiness. Yes, this was supposed to be a super serious moment, where we admitted our love for each other as teenagers and I couldn't believe this was happening.

Being with Kirill tonight had been easy for the most part. It had damn sure been more fun than I'd had in a long time. Even the insult and the fight had added a layer of excitement to my life that had been missing, had been wrapped up in working and delaying my own dreams and desires.

I was the sad sap that made my own life hard, and Kirill was the easy fun I'd been missing.

He frowned, and if I hadn't seen it for myself, I'd have never thought I could hurt his feelings. But I had, and that was the last thing I wanted to do. What I wanted to do was... him, a couple of times at least.

"I'm sorry. I wasn't laughing at you, that was at myself. I had such a crush on you for so long and I didn't expect any of this. I was sure you thought I was an annoying pest until that dance at your prom. But then you disappeared out of our lives, and it confirmed that you were just being my older brother's nice friend taking me for a twirl."

"I left because," he swallowed, and I watched as his brain fritzed out trying to decide how much to say. Even after three years, he still had a sense of loyalty. He wasn't out here trying to smear Ryan for whatever their fight was about.

"He made it clear that I wasn't welcome in your lives when I told him how I felt about you. He thought I was being a horny douchebag trying to get in your pants. Which, I mean, I did want to get in your pants, I still do. Fuck, I've been sporting a semi all night."

I couldn't help it. My eyes flashed down, and uh... if that was a semi, I was in for one wild ride.

"What Ryan wouldn't hear was that you're my... I mean, that I had actual feelings for you. I tried to push them away, but seeing you tonight has brought everything back." The anguish talking about that time was palpable in the frustration in his voice.

Ryan. He'd come home with a black eye and a lot of anger that night. What Kirill wasn't saying was their fight had involved kicking each other's asses. I just didn't realize it had been about me.

Our relationship changed the summer before my big over-protective brother went off to college in California. We'd always been close, and he'd never minded when I tagged along with him and his friends. Then, he shut me out, and got freaked out if I even wanted to leave the house. I thought it had something to do with him moving on to a new phase of his life, part that didn't need a pesky little sister.

He was getting an earful from me at Thanksgiving break this year if he bothered to come home. "I knew you guys had a fight, but he wouldn't ever tell me what it was about. He got weird after that."

Kirill reached for my hand but clenched his fist like he had to hold himself back. I didn't want him to. "He couldn't see you as anything but his kid sister that needed protecting. Admitting I wanted to be with you screwed with his head. Who and what I am, and what I wanted with you, scared him. He was just trying to keep you safe."

From Kirill. He didn't say that part. Who and what exactly did Ryan think he was protecting me from? The one man who saw me for me and not my muffin top or the junk in my trunk? The loyal friend? The competitive athlete at the top of his game?

Who and what he was? I wasn't buying that. Or maybe Ryan had bought into the hype that Kirill was nothing more than an asshole. "I don't need protecting. I can take care of myself. Have been doing it just fine since you two went off to college and left me behind without a goodbye or anything."

"You don't have to prove that to me. I saw you in action tonight. I was just as bad as Ryan back there, thinking you needed coddling." He shrugged and fiddled with a napkin on the counter. "I'm sorry I wasn't... man enough to come say goodbye to you back then."

He was so sweet and doing his best to show me he wasn't the asshole everyone thought he was. I'd always known that.

I'd always been attracted to that slightly rough side he had. It was sexy, and this was my now or never chance to have a taste of it for myself. No way I'd let it slip by me again. "You know, I was considering telling you we'd better call it a night, but..."

I took his fist and opened up each of his fingers, caressing along the callouses and deep lines he'd developed from playing ball all those years. I drew circles in his palm and looked up at him through my lashes, doing my best to flirt with him, tell him with my eyes exactly how I felt about him.

The lust he'd banked, hidden behind those confessions, lit up again. His voice dropped to a husky tone that made my lower belly tingle, anticipating his next move. "But you're not saying that."

I set my elbows on the counter and cupped my head in my hands, full well knowing I'd put my cleavage on display for him. "Nope. I'm not."

He stared at me a moment, and I swear his eyes flashed with a purple light before they went dark and lusty. Then he jumped up and over the Formica countertop, landing behind me in one fast, predatory move. He placed his hands on either side my hips, trapping me between the cash register and his body. "That's good, because we're just getting started."

Oh, yes. This was the Kirill I wanted to get to know. The cafe was only about the size of a galley kitchen with a couple of tables and comfy chairs, but suddenly it became a whole hell of a lot smaller. He was so big that he made me feel tiny, which was not something I was used to.

Everything with Kirill felt new or special and it all felt so perfect. I knew exactly where we were headed, and I didn't want to admit this was going to be my first time. But it felt wrong not to. I hoped hard that it wouldn't put a stop to the way he was touching me.

"Yes, we are." I spun in his arms and reached behind my back to untie my apron. "And I don't want to stop."

"I've been dying to kiss you and touch you all night, but I don't want to rush you into anything. We're just getting to know each other again. There are things about me you don't know."

"We know each other just fine. I've been saving something for you. I didn't really realize I was until just now. I blamed it on a lot of other things in my life, like not having time because of school and work, or the fact that most guys are assholes. But those were just excuses."

"What are you saying? You saved," he swallowed hard and studied my eyes, looking so deep into my soul I thought I would burn up under his scrutiny. "You saved yourself for me?"

"Yes. I think I did. I always wanted it to be you. You're the only one I've ever wanted." This should feel weird and awkward to say, but with Kirill, it wasn't. "Will you be my first lover?"

If I had my way, my only lover. I couldn't imagine ever being this intimate with anyone else.

There was a look of awe on his face, but then he smiled and nodded. That was all the invitation he needed because I didn't get a verbal yes or a no, but instead his answer came in the form of a scorching, teeth gnashing, count your tonsils, steal my soul kiss.

My lips and tongue dueled with his, testing, tasting. His flavor was so familiar, like Christmas and Halloween and the Fourth of July all rolled up in one. This kiss took from me as much as it gave. This demanding kiss said give yourself to me and I promise to take care of you.

Kirill shoved one hand into my hair, holding me tight, never letting me up for air. His other hand groped around on the back of my dress. "Where's the damn zipper on this thing?"

"It doesn't have one."

"Good." He ran his hands down my sides, to my hips and then my bare thighs. His body followed suit until he was squatting in front of me. He slid his fingers under the hemline and lifted the dress up several inches. "I can't fucking wait to taste you, to make you come in my mouth."

Oh, yes. Oh no. "Whoa, wait. Not in here. I serve food in this place."

I thought we'd go to his place, or mine. Although, we both had roommates. Honestly, the coffee shop would be just about as private as our homes, I supposed. And... I didn't want to wait.

"I'll help you scrub the counter with every cleaning product in this place. I'm not waiting another second. I've been hard for the last four hours and getting harder by the second. Give yourself to me, right now, *rybwy*. I promise to make you come so hard, so many times, you won't know your name, much less care if the counter needs cleaning."

I wrapped my leg around the back of his shoulder and decided to believe in the cleaning power of bleach. I bit my lip and gave him a crooked smile.

"You're dirtier than I thought if you think I'm letting you strip my clothes off in the middle of the coffee shop and do lots of fun and naughty things to me." Things I'd dreamed of, imagined, read about, but never done. Because I'd wanted to do them all with him.

He pressed a kiss to my inner thigh that sent waves of desire crashing through me. In one quick motion he pulled my dress up and off, tossing it onto the nearest chair. Thank goodness Hunter had made me wear this matching bra and panties set from the lingerie store.

I may be cool with my curves, but sexy lingerie sure as shit helped give me a confidence boost. There was no faking it till I made it now. The way Kirill looked at me in it was more than enough to know I looked hot. Ours were the only opinions that mattered to me anyway.

He eyed me up and down and then literally licked his lips. "You have no idea how dirty I am."

KIRILL

My heart was pounding so hard in my chest that, if I wasn't both a wolf and a student athlete, I'd never have survived seeing Adeline almost naked and confidently wearing lacy lingerie, wanting me.

"Come here and let me look my fill of you." I grabbed her ass and lifted her up onto the counter.

She leaned back and set her hands behind her, pushing her tits and her belly forward, showing herself off for me. For. Me.

My cock was ready to burst and all I'd done was one deep kiss and a whole lot of fantasizing. She hadn't even touched me. I'd love to have her spread eagle on this countertop, fucking her nice and slow, so she was begging me to make her come.

I needed to mark her so everyone else knew she was mine.

I would sink my teeth into that place just above her collarbone that had been calling to me all night. I'd fuck her hard and come inside of her, so her scent mixed with mine. I wanted to see her wearing nothing but a satisfied smile from being thoroughly well fucked, and claimed, and mated to me.

"Are you going to do more than look? It's not nice to make a girl wait." She was playing the seductress now and she had no idea how her sweet confidence turned me the fuck on. I palmed my cock through my jeans.

Maybe she did know.

Slow down, boy. She was wanting and willing, but she still didn't know about fated mates, or even that beings like me existed. Once I touched her, I would never, ever be with another woman. I would be forever hers. Fate had brought us together, made us for each other, but was I ruining her life by not allowing her to experience what else was out there?

Would she regret not getting to fuck other guys? The thought had my wolf rising up so close to shifting and peeing a god-damned circle around her.

"Oh, I'm going to do so much more than look, sweetheart." I licked my lips and placed my hands on either side of her hips, leaning in, and nipped at the side of her mouth. "But don't think this is going to be some quickie. I'm taking my sweet, delicious time with you."

I was no virgin and hadn't been with one either. I'd sowed my oats, fucking every other ball bunny that first year of college, trying to get Addy out of my system. Trying to tell myself that she wasn't my fated mate. I'd learned how to please a woman, but it had been meaningless to me.

She could make the choice not to be with me, even after I

claimed her, but it would fucking suck for the both of us. There was a not so quiet part of me, the beast inside, that said she knew we belonged to each other if she'd saved herself especially for me.

Now I'd wished I'd done the same. No co-ed I'd fucked since I got to college had fulfilled anything other than a very base need. In fact, I had become a grumpy monk this semester as I watched my friends find their mates.

I couldn't handle if she did the same. The thought of her so much as looking at another man, much less fucking one, had my wolf pushing me to mark her and claim her by fucking her brains out right here and now. I wouldn't do that to her until she knew what she was getting into. But that didn't mean I couldn't make her come a hundred and two times first.

"I want you so bad, Addy, but I don't want to hurt you. When I fuck you, I want you to be ready and enthusiastically consenting to every single thing I do to you."

"You won't hurt me. I promise I am very enthusiastic. I might technically be a virgin, but—" she blushed and grinned, her eyes flitting away. "I, uh, have plenty of experience with a vibrator."

Holy shit. My brain just exploded imagining Addy pleasuring herself with my name on her lips. This moment wasn't about me. What I wanted even more than to see her make herself come, was to see her come for me. I was going to eat out that sweet pussy until the dawn and keep my cock to myself.

Until I could show her my wolf and the world she'd be entering.

"You are so fucking beautiful, little *rybwy*." I fingered the lace at the edge of her fancy bra. What I wanted to do was rip it right off of her and shred it to pieces so there wasn't a single inch of her body hidden from me.

"Pretty lingerie helps."

"You'll be even more gorgeous out of them. Let me show you." I carefully slipped my fingers under the straps of her bra and slid them down her arms. The tops of the lacy cups dipped, and I skimmed my knuckles over her creamy, soft skin. What I wouldn't give to come all over her tits. There would be plenty of time for all of that if I had it my way. My way was to have her in my life forever.

I'd always known she was the one for me. Now I needed to prove that to her. The best way I knew how to do that was to show her by delaying my own gratification to make sure she was relaxed, happy, and satisfied. I'd be the most giving lover that ever was.

I kissed my way up her throat and gently tugged on her earlobe with my teeth. "Slide back down here and turn around so I can unhook your bra."

She pivoted and her ass was as enticing as her tits, plump and just waiting for my cock. My wolf howled inside to spread her thighs, push her down and mount her, rut into her, fill her with my seed. Not today. Maybe not for a long time, but I was willing to wait. I would have her in every way possible so that her body was mine and only mine.

I undid the clasp and let the lacy bit of fluff fall to the floor. My hands tingled, anticipating touching her, holding her breasts, playing with them until her nipples hardened. I wrapped my arms around her, lifting her breasts and rubbing my thumb across her nipples. She moaned and set her head back against my chest.

"Do you like to have your breasts played with?" I punctuated my question by pinching her nipples, and not lightly.

She bit her lip and groaned. The scent of her sweet peaches and cream arousal filled my nose. "Oh, God, yes."

I had to physically stifle a growl. Did she like it a little bit rough? I could get down with that. I continued to pinch one nipple but dropped my other hand down until it touched the top of her panties. "Let's see how much your body likes what I'm doing. Remember you can say stop at any time."

I dipped my hand inside the lace covering her pussy and pushed between her legs. Fuck. She was soaking wet. For me. No other man had ever touched this pussy and it was all mine.

I slid two fingers through her wet pussy lips and found her clit. Addy tilted her hips forward and rode my fingers like I imagined she rode her own thinking about me. The new angle pushed her ass right up against my dick. I couldn't help but notch it into the cleft of her ass. "That's it, baby. Ride my fingers, make yourself come all over my hand."

"Help me, please. I'm so close already." Her voice came out breathy, like she couldn't get enough air to say the words.

I pushed at her ass, dry humping her, my cock aching to get out of my jeans and into her. But that wasn't happening tonight. I flicked my fingers across her swollen clit. She was so damn sexy like this. Her breathing sped up and the nipple I continued to squeeze turned to diamond under my attention.

"Yes, Kirill, yes."

I lowered my mouth to her neck and kissed and licked her. My fangs extended, ready to mark her. I couldn't, I needed to, I had to.

Maybe just a scrape of them across her skin. Just a little taste of her. Fuck, I needed to push her over the edge because if she didn't come soon, I was going to lose it, and my wolf's instincts were going to take over. I whispered in her ear, "Come for me, baby. Right now."

I pressed my fingers hard against her clit, gripping it, pinching hard and bit down on her neck at the same time. I didn't mean to, I just wanted a taste. It was too late. Her body convulsed beneath me, and she wailed out her pleasure as I made my mark on her.

"Kirill. Yes, yes. I'm coming. Yes."

My cock screamed at me to keep riding her ass until I got my own release, but I tamped my lust down. My body might be angry, but I loved seeing hers shake and feeling the bite of her grip on my arms, like a wolftress would.

I pulled and pinched on her clit and her nipple, drawing the orgasm out. I loved hearing her gulping moans, wanted to hear her call my name over and over, knowing mine would be the only one she'd ever say as she came. My name on her lips. Mine.

But Goddess above, I'd fucked up. I released her flesh from my mouth and licked over the wound. My saliva would help her heal faster, but I'd marked her.

In a few short hours, that bite would morph into a wolf and a moon, looking like a tattoo. It could never be removed, and she would see what I'd done to her. Without her knowledge, without her permission.

I claimed that her consent in all of this was of the utmost importance, and I'd done the one thing that I couldn't take back.

I'd marked her as mine.

And I wasn't sorry.

ADDY

I sucked in giant gasps of breath, unable to do anything else, but ride out the best freaking orgasm I'd ever had. What the hell had Kirill done to me?

The biting and the pinching and biting. Did I mention the biting? Holy freaking cannolis. Plus, his demand that I come for him had sent me so far into the pleasure sphere I wasn't sure I was ever coming back down. This was nothing like masturbating, and I wanted so much more. I wanted him inside of me.

Kirill's fingers were still pulling and pinching at me, both between my legs and at my nipple. I'd just come and already I could feel another orgasm building. I wasn't a multi-orgasmic girl. One and done was my usual MO. Besides, if I was going to come again, I wanted it when we were joined as one.

"Kirill, please, wait. It's too much. I'm going to come again, and I want it to be with you."

He was silent for a moment, saying nothing. But there

was a low rumble coming from him, almost like an animalistic growl. "I want your mind and your body good and ready for me."

"I am, I swear. I don't think I can come again like this. I need you inside of me."

"Oh, you can, and you will. I'll give you everything you need." He pushed his fingers deeper, and then they were inside of me, driving in and out, making my body go straight back to that place where a climax waited just beyond my reach. "Mmm. You're so fucking tight. I can't wait to get my cock in you, but I'm big, sweetheart, and I don't want to hurt you. It's going to take a while before I fuck you."

I whimpered, knowing that nothing but having him fully claim me with his body would satisfy me. Never in my life had I thought about being claimed by a man, but that was absolutely the correct word for what I wanted from Kirill.

"Don't worry, I'm not going to leave you hanging. You're going to be satisfied and boneless when I'm done with you, and then we're going to do it all over again tomorrow night, and the next, and the next." He nipped at my ear and then scraped his teeth across the place where he'd bitten me before.

With every stroke of his fingers inside of me and flick of his thumb across my clit, he thrust against me. But it felt all too futile. I was still in my panties, and he wore his jeans like they were fucking armor. "Why won't you fuck me?"

He hissed in a long breath that turned into a deep chuckle. "The anticipation will make it even better when you do submit to me."

Was that it? He was kinky and thought he needed to keep

that part of himself from me? "I want all of you, Kirill. Not just your cock, but you."

"Fuck. Why are you so perfect? You break down all my control." He let go of my nipple and put his fingers on pause. Just when I was worried he was stopping us all together, I heard the clink of his belt opening, and the shred of fabric and maybe a zipper. His jeans clunked to the floor, followed by his shirt.

"I'm still not fucking you, but I am going to come all over your pretty ass while you ride my fingers." The long, hard, hot length of him slid along the seam of my butt, over the stupid thong that I wished he'd just rip off.

If this was what he was ready to give me, I would honor that he was the one who wasn't ready. I knew it was a big deal to a lot of guys to be a girl's first, and that was downright hot. He'd promised that we'd be doing this tomorrow, and again after that. I'd wait for him, just like I always had.

When the time was right for him too, that would make this all the more perfect. "I want to make you lose control. Let me hear you come for me this time."

"Fucking hell, *rybwy.*" Kirill buried his fingers deeper and this time, instead of thrusting he crooked them inside of me, finding a spot that made my whole pussy clench around him.

I cried out and he thrust his hips, sliding his cock between and over my butt cheeks. His free hand snaked around my belly, pulling me tighter against him and he pumped against me with every thrust of his fingers.

"That's it. Say you're mine, Addy. Always mine and only mine." He changed the angle of his fingers and thrust faster, harder, deeper. Each time, he pushed his cock over my skin and his thumb skimmed my clit, until I was ready to go insane if we didn't both come together.

I gasped for breath and pushed the words out in a throaty, tight keen. "Yes, yours. I've always been only yours."

"Mine." Kirill groaned out the word and shuddered behind me. Something hot hit the flesh of my rear end, and he pulled his hand out of me, smearing our release together across my skin. "Mine and only mine."

Before I could even react to the pure carnality of him marking me with his seed like that, he let go of the tight hold he had on my belly. Before I could even miss his body, he spun me around, picked me up by the waist and set my butt on the counter. He ripped my panties down my legs and tossed them over his shoulders and bent his head, giving me one long lick.

I'd never felt anything this good, even when I used one of those toys that looked like a tongue. The real thing was infinitely better. I wrapped my hands into his hair, and he snarled, licking and eating at me like a starving wolf. He slid his fingers in again and found that same spot that drove me crazy.

"Come for me again, sweet mate of mine. Come for me, now." The words filtered into my mind just like they did in my fantasies, and I lost it. My body clenched so hard I couldn't even breathe for a moment. Every muscle in my body jerked as the orgasm took over, and there was only bliss.

Mind. Blown.

"Babe. Addy. Are you okay?"

"Hmm?" I was still floating in the lovely afterglow. I

cracked one eye open to see Kirill, his face still wet from being buried in my pussy, floating above me.

He laughed and pulled me into his arms. "Your after sex face is fucking adorable. I wish I could wrap you up and cuddle you all night. But maybe not on the counter."

Oh, geez. We were in the middle of the cafe with our pants off. "Help me down. I'll be cleaning that with a lot of anti-bacterial products before the bookshop opens."

Kirill released me gently onto the floor and stepped away. The cool air of late night or early morning hit me, so that all I wanted to do was wrap myself up in him again. One big shiver swept over my skin before he pulled me up and held me in his arms. He tucked my head into the crook of his neck and rubbed my back. I wanted to stay there for hours. Except the sun was already rising and we'd spent the whole night together.

"We'd better get dressed." My panties were at my feet, but my bra hung from the latch of the pastry display case walk-in cooler on the other side of the cash register. "I need to get things cleaned up, and you have to go. The coffee shop opens soon."

He frowned and confusion flashed through his eyes. "I'm not letting you clean either yourself or the shop up without me."

Kirill crossed his arms and stared me down. He was naked as a plain donut, and I wanted to eat him up. "I meant what I said. You're mine and I'm not letting you go. We've both waited too damn long to be together and I'm not missing another moment with you."

I... didn't know what to say. We'd gone from zero to a sixty billion in the course of a few hours. I hadn't planned on going from slightly lost in my life and lonely to having a boyfriend who wanted to be by my side overnight. I wanted to be with Kirill. Completely and totally, but even as he made these declarations, there was something else he wasn't saying.

He'd kept the fight with Ryan quiet, he'd been reluctant to reveal his kinks to me... both of which I understood. I was all in, but was he really ready for the same? I needed him to open up to me if we were going to be together.

Kirill grabbed my dress off the floor and handed it to me.

"Thanks." I slipped the dress on, happy for the excuse to stay quiet for another minute. I was all up in my head, and I needed time to figure things out. Yeah, I loved him, and I was so happy that we'd had this night together.

But now that the flurry of lust and emotions was over, reality was sinking in. Worry skittered across my chest about what Ryan might say, do, think. Our sibling relationship had been tenuous for the past few years, and he'd been pissed as hell that I'd decided to go to Bay State instead of his university in California. Was I really willing to sacrifice my brother's love for Kirill's?

He was family. But Kirill could be my future. He was my future. I didn't want to give up either.

The jingling bell of the backdoor to the shop sounded, interrupting the spiral I was about to go down. Phew.

Wait. Oh shit. The cool air on my skin went absolutely frigid and it turns out my flight or fight response from earlier was gone. Now I was frozen in fear.

Because I was so getting fired.

Selena walked into the cafe, took one look at Kirill, and said, "Young man, you'd better tell me this girl is your fated mate and you've marked her, or both of you are fired."

Fated mates? Yeah. I liked that. I had known for a long time that we belonged together, and all it took was one night to rekindle all the feelings. No, that wasn't quite right, what I felt for him wasn't a schoolgirl's crush anymore. It seemed crazy to fall in love, real, soul deep love overnight. But we had. And he should know exactly how I felt.

I nodded to Selena, who didn't actually look mad. Not based on the cheeky grin she gave me and Kirill's junk. I positioned myself between the two of them, so she didn't have to... or get to eye my man. Then I took his hands in mine and looked into his warm violet eyes. "Kirill, will you come home with me for Thanksgiving? I want everyone in my family to know we're together. Ryan's supposed to come home this year, and I'd really like if you two could at least talk, if not be friends again."

Kirill answered by brushing his lips across mine and then dipping down and giving the place on my neck that must have an enormous hickey by now, a quick kiss too. Before he said anymore, he gave Selena a dip of his head too, acknowledging to her that we were more than just fuck buddies. "I want you to come home with me after the game this weekend and meet... some people who are important to my life. I have things I need to show you. If you still want me to go home with you for Thanksgiving after that, and make nice with your parents and Ryan, that will be up to you."

Umm. What in the world wasn't he saying? "Who are these important people?"

He glanced at Selena again before answering. "You know

Konstantin Troika and his... wife, Helinka? They took over the old Bay Inn?"

"Oh, yeah." The park and beach there had been really trashy and unkempt. The Bay's one real eyesore. People had said the inn was haunted until the Troikas moved in. "They've really made that old place nice again. Do you know them?"

"I do, and I'd like you to meet them." Something flashed in his eyes that I couldn't quite read. Was he nervous? Big, bad Kirill Zaliv didn't get the jitters. He was confidence on steroids.

Weird. I already knew his parents, so it wasn't like he had to take me home to meet them. But why the couple who'd only moved to The Bay a few years ago? They must be related in some way. Cousins, or an aunt and uncle maybe? Kirill also had a Russian last name, so I guess it was plausible.

Problem was, the last eight hours were a night-off anomaly. I still needed to come up with the dough to pay my rent, or my tuition, or both. "I have to work."

Selena sing-songed a response to that from the doorway to the kitchen. "No, you don't. You're owed some PTO that I just made a thing for all employees, so they have time to fall in love. I'll have Madison cover your shift. I have plans for her."

Kirill grinned like he was in cahoots with Selena or something, and then waggled his eyebrows at me. "Seems you're free. So will you come?"

I gave him a suspicious moue but nodded my agreement. He kissed me and kissed me and kissed me until Selena loudly cleared her throat.

"Maybe put some pants on before the early risers get more than they bargained for with their coffee this morning." She made her way into the bookshop as if she'd planned the whole affair and her work was now done.

I'd have to thank her for that later. Maybe after this strange visit to the Bay Inn.

KIRILL

I was so amped up after I took Addy home that my regular game day snooze was out. I liked the nocturnal life of a wolf, but school and football forced me into being awake when my instincts were to sleep. But if that meant I could stay up all night keeping Addy on my dick calling out my name, I'd skip some sleep.

I headed over to the field early instead, and that was where Eli, Nik, Luka, and Ty found me running laps like a mad wolf. I was all up in my head about how to tell her about the supernatural and not have her freak the fuck out like her brother had.

All but Luka had a human girl of their own, and they'd figured out how to tell them. I could use some advice. Since I'd been kind of an asshole when they'd been hooking up with their mates, I wasn't entirely sure they'd want to help me.

The lot of them joined in on my run. It wasn't like any of us were going to get tired out. Our wolves had plenty of stamina. This was nothing more than a warmup for us. Eli jogged up beside me and simply kept pace for a minute. Then he took the lead like the fucking alpha he was, and the other three moved into a phalanx beside and behind me.

There was comfort in being a part of a pack, even if it was just the five of us. It made my wolf happy to know we were a team that had each other's backs. That in and of itself gave my wolf enough peace to give me room to think clearly.

Eli took off, setting a brutal pace, going a hell of a lot faster than your average human. It was exactly what I needed. If anyone saw us, we'd get busted by coach for letting our extra power out where we could be questioned about it. Right now, I didn't fucking care. Why couldn't the world know we existed? Old rules for a different time, that's why.

Before Kosta and Heli took over the Bay and Fire Island packs, our alpha had been making moves to let the whole god-damned world know that we existed. He'd been a fucking sadistic dictator who thought we were a superior race and wanted to take over. I just wanted to be seen for who and what I was.

This secretive bullshit had ruined my life once before. I was afraid it would again. The only way out of this hell was to go through. If I was truly to be her fated mate, then I also had to believe that she would want me in all my messy, slightly fucked up glory.

Believe. I had to believe in fate, my love for her, and that she loved me back.

As if he knew I'd made a decision, Eli slowed the pace, and led the group of us to the benches and our waters. I flopped down and guzzled almost my entire bottle and poured the rest over my head.

"You good now?" Ty asked. "Wanna tell us what the fuck is going on?"

They were going to think I was being an asshole if I just blurted out that Addy was my fated mate. Or they were all going to give me tons of shit. Either way, I guess I deserved it. "Addy, the girl from last night, she's... mine."

Eli threw his head back and laughed. "No shit, Sherlock. But what's the problem?"

No shit? They all knew? I glanced around at each of them, and Luka was the only one who didn't have a look on his face like I was a complete dumbass.

Well, all righty then. Here was the real crux of the issue. "She doesn't know I'm a wolf."

Eli shook his head and tsked. Literally tsked at me like he was an old matriarch wolftress or something. He'd been hanging around Selena and that bookshop with Charlie too much. "Again, asshole, no shit. I still don't see what your problem is. None of our girls knew either. You show her and then help her learn about our world."

I couldn't admit to Eli, heir to the Chincoteague pack and rule follower extraordinaire, that I'd revealed myself to a human already and that it hadn't gone well. We were never supposed to let anyone find out except our fated mates. Even that had only come about in the past few years when Maxim and the other Troikas started a fucking revolution.

"Wolf up, dude." Ty punched me in the arm hard enough that I actually moved over on the bench a good couple of inches. "If she's truly your fated mate, she'll love it."

"And the way you two were gaga for each other, there's no way she isn't."

She might. She would. I did believe Addy would embrace the wolf side of my nature. "What about her family? They're from the Bay. She'll have a hard time hiding anything from them."

Jeez. I was being a shriveled-up ball sac. It wasn't her whole family I was worried about. Just one older brother who, despite my best efforts to not care about, still mattered to me. He definitely mattered to Addy.

Eli eyed me. "There's something else you're not saying."

"I hate this fucking secretive shit." I jumped up and paced, my wolf so close to the surface that if I didn't do something, I was going to explode and then the whole damn campus was going to wonder why there was a feral wolf running around biting people's heads off. "I should have fucking told her years ago, but I didn't. I just want to live my life, man. Play pro ball, have a dozen pups with my mate, and not hide anything anymore."

"Whoa. Is that what your problem has been all this time?" Nik threw his hands up in the air. "We all just thought you were a douchcanoe. A loyal one, but a total asshat."

I glared at him. I knew they all thought I was a dick, but that didn't help me now.

"Look," Ty said and crossed his arms. "I know what it's like to not want anyone to know who and what you are. And what I'm telling you is that once your mate sees the real you, nothing else matters."

Boom. The world froze, my heart stopped, my lungs refused to bring air in or out of my body.

Once your mate sees the real you, nothing else matters.

Nothing else matters.

That was the piece I'd been missing all of these years. I wanted so badly to be seen, but the only person I wanted to understand me all the way to my soul was Addy. She was my own true mate, and the person that I wanted to spend the rest of my life with. If she didn't know the real me... Nothing. Else. Mattered.

My wolf pushed to get out, and while I didn't shift, I did let the longest, loudest howl ring out from the depths of my soul. The other guys joined in, and before I knew it, thirty more of our teammates came rushing out onto the field, matching our cry. The game didn't start for three hours, but my guys were here for me in the one of the most important moments of my life. Most were simply human, and I'm sure they thought we were all just riling them up for the game, but that moment was the closest I ever felt to being the alpha of a pack of my own.

We got the whole team jumping, howling, and into a such a frenzy, we were going to eviscerate the other team. The second the game was over, I'd be sprinting to my mate, taking her straight to the sacred circle, and showing her exactly who and what I am.

"Eli!" coach shouted. "Why aren't you five dressed? Get in your gear unless you plan on sitting the bench."

"Yes, coach," The five of us said in chorus and hightailed it to the locker room.

When we got inside, Eli gave a look over his shoulder and then back at me. "If you want to go be with your girl now, dude. We can cover for you."

I didn't know whether it was because we were all wolf shifters playing in a human's world, or the bonds of friendship went a lot deeper than I'd ever realized, but I was flabbergasted by the amount of pure loyalty shown to me today. Eli would take serious shit if I didn't show up for the game, and quiet honestly, the Dire Wolves would probably lose. He and I were at the top of our game, and we scored a hell of a lot of touchdowns together.

"Thanks, man, but she's coming to the game with your girls today, and I've got plans to strut my fucking stuff and win this damn game for her." Nothing like a little competition to show off my prowess.

"If that isn't some medieval romance shit, I don't know what is." Luka smirked and shook his head at me. "I think I'll steal that move for myself."

"You got a girl, lucky Luka?" That was the first I'd heard of him being interested anything more than a ball bunny. Who had he hooked up with last night?

He narrowed his eyes at us and pulled his gear on. "Maybe."

"Faint heart never won fair lady, lads." Eli yanked his helmet on and gave it a couple of good knocks. "Now, get your asses in gear, gentlemen. Our team, and our ladies await."

"What are you a fucking historical lit major?" Since he'd hooked up with Charlie, Eli had finally let us all in on his dirty little secret of loving to read. I may be about to live my best life, but I still loved giving my friends shit.

He flipped me the bird. "Nope, just a lit minor, you illiterate werewolf."

I grabbed my chest and gasped. "Werewolf? Were fucking wolf? How dare you? I am a Dire Wolf to my core."

The other guys howled, and we jogged back out onto the

field to join in the warmups. Just before kick-off, I got a tingling feeling running up and down my spine.

She was here.

I searched the stands and found Addy and the other Dire Wolves' girlfriends in all their teal, silver, and black school colors and team wear. My dick went instantly hard imagining her wearing only my jersey and a well-fucked smile. She gave me a little wave and I decided to try something.

I reached out to her mind and tested the link between mates. "*Hey there, my sweet* rybwy."

Her head whipped back and forth looking for wherever my voice was coming from. She stared down at me and mouthed, "How are you doing this?"

I gave her a smile and a salute, along with the vision of her in my jersey with nothing on underneath. This time not only did her eyes go wide, but she blushed so sweetly I could hardly stand it. I was this close to jumping up into the stands and kissing her until she was begging me to take her home.

The whistle blew and our special teams hit the field. Time to play ball and show her what kind of man she was getting. Later tonight, I'd show her what kind of wolf she was getting too.

ADDY

I'd watched a lot of football in my life. A lot of Dire Wolves football. My dad went here, I always thought my brother would too, and of course, I tried never to miss one of Kirill's games. But I never had the time or money to come to the game, and I'd definitely never gotten to sit so close to the field.

Kirill running around in those tight football player pants on TV was one thing to lust over. In person? I was going to get dehydrated from all the drooling over him. Not to mention the way my heart pretty well exploded every time he had the ball.

I was on the verge of going hoarse after all the cheering and shouting I'd done. This was so much more fun than I'd had in ages. Now, there was only two minutes left in the game, we were tied, on the sixty-yard line, and it was fourth and ten.

The Dire Wolves had played a fierce game, but the Central Maryland Snallygasters were out for blood today. They'd already caused two of our players to go out with injuries, and I lost at least a minute of my life each time Kirill got tackled.

Somehow, he jumped right back up again, even when, from what I could tell, he should have been mashed so far into the turf, he should be flat as a pancake. But, boy, did he seem to be having fun.

Hunter elbowed her cousin, Eva. "Hey, if you only watch one play today, this is the one."

Eva had brought a vintage book to the game and had her nose buried in it the whole time. I'm not even sure why she came. But then again, it was almost impossible to say no to anything Hunter wanted anyone to do. Eva looked up for a moment, over at the scoreboard and then back to her book. Deadpan, she said, "Go sports. Move the thing to the other thing."

I snort-laughed. Girl didn't know what she was missing. And by that I meant hot football players. I was all for book boyfriends, goodness knows I had my fair share, but I mean... had she seen college football players? They were worth it for their butts alone.

The Dire Wolves snapped the ball, and Charlie hid her face in my shoulder. "I can't watch. Those Snallygasters have it out for Eli, I swear."

She wasn't wrong. Our quarterback rarely got sacked, and Eli had gone down twice today. But not this time. Kirill took off running toward the Gasters endzone, and Eli dropped back into the pocket. He let loose a nearly perfect spiral, sending that ball sailing down the field in one hell of a Hail Mary pass. No man should have been able to run fast enough to catch it.

Everyone in the stands jumped to their feet, and we were

screaming and cheering so loud I could barely hear myself yelling over the ruckus. That's when I decided to try something absolutely ridiculous. I closed my mouth, and in my head, I focused my thoughts on Kirill. *"Run, baby, run!"*

His voice came back to me right away. *"This one's for you, smart girl."*

He put on a burst of speed, outrunning the defensive players tailing him. Except for one damn Snallygaster who was almost keeping pace. The two of them had to be breaking freaking Olympic records right now.

The crowd went wild, and easy as if he was plucking the moon down from the sky, Kirill reached up and palmed the flying football in one hand, tucked it under his arm. The Snallygaster on his tail dove at the same time, grabbing Kirill around the waist and they went down together.

Kirill's hand shot out before he hit the ground under the weight of the other player, and the ball just barely crossed the white line.

"Touchdown, touchdown, touchdown Dire Wolves."

I barely heard the announcer. I couldn't hear anything over the whoosh, whoosh of my blood vessels rushing adrenaline through me. I hadn't imagined it. Kirill could talk in my head, and I could not only hear him, but I could also talk back.

Add onto that his incredible speed, the way he seemed to heal so easily, and the way he was so weird about whatever this secret he wanted to reveal to me was, I suspected he was more than the average football playing college kid.

Then there was the crazy tattoo that had appeared on my collarbone. I touched my fingers to the spot, and even through the jersey, I felt a tingle. Kirill was mid celebration, but he looked over at me and I swear on all that is holy, his eyes were literally glowing.

What in the wide world of sports was going on?

He tore his helmet off and jogged over to the sidelines along with the rest of the offensive team. The kicking team went out for the field goal, but Kirill and I weren't watching. We were frozen in our own space and time. I could literally feel his emotions, but he didn't say anything, in my head or not.

I guess the game ended, because the girls grabbed me and Eva and dragged us to the stadium exit. Rosie pulled me along. "Come on. We can meet the guys over by the locker room entrance."

We had to wade through a whole hell of a lot of fans, reporters, and other girls who were vying for the Dire Wolves' attention. The younger players came out first, and then one by one the stars made their exits to a cheering crowd. I was going to die if Kirill didn't hurry up and get his tight butt out here.

"Where are you, Kirill?" I grabbed my boobs and literally jumped up and down trying to see over the hundreds of people taller than me.

"Right here, sweet *rybwy.*" His voice came from behind me, and I spun. He was freshly showered, shaved, and had that after exercise gleam about him. I stared up into his still glowing eyes and saw so much more in them than I ever had before. "Come on, let's get out of here."

He took my hand and led me around the stadium and back toward the side of campus where the Wolves' Den and the Moon Bean stood. We went around back to the alley way where the employees could park their cars, but I certainly didn't have one, and I didn't think Kirill did either.

"Hey, why do you call me that? That ree-bwee thing you say." The way he said it was always warm or sometimes sexy as hell, but I didn't know what it meant.

Kirill chuckled, and chucked me under the chin. "It's Russian, and means something similar to sweetheart."

That was adorable, but there was more he wasn't telling me. I could tell by the extra added twinkle in his eye. "And...?"

"Well," his grinned but pressed his lips together, trying not to laugh. "Understand my family comes from a long line of sea fairing folk, and that means that that comes from the sea is precious to us."

Oh, cute. Maybe it meant something like pearl or jewel of the sea. I love that it had such meaning for him.

"*Rybwy* translates to little fish."

I smacked him on the arm. But I also made fish lips at him and he kissed them until there was no more jokes, only so much passion that I would forever associate little fishes with love.

"You wanna go for a ride? Ty is lending me his bike and some helmets so I can take you somewhere special tonight. The park near the Bay Inn has a secluded area I'd like to show you."

He wanted me to go off into the woods with him, all alone? With everything I'd seen today, any reasonable girl would say no. I should be scared out of my wits. Because Kirill wasn't human.

I took his hand in both of mine and brought his knuckles

to my lips. "I know what you are. You don't have to try to keep yourself secret from me anymore."

The muscles in his chest, shoulders, jaw, and arms tensed. "What do you think I am?"

I released his hand and pulled the neckline of my shirt to the side, revealing the tattoo of a howling wolf with the sea at his feet and the full moon behind, all at the outline of the bite mark he'd given me last night. "Werewolf. You're a werewolf."

Kirill's eyes flashed, the purple bursting to life. He ripped off his t-shirt and his face and arms partially shifted, fangs and claws appearing. He snarled and shook, like this transformation caused him pain.

I touched my hand to his cheek and stroked my thumb over it. "I'm not afraid of you. I love you, no matter what."

The intensity of the animal pushing to get out receded and he placed his hand over mine as he got himself back under control. "You love me? Even knowing I'm just as much beast as man?"

His voice was harsh and broken, but not because of this animalistic side. No, my Kirill was worried I would reject him, run away, never want to see him again.

Just like Ryan had.

Oh my. This is why they'd fought. He'd revealed this secret to my brother. And Ryan had not only run away to the other side of the country, but he'd also made sure that Kirill and I never saw each other again too. I'd deal with Ryan later. Right now, I had a puppy to pet. "I do. I always have. I always will. You might be a wolf, but you're my wolf."

Kirill swept me into his arms and kissed me, so deep, so needy, and so desperate. "Thank the Goddess. There's so much more to explain, but it will be easier when we're somewhere more private. Come on."

He grabbed a helmet and handed it to me before grabbing his shirt back up and putting his own on. With easy moves, he straddled the motorcycle and started it right up, then held out a hand to me. I'd never been on a bike like this, and I had a feeling this was not going to be my only first tonight.

We zoomed out off campus and toward the Bay Inn. It only took a few minutes for us to get to the open space area, but by the time we pulled into the inn's parking lot right near the beach, the moon was starting to rise over the water. The way it sent sparkles out over the water was one of the most gorgeous sights I'd ever witnessed.

The front porch light of the inn flickered on and the couple who owned it came out. The woman, Heli, went over and sat down on a lovely porch swing, but the man, Konstantin Troika stood at the top of the steps with his arms crossed.

Kirill gave the man a low nod of his head and held it there for a long minute. Konstantin's eyes glowed with the same purple as Kirill's, and I had to hold in a gasp. This man was a wolf too. Not just any wolf either. His presence carried an importance that even I could feel.

"Kosta, don't torture the poor guy," Heli called. Then she directed herself toward the two of us. "The sacred circle is all cleaned up and ready for, uh, visitors if that's where you're headed. Have fun."

I couldn't take my eyes away from the man who seemed to have Kirill in some kind of a thrall. Until Heli stood up and gave her husband a smack on the arm. Soon enough,

Kirill lifted his head and put his arm around my shoulders. Then Konstantin smiled and gave us a nod that I could only take as approval.

"Should we go over there and like actually talk to them?" I whispered.

"We'll come back to do that later." He lowered his hand to the small of my back and guided me down the beach toward an area that wasn't open to the public. "But I want to show you my full wolf form, and then I need to fuck you and feel you coming on my dick. I need to know your body is mine."

Oh. Oh, yes, please.

We entered the area and went through some trees that, once we were within, opened up into a circle with only the sky above visible. It was beautiful.

"Take off your clothes and let the moonlight pour over your lush, soft body." Kirill ripped off his shirt, dropped his jeans to the ground, and kicked off his shoes, all in the fastest moves I'd ever seen.

I didn't even get a chance to react before he reached for my t-shirt hem and lifted it up and over my head. Today, I didn't have on anything but basic white cotton underthings. But it didn't matter. I wasn't going to be wearing them long anyway.

As he stripped me, the moon rose over the top of the trees, and I forgot how to breath. Kirill's entire body glowed with an ethereal light. He bent his head and pressed a kiss to the wolf mark on my neck.

"I'd heard stories that true mates glow for each other in the moonlight, but I didn't think that was anything more than a fairytale until now. You're fucking beautiful bathed in the Goddess's light."

Oh my Goddess. I loved every bit of this night. "You're glowing too. You're saying that's for me?"

"Only for you." As he said those words, he winked and then he dropped down to all fours. I cringed as his bones cracked and his skin split, reshaping his body into that of an enormous black wolf.

He was just as tall as I was, all fur and teeth and claws. But those eyes. Those were still Kirill's eyes. I carefully reached out and touched the soft spot between his snout and his forehead. He relaxed into my touch and in another moment, he was back in his human form, my hand still on his forehead.

"That was amazing. I was worried you be all scary like the werewolves in the movies."

"We aren't actually like those myths at all. We're wolf shifters, a gift from the Goddess of the Moon. There's a lot to teach you, but the most important thing is that you can't reveal our existence to anyone."

"You did." I stroked my hand into his hair, needing to be as close to him as I could. "You showed yourself to Ryan, didn't you?"

"Yeah. He didn't take it very well. But he did promise not to tell anyone else. If I stayed away from you."

"Ryan doesn't make my decisions for me. I love him, but he was wrong to do that." I'd kick his big butt for it at Thanksgiving.

"You always were a badass." Kirill pinched my butt and when I squealed, he picked me up and lowered me to the ground. "Are you ready, *rybwy*? Ready to be my mate?"

I nodded because I couldn't make any words come out of

my mouth. This was everything I ever wanted. "Yes. Make me yours, my big hot shot of a wolf."

Kirill took my hand and brought it down to his huge cock. I'd seen it yesterday, sure. But now, up close, and about to be mine, it was so much bigger than I'd imagined. He stroked my hand up and down his shaft a few times and groaned. "Keep doing that, while I touch you. I need you to be wet and wanting if I'm going to fuck you like I want to."

"I've been wet for you since you scored that touchdown." A lot longer if I was honest. "Plus, that motorcycle ride and seeing your wolf, your true self, helped too. I'm more than ready for this."

Kirill swiped a hand between my legs, drawing two fingers through my wet pussy. His eyes flared and he brought his soaking fingers to his mouth and licked them. "I've been scenting your arousal for hours, but I didn't know you were this needy for me."

"I need you. I need you right now."

He pressed my legs open with his knees and then notched the head at my entrance. Slowly he pushed his cock into me, all the way to the hilt in one long thrust. Then he stilled. "Fuck, your so god-damned tight. Are you okay?"

Was I okay? I was dying in all the very best ways. It was like our bodies fit together so perfectly that there was no doubt we belonged together forever. "I'm more than okay. I'll be great if you do a whole lot more. Like make me come."

Kirill growled and the glow of his eyes, that I understood now was his beast coming out to play, shimmered and sparkled.

"I'm going to do more than make you come. I'm going to

claim you, I'm going to fill you with my seed, so that every other wolf will know that you belong to me, and me to you."

He pulled out and I didn't even have time to miss our connection before he flipped me over and put me on my hands and knees in front of him. With a snarl, he grabbed my hips and thrust into me from behind, deeper than he'd been before.

"Your next orgasm is mine. You're going to come, but not until I say you can. Do you understand?"

His words shot straight from my brain to my pussy like an electrical shock of the best kind. This dominant side of him was exactly what I wanted and needed. I loved the way he demanded to take care of me. "Yes."

"Good girl." He grabbed my hair, holding it tight in his fist and dragged his cock in and out of me, filling me, driving me higher with each push. I wrapped my feet around his waist wanting to hold him to me, never let him go.

"God, if your cunt is this fucking tight," He palmed my butt with his other hand, "I can't wait to take your plump little ass."

I could do nothing but whimper. Not even the romance novels I'd read were so dirty, and no one had ever said anything like this to me before. I wanted more.

With a growl, he wrapped his arm around my hip and slipped his hand between my legs to find my clit. He slid his fingers over that oh, so sensitive area, once, twice, but not enough to make me come.

"Please, Kirill, I'm so close."

"Don't come until I tell you to. I want this first time to be perfect for you."

I gulped in air, my pussy fluttered around his cock. His words and his sincerity were driving me into ecstasy just as much as his body. I wasn't going to last much longer. "It is, because I'm with you."

"Goddess, I love you Adeline, I fucking love you." He rocked into me fast, hard, and harder, losing his own control over the encounter. He released my hair and gripped both of my hips. A million tingles sparked across my scalp, increasing the sensations throughout my body. I was reduced to a puddle of whimpers and moans. "That's it, you're almost there. A little more, baby. Give me a little more."

I didn't have anything left to give. I cried out as my body took over. Muscles I didn't even know I had contracted and pulsed. "Please. I… I… I'm…"

"Yes, now, Addy. Give me your orgasm, give me your body, give me your love. Come for me, now."

I shattered, exploded, imploded. There was no him and me, there was only us. Our bodies creating a whole new universe. My vision went black and all I saw was stars. All I could feel was pure ecstasy.

Kirill thrust into me harder than ever before, and his cock felt different this time. I was so much fuller. I clenched around him, and he cried out his own release. "Mine, Addy, mine."

KIRILL

Addy and I were inseparable for the next few months, except when she was at work and I was at practice. But she came to all my games, and I developed an appreciation for Sundays spent with her at the bookstore. Selena had promoted her to cafe manager and gave her a raise that went with it. Her cafe was very conducive to studying and her mochachocolattes were the bomb.

Christmas was rapidly approaching, and Addy's emotions were on crack from her worry about how her brother would react to our relationship. She hadn't told him off at Thanksgiving like she wanted to because the jackass hadn't come home. Sure, sure, his team had a big game that week, but I had a feeling he wasn't sad about that.

I'd watched him play on TV with a lot of interest. If they won, the Dire Wolves were going to play Ryan's precious East Cal State Dragons in the Titan Bowl right before Christmas. And the game was right up the road in the New York Destroyers stadium. I already had tickets for her and her parents on the Bay State U side.

This particular dragon from our past was mine to slay, and I had a plan.

The next morning, after the Dragons won, I sent off a text, knowing it wasn't even the butt-crack of dawn in California yet, and headed to the cafe for some back room making out with Addy before I had to head to the field for practice. My phone buzzed in my pocket a few seconds later.

Ryan: What do you want, hot shot? Hoping for some tissues for your whiner baby quarterback, dude?

Me: My QB is going to kick your sorry asses.

Ryan: Good luck with that.

Me: We need to talk

Ryan: FML - you finally did it, didn't you?

I didn't pretend for even a second that I didn't know what he was asking.

Me: It's been a long time coming. You should have told me she got into Bay State U.

Ryan: Hurt my little sister and I will wipe the field with your face on Christmas. Then every day after that just for fun.

What the shit? Was Ryan actually giving me his blessing to be with Addy in his own fucked up way? I stared at the screen for at least five minutes before replying. Because, holy shit, he was.

Me: You're okay with Addy and I... being mates?

Ryan: She's a grown ass woman, it's not my place to tell her what to do anymore. It's not like I didn't see this fucking coming when you turned into a fucking wolf and said she was yours. Just treat her right, you douchecanoe.

Me: I will. I am.

Ryan: You'd better be planning on naming your first kid after me.

I'd fucking name all of our kids after him just to have his blessing. Little Ryanina would have her uncle wrapped around her little finger.

Me: See you at Christmas

The day of the Titan Bowl couldn't come soon enough. I'd show Ryan and the whole damn world just how much I loved Addy. I even had Kosta's blessing to do so. Turned out he'd been pushing his brother, the Wolf Tzar, to start letting more humans into our world. I wasn't allowed to reveal my wolf, but I didn't have to hide from the spotlight. He even agreed to let me enter the draft in the spring and possibly play for the pros.

It took a damn lot of strings pulled, and my special privileged use of the patented Eli Chincoteague, QB charm, to talk the camera guys at the stadium on game day to give me some airtime. As much as I wanted time on the field, I prayed the Dragons had the ball and I'd be on the bench when the last whistle before halftime blew.

The girls and a bunch of Dire Wolves' pack family members, their faces painted Bay State teal and silver, sat front and center at the fifty-yard line, waving giant foam fingers. I had all of two minutes during the last commercial break before half-time to rush over to the sidelines to her. Coach was going to kill me, because I certainly hadn't asked his permission, the old grump, but it would be worth it if she said yes.

Ryan and I clashed on the field and I was pretty sure he was testing my mettle. He'd gained muscle, speed, and gotten a hell of a lot bigger out there in Cali eating his granola and avocados. On the last whistle, where I'd flattened him, I offered my former best friend a hand up. He took it and when he was up, socked me in the shoulder, guy-thanks style.

I slugged him back. "Hey man, keep your eye on the Kiss-Cam right before half-time."

He didn't have time to reply before we had to head back to our respective benches, but I knew he heard me by the way he gave me the finger.

The clock to half-time clicked its way down and of course Eli decided to run in a fucking touchdown right before the last commercial break. I had to sprint off the field of play to get to Addy in time. I snagged the ring out of my bag and rushed over to the sidelines where she stood. There was too much space between the stands and the field, and I couldn't take her hand, but I yanked off my helmet and got down on one knee.

Marriage and weddings and rings weren't wolf tradition, but they were human, and I wanted to make her as happy as I was having her as my mate. We'd have a wedding, but it would end in a traditional wolf mating ritual under the full moon.

"Adeline," I shouted. The scoreboard nearest us lit up with the Kiss-Cam border and zoomed out to show both of us. "Will you marry me?"

The shot narrowed to show Addy with her fingers wiping at happy tears, nodding, and yelling back her answer, "Yes, yes, so much yes."

Another camera angle popped up next to the picture of Adeline, showing ECS middle-linebacker number sixty-two, Ryan Austin. I don't know who gave the camera guys insider info that he and Addy were related, dammit. My stomach sunk down to my cleats waiting for Ryan's reaction. I'd been sure he was good with me and Addy, but now in the moment of truth, I worried I was wrong, and he wasn't ready to have me as an in-law. But maybe a wolfskin rug for his dorm room instead.

Addy looked across the field at Ryan and smiled at him. He pulled off his helmet and gave her a smirky grin back and nodded his head. The crowd erupted into cheers and I used just a smidge of my wolf strength to jump over the retaining wall, up into the stands, and put the ring on Addy's finger.

My entire offensive line, including Eli, Ty, Nik, and Luka came over and howled and did a touchdown style dance, which distracted the cameras and the crowd. I barely got in a kiss before the commercial break ended and the whistle blew for the next play before halftime.

But that was okay because there would be plenty more kisses from Adeline for me. I jumped back over the wall and turned to blow her one last kiss before returning to the team. When I did, not only were there happy tears in her eyes, but the purple glow of the Bay pack wolves was there too.

I gave out a sharp, elated howl, and not only did Addy return my cry, but so did half the stadium. Only she and I knew they were celebrating more than a great game and an engagement. They were celebrating our love.

JUST HOW IS it that Selena seems to know who belongs together?

Read about her match making in the Alpha Wolves Want Curves series - start with Dirty Wolf

Turn the page for a preview of the first chapter of Dirty Wolf to get a taste!

DIRTY WOLF PREVIEW

WOLVES, DRINKS, AND OTHER DELICIOUS THINGS

Ahh. Finally she could breathe. The cool night air brought the heat in her cheeks and her temper down to a manageable level. Gal seriously knew better than to walk through the Reserve at night, but here she was. The posted rules stated that the area closed at dusk, and trespassers would face severe consequences. Lately that kind of threat meant less and less to her. After the blowout she'd had with her dad tonight, she was feeling an extra special kind of rebelliousness and consequences could go blow themselves.

So, yeah. She'd snuck out of her room like some teenager, and cut through the Reserve even though it was nine o'clock at night and dusk had long since come and gone. But come on, seriously. What twenty-three year old woman with an advanced degree wasn't allowed out at night to hang with her friends?

Her. That's who.

She found herself stomping, but it wouldn't do to trample some poor little caterpillar or crush some flowers because of her foul mood. It wasn't their fault. It was hers for not realizing what moving in with her parents would be like. She was saving every nickel and dime that didn't go toward paying her school loan. She'd sold her car to save on gas and insurance since she lived within walking distance to the library. Tonight was the first time since she'd gotten back to Rogue that she'd even gone out. It wasn't like she wasn't trying.

Trying too hard according to her dad, who'd told her more than once tonight she was making him bald. What really irked her was that her mother had simply sat there on the couch, knitting of all things, and hadn't said a word as her father had berated her lifestyle. Choosing to get a masters degree in Library Science and not being married were not bad choices. Ugh.

Unless your father would rather have you still a virgin, married to a nice Persian boy, and staying at home doing the dishes. No way, *pedar.*

A rustling behind her in the underbrush had her speeding up. If she made as much noise as possible, maybe that would scare away any animals following her. Eek, she hoped it was an animal. As far as she knew, Rogue, New York had never had a serial killer. Double eek. Maybe that meant they were due for one.

The leaves on the trees shivered in the wind and the shadows in the underbrush seemed much darker than they should. She was such a freaking dumb bunny. She should have just called an Uber to take her to the old town district.

It just felt so deliciously naughty to do a little law breaking in what had felt like a benign way at the time.

Now here she was in the middle of the dark forest of the Reserve and pretty sure someone or something was following her. Gal whipped out her phone and dialed Zara's number. "Come on, come on. Pick up."

She really wished that she hadn't listened to those teenagers at the library last week who insisted these woods were filled with wolves. No, not just wolves, werewolves. She'd laughed along with the kids and helped them find a werewolf anime series to read. Might as well take advantage of their fascination with the supernatural to get them to read.

If they were right and she got bit by some creepy ass animal and turned into a shape shifter, she was going to.... to.... kill someone. Gal laughed at her own ridiculousness and dialed the phone again. Zara picked up and the sounds of a busy bar burst through the phone.

"Hey, where are you?" Her friend shouted into the phone.

"On my way. I had a big fight with my dad, but I'll be there soon. I could seriously use a drink." And to have her head examined. And a drink.

Something swished across the path behind her and her conversation went on autopilot while her brain compiled a to-do list for escape and evading. She said the required yeses, nos, and kept her voice cheery, but she also hurried a little bit faster. The instructor at the all women's martial arts school she'd taken classes at in Ann Arbor would be really disappointed if her star student was murdered because she's made a really bad decision to go out walking alone after dark.

In the woods.

Where werewolves lived.

Don't be silly. Gal could still use the skills she'd learned in class about spatial awareness and threat assessment to get out of the Reserve safely. The first thing was to make sure her friends knew exactly where she was. She spoke so loudly, the whole city would know her position. Take that weird, creepy stalker.

"Yeah, ha ha. I'm almost to the parking lot at the edge of the Reserve." She could see the lights of the businesses in the old town district and the road up ahead. She was going to make it and without spotting any monsters of any kind.

That's when she caught sight of the wolf.

She barely glimpsed him out of the corner of her eye. A flash of silver against the brown and green of the forest.

She waited for her heart to stop, for the scream from the innermost depths of her soul, or to simply faint right there on the little dirt path.

None of those things happened.

A sense of calm, like she'd been hit in the face with a whole lavender bush, washed through her. She had zero doubts that the animal was there to protect her, not harm her. What a strange thing to think, but she knew it was true.

Clearly she was hallucinating and needed that drink more than she thought she did. Moving back home, starting a new job, and saying goodbye to her care-free and independent college life had taken more of a toll on her psyche than she had previously thought. Time to de-stress with a good old girls night out.

In a few more feet she was in the parking lot and jogging across the street. Her favorite little bar, the Sleepy Folk, an old speakeasy from the days of prohibition was just another block up the street. She pushed into the little pie shop at the front and headed straight for the back stairs that led to the bar below. Although, later she was totally having a fried apple pie. Mmm. Two in the morning, slightly tipsy, bar food was the best.

She should know, her ass showed just how much she liked tasty beverages and tasty treats. Not that she'd been a skinny-mini to start out with, but she'd put on the freshman fifteen and more. Her college friends had gotten her hooked on sweet shots and she'd never looked back.

The bar was packed but Zara and Heli had a coveted table and spotted her right away. Zara waved and Gal pushed through the Friday night crowd to get to them. They were the best of friends and had her chocolate martini waiting. She'd taarof with them later to decide who paid. "Hi, you guys. I missed you both so much."

They all went in for a round of hugs. Heli first, then Zara who held on for longer than the regular old friend reunion squeeze. Seems they all needed a girls night out. Fruity flavored alcohol was a great cure all. When Zara released her, Gal raised her glass and they clinked glasses. "To many more girls nights out."

"I'll drink to that," Heli said and sipped her pink drink. Zara's beverage looked quite a bit stronger. Something amber on ice. Whiskey. Yikes. Hanging out with her friends when they weren't drinking moved up on the priority list. She'd do her best to pull whatever was wrong out of Zara later.

Gal squeezed Zara's hand and made a silent promise to be there for her. "Okay. I want all the town gossip from you two. Six years is far too long to be gone. Give me the low down on who is sleeping with whom and who else is mad about it. The preschoolers at story time don't know squat. Totally unreliable for gossip, those kids are."

Heli exhaled and smiled, a thank you in her eyes. "Well. Remember Cynthia, third in line for the mean girl title my year?"

"The one who bleached her hoo-ha so her carpet would match her curtains?" They all knew, because every horny jock on the football, basketball, baseball, and even the soccer team knew. High school boys were worse gossips than any of them ever were.

"Yeah." Heli rubbed her hands together and her eyes flashed with the kind of mischief Gal loved her for. "She married Mark Grubler."

"No." Gal gasped in fun. "But his family is uber religious. He used to go to church before school every morning."

Heli took another sip of her drink and popped a piece of fruit in her mouth, chewing and making them wait. "I know, Cyn is a devout Sunday school teacher now and the perfect little homemaker. She's the president of the PTA."

"How is that even possible? You have to have a child enrolled.... oh. What? They were doing it in high school?"

Zara laughed and finally joined in the conversation. "Yep. Little Noah is six and started first grade this year. He's some sort of math prodigy or something. Can you even imagine?"

They giggled and laughed and gossiped until Gal's cheeks hurt. Man, she needed this. She absolutely needed to make more time to hang out with her friends and rekindle all the good times they had together. Who would have thought three girls who'd bonded over the horrors of the aerobics unit in their mandatory high school PE class would be such good friends after six years apart?

"Speaking of old gossip. Look who just walked in." Heli gave the tiniest of motions with her head behind Gal. "Wait. Don't just turn around and stare. Be cool about it."

Cool? Right. Gal picked up her glass, downed the rest so it was empty and turned toward the bar like she was going to get another one.

Standing where she expected to see the bartender was the boy, uh- huge, hot, man…., had he gained a lot of muscle..., man she'd had a crush on since about the third grade. He caught her looking and his eyelids lowered to half-hooded and he grinned.

Every butterfly in the northern hemisphere flew straight into her stomach and a good fifty percent of those migrated south. Gal spun around and widened her eyes at Heli. "You could have told me it was Max. Cripes. He isn't coming over here, is he?"

Heli nodded. "He sure is."

"Ack. Do I have anything in my teeth? Did I spill down the front of my shirt. Dirt on my head, I always do that."

The words poured out of Heli's mouth, hurrying to answer. "You look great. His mouth is probably already watering. Here he comes."

"Ladies." A hand landed on the back of her chair and she could practically feel the heat coming off his extreme hotness. "Can I get you another round?"

"Hi Max. That's nice of you." Heli grinned up at Max. Gal didn't have the guts to do the same.

"Heli, Zara." Max gave Zara a bit of a nod and a conspiratorial grin. The Troikas' parents had never approved of

Max's older brother Niko and Zara seeing each other. Max and Kosta didn't agree with their parents. One time they even pretended to have a broken down car in the next town over to get their mom and dad out of the house so Niko could take Zara to the prom.

His rebelliousness was one of those qualities that had drawn Gal to him in the first place. Back then she couldn't imagine defying her father. Dating a Troika would probably send him into fits. She was an adult now. She could do what she wanted.

Sort of. Man, she really needed to figure out a way to move out of her parents' house faster than what her librarian's salary afforded her.

"You drinking chocolate milk there, Galyna?" Max tipped his head at the few dribbles left in the bottom of Gal's martini glass.

She did love a good flirt. So why was there a funny wiggle in her tummy where her flirter should be? She couldn't seem to get it kick started. "I've graduated to chocolate martinis, thank you very much."

"Mmm. Sounds delicious. Can I try it?" Max eyeballed the glass in her hand, or maybe he was staring at her chest.

Okay, that grin he was giving her was way too sexy, and he knew it. Definitely her chest. She had dressed sexier than her usual sweater sets. Certainly not because she'd hoped to see him tonight. No, not at all. "Afraid there's not much left."

"Just enough." Max took the glass, his fingers barely brushing against hers and oh, so slowly ran the tip of his tongue over the rim and then dipped into the well, once, twice. The pink of his tongue was visible through the bottom and he swirled it around licking up every last drop.

The inside of that glass wasn't the only thing that was wet.

Her eyes must be the size of the moon tonight. Gal half coughed, half laughed.

"That is delicious. Come on over to the bar and show me how to make that." He held out his hand to her.

She almost didn't want to touch it. No doubt putting her skin to his would be electric. She didn't need to be any more turned on by him than she already was. "I'm pretty sure your bartender can show you. He made me this one."

Someone kicked her under the table. She didn't know which sister did it though because they were both making are-you-insane faces at her.

"He's busy. Besides, I'm sure yours will be much, much sweeter." Every word out of his mouth dripped with delicious sexual innuendo.

Her hand reached out for him of its own accord. The traitor. It was in league with the butterflies in her stomach and her girly parts, which were all on team Jump Max's Bones.

The naughty look on his face said he was on that team too. He took her hand and pulled her up from her chair. She'd been right, something like electricity but more fun zipped through her sending the nicest kind of shivers along her skin. If simply touching his hand was like this, what would sex be like?

Gal mentally eye-rolled herself. It wasn't like they were gonna go into the back store room and get it on. She didn't even know where the store room was and this wasn't a porno. Max dragged her through the crowd and behind the bar. They stood side by side in the small space, so close their arms and hips touched. Max pulled down two martini glasses from the rack overhead and she felt every one of his movements down to her core.

"What's next, Galyna?" His tongue peeked out licking his bottom lip and his eyes flicked between hers and her lips. Why did it sound like he was asking a whole lot more than how to make a martini?

"Chocolate vodka, vanilla bean if you don't have that. Chocolate liqueur, creme de cacao, cream, and chocolate syrup." If she were in her sorority house back in Michigan, she would have also dipped the rim in chocolate sprinkles, but she doubted they had any of those behind the bar.

Max grabbed both kinds of vodka without even leaving her side. Then he winked at her and sunk down, down, down her body. His hand went to her leg, using her for support. Those butterflies in her tummy burned up in the flames his touch ignited.

He slid open a cooler where all the refrigerated ingredients were kept and even the cool blast of air did nothing to lower her internal temperature. It's not like she thought he was going down there for anything other than the freaking chocolate syrup, but her libido sure didn't seem to know that.

Up came the cream, liqueur, and chocolate syrup. Kind of like he knew that's exactly where they kept all the ingredients. Gal held in a snort-laugh. Of course Max knew where everything they needed was and probably exactly how to make this drink. He owned the bar for goodness sake.

Fine. It wasn't like she didn't know they were playing a game anyway. She'd just smartened up to the rules a little better. She could do this. Max wanted to get his flirt on? Two could flirt better than one.

He took his sweet time standing back up, his eyes wandering over every single one of her curves. Gal straightened her back so by the time he got above her waist, her girls were proudly thrust forward. She wasn't disappointed by the extra sparkle in his eye as he lingered on her chest. Again.

Her hips, thighs, and butt might be bigger than was considered acceptable by main stream media and her family, but she had killer boobs. Max stared at her chest long enough that she cleared her throat. He swiped a finger across the tip of his nose and then his lips before finding his way to her eyes again.

The lust in his gaze was so powerful it seemed like his eyes were glowing with it. Gal blinked and the glow was gone, but the lust remained. "Here's everything you need, *kiska*."

Gal swallowed, not quite trusting herself to reply yet. Max leaned forward. Whoa, he was coming in for a kiss. Right here, in front of half the town. His eyes never left hers and he reached around her side, skimmed his palm along her bare arms. Her heart rate soared right up to maximum speed and at the same time she forgot how to breathe. She'd imagined kissing Max more times than she could count.

His eyes twinkled, her eyes surely matched with her own gah-gah for him sparkle. Gal parted her lips and sucked in the soft woodsy scent of him.

Max shifted and held a crystal clear martini glass right in her face. "Salt or sugar?

Gal raised one eyebrow at the bastard and sucked on her

teeth. She was salty alright. "Neither. Gimme the chocolate syrup. I'll prep the glasses, you mix the drinks. I think you know what to do."

His lips pressed together in a close-mouthed grin stifling a laugh that screamed he knew exactly what he was doing. Why was she staring at his lips anyway?

She turned and grabbed the bottle of syrup and the glass out of his hand. She put all of her concentration into pouring a thick bead in a long swirl from the base to the rim, drizzling the Hershey-goodness along the edge so it dripped enticingly down the outside. A peek out of the corner of her eye showed him watching her while pouring the ingredients into the shaker. Good.

The bottle gave a satisfying splursh with her next squeeze and the chocolate covered the ends of her fingertips. "Oops."

She brought her finger up to her mouth and wiped her fourth finger clean by swiping it down the inside of her bottom lip then licking the end clean. Max knocked the shaker and had to fumble to save it. It was a wonder he didn't spill it everywhere since his eyes were locked on her mouth and fingers and not looking at the countertop at all.

Ha. All's fair in love and war. This was a little of both. Gal moved to lick her middle finger next but Max grabbed her wrist and sucked both messy fingers into his mouth. His tongue swished back and forth and then pressed against her fingers as he sucked on them. Those sparkles in his eyes went dark as midnight and she could hear his rapid breathing as if no one else existed around them.

The things that man did with his tongue had Gal's knees going weak.

"Mmm." He hummed around her fingers and the vibrations went straight through her. One by one, he popped her fingers out of his mouth, licking the tips, imitating her earlier tease, and then licked his own lips. "You are delicious."

"Uh-huh." Crap. Her voice came out breathless and wow, she sounded super-smart.

He moved even closer to her so their bodies were only centimeters apart. "I'd love to just eat you up."

The yes-please was on the tip of her tongue when his phone rang. Max's eyes narrowed and he silenced the ringer. Irritation flashed across his face and he sighed. "Duty calls, kiska. I have to go, but I will be seeing more of you."

"Okay." She sure wished she had a flirty retort to his declaration, but she wanted him to see more of her. Much, much more.

Max grabbed a napkin and a pen. He scribbled something on it and pressed it into her fingers. Then he kissed her palm, put one hand on the bar and leapt right over it and into the crowd. He was through the crowd and out the door before she even got her wits about her. She gave the drinks they'd mixed a shake and poured them into the glasses she'd prepped. She made her way back to the table and set the martinis down for her friends. She was riding a natural high and didn't need anything more to make her night feel good.

Heli was practically vibrating with excitement. "Holy crap. I thought you guys were going to start making out right there at the bar."

Zara nodded and picked up one of the drinks tasting it. "The way you guys were eye-sexing it up got pretty much everyone in here hot."

"Shut up. You're going to make me blush." Gal put her hands on her cheeks but there was no hiding her high color. She opened the napkin and found Max's phone number written on it, with the words, put this in your phone printed underneath it.

"Too late." Heli took the other drink and downed half of it. "So, when are you seeing him again?"

Not soon enough.

Keep reading Dirty Wolf in Kindle Unlimited, eBook, paperback, and/or audio!

ALSO BY AIDY AWARD

Dragons Love Curves

Chase Me

Tease Me

Unmask Me

Bite Me

Cage Me

Baby Me

Defy Me

Surprise Me

Dirty Dragon

Crave Me

Dragon Love Letters - Curvy Connection Exclusive

Slay Me

Play Me

Merry Me

The Black Dragon Brotherhood

Tamed

Tangled

Twisted

Fated For Curves

A Touch of Fate

A Tangled Fate

A Twist of Fate

Alpha Wolves Want Curves

Dirty Wolf

Naughty Wolf

Kinky Wolf

Hungry Wolf

Flirty Wolf - - Curvy Connection Exclusive

Grumpy Wolves

Filthy Wolf

The Fate of the Wolf Guard

Unclaimed

Untamed

Undone

Undefeated

Claimed by the Seven Realms

Protected

Stolen

Crowned

Vampires Crave Curves

Vampires Are Forever

The Vampire Who Loved Me

By Aidy Award and Piper Fox

Big Wolf on Campus

Cocky Jock Wolf

Bad Boy Wolf

Heart Throb Wolf

Hot Shot Wolf

Big D Wolf

Contemporary Romance by Aidy Award

The Curvy Love Series

Curvy Diversion

Curvy Temptation

Curvy Persuasion

The Curvy Seduction Saga

Rebound

Rebellion

Reignite

Rejoice

Revel

ABOUT AIDY AWARD

Aidy Award is a curvy girl who kind of has a thing for stormtroopers. She's also the author of the popular Curvy Love series and the hot new Dragons Love Curves series. She writes curvy girl erotic romance, about real love, and dirty fun, with happy ever afters because every woman deserves great sex and even better romance, no matter her size, shape, or what the scale says.

Read the delicious tales of hot heroes and curvy heroines come to life under the covers and between the pages of Aidy's books. Then let her know because she really does want to hear from her readers.

Connect with Aidy on her website. www.AidyAward.com get her Curvy Connection, and join her Facebook Group - Aidy's Amazeballs.

ALSO BY PIPER FOX

The Ironhaven Wolf Pack Series

The Dragon Space Order Bride Series

Bears of Crooked Creek series

Last Warriors of Delaria series

Seven Brides for Seven Demons series

Immortal Blood series

Alien Warriors of New Delaria: a BBW scifi RH series

Midnight Huntress: A paranormal reverse harem series

Stolen Legacy: A Why Choose Paranormal serial

Academy for Reapers series

ABOUT PIPER FOX

Piper Fox writes short steamy paranormal romances for sassy, strong-willed women who love sexy alpha men, fated mates, and insta-love. When she's not writing... oh, who is she kidding, she's always writing or reading in her favorite genres - paranormal and sci-fi romance.

Get a free book by joining her Foxy Reads at PiperFox-Author.com

Join her on Facebook for of hot heroes pics, book nerd memes and other foxy fun! (like monthly giveaways and ARCs!)
Facebook: facebook.com/PiperFoxAuthor

ACKNOWLEDGMENTS

It's always great to have writing friends to do projects with! Piper and Aidy would like to thank M. Guida, McKenzie Rogue, Michelle Ziegler, and Candice Bundy for being great friends and we're both looking forward to more retreats and projects together with you!

Readers - if you haven't checked out any of these authors, we think you'll love each and every one of them!

From Aidy:

I am so very grateful to my Patreon Book Dragons!

Shout out to my Official VIP Fans!

Thank you so much for all your undying devotion for me and the characters I write. You keep me writing (almost) every day.

Extra Hugs to you ~

- Anna P.
- Barbara B.
- Jeanette M.
- Corinne A.
- Hannah P.
- Jeanette M.

- Kerrie M.
- Natasha H.
- Sandra B.
- Sarah M.
- Tracy L.
- Frania G.

And enormous thanks to my Official Biggest Fans Ever. You're the best book dragons a curvy girl author could ask for~

Hugs and Kisses and Signed Books for you from me!

- Alida H.
- Cherie S.
- Dale W.
- Danielle T.
- Daphine G.
- Jessica W.
- Katherine M.
- Kelli W.
- Marilyn C.
- Mari G.
- Melissa L.
- Rosa D.
- Bridget M.
- Stephanie F.
- Stephanie H.